DON'T HATE THE PLAYER
HATE THE GAME

DON'T HATE THE PLAYER
HATE THE GAME

BRANDIE

www.urbanbooks.net

Urban Books
1199 Straight Path
West Babylon, NY 11704

ISBN-13: 978-1-60162-045-3
ISBN-10: 1-60162-045-4

First Mass Market Printing April 2008
Printed in the United States of America

10 9 8 7 6 5 4 3 2 1

This is a work of fiction. Any references or similarities to actual events, real people, living, or dead, or to real locales are intended to give the novel a sense of reality. Any similarity in other names, characters, places, and incidents is entirely coincidental.

Submit Wholesale Orders to:
Kensington Publishing Corp.
C/O Penguin Group (USA) Inc.
Attention: Order Processing
405 Murray Hill Parkway
East Rutherford, NJ 07073-2316
Phone: 1-800-526-0275
Fax: 1-800-227-9604

Acknowledgments

GOD—you have been my guide through this entire journey called my life. Though it is far from being over, thank you, thank you, thank you! I will stay faithful and loyal to your guidance, Amen.

Vera—William—William—Vera, you two have released a monster onto the world. Every word spoken, every action taken, I have listened and watched intently for the next lesson. I thank you both for giving me choices to become Brandie and pushing me to become what you wanted me to be. Mommy all your teaching-preaching, our bonding and arguments, your smartness, caring, sharing and love has made me a woman. Daddy I'm still daddy's little girl, your girl and you are still my genius. I love you Mommy and Daddy—thank you!

Brandon Rayford, lil brother-bestfriend, thank you for allowing me to be a mother without any children of my own. I love you very much and will always be by your side, ready for any battle. You a grown man now! Go run that roc for Tennesse State and take it to the top in the NFL. William Rayford Jr. (Gookie), Big brother, we've been through a lot of living and learning with so much more to go. I love you and I always got your back!

Carrie Layfield(Grandma)Love you sugar, you've held your family down, now it's our turn to hold you up! Willie D Layfield(Big daddy, rest in peace, your Sweeten). Orenstien Walker (Grand-ma) We miss you very much. My cousins—Rona and LisaLewis ya'll are the truest, letting me know when my shit stanked and when I was on point-thank you—Robert, Jada, Ronald and Rashun. Dequandre(Pooda)Turner, Debra, Jareka and Chantiss Butler, Keith Turner(Pekey—I love you, Be good! I am and will always be here for you.) Bo Turner and his wife and family. Kirra and Tyler Riley you are always in my heart and on my mind. Mary, Regina, Pete and Robbie Layfield. Willie (Poke), Tanya, Brianna, Lil Rod, Roderick, Marqeta, Linda Layfield. Kenny, Sherman, Derrick, Monica, Diamond, Jeremy, and Joshua Burkes. My uncles—Tommy, Charles, Willie, and WC(may you rest in peace-I know you would be proud of me). My auties, Babygirl(Jerelen Lewis) Thank you for all your support. Annie Burkes. Mary Layfield—Even though I was unable to meet you here on earth, I always feel your sprit around me—I heard I took on your attitude-fashion sense and writing abilities? Sister (Shirley Turner), I miss you so much. I wish you were here for more reasons than one, I think about you endlessly. I know that you would be the first one to congratulate me and help me celebrate—love you so much!

Dj Mims—you've hung in there with me for 6 long, hard, trying, unbelievable years. I appreciate all the shoulders you gave me to cry on, the long nights you sat by my side to make sure I was alright, the worrying you did when I was down, and all the jokes that made me laugh and all your love and support. Thanks for sticking by my side even when I was nasty and mean. Your time is coming. I love you! Thanks to Mr. and Mrs. Mims, Jovan, James, Nene and Carlton Hubbard. James Mims you are truly missed here on earth, but a little person told us that you visit on a regular.

Girlfriendsssss! Emily Davis Fowler—Brittany-Caleb, Akaila and Perrell Fowler. Emily you have been a life saver ten times over. From our first meeting in the 5th grade until now us being 2—hahaha, I've loved you, thank you for being my friend-staying up late nights reading and correcting my mess. I will buy you that red dress for the awards show! Kanika Mosely—Lexy and the Mosely family. Girl you have been a solider by my side in all my battles. You are a true friend and therapist. Thanks for all the advice and laughs we've had till 6:00 in the morning. And don't worry about Lexy, we will keep her humble. I love you very much—thank you. LaTanya Fraizer-Hayvn lil cutie, girlllllllllll what haven't we done. We should be old and gray by now! We've had a lot of fun, a lot of scary times, a bunch of tears, but all in all we came out of youth ok. If I wrote about our child hood it would take at least 5 books just to tell the beginning. You will be a great mother to Hayvn, and I will handle being the auntie that let's her get away with murder! Tracie Lias—Cameron, It's crazy how we met, but we've been together ever since. You're crazier than I am so that makes you a perfect friend. Love you. Edith Weston—Corye and Ty thank you for all your support and friendship since we were in the 5th grade. We've been through a lot and come through it all. I really do appreciate your friendship and I will always be here for you. Shonda Brock—Josuha, I love you so much, we've some how grown apart in the last few years, but soon we will be able to bond again. But I live through all of our memorys—17yrs worth.

Urban Family—Carl Webber, Roy Glen, and the rest of the Drama Clique, thank you for the opportunity for the world to know my talent. This has been hard as hell! But worth every effort put forth. Thanks. Marcus-Nubian Bookstore, thanks for all of your support through the many years of waiting. You're the best. Thanks for the hook-up to my success.

To my fans-readers, this book was like a bad nightmare turned fairytale ending. I hope that you enjoy it, it only gets better. GOD 1st

Brandie

Chapter One

THE SESSION

"FUCK me, Daddy! Mmmmm . . . yeah—just like that," she moaned as she licked her full red lips. "YEAH!! HIT IT! Sssss . . . deeper . . . harder. Yeah, like that." Her rotund brown ass bounced up and down as she moved her wide hips round and round on the hungry dick.

"Dat's it, girl." He smacked her ass and watched it jiggle as he continued to poke her big backside even harder. "Work this got damn dick!"

"It's yourssssss, ooh, Daddy! Anything . . . you want . . .

"Get on yo' knees, bitch, and take me in yo' mouth."

The young, sable beauty did as she was told. Her full red lips, took a mouth full, almost choking on the large penis.

"Like this, Daddy?" She pecked and licked carefully, scared to jab too much in her mouth at one time.

He pushed her head down and forced his dick down her throat, making her choke. "Daddy . . ." She tried to pull away from the clog in her throat. "I can't breathe. I can't—"

"Ain't no can't in my world," he said in a harsh tone, while pushing his dick deeper in her throat. "And if you throw up, bitch, I'ma stump yo' ass out."

Her big eyes swelled with tears as she tried to hold his swollen dick in her throat, and at the same time, not throw up.

After he tortured the young cutie for a few minutes longer, he pushed her back on her knees and rammed his enormous penis into her doggie style.

"Ahhhh, Daddy . . . ooh!" she yelled out in pain, not pleasure. The look on her face and the way she kept scooting away told the story.

He slammed her backside continuously, making her ass cheeks jiggle uncontrollably to his hard rhythm.

"Mannn, that broad is fine as hell," young Chocolate commented as he sucked back the spit on his bottom lip.

"I feel ya, Chocolate." Money nodded in agreement, not able to take his eyes off the 32-inch TV screen.

"I jus' wan' a girl wit' a big ol' ass and some big titties." Taeko slurped up the drool from the corner of his mouth and outlined an imaginary figure of a big-booty girl.

Chocolate and Money looked at each other, then back at Taeko. Tormenting him was Chocolate's duty. "Nigga, you betta wish fo' a girl, period. Then, if you get that far, you betta hope she come wit' teeth and hair." They all laughed and continued to focus on the TV.

"Mmmmm . . . yeah, Daddy, fuck dis pussy. Sssss . . . Mmmmm. Make this pussy cum, Daddy!"

Chocolate focused his eyes on the natural, long-haired, sweet-lookin' sista on the TV. At the tender age of thirteen, Chocolate was mesmerized by her long, thick legs. And her caramel complexion had him on edge. "I jus' don't understand why a woman so beautiful would get caught up wit' Taeko's greasy, jherri-curl-head uncle."

Before Taeko could defend his uncle, Money offered his lame excuse. "Nigga, dat's called the power of the tongue."

"I see dat," Chocolate acknowledged, watching the man circle his tongue on the woman's clit, "but—"

"Naw," Money interrupted, trying to sound like a professional in the field of women. "It's all about game! Taeko's uncle pull hoes left and right, cuz. He a pimp—a real pimp. Make dem hoes fuck him and sell they ass for cash. He smooth, know how to talk to 'em. And dat's jus' how I'ma be in a about four years when my grandparents set me straight wit' all dat dough."

"Yeah," Taeko said as he jumped up to grab a bag of Doritos and stuffed a handful of chips in his mouth. "My uncle be havin' women, all shapes, sizes, and colors. I wouldn't have stole the tape if I didn't think she was bad." Taeko flashed a big smile across his greasy lips.

"If all you wanna get is hoes, then you right. Another year or so is all it's gon' take. I want the real deal though—a beautiful sista that respects herself, and will use my brand new dick like it means mo' to her than it does to me. So it can take a lifetime if it has to, fah me."

Money sucked his teeth. "Man, you gots to stop hangin' 'round yo' mama."

"Hangin' around a woman is the best way to know one," Chocolate pointed out and snatched the almost empty bag of Doritos from Taeko. "I mean they all look different, but they just want you to pay attention to 'em. Their basic happiness is a good man."

"Yeah, one wit' some good pipe." Taeko let go a goofy laugh and grabbed his crotch.

"Taeko, you gotta lot to learn."

Chocolate

Them niggas took pussy, women, and life for granted. I loved 'em like my brothers, but they had a lot to learn. I'm sorry they didn't get a chance to meet my uncle Bee. He was my mother's brother—the coolest cat ever. He was the one that schooled me about women and the adventures of "the panty hunts."

Bee used to show me nudy magazines and porno tapes. He even let me hide in the closet to see him and some of his "freaks" as he called them, do their thang. But, he also let me see his dick when it got a big raw sore on it. And that's when he told me that he wished he had stuck to being with just Nia, the love of his life. He said she was sweet, took care of him, cooked for him, would wipe his ass if he was sick, and that she had the best piece a pussy in the world. Said he wanted to bottle it up and put it on the shelf to make millions.

Bee said that if he could do it all over again, she would have been his first and only one. She was the gold package. He said that all men longed to have that one special girl with all the right qualities, and that she would be worth the wait. I took that to heart, and knew that if uncle Bee said it, then that's what it was.

A year after Bee finally got Nia to marry him, he got real sick and died of AIDS. That's why I told them niggas, pussy ain't worth dying for.

But I'm gon' make sure that all three of us—me, Money and Taeko—gon' leave our mark in this world, being superstars, staying best friends, and defying all the odds until the day we die.

Money

That pretty nigga, Chocolate, always tried to preach to somebody. If he wasn't my boy, I'd swear he was gon' be gay. Always talkin' that love shit. Fuck dem hoes! Man, I was born to ball till I fall. The pros already talked to my coaches and I was only fourteen years old. Tae gon' be right wit' me playing pro basketball. He better be, 'cause he ain't the smartest person in the world. And Chocolate gon' be our lawyer, taking care of all our loot.

I will use my money for the good of others—buy houses for poor families, help people off drugs, and build community centers for kids to have a place to be all they can be. All of us gon' be great, make a difference in this world. Grow up and be pros, fathers, and best friends to the day we die.

Taeko

My boyz think I'm slow, don't know what's going on around me, but I pay attention to what I need to know. I know I'm gon' leave dem niggas in the dust when I go straight to the pros and skip college. Pro teams are already trying to set me straight. Just 'cause I can't identify my own daddy don't mean I can't be a man in my own right. My mama and the streets raised me well. While Money gon' be ranked number one in football and Chocolate is gon' be one of the tightest lawyers ever, I am gon' be the greatest basketball player to ever touch the ROC, ranking right up there, neck and neck, with Jordan. No matter how hard my boyz is on me, we gon' ball till the day we die.

Chapter Two

Chocolate

". . . And today is the beginning of your life as adults. Always be responsible for what you say, and always think before you react. Congratulations to Benjamin E. Banneker High, class of '94. Let's give a big hand to Taeko Devoe for being drafted to the Atlanta Hawks. That is a very big responsibility straight out of high school. And to Money Loane . . . congratulations on the signing to Florida State University. Make us proud you men. I am very proud of each and every one of you!" Mr. Wilkerson, the principal of our school, raised his hand and motioned us to stand. In response, we threw our hats into in the air, yelling and screaming, happy to be considered grown-ups.

Afterwards, in the front schoolyard, which was filled with happy families and graduates milling about, my mother gathered our little group together for a picture. "Stand still, Chocolate. Money and Taeko, both of you need to move in closer. Joi, get your butt over here in this picture." Joi has been Taeko's girlfriend since ninth grade, and now, she was his baby's mama of two years, with one due any day.

"Ma, come on now. We got parties to go to . . . and dis suit is hot." I threw my hands up in an exaggerated protest. Inside, though, I was really proud.

My mother smiled, tears rolling down her face. "This is the least you guys can give me—a picture of all my boys in their graduation cap and gowns. After all, I've been waffle house, tutor, chauffeur, nurse, ATM, babysitter and mother." She pouted for a second then realized she could get what she wanted if she put some bass in her voice. "Y'all better get it together and smile 'til I tell you to stop. Now come on."

"Vegas, come on over here and get in dis picture, boy. You gon' be wearin' this hat next year," I yelled to my youngest homeboy.

Our mothers were best friends; they grew up in Columbus, Georgia, and moved to Atlanta at the same time. His aunt lived next door to me, so he was always around like family.

Vegas was a true solider. He kept it gangsta in the streets and was as smart as hell in school. He went to Tri-Cities High School, our rival. But I'd known him since I can remember. He was a year younger than me, but wise beyond his years. We tried to keep him focused, keep his little head off the girls, and the big head on the books. He was going to become the doctor of the group—nothing but a 4.0 since the first day of school. I told him that the star birthmark on his left cheek drove chic's crazy, but the true meaning of it was that he was destined to be great.

After taking a thousand pictures with everyone—including people I didn't even know—we were free to go. Vegas dapped out because he had to go check on his little sister, probably some broad.

Me, Money, and Taeko rode out. Money had us rolling in style in his '95 Ford Explorer, a graduation gift from his grandparents. Money was my dawg for life. We grew up running thangs in College Park, after moving from Columbus, Ohio in the fifth grade. Now, we're men.

"Man, I know these broads gon' be wearin' that 'come-get-me shit,'" Money said, rubbing his hands together.

"Skeet call you?" I inquired as he scanned a stack of CDs.

"Naw. What up?"

"He talkin' 'bout he might need you to come scoop 'im up if Vegas don't come through."

Money nodded his head and turned up the music.

Skeet, a stuttering, cool li'l nigga from the neighborhood that went to school wit' us until tenth grade, said the streets were calling 'im. What more could we expect with a prostitutin', crackhead mother, and a robbin', baby-makin' daddy?

Money turned into Shannon Lake Apartments with Above the Rim's sound track, "Pimping in My Bone," blasting. We pulled up to the pool party already in progress, and all heads gave us their attention.

"Aye, dere go Skeet an' 'em," Taeko yelled like a groupie.

"Nigga, damn, they suckin' yo' dick or sump'n?" I playfully teased him.

Money laughed out loud, making sucking noises with his mouth, and Takeo waved us off.

We got out the truck hyped, and greeted our boys. "Whoooooo!"

"What up, folk?"

"Chillin', home boy."

We all gave each other dap. "'S'up?"

"What's happenin', ghetto superstars?" Lan joked.

Lan stood six-foot five, a true-to-the-heart gangsta, hustla, lover, and mama's boy. His daddy ran drugs on the streets of Atlanta and Ohio, wit' his son right on the back of his heels. Lan's only downfall was he hung tight wit' two low-down, cold-hearted, scummy niggas, Stone and Sham. But unlike them, Lan had a conscience and love for life.

"Let's go turn dis shindig out." Vegas hopped down off his car, and flicked a cancer stick to the ground.

This girl I use to kick it wit', Nikki, was hosting the pool party. We were tight until she started gettin' too hot with her mouth—and not in a good way.

Eightball and MJG's "Coming Out Hard" filled the air. Nikki had the party jumping with some fly-ass honeys, and the food was off the chain.

All of us walked in like superstars. Money and Lan grabbed beers for everybody while we scoped out the girls in the pool with the big ol' titties in the itty-bitty bikinis.

"Tae, pick up your lip and wipe the slob off your

chin." Me, Money, and the honeys that were standing next to us, busted out laughing.

"Whatever, Chocolate. Fuck you, man!"

"Naw. Fuck one of them." As I pointed to the girls in the pool, a soft tap on my shoulder distracted my attention away from an eyeful of ass and titties to a round, cinnamon face with gray, almond-shaped eyes.

"Chocolate, can I talk to you for a minute?" She looked good as hell with her thumbs resting in her back pockets, shifting her weight from side to side . . . but hell naw. This was the same girl that threw bleach on my Polo jumpsuit.

"Naw. 'Cause I don't have no money to keep buyin' clothes that turn white in an instant."

Damn! She looked good, but not good enough to let her keep fucking up my mind and my shit.

"I swear," she said, as she held her hand over her heart, "that I will be on my best behavior."

"Yeah, man," I sighed loudly, "but I ain't wit' no drama tonight. We just graduated, everybody chillin', and I wanna—"

"Look, I don't want to fight with you, either. I just want to get some kind of closure before I leave for Howard."

She looked so innocent and fine; it was hard to resist.

Vegas, Skeet, and Lan started clownin'. "Yes, Nikki, I'll be your baby daddy."

"Jus' put it in ya' mouth," they all sung in unison.

"Chocolate, she want chu to melt in her mouth, not in her hand. Ha, ha, ha!"

Annoyed by the three stooges, I said, "Let's go outside. Money, let me get your keys, Dawg." I needed to get her away from any witnesses in case she wanted to show her ass, and I had to show mine.

Money threw me the keys to his new truck without any hesitation and said with a serious look, "Aye, Chocolate, man, don't be fuckin' in my shit. I ain't got my first piece in it yet." He smiled a devilish grin.

"Man, fuck you!" I waved him off.

Cock-blocking Taeko ran up behind me. "Aye, let me get a ride to the sto'."

I shot him an aggravated look. "Hell, naw. Stop blocking!"

Taeko turned around like a lost puppy. "A'ight, Dawg, but you ain't gotta be frontin' on a nigga."

Taeko was a chump that happened to know how to carry his balls, in all sports.

Me and Nikki walked through the iron gates like we were walking into purgatory. As we walked out, she put her finger through my belt loop like she owned me, but I just kept walking, not wanting any of her drama.

I opened the passenger door and let her in. I had to admit she was as fine as hell; wearing a pink halter-top, with dark-blue jeans hugging low on her hips, and a pair of glitter sandals that matched the writing on her top. Nikki was a beautiful sister, but had the ugliest, nastiest attitude known to mankind.

The A/C blew her scent into my nostrils, getting me aroused. The aroma was breaking down my defenses.

As I started to pull off, Caymin, my girlfriend of

eight months, stood at the gate with folded arms, a tapping foot, and tears in her eyes. I thought about pulling back in, so I slowed down because I cared a lot about her. But I had to handle the Nikki situation so that we could be together without any interruptions. I had to take Nikki away from the party so that she wouldn't make a scene in front of everybody and make them think there was something between us when it wasn't.

I broke eye contact with Caymin and continued to back out.

"So what's up? I thought we nipped this situation in the bud two months ago."

"We did, but I was just over your house two days ago sucking your dick . . . if that's what you call nipping it in the bud."

A smile crept across my face. *She do got that fly head.* She started rubbing my upper thigh. "I thought you weren't goin'." She started fondling me, catching me off guard, waking up the cat killer that lay beneath my jeans. "Stop, man. Gon' now."

She smiled as she stroked my manhood, thinking that she was winning me over. "You like that?" She continued to aggressively stroke my penis until I was full and ready. "I'm dripping wet—just for you." She shoved my free hand down her pants, letting my fingers become drenched in her warm juices. "Ummmm! Yeah, I knew you wanted this."

Her cocky words brought me back to the reality that I already had a girl, who could really be the one. Snatching my hand out of her pants, I snapped, "Cut that shit short, Nikki!"

She circled her warm, wet tongue in my ear, ignoring my helpless plea.

"Dammit, Nikki, I said stop!" I pushed my elbow into her chest, and she fell back into her seat.

"I know I look better than Caymin, finer than she'll ever be," she boasted as she huffed and puffed with her arms folded.

"Looks don't mean shit."

She almost jumped into the driver's seat with me, trying to smother my lips with hers. Her hip bumped the steering wheel and caused me to swerve. "Man, sit cho monkey ass down before I wreck this truck or go to jail for your crazy ass!"

"Why did you leave me? Cheat on me with Caymin?"

My temples got tight, like they were going to burst if she said another word. "Nikki, look, we did not agree on a commitment; we had a companionship. You wanted what I couldn't, or rather, wasn't willing to give you." I could see in her eyes that my words hurt, but it was the truth.

While I drove through the small town of Union City, I obeyed the speed limit, giving her time to get everything off her chest.

"Chinoe, I loved you. Still am in love with you," she pleaded, and grabbed my hand like it was her last hope. She called me by my real name, so I knew she meant every word from her heart. "Chinoe, do you hear what I'm telling you? I want a future with you."

Nikki slowly let the drama unfold; tears began to fall. "I love you and I don't know how to change that. You treated me like a queen. You touched me in ways no one else has." She let my hand go but kept the drama rolling. "Will you at least look at me? Tell me that we can try to work this out. I will stay here and not go to school. Chocolate, please—"

"Naw." She went right over my head. I wasn't the one. I didn't love this girl; I only liked her appearance and how good her body felt next to mine. *Shit!* I wanted her to go to Howard. She was smart and deserved to succeed in life. *I don't understand why women are willing to give up their lives, 'cause a brother ain't willing to give up nothing but dick.*

I wanted to stop the car and shake some sense back into her. "You want something to eat or drink?" I asked her as I slowed down and pulled into McDonald's parking lot to calm my nerves.

"Chinoe, I don't want anything but you. Stop trying to change the subject. Tell me something I want to hear."

"I ain't, man—I mean . . . I can't do that, Nikki . . . give you something that I don't have." I turned the truck off, hoping to give myself, and her, a little time to get this over with.

I looked into her hopeful eyes ready to explain to her that I was a selfish man. I wanted to get my feel of different women; thick, slim, tall, short—hell, all girls for that matter!

Nikki swung her long hair to her back and folded her arms. She turned toward me as if we are about to play chess and she had already figured out how to checkmate. She placed her hand on my shoulder, looking like a damsel in distress. "Chocolate, please tell me that I'm beautiful and you want us to be together. You don't have to promise me forever, just right now. We can make forever happen later in our future."

"You don't get it, do you?"

She crunched her eyebrows and pursed her lips. "What is it about Caymin?" Then she started acting like three different people in one. "Damn it, Chinoe, is she really that *bad*? I know I got her." She rubbed her hands over her hair. "Okay, I'm really tripping about a bitch that live in the projects. You a stupid-ass nigga if you choose that bitch over me."

"Nikki," I said slowly, "I don't owe you shit." I looked into her eyes and could tell that she was not getting the picture. "Fuck this! I'm taking you back to your party because you starting to bug the fuck out."

Nikki reached for my hand and stopped me from starting the engine. She snatched the keys and threw them into the parking lot.

"Nikki, what the fuck is wrong wit' chu, girl? This ain't my shit!" She popped her lips, folded her arms, and sat back in the seat real hard.

I opened the door and got out the truck to look for the keys. My head started hurting so bad that I felt nauseous. I didn't see the keys anywhere. "Nikki, where the keys?"

"When you talk to me straight, then I'll worry about those damn keys."

"Bitch, you betta help me find dem goddamn keys!"

"Bitch? Chinoe, who the hell—? What is wrong with you? Have you lost that much respect for me?"

I walked fast to the passenger side of the truck, and slammed my fist on the top of the truck. "Look, Nikki, I ain't in love with you. Never have been, and I don't see a future with you. You a beautiful girl. Sexy as hell. Smart and fun when you not buggin'. You got a lot to offer a man, but I am not that man."

Nikki looked into my eyes and asked, "Can we hug and kiss one last time? I need this. Please."

The only thing I could think about was Caymin. I liked her a lot and didn't want to hurt her. "Naw, Nik, you know that I'm wit' Caymin."

"Fuck Caymin wannabe-me ass and Joslen young ass, too."

"What?"

"Don't what me, Chocolate! I know about that young-ass girl, Joslen, at Creekside. She's a cheerleader. I met her at the cheerleading conference back in January. I sat there and listened to her dumb ass brag about this wonderful guy name Chinoe, but I never mentioned it because I wanted to stay with you and not be a nuisance."

"Man, you sick. Girl, help me find this boy's keys, and let's go."

Nikki was naïve and a little slow when it came to men. After I got involved with her, I heard that she used to let a dude use her car and money like it was water. Then she started stalking him, breaking out windows at his mother's house, and going up to his job to get him fired.

By the time I found out about her obsessive nature, we had already started tittie-sucking and finger fucking. She flipped out when she found out I was a virgin and didn't want her to be my first.

Yeah, I was still a virgin, probably the only one living besides children under the age of eight. I wasn't no queer or nothing; I loved women more than the next man. But my uncle Bee's words and the sight of him sitting on his death bed was enough for me to want my first time to be with the one woman who took my breath away, not my life.

"Chinoe, if you don't want me I can understand. No, really I don't, but I can't make you love me. The keys are on top of that bush." She licked her shiny lips. I saw tears fall from her face and it kind of got to me, but I had to be hard and protect myself. I needed to keep reminding myself that she was as crazy as hell.

As soon as we were about to ride out of the parking lot, my eyes bucked, and my heart dropped down to my balls. Caymin and two other girls pulled into Mickie D's with drama written all over their faces. I stopped the car to face the monster I'd created.

"Chinoe, what the fuck are you doin'?" Caymin stared at me with crayon-red eyes.

"Caymin, look, I had to take care of an unresolved issue with Nikki."

Before I could get another word out, Fee, one of Caymin's friends, was at Nikki's door banging on the window and screaming, "Bitch, open up the door!"

"I have feelings, too, Chinoe. And Nikki know we together. I thought you already took care of this so-called situation," Caymin said, tears glazing her eyes. Talking to Nikki, she said, "You always on somebody else nigga, smiling an' shit."

Fee was hitting and kicking the passenger door of the truck, trying to get at Nikki. Nikki was licking her tongue at Fee, making her even madder.

"Aye, Caymin, call Fee off. This ain't my shit for her to be fuckin' up!"

Nikki pushed me back and leaned over me.

"Look, Cay-men, we are just friends. It seems he prefers to be with trash over class. And anyway, bitch, you took him from me, so calm your fuckin' nerves."

Fee snuck around to my side of the truck, reached over me, and grabbed some of Nikki's hair. "Uh huh, told you, stupid bitch, I was gon' get that ass one way or another." She was yanking hard as she could.

Caymin jumped out of the car. "Let's see if you like dis bitch baldheaded."

Nikki fumbled for the button to let up the window as she fought hard, fist to the face and elbows to the head.

She finally found the button and got it up, but caught a good bit of her own hair in the window.

"Leave, Chocolate!!! Pull off!" Nikki yelled, thinking that if I pulled off fast enough, Fee would have no choice but to let go.

"I can't see with you in the way."

While Fee stood guard, holding on to Nikki's exposed hair, Caymin started ferreting around in her car.

"Man, let dat girl hair go, Fee," I urged, with laughter in my voice.

When Caymin returned with something in her hand, she heard my plea and replied, "Oh, ain't that sweet, muthafucka? You takin' up for this stupid bitch. You full of shit—with no heart and no conscience."

All of this shit was getting crazy. "Caymin, look, I'm going back to the party to drop her off and I suggest you take your ass home and calm down. I'll be over there to get you."

"No!" She shook her head side to side wildly. "Hell, naw. Make that bitch walk!"

Even though I didn't like or really care about Nikki, it would have been murder to leave her out there with them.

"Naw. Fee, let her hair go and take y'all asses home and stop fucking around." As Nikki moved around and tried to free her hair, I got a better view of what was in Caymin's hands. A clear-pink lighter lay comfortably between her thumb and first finger.

"Fuck you! Don't bother calling me; I'm through with your triflin' ass!"

Before I could react, Nikki's hair went up in flames. "Oh, shit!" I stepped on the gas, not knowing if oncoming traffic was heading my way.

"Aaaaaaah, my hair, my hair! Aaaaah, aaaah!"

Once we were away from Smokey and the bandits, I slammed on the brakes and let down the window. Me and Nikki, both, tried to smother the flames, but neither of us could smother her loud crying.

Caymin drove past us, smiling as Fee threw a milk shake out of the window. "Here, bitch. Cool your hot ass off. Ha! Ha! Ha!"

Chapter Three

Chocolate

It had been a month since the night of graduation, and I felt like I'd graduated into a life of heartache and uncertainty. Even though me and Caymin were kicking it again, she was still making me pay for 'playing games' as she put it. Plus my mom had been bitching all week about me getting my stuff together for school, and I was still a playa wit' out a ride.

"Your lazy butt is not going to lay around here doing nothing. I cannot believe you didn't send those papers to Morehouse. Boy, what are you thinking?"

"Ma, I changed my mind. I want to go to a tech school until I'm ready to take on all that work of being a sports agent."

"Just like your blockhead daddy—pretty, and think everything should come easy to you. But you have something your daddy didn't have—brains." Mentioning my dad's name made her whole demeanor change. "Boy, you better wise up and listen to me. I have been around more times than two, and you know I am telling you the truth. I would never steer you wrong. Leave those fast-ass girls alone.

"I keep telling them to stop calling here at three in the morning. I know their pussies are on fire and just gotta have your hose to put it out, but I know they can wait until daylight to call."

I was shocked at her choice of words. "Mama, please. I told you I'm not hitting nothing. I'm offended by your accusations."

"All right. Be smart-mouthed. I know you in heat."

I had a cool mom. She just bugged out sometimes when she talked about my dad. I tried to stay out of it because I wasn't into taking sides. She wasn't much older than I was when they had me. I guess that's why I felt comfortable saying and telling her anything.

My dad was a true player. He owned a luxury car lot in Dunwoody and loved me more than life, maybe because I was his only child; my mom was a homebound teacher who thought she was a saint sent to earth to save all kids.

"So, Chocolate, what classes are you interested in taking at this technical school?" she asked in a smart-ass tone, saying technical like it was a disease.

"Computer information. I figured, once I have a year under my belt, I can transfer my credits to Morehouse."

"Well, at least you do have a plan. Just don't fail. You owe this to yourself. You have worked so hard at being a good student and succeeding at everything you do; that's why I'm so proud of you." She leaned over and kissed me on the forehead. "Oh, yeah, your blockhead daddy called. Said he had a surprise for you." She gave me a smile as she walked out the door.

A surprise? The only surprise that he could give me is a heap of money or a brand-new ride. I flopped down on the sofa, *BET* caught my eye with hoes dancin' and shakin' they ass.

Surprise? I called my pops immediately.

"Hello, Starr Rides," he answered, his voice scruffy and tired, yet proud and arrogant.

"Hey, Pops, what's up? I hear you got something for me."

"Yeah, boy, a ass whupping. Ha ha ha." He laughed hardily.

"Naw, old man. You might lose that battle."

"Can you get down to my house tomorrow?"

"Yeah. I'll ask Money to bring me by."

"Yeah, do that. He ain't call me in a while. Talked to his grandfather yesterday. Told me he goin' to Florida State. That boy gon' go pro." My father sounded like a proud dad. The closest thing to one that Money ever had.

"Yeah, and by the time he hit it big, I'll be representing him."

"That's my boys. Hey, do me a favor. Try and hold it down over in College Park. Seal worried about you and them girls. Said they be callin' all times at night, riding by the house, fussing, and being loud. Boy, you're lovin' that hard?"

"Man, you know how Mama be exaggeratin'. I had a few problems earlier this month; you know how these girls are."

"You didn't answer my question."

I hesitated because I didn't want to tell my daddy no, and have him think I was gay, but I didn't want him to think I was a ho-monger, either.

"Old man, you all up in my business. I'll be over there tomorrow."

I hung up the phone and laughed. Thinking about how him and my mama always tried to figure me out. I went back to my room and turned on the stereo. Outkast's "Southerenplayalistic" filled the room. Dem boys were deep, and right then I needed some mental therapy.

Ring . . . Ring . . . Ring.

"Talk to me."

"Nigga, don't nobody wanna talk to yo' ol', sweet-talkin' ass. You can let me speak to yo' fine-ass mama, though."

"Shiiid! Nigga, you can't afford what it's worth. But I'ma get at cha sister when she get three mo' years on 'er," I joked with Vegas.

Vegas was a hater when it came to his little, fine-ass sister.

"Ahhh, a'ight, nigga, I got chu." He laughed it off and changed the subject. "What time y'all niggas gettin' out?"

"I 'on't know. I—" The phone beeped. "Hold ya nuts, nigga," I told Vegas.

"Talk to me."

"What's going on?" It was Money.

"What up, Cash Money? What's poppin'?"

"It's Friday, so let's ride, Dawg. Vegas talkin' 'bout ridin' out to the Briar."

"That nigga on my other line now, hold on." Clicking over to Vegas, I said, "Yo, man, dis Money, talkin' 'bout making moves. I'll hit you back."

"Let me know if ya'll ride out to the Briar."

"I'll holla." Clicking back to Money, I continued, "Nigga, ya'll can have that heat. My black ass gon' stay right here in the A/C."

"Pretty nigga, get yo' punk ass up and get dress. I'll hit you up about seven-thirty tonight."

"Aey, nigga, you take Shawn to the movies last night?"

"Yeah, I took 'er, so I could get some pussy. And she worked the hell outta this dick too."

"Fool, you wild. Caymin told me that Shawn in love, nigga. You better slack up."

"Man, she know she ain't nothin' but a piece of pussy. Something you wouldn't know nothin' about." Money laughed out loud.

"Whatever. Fuck you, nigga. I'm privileged not to have had all that shit you done had: crabs, gonorrhea, and all that ol' other fucked up shit. And, to top it off, too many dead babies to count on two sets of hands. You can keep that shit, man; I'm looking for a pot of gold."

"All yo' life you will be. Late'a." Money slammed the phone down.

I knew I hurt that nigga's feelings, but Money still hadn't learned his lesson. He was still fuckin' hoes wit'out rubbers and he knew they was hot in the ass. I'd rather stay a virgin and not have to deal with penicillin. A lot of cold showers and a lot of prayer would bring me the pot of gold I deserved.

Chapter Four

Money

C*hocolate think he know everything about women and he's never even been in a piece of pussy—besides comin' outta his mama's,* I thought as I clicked off the phone. *I'm startin' to think that nigga is gay.*

Mmmph. Pretty niggas always thought they had it nipped in the bud. But I wasn't kissing no bitches' ass. Women loved that rough shit, and it didn't hurt that my six-foot three inches looked down on 'em, while my wide arms hugged 'em tight.

When they would first meet me, they could already see me tossing that ass, rubbing it against my smooth, pecan-brown skin. And hoes loved my bright, gap-toothed smile. Plus my wardrobe was always dressed to impress and my ride was the baddest thang on the street. I was ballin'.

Fuck dat nigga! Gon' tell me about Shawn. Shit! He better had been worryin' about Caymin's psycho ass.

Ring . . . Ring . . . Ring.

"What up? Tell a nigga sump'n."

"Money, I'm pissed at you. What happened to you calling me back last night?" the angry, yet sexy, voice asked.

"Aey, baby, I layed down and fell asleep on the couch in the basement. I guess I didn't hear the phone—it was upstairs."

"Someone told me they saw you at the movies last night."

I paused for a second, tryin' to think of some sweet lie to win her over. "Salone, baby, I was right here 'sleep. And, anyway, I thought we were on another level, not worryin' about all that other shit."

She hesitated like she wanted to dispute it, but I guess she didn't want to hear the truth. "Well, I have to get back to work. Will you come by and see me about seven-thirty? I'll be in the store all by myself. You can come by and pick out an outfit, we got some new stuff in."

"Yeah, me and Chocolate'll be there." Click.

I knew I needed to slow down, 'cause them girls were gettin' smarter and more devious than ever, just to be wit' a nigga.

It was about 3 p.m. when Shawn started ringing my phone off the hook, so I turned the answering machine on and jumped in the shower.

While the warm water flowed over my head, the past came into focus. Since third grade, my life had been football. Every team I played for I became the star and kept the team undefeated. Women automatically fell in my path, but the first and only woman to steal my heart, virginity, and love was Luvly Mancini.

I remembered the first time I laid eyes on her. Me and Chocolate were fourteen, ballin' at Mosely gym.

"Shoot, punk nigga," a restless opponent yelled.

"Woooooo," Chocolate yelled, clapping his hands, anxious to get the ball.

My timing was good, my mind focused, and just when I was ready to make the basket—*bam!* My eyes caught sight of a bronze-colored girl. She walked through the doors with two other girls. Her beauty cast a shadow over them, her complexion; fresh as a new penny, her waist-length hair rested seductively on her back.

"Damnnn, look at what just walked through the door," an older guy shooting for the opposite team said. It seemed like everyone in the gym gave the three girls their game attention.

This dope nigga name Diamond, who we played ball against sometimes, noticed them hard as I did. "Damnnnn," he screamed in a higher-pitched voice, "Shawty bad! She pretty as hell. I need to put her on my team." He dapped his partner in crime, Jae.

"What? You gon' make her baby mama number four?" I asked.

He noticed the sound of infatuation in my voice and the disgust on my face. He took it as a challenge, frowned, and walked up on me chest to chest. "What, young nigga? What? You gon' make 'er a cheerleader?" Diamond backed up a short distance, and threw the ball hard into my chest. "Play ball, li'l nigga. Make these shots and go get yo' cheerleader. But if you fail, I'ma save a ho!"

Diamond was a Cuban, fake Scarface-type nigga that was a couple years older than us. He already had three baby mamas, and he was on his way to becoming a drug King Pin. But what no one knew was that he looked hard on the outside, but was marshmallow on the inside. He had no heart.

Diamond used to front this young kid, Al, that lived a few blocks up from me, one ounce of cocaine; known in the dope world as a cookie. At first, Al would take two cookies at a time flipping them like clockwork, earning Diamond hella money, and his trust. But Al had a plan all along to gain all trust and break away.

One day we were shooting ball in Al's yard and Diamond pulled up, "Yo, nigga, you got my cheese this time."

"Man, I ain't got chu," Al said nonchalantly and shot a basket.

"You said that last week, the week before that, and the week before that. I want my goddamn money!" Diamond shouted.

"Muthafucka, you deaf? I said I ain't got it." Not giving Diamond eye contact, Al took another shot.

"Li'l nigga, you talking to me?" Diamond quickly jumped out of his car, running up on Al, knocking the ball out of his hand.

Al chuckled, "Nigga, you betta back the fuck up off me."

Right at that moment, I knew Diamond didn't have the heart to be "the dope man", only the smarts and connections to make the money. He'd given Al too many chances. A real baller, dope man, would have had Al's throat slit the first time, no questions asked.

"Ya'll boys ready to bounce?" Al asked me and Chocolate.

"Nigga, you betta have my money Sunday."

Al walked up to Diamond's face, both of them exchanging each other's breath. "I ain't got it. Ain't gon' have it. But I tell you what the fuck, nigga. Go tell the police to come and get it or betta yet, get it in blood, my nigga." Al spit on the ground in front of Diamond's shoes.

Diamond didn't flinch; he didn't say a word, just hopped back in his car, and sped off. He never told Jae or anyone in his crew about him being punked by a sixteen year old. We kept the incident a secret and Al kept the money, came up fast, and moved to Florida where he became known as "the dope man."

The whole game I kept staring at her. And her staring back made it more difficult to concentrate. Chocolate walked over to the cuties and got some info, just in case I lost. Which I did.

"Damn, man, you let Diamond sorry ass whup you in front of shawty?"

I was mad as hell. "Shut that shit up, faggot!"

"Fuck you, punk nigga!"

I looked around everywhere trying to spot her, but she was gone. When we got outside, there she was—posted up on Diamond's Mercedes.

"Man, I knew she was gon' fuck wit' that nigga. Shit! I look good, but that nigga got the power, money, cars—and his own damn house." What was

I thinking? I was only fourteen with nothing to offer her, and he was nineteen and could give her the world.

Chocolate pretended to hold a microphone and talk proper. "Damn, Money Loane, are you actually pressed?" He was getting a kick out of me jocking this girl.

"Man, naw, but she just tight as hell. Something about her is right."

"Naw, dog, my girl Lisa is finer," Chocolate boasted.

I stared at her as I walked by. She was giggling and acting all shy, with Diamond in her face, but I still had her attention.

"A'ight den, young boyz, y'all hold it down. Luvly, get in." Diamond had the slickest smile on his face.

"Luvly? Her name Luvly?" It was a name I would never forget.

"Oh, yeah, Romeo, here," Chocolate said, giving me a piece of paper with her name and number and a little message:

Luvly
777-964-4323
You are a serious cutie pie.
Give me a call when you through playing games!

"What the fuck she mean 'playing games'?"

"She said she know you talk to Tayana."

Yeah, she knew that, but what she didn't know is that I would drop everything for a chance with her—even football.

* * *

Three months later, me and Chocolate went to a big house party. Everybody who was anybody was there. "It's packed as sardines in here." The strong smell of cologne over musty armpits hit strong.

"If the room was full of women I wouldn't mind," I said as Dougie Fresh's "The Show" came on. The first chicken head I saw I grabbed and hit the dance floor.

After an hour of dancing, mingling, and feeling on a little booty, she walked through the door. "Chocolate, there she go, Dawg. There she go!"

"Who?" asked Chocolate, who was all up on some thick girl with buck teeth.

I was walking toward her, ready to finally make that move. I'd been holding her number, looking at it everyday, wanting to call. Just as I was about to walk up on her, Diamond came through the door seconds later, grabbing her tight by the waist. I turned around ready to dip.

"Man, did you see all them bad hoes up in there?" Excited, Lan clapped his hands.

"That bad bitch from Decatur . . . what's her name, Vegas?" Chocolate asked as he shuffled through the many pieces of paper with phone numbers on them.

"Niggaaaa, she was ugly as hell," Vegas said disapprovingly.

"Naw, homeboy, she had a tight body, but her face was fucked up," Lan concluded. Just then a carload of girls from the party were getting dropped off. So we slowed up to talk to them.

We were mackin' when a silver, big-boy Benz pulled up with its brights blinding us. "Man . . . who the fuc—?"

"Need a ride?" a sexy voice asked.

My heart dropped, and my soul smiled. But a straight, hard face stayed planted. "Naw."

I started walking again. I needed to know how bad this girl wanted me.

"Yo, why you ackin' like dat? I been gave you my phone number. Why you ain't called me?"

" 'Cause you ain't gon' have me layed up in no ditch. By no means do yo' pussy-ass nigga scare me, but I ain't gon' waste my time defending sump'n that I ain't never had."

She kept the car rolling at my speed. "Look, I been tryin' to get at you, but you were seein' Tayana."

I threw my hand up at her and kept a steady stride.

"Money, get in and take a ride with me."

"Girl, you ain't nothing but—"

"Fifteen."

"Ooh, and that makes it legal for you to be driving."

"Come on, pleaaase."

I hesitated at first, but her pretty eyes and enticing voice pulled me in. I kept looking around making sure no one but my boyz saw me get into Diamond's car—wit' his woman. I threw my head up to Chocolate to make sure he knew that I was going with Luvly.

"So why haven't you called me?"

"Man, you been kickin' it hard wit' ya boy, so what was the use?"

"Me. I've been coming to see you play football for quite a while. I've been at every game."

"So now I should feel privileged that you been watchin' me?"

"No, I'm the one that's privileged to be able to watch you."

I watched her grip the steering wheel firm and tight, wishing it was me that she was holding. She was gorgeous. "Yo' nigga gon' kill you."

"Who said he had to know?"

She pulled into Union Station apartments. "Come on."

When we got inside the apartment, it was pitch black. Luvly grabbed my hand and didn't hesitate a step; she knew exactly where she was going. Seconds later, music started playing.

"Sit right here." She pushed me down onto a bed. I wasn't putting up a fight.

I asked, trying to remain calm, "Why no lights?"

"Don't need any. I know where everything is in here and on you. Ooh, that's my jam." "Love Me In A Special Way" by Debarge came on.

Before I could get another word out she was kissing me. When I reached up to push her back, I touched nothing but skin. She had taken all of her clothes off. Her skin felt warm and silky. I lay back and let her take control.

"I've waited so long for this," she whispered between kisses, blowing hot air into my ear, and making my dick want to pop. "I promise all those other girls won't mean nothing after tonight."

Other girls? Little did she know, she would be my first.

Once she had all my clothes off, she sucked and licked my nipples like a dude would do to a woman. I was about to skeet her ass into the ceiling when she put my above-average-sized dick in her mouth.

"Oooh, oh, oh, shiiit!" I moaned. I grabbed a handful of her hair, and tried to bury my face in the pillow. "Girl, if you don't want me—ohhhh— to nut in your mouth, you betta stop."

Taking heed to my warning, she slid her body on top of mine. "Here, put this on."

I wanted to feel that thang bareback, but I put it on at her request. I tried to lay into her nice and smooth, but her pussy was tight, like brand new. She couldn't see the big-ass smile I was wearing.

She was pushing on my stomach. "Sssttt, it hurt, Money."

Easing up, I moved back—just a little bit—not wanting to lose contact wit' that thang. "Sorry. I don't want to ever hurt you." I kissed her on her forehead as I held onto her hips, trying to spread her open as far as she could go, so that I could fit without hurting her. Wiping sweat off my forehead, I proceeded to push on it.

"Ahhh, Money, ummmm." Her nails scratched my forearms. I put my arm around her waist and arched her back so that she was as close as possible to my chest, to comfort her.

"Damn, Luvly, yo' pussy so goddamn tight." I was slobbering, catching the drool with one of her breasts between my hungry lips.

She wrapped her legs around my waist, stopping me from pushing all the way inside of her. All I could think about was, how deep does it run? Good thang I had on a rubber; I busted the quickest, strongest nut—ever.

My young mind was gone. I was in love with not

only her pussy, but with her beauty and passion for me as well. After that night, Luvly became my canvas—no matter who came along my way or hers.

Diamond heard rumors in the street about us fuckin' in his bed on more than one occasion, but he kept his distance from me. I guess she had put that thang down on him as well.

If all else failed, my future would be bright, thanks to my grandparents, my backbone. Mama Gene and Papa Sam had money. Lots of money. Papa Sam was the one that named me Money. When I was born, he said, "One day this boy gon' bring all us a lot of money." Papa Sam played my birthday and hit the lottery for 2.5 million dollars. I've never needed for anything since but attention, the attention of a mother.

My mother left me a long time ago. She let a man turn her on to drugs. I just can't see problems getting that damn bad. I remember she came back to visit me one summer when I was six, right before school started. I really thought she was going to be my mother and raise me. My grandfather gave her five hundred dollars to buy me some school clothes. When we got to the mall, she told me to pick out some stuff while she went to the bathroom. She never came back.

The police called my grandparents, but Moe, Chinoe's dad, came and picked me up. He hugged me, told me everything was going to be okay, and kept me at his house that night and for the next week. Moe filled the shoes of my absent father. He was always at my little league football games and even at my first girl-boy dance. He's the one who sat me and Chocolate down together and talked about what to expect our first time having sex and falling in love. And Ma, Chinoe's mother, had been my mother, always giving me love and showing me compassion. Once I go pro, there will be no limit as to what I would do for all of them.

No mother should damage her child's life. Me, being a real man, I needed that sweet love from a woman. Seal did her best as a mother figure. I guess not having a real mother is the reason I used girls like I changed my drawers. Not having any respect came from not having the one woman that's supposed to be my everything—be nothing.

Hoes loved me and my boys. Shit! We were jocks, the most popular, everything. We were what every young boy dreamed of becoming.

Chocolate, looking for a pot of gold, had shit screwed up, if you asked me. *Hell! Screw these chics and find gold on the way.* That was my theory, and I stuck wit' it.

My plan was to go to FSU, ball for them white folks, and go pro after two years. Yeah, that was my plan.

Chapter Five

Chocolate

It was 6:20 p.m., and I knew Money would be on time and ready to roll. Looking through my closet, I was thinking, should I pimp my Fubu nylon outfit or my Polo gear? It's Friday, and I knew chics were going to be lining up for me to choose. Fresh Fubu it was. Maybe my pot of gold would come sooner than later.

After jumping out of the shower, lotioning up and splashing on some Nautica cologne, I heard a loud engine in front of the house. Before running to the front room to see who it was, I heard another car pull up.

Caymin met me at the door, with Joslen right behind her. *Why do girls always show up without calling?* They would avoid a lot of confrontations if they followed a few simple rules.

"Chinoe, who is that?" Caymin asked, pointing at Joslen getting out of the car.

"Just go in the house."

Caymin walked in the house way too easy. I knew her nosy ass would be hanging on every word from behind the door, so I walked out into the yard to meet Joslen.

"What's up, baby girl? Why you poppin' up wit'out callin'?"

"My cousin live around the corner, so I thought I would just stop by and see you," she answered innocently.

"Your cousin, huh? Well, this isn't your cousin's house. Next time, boo, why don't you call me first?"

"Chinoe, I may be young, but I'm not stupid. You don't have to play me stupid, okay."

Joslen was cute, but there were no strings attached.

"J, look, as you can see, I have company; so I'll hit you later." Running my fingertips across her chin, her young naïve eyes filled with tears. She turned and walked away.

"What's up, Dena? How you doing?" Her older sister rolled her eyes and turned up her nose.

"Chinoe, you full of shit! Leave my little sister alone. She young and don't need no trifling-ass nigga fucking up her life; leave her alone!"

"She looks like a big girl to me; she can make her own decisions," I said, winking my eye. "Check y'all later. Be safe."

I walked back in the house rubbing my head and heard things being shuffled around in my room. I quickly, but quietly, walked around the corner to my room. Caymin didn't hear me come in the house because she was too busy going through papers on my dresser. I stood at the door, watching her talk on her cell phone and ramble like a rat for cheese.

"Well, this is his muthafuckin' girlfriend and—"

"Bitch, please. Chinoe ain't goin' nowhere but between these legs so—"

"Caymin," I yelled. "Whatchu doin'?" It scared the shit out of her, and she jumped, dropping the phone.

"You scared the shit out of me. I was—ahmmm—I was looking for a piece of paper and pen to write with."

"Caymin, what's wrong with you? I told you I didn't like all this psycho shit." I snatched up her purse and cell phone and grabbed her by the arm. "Come on. You leavin'."

She scrubbed her feet on the ground like a mad dog. "Chinoe, why you got to lie to me and do me so wrong?" She had a balled-up piece of paper in her hand. I snatched it from her.

"Why you always lookin' for shit, Caymin? Got-damn!" I pushed my finger into her forehead, wanting to knock the shit out of her. "Get yo' shit and get out!" I had to check myself because my volume and tone got out of control.

She fell to the ground like a wounded doe. "Chinoe, I have put up with your shit long enough. I thought I had to be mighty special for you to choose me over Nikki. But I guess she was the lucky one to be out of your life." She started wiping her tears away with the back of her hands. I felt like picking her up and hugging her, telling her everything was going to be all right—but it wasn't.

"Caymin, give me your hand." I said, standing over her. "Come on, give me your hand. Come on, get up, baby." She just looked up at me with red eyes. She was so beautiful, her warm, caramel skin so smooth, like butter.

Pulling her to her feet, I hugged her tightly as she put her arms around my neck and pressed her soft body against my hard chest, six-pack, and my hardness. She slowly kissed my ear lobe, then my cheek. "Chinoe, please don't treat me like this." She continued to place kisses on my cheek then to my weakest spot—my neck.

I grabbed her waist and squeezed her close to my body. She smelled like sweet peaches and crème ready for me to taste. Moving backwards toward my waterbed, we fell. The motion seemed to open her legs up to my body. She wrapped her legs around my waist, shoes rubbing up and down my back. I kissed her wildly.

"Baby," she said, holding me tighter, "make love to me. I know you said you wanted to wait, but, Chinoe, I'm so ready to be with you."

Damn! I wanna hit this worse than ever. She was smelling and looking so good, lying on my black silk sheets. Placing my fingers over her lips, trying to hush her thoughts away and kissing her lips down to her neck, I slipped her spaghetti straps off her shoulders. The stereo was thumping R. Kelly's "Bump and Grind" re-mix. Perfect timing.

Caymin started grinding up against my dick. The little skirt she had on allowed me to feel her warmth and wetness through her panties and my nylons. Tracing her inner thigh with the slow motion of my fingertips, I played with the side of her panties, making sure she was ready. I licked my fingers and rubbed them against her clit, putting one finger inside her. She started moving back and forth, using my finger like it was my dick. Her moans grew louder. I licked the finger that was inside her. Then I put two fingers back inside her. She started to grind and ride my fingers harder—faster. She was wet as a waterfall.

Caymin started grabbing for my pants, but I moved her hand and held it in the air, licking her fingertips and sliding my tongue down to the crease of her arm. I sucked until a passion mark appeared. She hugged her legs around me tighter. Her breathing became erotic, like a panting wolf.

She reached for my pants again. This time I let my guard down and let her fingers find their way. She looked up at me with her big, baby-doll doe eyes. "Chinoe, I love you, now and forever. I don't want to lose you—us." My dick was full in her hand. "Damn, Chinoe! You so hard and big."

Before I knew it, we were switching places. She kissed my lips and sat on top of me. She looked like a princess sitting on her throne. As she rubbed my face, I ran my fingers through her silky hair: another one of my weaknesses. She leaned her breast over my mouth, and I squeezed them together and put them both in my mouth. I knew she loved it, so I did it forcefully until I heard her cry out.

At that moment I knew that she must be my pot of gold.

Caymin slid down on my body slow and sexy, her mouth so warm and wet. The feeling was so strong, I didn't want to let her go—out of my house or my life.

"Lord, have mercy on me." My words were louder than a whisper.

"I will help you, Babe. I'll give you everything you need and want; all you have to do is love me."

Love her? I didn't know if I loved her. Was that supposed to be part of it? "Oooh, shit." Her full, soft lips kissed me up and down, licking from the tip of the head, circling from top to bottom, deep throating me all the way. She licked my nuts and had me about to scream. I took control of her head and forcefully pushed it up and down.

"Cum for me, baby! Cum for me!" she cried out.

I layed back and relaxed all my muscles, releasing all I had in her mouth. She swallowed gracefully, while I almost choked on my own spit.

"Damn, Caymin. Babe, you always make me feel like a million bucks."

"Anything for you, Babe." She slid off her purple satin panties leaving them on the floor.

She had given me head so many times before, but this time I wanted a bigger nut—inside her. I grabbed her off the floor and swung her on the bed; then rubbed my head against her pussy lips, getting ready to enter heaven.

The front door slammed shut.

"Oh, shit! Chinoe, that's your mom."

"I don't care who it is. I'm ready to come inside of you and never come out," I grunted.

"I don't want her to see me like this." She pushed me up and started looking for her bra and panties.

"Chocolate, I brought you some Wing King." As my mother's voice became clearer, I quickly put my pants back on and ran out of the room to meet her face on.

"What's up? Why you out of breathe? Isn't that Caymin's car outside?" The big smile on her face told me she thought she knew what was up.

"Dog, ma, why twenty questions? She back in my room."

"Y'all weren't fighting were you? Chocolate, I told you I wasn't—"

"Man, Mama, chill out. That girl a'ight."

Caymin came around the corner. "Hi, Mrs. Starr. How are you?"

"Fine. A little better than you. Fix your shirt, it's inside out." Caymin smiled with embarrassment.

Mama gave me a silly smirk and walked back into the kitchen.

"Baby, you want some wings and soda?" she asked Caymin, who hugged me and gave me a kiss.

"I really wanna eat you," she whispered in my ear. "Yes, Mrs. Starr, I would like some."

It was going on 9:15 p.m., and it seemed like hours had passed since I almost laid my foundation with Caymin. I ain't gon' rush it, though; if it was meant, then it would be.

"Damn! Where is Money?" That nigga probably layed up in somebody's pussy.

Chapter Six

Chocolate

"Come see me, Money. It's hard not seeing you everyday. Babe, I need you."

"All right, Salone," Money said, frustrated, switching his cell phone from the left ear to the right. "I'll be at the mall in fifteen minutes." *Click.* Money hung up the phone like he was frustrated.

"Nigga, you need to stop. Them girls gon' kill yo' ass one day."

"I got this thang under control, Dawg."

"Do you, my nigga? So when you leavin' for FSU?" I asked, not wanting to go into the same old debate.

"Well, training camp starts August tenth."

"Damn, nigga, that's less than a month."

Damn, my main nigga was about to be out the door. It was gonna be weird not having him by my side, I guess. I could use his moving down there as an advantage. I could visit Tallahassee and meet new people, maybe find my piece of gold.

"Man, I'm proud of you. I know Mama and Papa Loane are, too."

"Yeah, they all excited. I'm just sorry that my niggas ain't gonna be there. I hate trying to blend in, being the new cat. But looking on the bright side; new bitches." He gave us a wide smile.

"Man, you gon' be tight. You know how to ball. Just go down there and show them oranges how these peaches squeeze."

We gave each other a College Park handshake.

We pulled into Southlake Mall. I knew who we were there to see. Shit, I just wanted some free clothes.

We jumped on the escalator heading to Dollwear. On the way down the aisle, I happened to look downstairs and see the most beautiful creature. I kept my mouth closed; knowing Money would want to try his luck. So I let him walk in front of me.

"Aye, Money, I'll be in . . . in a minute."

He looked around trying to see what I had spotted. "A'ight den, nigga."

With my eyes glued to her, I walked to the escalator, taking in her long, jet-black hair and smooth, honey-caramel skin. She looked like she was beautifully mixed with Indian or Samoan, but I knew she was definitely glazed with black sweetness.

She was well shaped. Her hips stuck out, not protruded—just thick, shapely thighs, and a butt that sat perfectly plump. Her stomach wasn't ironing board flat; it was molded into her thick and juicy frame. As I got on the escalator, I saw her heading towards a store named Lerner's. I hoped she was by herself. Shooot! I didn't even care; she was just that beautiful. I was gonna step to her anyway. "Damn, this escalator packed and moving slow as hell."

Two little boys were eating ice cream and jumping around like they were on the playground. I wanted to smack their bad asses.

"Shit!" Those bad motherfuckers wasted ice cream on my shoes, I noticed as I stepped off the escalator.

Their mother covered her mouth. "Oh, young man, I am so sorry." She knelt down and started wiping my shoes.

"Ma'am, that's all right, thank you. No problem." I shoulda beat the hell outta those bad-ass kids. My Timberlands were stained, but I was pressed for a meeting with a queen.

I walked into Lerner's. I didn't see her in the front, so I walked toward the back counter, hoping that she was around the corner: maybe in the dressing room. "Ma'am, did a young lady with long, jet-black hair, caramel complexion just come in here?"

"I don't know, but you can ask the salesgirl at the register; she might have assisted her."

Let's see if the register girl knows anything. Her back was towards me, but something about her looked familiar. "Excuse me Miss, but did you happen to see a young lady come in here with a purple T-shirt and blue jeans?"

As she turned around, I turn to scan the store once more.

"I think she—"

I turned back around, meeting eye to eye with her. "DAMN!!" I wished I was still at the bottom of the escalator with the mommy and the two bad-ass boys.

Chapter Seven

Money

Salone, *lookin' good in dem Calvin Klein jeans and black, fitted halter-top,* didn't see me walking up behind her 'cause she was wit' a customer. The lady started smiling because I was holding a single long stem rose. I put my fingers to my lips to shush her. I grabbed Salone by the waist and kissed the nape of her neck. She turned around and caught me with a soft punch to the stomach.

"Money, you so crazy. You scared me."

"Aye, Babe, you were just looking so good from the back, and your waist looked lonely."

"I'm sorry, ma'am, but I will call you when we get those Christian Dior shoes in." The lady kept smiling and told me, "This here is a sweet girl. I hope you keep her smiling and sweet all her days."

I nodded to the lady and hugged Salone off her feet. She was petite, but had a fat ass and thighs. A little lacking in the chest area, but her juicy lips and sexy eyes made up for it.

Salone's parents died two years ago and left her an inheritance. She took the money and invested it in Dollwear Clothing. She also had a shoe store on Jimmy Carter Boulevard called Toe to Toe. Twenty-three years old and her life seemed set. But if she thought her life was picture-perfect with me, she had another thing coming. I was eighteen years old and nowhere near ready for married life.

I knew she had to do inventory, but I wanted to make her feel special by asking her to go out. "What time you get off?"

"Money, I told you I had to do inventory. Kayeshia won't be in until nine-thirty to help, and Paula has to go home because of baby-sitting problems. So I have to be here all night."

"Well, I know you hungry. You wanna go get a bite to eat when you close up?"

"I don't know. I have so much to do and I want to have everything put out by tomorrow. You know how black folks be spendin' all their child support, alimony, and welfare checks on Saturdays."

"Yeah, you wouldn't know about those kinds of problems now, would you, Ms. Entrepreneur?"

She walked around the counter, which is up on a platform and met me eye to eye, all of my six feet, four inches. I reached for her hand and kissed the inside of her palm.

"Well, can I bring you something back up here? I don't want you dehydrated or famished."

She cracked a smile and licked her lips. "Yeah, please get me some Popeye's. You know what I like, right?"

"Yes, darling. Two-piece dark meat, cajun rice

and beans, one biscuit, and one large tea, no lemon."

She smiled, leaned over, and gave me a kiss.

"See, your lips already need some water; they're dry and peeling. Sweet, though."

She slapped my head. "Shut up, boy. It's just my lip gloss peeling."

Aside from having the sweetest kisses, Salone was a sandy-colored redbone with a short cut that was always changing colors. Her long, healthy eyelashes along with the moles and freckles that some viewed as ugly, complimented her slanted, marble-black eyes. Sexy and ripe. She dressed to impress and had beautiful toes that are always perfectly painted, summer or winter. All that prissiness turned me on. And the free clothes and shoes don't hurt either.

We'd been messing around for about two years, off and on. She knew about my female lovers, friends, and I never asked about hers.

"Well, sweetie, I'm gone. I gotta catch Chocolate. He done seen some broad and ran behind her."

"This might be his lucky chance; don't hate on him."

"Naw, that's my cat, but he oughta be tired of chasing the invisible delight of his life."

"I'll be waiting for my food. If you come back after nine-thirty, I'll have the back entrance open."

"A'ight, later."

As I walked away, I thought about everything me and Salone had been through—nothing. No drama, no babies, and no ties. Just loving, loving, and more loving. She was a perfect mate for life. I knew she was attached to me because of all the things she'd done for me. I was attached to her also, but my heart wasn't in it. I knew one day that I would make someone a perfect, faithful, loving man. But then again—maybe not.

Chapter Eight

Chocolate

I couldn't believe my eyes. Her hair was so short, laid, but short. And she had a Barbie-doll face: lipstick, thick lashes, and eyeliner—all that fake shit.

Her eyes were glued to my face. And the nasty attitude she wore on her face would be forever glued to my heart. That was one nametag that I didn't need to read. I knew that face well, that body, and that scent. I could smell her from behind the counter. She'd put on a few pounds, but it looked damn good on her.

Shit! If I was stupid I'd tell her that I wanted her back in my life, but I would only be dreaming for both of us.

"So, Mr. dog-ass Chinoe—naw, naw, I'm sorry. I don't even want to be nasty. Things are good for me, and I'm on my way up . . . thanks to you."

Like a slave, I wanted to run away. "Yeah, you

look real good. Your weight fills your face out. I have to be honest though—"

"Whoa, honesty! I better listen and take it for what it's worth."

"The makeup—lose it."

She got a look on her face of disbelief, my cue to get the hell on. Before I could get out of sight, Sandra, the other sales girl walked up. "Nikki, did you help this fine, young gentleman find his lady friend?"

Nikki looked like she wanted to spit venom. "Yeah, many months ago."

"Thanks, Sandra, and have a nice day, Nikki." I jetted as fast as I'd come, hoping to catch my mystery girl going down the escalator.

Soon as I got to the top of the escalator, Money was hanging up his cell phone. "Man, Taeko just called me talkin' 'bout come scoop him up; his car broke down in Niggaville."

"Greenbriar Mall," we both said in unison.

"Man, Money, I just met my wife. Well, I didn't meet her thanks to Kane and Able."

"What, nigga?"

"Man, these kids wasted ice-cream on my shoes, and I lost my dream girl right before my eyes. She was bad, Dawg, a Clydesdale stepping, a stallion wild. Beautiful baby! Simply beautiful."

"Nigga, I knew that's why you shot off like you spotted gold."

"Hell, yeah, Dawg. She is the pot of gold."

"Man, that could be fool's gold and you the fool chasin' it." We both cracked up. But in the back of my mind I knew she wasn't any fool's gold, but I wasn't gon' be chasin'. Let someone else be the fool.

Chapter Nine

The Session

Junior Mafia played in the Explorer as the boys sat in Gresham Park, inhaling, coughing, and getting high as kites.

"Y'all niggas gon' die from too much weed smoke to the brain. And, Taeko, you know you don't need no more dead brain cells," Chocolate joked as he inhaled the second-hand smoke.

"Nigga, you jus' jealous 'cause yo' pretty ass can't hang," Taeko challenged as he inhaled a mouth full of smoke.

"Hell naw, dat nigga scared. Just like he scared of pussy." Money agreed with Taeko, taking a long, hard pull. "Come on, Chocolate, man. Take one hit." They both sat looking silly, staring into Chocolate's face like two lost puppies.

"Naw, somebody got to have a level head out of the three of us." Chocolate looked at them like a disgusted parent.

"Nigga, go 'head wit' dat shit. You gon' stay at the same level fo' the rest of yo' life—ON FULL!"

"Ha! Ha! Ha!" They both laughed hard about their same ol' faithful subject.

"Y'all love holl'in' that shit 'bout me not gettin' no pussy yet. What y'all seem to keep forgettin' is that I have to beat the pussy off with a baseball bat. I should be a professional baseball player. Y'all need to be practicin' abstinence. Shid! That's why you a daddy already. I ain't gon' even get on the fact that you got a damn abortion clinic named after you . . . and a health department."

After a long pause, Money spoke up. "Man, you better tell me that the contact you gettin' off this weed makin' yo' lips leak bullshit."

"Nigga, you wanna buck?" Chocolate balled his fist up and swung at Money. Money waved him off, feeling too lazy from his high to wrestle. "Jus' hit the damn blunt, Chocolate; it ain't gon' kill you."

He stared at the blunt, weighing his options. "Man, give me the shit."

AN HOUR LATER . . .

"Man, dis the first and last time I mess around wit' y'all fools," Chocolate said, pulling hard and deep on the blunt and giggling to himself. "But you know what? I can actually hear what Craig Mack is sayin' in this re-mix." Laughter filled the truck.

Chocolate raised up out of the seat slowly; looking dazed and pointing toward the woods. "Shhh, man. Y'all see dat shit?"

Both boys looked into the direction that Chocolate was pointing.

"I know I just saw somebody by dem trees." Chocolate waved his hand in front of his face and burst out laughing.

"What, nigga?" Money asked, focusing to see if it was some haters or the Po-pos."

Popping his lips because Chocolate was blowing his high, Money said with authority, "Nigga, you trippin'. Ain't nobody out there. Control the weed; don't let the weed control you."

"Ahh, ha! Ha! Ha! Dis nigga is really feelin' this shit, Money."

Chocolate busted out laughing, "Man, I'm high as hell. I feel like Superman, like I got x-ray vision or some shit. Ha! Ha! Ha!"

"Ha! Ha! Ha! Chocolate, you fucked up. Welcome to our world," Taeko laughed.

Sitting up straight in his seat, Chocolate licked his dry lips. "Boy, I'm hungry and horny as hell. I need some pussy to poke or munch on."

Knowing that he was a virgin, they both looked at him like he was stupid, but felt what he was saying.

A bright red and yellow 18-wheeler, going over the speed limit, lights bright, horn tooting loud, looked as though it was coming through the trees. "Oh, shit, oh shit, y'all let me the fuck outta here!" Chocolate jumped out the window and hunched down beside the door with the blunt still in hand.

"What is dis nigga doin'?" Money asked, reaching out of the window and snatching the blunt out of Chocolate's hand. "Boy, don't touch this shit no mo'."

Grumbling stomachs, Chocolate's laughter, and UGK's "Pocket- full of Stones" occupied the truck.

"Man, I got to do sump'n 'bout dat got damn Salone. She been trippin' lately," Money said as if he was in deep thought.

Chocolate perked up and paid attention. Taeko, stretched out across the back seat, lighting up his second blunt.

"And what I can't understand is we have a understanding of being friends . . . open to see who we wanna see. She askin' me 'bout Luvly and shit. SHIT!" Money let the blunt burn too long and a big lump of ash sizzled through his Falcon's jersey.

There it was, Luvly, the forbidden subject. But Chocolate was feelin' himself, so he rode the subject. "What about Luvly?"

"I love 'er."

"Dis weed must be the strongest shit around," Tae said seriously.

"Naw, I'm for real. But what a nigga s'pose to do when she attached to Diamond's nut sack. I ain't gon' give that nigga total credit for raising her. I'll give that nigga some credit, he did take care of her financially, but I put in the time, shoulders, heart, and the dick. But what should I expect from women, when my own mama ain't shit? Besides Seal and Grandma, it seem like every woman that has ever been in my life has fucked me—with no Vaseline." He stepped out of the truck and slammed the door. "Fuck 'em all."

Money's weakness was finally front and center—Luvly and the absence of his mother.

"Damn, did I see tears in dat nigga eyes?"

"She do be hurtin' dat nigga, doh," Taeko answered with sympathy.

"Aye, Tae, I saw my wife today."

"What she look like?"

"Ahhh, man, she was perfect. Thick and smooth. She had long, black hair with caramel skin. Ummm. Damn, I missed her just like that!" He snapped his fingers. Talking about his mystery star brought him back to his senses.

"Yo, you gon' see 'er again. Atlanta ain't that big, Dawg."

"She might not be from Atlanta; she could be jus' visitin' or somethin'." Chocolate thought to himself, *Damn, finding this girl is gon' be harder than taking candy from a baby.*

"Money, bring yo' ol', heartbroken ass on."

Chapter Ten

Luvly

Slap, Slap, Pop.

"Diamond, no!" I screamed, trying to crawl away from him. He ripped my shirt, and I felt a long, burning pain in my back. He kicked me in the stomach to slow me down. Snatching me up fast, he slapped me across my face, splitting my lip.

"Why you always believing them bitches in the street?" I cried.

I tried once again to run from him. "Bring yo' ass here!" I held my head with both hands, trying to avoid direct contact with his huge, hard fist.

He caught me and shook me like a baby rattle. "Stop, muthafuckin' lyin'. I know you was wit' that muthafuckin', nigga. You gon' make me fuck you up. Keep playin' with me, Luvly." Grabbing me by the throat, he threw one last forceful blow to the side of my head. I screamed out in severe pain.

"When I get back from Cancún, yo' punk ass gon' get pregnant; ain't gon' be no more of this shit." He snatched my birth control pills off the marble and iron end table, and threw them on the floor. "Then we'll see if Money's punk ass gon' wan' chu." He dropped me out of his hands like a rag doll.

He picked up the pills off the floor, set them on fire with a lighter, and threw the ball of fire at me. As I tried to dodge the ball of fire, it singed the hairs on my leg.

Without looking back, he walked out the door to be with Jordan, one of his baby mamas. Little did he know I wasn't using the pills as my method of control, termination and miscarry were becoming my best friends.

I layed in the same spot for about an hour with my aching, bruised face to the cold marble floor, wishing Money would come rescue me.

The phone rang constantly, but I wasn't in the mood to speak with anyone. *But maybe it's important. Like, maybe Diamond fell overboard and got ate by a shark.*

Ring . . . Ring . . . Ring.

"Hello," I sniffed.

"Girl, what's wrong with you? I guess I should know. I jus' saw Diamond pick up Jordan with all her baggage."

I didn't know if my cousin Precious told me about Diamond cheating every minute because she wanted me to see him for what he was, or because she enjoyed seeing me miserable.

"You like that nigga dawgin' you out, puttin' his foot on your neck, almost cuttin' off your air. If I had a fine-ass nigga like Money sniffin' the seat of my drawers, I wouldn't hesitate." She shuffled the phone, but continued her preaching, "But I can understand why you hesitate on Money, 'cause he need to grow up and figure out what he wants in life," she added.

I knew she was right. Money was whom I wanted. He had a stronghold over my heart, but Diamond had an even stronger hold over my soul.

"Why you cryin'? He beat yo' ass again?" Precious asked, not surprised.

I wanted to hang up in her face, but Precious was the only person Diamond let me hang out with. Besides, she gave me reality checks.

"Yeah, ain't that always the case over my way." I looked at myself in the wall mirror, rubbing the knot that lay underneath my hair on my head. The only visible scar on my face this time was my lip, and ice would heal that in no time.

Normally, when he left to go out of town, he would leave his handprint, or some kind of visible scar on of my face so that I wouldn't go out.

As I got up to wash my face, I felt the stinging sensation on my back again. The long, deep, raw, bleeding, gash looked horrible.

"You need to call that boy and tell him you wanna be with him. And tell him to talk to Chocolate's fine ass for me."

"Girl, you know you too wild for Chocolate. He likes clean, mature, wholesome girls."

"Shit! I'll be wholesome for his fine ass. I'll wash off all the makeup and take out all the weave."

"Yeah, and then he'll probably shoot you, mistakin' you for the boogie man." We both busted out laughing.

"Precious, I'm about to go to bed before I worry

myself to death about these men." Before she could say her piece, my phone beeped.

"Hold on, girl . . . Hello." There was no answer. "Hell-o-o?"

"Hey, beautiful, how are you?"

I smiled from ear to ear because I knew that strong, rough voice, with muffled ears. "Hey to you, too."

"Ya boy gone, ain't he?"

"Yeah."

"Are you busy?"

"No, I can talk. What's up?" There was a pause. "Hello, Money?"

"You. I want and need you."

"Money, let's not start this again. You know you're not ready for a real relationship, but we can at least give it a good start by being honest with each other. Salone is still in your life. She has practically been there since I have."

"Why every time the conversation get serious about us, you start talkin' shit about Salone? I don't bring up that low-down-ass nigga you so hooked on. Man—fuck! I shouldn'a called. Bye, man."

"Money, no! I'm sorry." Before I knew it, I was telling him to come over. I knew that people were always watching, and that Diamond would kill me—literally. "Come over and let me see your eyes."

We both hung up. The phone rang again and scared the shit out of me.

"Yeah."

"Girl, you crazy or something? I ain't a damn phone operator." Precious was still holding on.

"I just told Money to come over here," I said, covering my mouth in shock at my own actions.

"Get it, girl. Get yo' groove on. Diamond is out of town screwin' that old, nasty freak, anyway. He probably got her in one room and Pila in another. Look at it this way, you are going to make love to a man you love."

I ran to the bathroom and took a shower. With me being in Stone Mountain and Money in College Park, it would take him at least twenty-five minutes to get here.

The hot water felt good hitting my body—except for the deep cut on my back. I cried one last time and let the water wash away my tears.

After my shower, I rubbed on some Bath and Body Works' Pearberry and put on a white, ribbed tank top. He thought it was sexy for women to wear white Tees.

I put fresh sheets on the bed, lit Pearberry candles, and turned off all the lights. 104.7 set the mood with slow jams pouring through the speakers. I ran downstairs to clean up the glass from the mirror that Diamond threw me into and looked around to make sure everything was set.

The doorbell startled me. I ran to the door, but not before I looked back once more to make sure everything was straight—it almost scared the shit out of me. Diamond was staring at me through the silver frame. I ran over to the table and slammed them face down, took a deep breath, and opened the door.

Money's cologne pulled me straight into his arms. The wet rain on his skin, mixed with the fresh Nautica cologne smelled so good. His full lips swallowed me up. I couldn't wait to feel those lips between my thighs.

Taking a good look at me, he asked, "What the fuck hap—"

I placed my finger over his luscious lips. "Please, Money, jus' make it go away," I pleaded with tears, hunger, and passion in my eyes.

Money picked me up and I wrapped my legs around his waist. He knew my body like he'd molded it from clay. We had been in this position so many times before, but this night felt stronger—special. He knew exactly what I needed. He walked us up to the bedroom with me still hugged tight to his waist. "Damn, girl, you smell good." With a big smile on his face, we both said, "Pearberry."

I hugged him even tighter. "Choosey Lovers" filtered through the speakers as he layed me down and sung to my body and heart as The Isley Brothers sung the shit out of that song.

He layed me on my stomach and told me relax. He began to lick the lower part of my back, to the dip of my ass. "What the fu . . ." Money let out a long sigh as he rubbed his fingers over the gash on my back.

"Sssss." I jumped, turning to face him.

"How long you gon' let this shit keep going on, Luvly?"

I hugged him tight around the neck and gave him a peck on the cheek. "Make love to me, Money. Let's not let Diamond ruin this for us."

After kissing my wound, he gently guided me back to my stomach, pushing me up on my knees. He held both my ass cheeks in his hands, spreading them apart. I knew what I was in for and I was ready.

He rubbed his face against both my butt cheeks,

preparing me for ecstasy. His tongue lightly circled around the entrance of my ass hole. "Ahhhhhhh."

I fell to the bed unable to control my laughter. "It tickles."

"If you don't like it—" He said unsure of what he'd just done.

"I do, I do. Okay, come on, let's try it again."

He held on tight to my hips, returning to his original position. This time he applied more pressure with his tongue, replacing the tickles with pure sensations of pleasure.

"Oooh, hmmmm, yes. Money, keep it right there." Once he knew that he had me in his zone he dug his tongue deeper into my hole. "Hell, yeah. That's it, baby," I yelled, getting excited.

As I started to move back and forth on his tongue, he shook his head from side to side bouncing my cheeks from left to right on his face. "Ooohhh, shit! God . . . ummm . . . yessssss."

My pussy must have been calling his name because he answered it with sweet tongue kisses. Pressing his full, flat tongue up and down my pussy sent me into a frenzy. "Ahhhhhhh, Money. Ooohhhh . . . Babe. Hmmmm, it feels so good. Suck it, baby! Eat it!" Dripping wet, I grabbed his head and pushed him deeper into my love.

He turned me over for me to sit on top of him. I licked him from his lips to his ears, driving him crazy. Trailing down his neck to his stomach, I French- kissed his navel. "Sssss. Mmmm." He knew the direction I was headed, so he stretched his body out.

I began sucking his dick, keeping my strokes steady and firm.

"You gon' make me cum. Come up here and

ride it out of me." He grabbed my hair and pulled me up. I rubbed my pussy against his stomach, moving around in circular motions giving him a preview of how good it was going to be.

He pulled me back into his stomach. "I love you, Luvly. I'm sorry for everything I've ever done to you. I want to be with you, Babe, take you away from this bad life. When I go pro, Babe, I swear, I will come for you."

I believed Money, but I couldn't just up and leave my security.

Shit! He had been going between me and Salone for so long that I was used to the unspoken arrangement.

Even though Diamond was a dirty muthafucka', he took care of me in more ways than one. I had become accustomed to wearing Marquis, Baguettes, Louis Vuitton, Via Spiegel, Prada, Chanel; I was spoiled with endless ends. And his sex, ummm, it was off the chain. It made me forget any slap, punch or calling me out my name.

He also sent me to school for nursing, but I refused to go to school everyday with black eyes, busted lips, and, worst of all, a fucked-up mentality. When your heart is messed up, the mind shuts down and can't function.

So, I decided to go to nail school instead. After I got my certification, he had me a shop built on Old National. He named it Diamond Nails, of course. Women were flocking to the shop just because they had either slept with Diamond or wanted to.

I was living a life only dreams were made of. I

didn't have to lift a finger; I had my own personal maid. The big-ass house I lived in with him was laid to my liking, and I was driving a Jaguar. What else could a young woman want? A loving husband, maybe.

Before I knew it, Money was inside me—full and hard. I rode him like I was born to be his personal cowgirl. He held my ass and hips with a full grasp.

With just a few strokes, "I'm about to cum, Money. Mmmm I'm getting . . . so weak." He grabbed me so tight that he put nail marks in my hips; scars I didn't mind one bit! I came. We came. He came inside of me, and I accepted all of him.

Chapter Eleven

Chocolate

Tap, tap, tap, tap.
"Hmm."

Tap, tap, tap, tap. It sounded like fingernails tapping on my window. It stopped, so I lay back down. A few minutes later, tap, tap. Looking over at the clock I could see it was three o'clock in the morning.

My bed was next to the window, so I pulled up the blinds, "Oh shit, it's my lady!" She was standing in a white, see-through negligee that lay on her skin like satin, and some white bikini-cut panties sitting low on her hips. Her hair was pulled up into a sleek ponytail, the end twisted into a curly Q. Her glossy lips were pouty—ready for a kiss.

"What are you doing out there? You need to be in here where I am."

Damn, she sexy as hell! I rubbed my eyes to make

sure it was truly her. When I opened my eyes she was standing beside the bed. That perfect, white smile was driving me wild. Her baby-doll-pink toes, I wanted to suck 'em clear.

"Chinoe, I'm sorry you've waited on me for so long."

"Yes, Babe, I've been making deals with heaven and hell to get with you."

"Well, I'm here, Chinoe. What would you like me to do?"

"Come and let me taste you."

She blushed. "Chinoe, I'm so in love with you."

"I love you, too—wait a minute. I don't know your name. I tried to get to you in the mall, but these—"

"Shhh, don't say another word."

She bent down and kissed me so soft and passionate; I could feel her soft lips melt into mine. They felt like cotton.

She sat on top of me. I was rock hard, scared to enter her; *I might bust a hole in her womb.* She moved her pussy lips on the top of my head in a circular.

"You about to make me—"

Buzzzzzzzzzzzzzzzzzzzz, the alarm sounded, "Damn, I was having a phat-ass dream."

Chapter Twelve

Chocolate

My mama was in the kitchen, throwin' down. The smell of homemade biscuits, bacon, eggs, and pancakes replaced the oxygen flowing through my nose.

"Well, sleepyhead, you're finally up?"

"Yeah, unfortunately."

"What's that suppose to mean? Boy, you should wake up praising God that you were able to wake up."

"Yeah, Ma, I know, but I was havin' a dream that a man wouldn't wanna wake from."

"Um, um. What time did Caymin leave?"

"She left about forty-five minutes after you did."

Mama was tryin' to make conversation, beating around the bush. Something was on her mind. "What's up, Ma? Whatcha need? Whatcha want? What can I do for ya?" I asked, kissing her cheek.

She took a serious tone. "The only thing I need is a place in heaven. Everything I want I have: a great job, wonderful friends, and a very comfortable lifestyle. And for your last question, a good-looking young man to cut my grass."

"You got it." I smiled like a Cheshire cat. I'd been promisin' to cut it for weeks now.

"Now for the lighter side of things, I would like a vacation in Cancún, a Mercedes Benz, and a house in the hills."

"Ma, you trippin'. When I make it big, your list will be the first one filled."

"And what you could do for me is—" She came closer to me and leaned on the opposite side of the breakfast bar, grabbing my face like she used to when I was little and she meant business. ". . . From you, I want a success story. For you to live out your dreams, not to be a failure to yourself. To have one strong BLACK woman by your side that'll kick your stubborn butt when you get out of line."

I looked into my mom's strong, worried, proud, black eyes and truly knew she wanted me to be successful at everything I did. My mother never let me be a wimp. Shit! She used to rough me up more than my dad. She used to tell me, "If I love you and can rough you up, then you can get roughed up by this world and not feel disappointed when it lets you down."

"I understand what you sayin' Mama. I understand."

After I ate, I jumped in the shower. The hot, steamy water felt good running down my tense shoulders. It reminded me of when I used to play football and felt sore after practice. Lathering the soap up in my washcloth made me think about how good my dream was the night before.

I couldn't get over that dream. It was so real. I mean I could feel her body against mine, and her soft lips on mine. Squeezing the sudsy washcloth, my dick became hard. I just needed to see her again. Shit! I would definitely ask that girl to be my life-long partner.

I was expecting Money to swing by at about 11 a.m., so I could go check out my pop's surprise.

Thinking about my life was starting to consume my thoughts. Like, what type of man was I going to become? Or what type of woman would I marry? What would my kids be like? Would my son act like Money or me? That was a scary thought. What I really wanted was three girls: a basketball player, a ballerina, and a lawyer or doctor, three well-rounded, strong women.

Just as I got out of the shower the telephone rang.

Ring . . . Ring . . . Ring.

"Talk to me."

"Hi, Mr. Chinoe. Chocolate Starr."

Excited to hear this sweet lady's voice, I asked, "What's up, Babe? How you been doin'? Two weeks is the longest you've ever stayed away from me. This time it's been over two months. So is it another man or what?"

"Naw, you know y'all are the only men a woman needs for survival," she laughed.

"You know it, Babe. We yo' ghetto supermen," I said in a cartoon voice.

"Where is Money, anyway? He act like he can't sit still long enough to keep in touch wit' me."

"You know how dat pimp do." She hesitated like something was on her mind.

"Luvly, what's up? Who broke your heart this time?"

"Nobody. My heart has yet to heal from Diamond . . . and is still open to Money."

Luvly had always been like a homeboy to me. She was always there for me to talk to about females, and I was always there for her to talk to about Money and Diamond. She was definitely sweet, sometimes a little naïve, but always loving. Mixed with a black mother and an Italian father, she was simply gorgeous. Five-seven petite and well-packaged, she was very shapely.

Luvly used to have high spirits, smiling all the time, going to all the parties, and just enjoying life—until she fell in love with her two weaknesses.

Money and Diamond competed to be with Luvly, but back then Diamond was the man with the plan. We were a year younger than Luvly, and Diamond was many years wiser than all of us. His big plan all along was to beat her into submission.

Luvly had been living in her own apartment since her junior year of high school—with Diamond. This kept us from knowing what was going on with her. The way she kept in touch with me was through my mother. She told Diamond that my mother was her tutor, helping her to get her GED.

Two years ago, by the grace God, it took all me and Money had, to keep her alive.

As we approached the hospital, Money spotted a

green 600 series Benz with a CUBMAF license plate, backed into a parking spot.

"That muthafucka' got the nerve to fuck 'er up and then be at the hospital." Diamond was grabbing a young nurse, for information on Luvly.

Soon as he whipped into the parking lot, barely letting the car stop, Money took off running, with Diamond unaware that he was under attack. Just as the nurse stuffed a wad of cash into her overcoat, turned and walked back into the hospital, Money punched Diamond in the side of the head.

"What the fu—?" Money opened the door to the car and pulled Diamond out before he knew what was going on.

"Nigga, you gon' pray about this ass-whuppin' you about to get!" Money grunted as he yanked Diamond out of the car.

As soon as Diamond hit the ground, our feet were on his head and neck. Diamond fought to get to his feet by pulling up on the car door. He kicked back, hitting Money in the knee, bringing him to the ground with Money still throwing blows to Diamond's head.

Money punched Diamond until his own skin broke and began to bleed.

Diamond kept trying to get back to his car. But we knew that if he got to his car, bullets would fly.

We stomped him damn near unconscious. It looked like "Ole Dawg" and "Kane" from *Menace to Society* when they stomped dude when he tried to confront Kane about getting his cousin pregnant.

Mrs. Mancini, Luvly's mother, ran out the hospital with the same nurse Diamond paid, and a male orderly.

"STOP! Stop!" Mrs. Mancini yelled, only touching my shoulder for fear that she would have been trampled if she tried any harder. I backed off, but not before giving him one last kick to the chin.

"This is not going to help Luvly. She needs you here by her bedside. Savoy, Savoy!" she yelled for Mr. Mancini.

Unaware of what was happening, he was already hurrying out of the hospital doors behind his frantic wife. But when he caught sight of us fighting, he understood that we had to be stopped or somebody was going to die.

"Hey, hey, come on, Money." He wrestled between Money and Diamond, taking a blow here and there until they were on either side of him.

Diamond, breathing heavily and full of blood, panted, "Muthafucka . . . you . . . gone." He grabbed his chest, trying to catch his breath. "This shit . . . ain't over, nigga."

Security finally got to the scene asking questions, and the nurse that Diamond paid earlier was crying and begging him to please leave, for the sake of her job.

"G'on! Get outta here!" Mr. Mancini waved his hand at Diamond. "You oughta be glad I ain't shoot you between the eyes."

"Come on, boys. Come on." Mrs. Mancini was hugging me like I was the one on the floor bleeding and begging for my life.

Mr. Mancini was holding Money around the waist.

"Nigga, this ain't finished. It ain't finished by a long shot!" I meant that to the heart. He was going to be made to pay.

When we walked into Room 704, it was like a

scary fairy tale. She was lying in the bed with perfect hair, hands very still by her side and the white sheet pulled neatly above her breast. Her face was swollen-purple, and her hands had abrasions on both of them, where it looked like he held her down or scratched the shit out of her.

Me and Money kneeled down on opposite sides of the bed. Money had tears in his eyes. "Luv, I love you, girl. You got to get up." He let out a loud sigh and layed on her chest. "Please, baby, get up, and open your eyes."

My eyes started to tear up, but I cleared my throat and choked it back. I loved Luvly like a sister, but Money had a deeper relationship with her. Whenever Diamond was fuckin' up, Money would be fuckin' and lovin' her.

Her parents were exhausted and needed a change of clothes. She had been there for two days. We didn't know about it because we were out of town playing a football game. We told them that we would stay and that my mother would be there in about thirty minutes. They agreed and left with long miserable faces, but not before they both kissed their helpless daughter and gave their two extended-family sons a hug.

Money got on the phone and began putting some things in motion. "Taeko, Luvly in the hospital. That nigga, Diamond, beat the shit out of her."

"What the fuck! Man, I'm on it. You know you ain't got to say a word."

I grabbed the phone and took a deep breath for what I couldn't believe I was about to say. "A, Taeko, man, don't kill that nigga. You know she love 'im and would hate us even more for killin' 'im."

"Fuck that! These niggas got records and don't give a shit about that nigga! I can't believe you pleadin' for that pussy-ass nigga's life."

"Look, Taeko, you know how she is now. Don't fuck her no more than she already is."

There was silence on the phone for two minutes. I looked down at Luvly and it was as if she was speaking to me through her coma.

"Taeko, you hear me, Dawg?"

"Yeah, I heard you, loud and motherfuckin' clear. Spare that pussy his sorry-ass life."

"Just remember though, if she don't make it, he don't make it."

I put the phone down with relief. Relief for the sake of Luvly.

Two months after she recovered she was in that nigga's arms again, forgiving, but never forgetting.

Later on, I found out the reason he stomped her was that he found out Luvly and Money had been screwing since the beginning—in the place he paid for, in the same bed where he layed his head.

"Money is about to stop by and take me to my dad's lot."

"And you are saying that to say what, Chocolate?" Luvly tried to sound uninterested, but couldn't hide the interest that aroused in her voice.

"I mean you know how I'm the last one to know what's really goin' on. So—shit—maybe y'all gettin' busy again."

She paused as if I didn't know something I needed to. "Well, I do need to tell you something, but I don't want a lecture. Okay?"

I already knew what it was. Diamond had put

the word out on the street that he was about to add to his baby collection.

"Yeah, I promise, no lectures."

"You ready to be a godfather?"

"Nope, not if it's the seed spun from asshole."

She laughed, but I knew it hurt her. "Come on, Chocolate. It's part of me, so I know you got to love it."

"Yeah, girl. Damn. You fucking up big time now"

Ding Dong, Ding Dong.

"Hold on." I threw the phone on the sofa behind me because I knew who was at the door, and I didn't want him to say anything out of the way.

Ding Dong.

"Damn, nigga! Don't break my bell; ain't no pussy in here."

"If it was, I know it'd be untouched."

"Man, go head wit' all that. Boy, guess who I'm on the phone with?" He raised his eyebrows. "She done finally rose from the dead." His spirits died right on the spot.

"Man, I ain't studin' her," he said, dismissing her with a wave of his right hand. "I'm tired of all the drama and wishy-washy shit."

"Not Money, not pimp tight, tired of a fine woman," I said, rubbing my chest like Rico Suave. I leaned over and looked in his face. "You all right, folk? You sick or some shit you ain't told me?"

"Naw," he said, turning up his top lip. "Just tired of her using me for backup."

Understanding his tone, I handled the phone call. "Luvly, I'm about to be out. Hey, you still live with Diamond?"

"No, he stay in Stone Mountain with baby mama number two."

"Well, give me a call later and I'll come by."

"Was that Money?"

Money's eyes met mine. I pointed at the phone and he started waving his hands in a motion to suggest he was not there.

"Naw, that was Mrs. Hemton lookin' for Mama."

"Just please don't tell him I'm pregnant; let me handle that."

"You got it." *Click.*

Chapter Thirteen

Chocolate

Our Saturdays usually consisted of washing cars, shooting a little ball, playing a game of football, or volunteering at the Boys' and Girls' Club and homeless shelter, but today we headed downtown to my father's lot. The ride had been quiet for the most part. I knew Money still loved Luvly. Always would. But I also knew he was tired of being her crutch when she was hurt.

He told me one time that he would marry her. We were drinking and he was smoking that night, but I knew he meant it.

Beep . . . Beep . . . Beep.

My pager sparked a conversation.

"Hey, you start back messin' wit' Nikki?"

"Hell, naw. Why? Who tellin' lies now?" I asked, hoping the information hadn't got back to Caymin.

"You know Salone know everybody business but her own, but I guess Nikki was, or is, trying to get on with Salone at the mall. She said Nikki talked about you all day at lunch."

"Man, I saw her at that white-girl clothing store downstairs at the mall yesterday. She ain't even my type anymore. She done cut her hair and wearin' all that shit on her face."

"I mean what do you expect her hair to look like after that shit Caymin pulled graduation night."

Beep . . . Beep . . . Beep.

"Speak of the devil—Caymin pagin' the shit out of me. I know she don't want nothing, but some money for the mall."

"I'd have to be hittin' that ass if I was givin' up presidents?"

I didn't feel like I needed to explain myself to Money, but I didn't want to hear that shit. "Man, don't start that cake-daddy shit. If you understood what she had to deal wit', you'd be pushing me outta the way to give it to her too."

We finally pulled up to my dad's car lot. A flock of new SUV's, Lexuses, some oldies but goodies, and a few Jaguars sat pretty.

"Damn! Pops comin' up like a fat rat."

"Shit! Nigga, that last name Starr ain't Starr for nothin'."

My dad was already on the lot making deals and making earnings for my education.

"What's up, Pop? How you doin'?"

"Not as good as you, Money. I don't have all the ladies you got."

We laughed as we walked toward the SUV's. "Hey, Money, how your truck holdin' up?"

"It's runnin' like a champ."

"Yeah, your grandfather had me special-order that paint and design."

When I got back to the lot, Money was talking to some woman like he knew what he was doing.

"That Money somethin' else."

"Yeah, something crazy."

"Shit, if that boy sell that woman a car, I'll give him the profit."

"Well, I need to be out here sellin' then."

"Naw, you gon' take your butt to school and make money to set me up like a kingpin. Come on over here and let me show you something." We walked to the side of the building to the garage. He usually kept celebrities' cars and high-profile cars there. "Open the garage door."

Behind the garage door was sitting a 300zx, twin-turbo.

"Daddy, this car tight. Who's? Some football player?"

"You really like it? What about the color?"

"The color and rims are tight."

"You want to take it for a spin?"

"Hell, yeah."

Man, that car felt like I was floating on water. It was smooth even over bumpy roads. It had the same system as Money's truck, the sound crisp and clean. That car was made for me. I would have loved to have that thang in my possession, but I knew a car like that would only bring problems.

I whipped back in the parking lot. Money and my father were standing in the middle of the lot like two proud poppas.

"Aye, Dawg, dis car tight!"

"Yeah, it is." Money started laughing. "Open up the glove compartment and see who owns it. I think your pop said it belongs to a famous entertainment lawyer."

"Did you sell that car?"

"Yep." He punched me in the arm. "A Jag, nigga. That's dead presidents all in my pocket. Shit, I might take her old butt out. She ain't that old. Thirty-four."

We both leaned back to check out how old her backside looked. "Twenty-four."

I looked into the glove compartment trying to see who owned this baby. An envelope with Chinoe Chocolate Starr is staring at me with "Attorney-At-Law," written in fancy letters under my name. Opening the envelope, almost shittin' on myself, there was a check for thirty-five thousand dollars, and one thousand dollars in cash with a note attached:

> *To Chinoe Starr:*
>
> *You are a loving second grandson. We hope that you succeed in everything you do. Anytime you are in need we are going to be here indeed. Take care of yourself and Money. Hurry up and become that big-time lawyer. Money is probably going to need it.*
>
> *Love, Mama and Papa Loane*

I was speechless. What's this? Two more pieces of paper were behind the money. One paper was a contract for a condo of my choice; the other paper was the registration for the car with my name on it. I almost choked.

At that very moment, I felt like I had really graduated into adulthood. I had no choice but to grow up, get serious, make my impression in life, and then flirt with the world, leaving Caymin's bullshit, and all the old issues behind me.

The only thing I couldn't let go of was the beautiful girl I saw at the mall. If it took everything in my life, I was going to find her.

Chapter Fourteen

Luvly

"Ma, I don't need your sarcasm right now; I'm in trouble," I screamed into the cell phone.

"Yes. You are! You need to listen to what you said. You are in trouble—again. And you need to watch your tone with me; I'm not one of your little hot-in-the-tail girlfriends."

"Yeah, Ma, I understand all of that, but what am I suppose to do?"

"Tell the truth, and let God be with you. We've tried so hard with you, Luvly, but you keep refusing our help. You know your father and I love you very much, and you don't ever have to want for anything."

I pulled into a gas station, crying. "I know. I know." *Click.*

Lord, have mercy on my soul. Who do I tell

about my baby? Diamond or Money? *I know in my heart that it's Money's, but Diamond will kill both of us. That's why I can't get rid of it this time. My best bet is to just play it as it comes. I know I'm going to pay for this shit in the end, but what do I do while I'm faced with it in the present?*

Money had been messin' wit' this trick named Salone that kept callin' my fuckin' phone threatenin' me. That bitch was crazy. And I couldn't call Money and tell 'im that she fuckin' wit' me, or that I heard in the street that she fuckin' Diamond, 'cause he would only think I was playin' get-back games wit' him.

I looked into the mirror to make sure I looked half-decent before I went into the store. It was packed and anyone could be at this little freak-nick gas station. I wiped my face and headed inside.

"Damn, Luvly, you gettin' thick as hell. You need to let a nigga get at chu," A boy I knew from the neighborhood said.

"Dee, please. Boy, you couldn't handle all this woman if I gave it to you piece by piece." We both laughed as I walked into the store.

Being upset and not paying attention, letting my guard down, I let my surroundings get the best of me. Just as I walked out of the store, a black Jimmy with tinted windows hit my Mercedes from the back, which made my car hit the car in front of me.

"What the fuck? You can't see or something?" I yelled. The girl in the car in front of me just laughed like it was funny. The girl in the other car just looked at me like she wanted to beat my ass.

"Fuck this!" I walked fast to my car, reaching

into my purse to grab my cell phone when someone kicked me in the back. "Ahhh!"

My only thought was about my baby. As I fell into the front seat of my car, I could see people moving closer to the pumps, but not close enough to get involved.

"Get yo' trick ass up!"

The voice sounded familiar. Like the same voice that was threatenin' me every night. I tried to search the car floor for the heavy flashlight that always rolled under my seat.

"I told you that I was on yo' ass and you would slip up real soon." Smack! The slap came before I had time to get back out of the car.

Not paying attention to my passenger door, the girl that was parked in front of me grabbed my shirt and hair from the back. While Salone and one of her disciples started punching me in the stomach, and scratching my face, my legs were kicking at full force.

"You won't have this muthafuckin' baby, ho."

She was so determined to hit me in the stomach that I was truly afraid she was going to succeed. My cell phone hit the ground; it gave me both hands free to finally get to the flashlight. I hit the girl holding me from the back, cracking her wrist.

"Ahhh, shit!"

Salone was still punching at full force: "I hate you, you stupid-bitch! Money is mine—"

With no one holding me from the back I got loose and punched Salone in the face, my fingernails deeply wounded her under her left eye. But being in the car, I was at a disadvantage. Another one of Salone's friends grabbed me from behind again. Salone took all of her strength and came down full blast with both of her hands into my stomach, which left me screaming louder then I screamed when Diamond jumped on me.

That took all the fight out of me. While one girl held my hands back, another girl took my Chanel sandals. Salone yanked my legs like a rag doll and my body hit the ground like a pound of logs. She ripped my diamond-hooped earrings out of my ears, but when she bent down to go for the sapphire ring that Money gave me, I bit her in the same spot I had just scratched her in.

Dee ran over with a couple of his boys and stopped it, but it was too late. My stomach started cramping and when I looked down, there was blood between my thighs.

Chapter Fifteen

FOUR YEARS LATER

Chocolate

"When you comin' home, boy?"

"After my agent gets everything in order with my contract and money—something you should have been handling. Man, a mind is a terrible commodity to waste." Money sounded more mature and focused. Going to the Super Bowl had helped him prove to himself that he could achieve anything he set his mind to.

I knew he'd be busy flying here and there, doing interviews and commercials, so there was no telling how long it'd be before he came home.

"Hey, did you go by the mall and take Salone her birthday gift?"

Oh, shit! I forgot. That silver box was still sitting on my bar. I knew if I told him no he'd be tripping like a little bitch. "Yeah, I took it up there yesterday, but she wasn't in the store. That skinny, freckled face chic said she would be back later on today."

"Yeah, nigga, you forgot."

We both paused thinking about all the latest information we needed to share before we departed.

"Aye, Luvly been askin' 'bout you."

"Yo, Chocolate, leave that conversation in the wind blowin' anywhere but up my ass."

"Nigga, you can't keep pushing the issue away because the problem is still going to be there."

"If she want that sorry, dope-dealing, woman-beating-ass Diamond to fuck her and her life up, and take care of Sap, then that's on her dumb ass."

I knew that was the end of that conversation.

"Have you made plans for Daytona and Cancún?"

"Yeah, my agent called last week. We got a beach-front house in Daytona. I was trying to see where Jay-Z was getting his house so that we could be in the vicinity of all the concerts and booty-shake contests."

The laughter crept back into our voices.

"Well, let me get to the mall so your boo can put on an academy awards show about her present."

"When she get it, tell her to open it in front of her computer so that I can see her reaction."

"Yeah, nigga, later."

"Later."

Quite a few things had changed in CP. Everyone had grown up physically, but mentally I think we were all stuck in a maze.

After Lan got out of jail at the end of '94, he and his baby's mother got back together. One week later he beat her again, and she slit his throat in the middle of the night while he slept.

Vegas's life had been bittersweet. In the summer of '95, his mother and her boyfriend were arguing about her seeing another man. His aunt, the mother's sister, was standing in the middle of them while they argued. The aunt was secretly seeing the boyfriend on the side as well, telling him everything her sister was doing. The boyfriend pulled out a gun and shot both of them in the head, and then turned the gun on himself. Vegas came home from a Friday night out wit' the boys to find the door wide open with his younger sister screaming, lying on top of their bloody mother.

Since both of them were minors, they had to go live with their father in Korea. Then, Vegas started attending some big university up North. He wrote me a couple of letters, but I hadn't heard from him since.

Unfortunately, I didn't transfer to Morehouse, I finished up a degree in Computer Programming at Clayton State University. I was still a virgin, on what seemed like a hopeless journey for perfection. Lately, I'd been offered some modeling gigs and getting paid a pretty penny.

Money, Luvly, and Taeko were doing well despite some poor decisions. Money went pro after he graduated from FSU with a degree in Sports Therapy. He had offers from every team in the league, each one trying to outbid the other, offering homes, cars, extra signing bonuses, women—anything they could to get 'im. With all that at his feet, he decided to sign with the Falcons so that he could be close to his family. Lately, he'd been playing with fire and he knew it.

Luvly had a little girl and named her Sapphire, making me godfather, of course. That little girl was the number one lady in my life. When Sap turned one year, she looked like Money carved her out of his chest, but Luvly still denied the fact that he was her father. Maybe she really didn't know who the father was, but I doubt it.

Diamond used Sap as a hold on Luvly. He was barely around to see that little girl. The only time he wanted to be bothered with her is when he screwed or beat on Luvly.

After she had Sap, she was miserable and barely holding on to her sanity. My mother and Grandma Loane had Sap the majority of the time when she was first born. I picked up responsibility with her when she was able to walk. Diamond wasn't around enough and didn't care enough to know who was taking care of Sap.

Luvly moved to Stone Mountain, thinking she could outrun her trouble, but it followed her. I tried to help Luvly as much as possible, keeping Sap on Tuesdays and Thursdays; my mom kept her on Mondays and Fridays. And I kept my mouth shut and out of her business about Money and Diamond.

Taeko also went pro. He played for the Hawks. Pimped a Bentley and wore diamonds and platinum from head to toe, the boy was ballin' in more ways than one. He signed the biggest contract in the history of the NBA and bought a four-story house with an elevator, theater, inside and outside basketball courts and more out in Henry County. With all that, he still slipped and let the groupies get to both of his heads.

Chapter Sixteen

Chocolate

It was Thursday and I had to pick up Sap, so I decided to deliver those four-karat earrings to Salone. I went to McDonald's first to pick up Sap's favorite cheeseburger happy meal. While I stood in line, I looked out into the parking lot. High school didn't seem that long ago, but Nikki and Caymin did. All that drama for what? Nothing. Not a damn thang came of it. If I could go back to graduation night, boy, would I change the whole thang!

"Hey, Chinoe, how you doin'?"

I turned around and stared into the eyes of Joslen Frank, still as cute as she was in school. "What's up, girl?" We embraced each other.

"Well, you know I'm back here in Atlanta now."

"Oh, yeah, you went to L.A. for acting, right?"

"Yeah, right. So what are you doing now?"

Shit! I wanted to say that I was a big-time, high

profile, entertainment lawyer. "Well, I graduated with a B.A. in Computer Programming. I'm self-contracting, trying to decide if I want to stay in Atlanta or not."

"Well, you should stay in Atlanta. Black people are making Atlanta hotter than ever." Her smile could have broken any hovering cloud. "So you married? Kids?" Joslen asked.

The cashier cleared her throat, and tried to hand me Sap's happy meal.

"Oh, no. This is for Luvly's little girl, my goddaughter."

"Oh, yeah, she did have a little girl by Diamond, right?"

"Unfortunately."

"Well, here's my card. Let me write my home number on the back."

I took her number to satisfy her ego, and dropped it in the trash as I left. She was definitely not the one, and I'm not the one to pretend.

I headed up Old National to the daycare center. When I walked in, Sap was running around being bossy as usual.

"Hi, Mr. Starr. Sapphire has been using foul language today. I don't know why she is so hostile lately, but we are not going to tolerate it," Mrs. Tate said, smiling. But I knew she meant business, seeing that this was an academy for excelling and gifted children.

"Thank you, Mrs. Tate. I will address this with Sapphire."

Sapphire looked around the corner, and almost broke her neck to get to me. Her little lips almost swallowed up her face with a huge smile.

"Hey, Uncle Cha-late."

Before I picked her up into my arms like I always did, I stopped her in mid jump. "Hey, li'l lady, have you been bad today?"

She put her finger in her mouth and shook her head no.

"Sap, is Mrs. Tate telling stories on you?"

She started to twist her long ponytails.

"Sapphire, I'm very disappointed in you, but I can forgive you for a hug, an apology, and a promise to never use those words again."

Mrs. Tate pulled her close for a hug then gave her a lollipop. They loved Sap at her school. She was very bright, talkative, and sweet, thanks to my mother.

I scooped her up in my arms and headed for Southlake Mall.

"Uncle Cha-late, when Uncle Money come home? I miss him."

I looked at her through the rearview mirror. She was stuffing her face with fries. She had no idea the predicament her mother had put her in.

"He's coming in two weeks."

She started bouncing up and down shaking her head from side to side. "Yeah! Yeah! Uncle Money come home. D'mond is bad."

"Did Diamond hit you, Sap?" I hit the brakes, almost killing us both.

She shook her head no. "Mommy, in the face."

I knew I had to talk to Money and Luvly before I went to jail for some shit they could have handled a long time ago. That little girl deserved the best, and Diamond was far from that. As we walked through the mall, Sap started going crazy. "Uncle Cha-late, I want the doggies! The doggies!"

"Okay, pun'kin, after I go into this store."

Walking toward Salone's shop, I caught déjà vu. There she was—my heaven. I rushed Sap into the store. "Salone, watch Sap, right quick."

"Yeah, okay."

I ran down the steps, this time almost breaking both legs. I could only see her from the back, but I knew it was her.

"Excuse me, Miss . . ." She turned around, shooting my spirits straight to hell. "Oh, I'm sorry to bother you, Miss, I thought you were someone else."

"That's okay," she said, extending her hand. "My name is Sophie."

"Hey, how you doin'? I'm Mac. Nice to meet you."

Her four girls were running around, out of control and screaming, my cue to get the hell on.

"Well, I have to go and get my three boys and girl from the toy store upstairs." I knew that would discourage her. Women looking for someone to take care of them and theirs and don't want a man with as many kids as they have.

Damn! I was disappointed and relieved at the same time. That wasn't even that woman's real hair; my doll has natural hair, from the roots.

When I got back to the store Salone seemed content playing with Sap, even though she held pure hatred for her mother. The love she held for Money was enough to keep her cool about Sap.

"Uncle Cha-late, I want that dress, and that dress, and that pants," she giggled and continued to play dress up.

"Yeah, Uncle Cha-late," Salone said laughingly, "buy me a dress, too," she continued mockingly. She knelt down in front of Sap. "Here, take these dresses and pants outfits home and show your mommy, tell her Auntie Salone gave them to you."

Sap took in her whole face. "What did that to face?" The little girl asked as best she could, pointing her little finger to the scar under Salone's left eye.

With a sad look in her eyes, there was no way Salone could tell Sap that she'd gotten that scar from trying to abort her from her mother's womb. "She is getting so big." Salone rubbed playfully on Sap's stomach.

"Yeah, old enough to relay that sneaky-ass message you tryin' to send to Luvly."

Salone stood against the tall counter; arms folded, took a long sigh, and blew her bangs up into the air. "It's not that I'm being sneaky; I just want her to know that I'm still here and I'm not going anywhere."

"Well, I'm not gettin' caught up in y'all mess."

"Yeah, well, she looks just like Money. Is she Money's or what? Why that ho . . . I mean, why hasn't she got a test yet?"

"You know that if I knew the answer I still wouldn't get in y'all business. That's my boy, and my loyalty is to him," I insisted, as I grabbed for Sap's hand.

"Yeah, y'all low-down niggas always stick together."

"Salone, you know I'm not low-down; I'm a good brother just looking for my queen."

"Ahhhh, man, please don't be givin' me that queen bullshit; I know the real deal."

I reached in my coat pocket and pulled out the pink box. "Here. This is from your low-down friend—Money."

She broke into a smile and took the box.

"Oh, yeah, don't open it until you get in front of the web-cam."

Her expression convinced me that this would comfort her for the week. "Come on, Sap. Tell Miss Salone thank you."

With candy all over her hands and mouth, she waved good-bye.

"Come on, messy mouth. Let's get you cleaned up."

We went to the bathroom in the back of the store to wash her hands and mouth. Looking at how beautiful she was with big, black eyes framed by long eyelashes, coffee-colored skin, and long, sandy brown ponytails. Her lips and nose had Money written all over them.

I heard a new voice from outside the curtain, asking about some shoes. It sounded so sexy. A little rough and hoarse, but still very womanly. I tried to look around the corner, and almost tripped over a box. I couldn't see who it was because of all the clothes obstructing my view. "Come on, Sap. Hurry up," I whispered to myself.

By the time I grabbed Sap and we walked out, the lovely voice was gone.

"We out, Salone."

"We out, S'one." Sap always repeated everything she heard.

"Are you still coming down to the shelter Saturday to help with the food? Taeko can't be there, so we need an extra hand."

"Yeah, I'll be happy to help the homeless."

When we got to my condo, I gave Sap some cookies and juice, and put on Teletubbies before I sat down at the computer to check my emails.

I'd been a little anxious about my e-mails and assignments. Being lonely for companionship was really starting to bother me. The sex thing was still not an issue. *Head* was keeping my head straight to be twenty-one and still looking for that pot of gold, actually, I'd upgraded to platinum. A gold piece would be good, but platinum would be more rare and precious.

Ring . . . Ring . . . Ring.

The phone interrupted my concentration.

"Starr residence."

"What's up, Dawg?" Taeko asked. "I was just calling before I headed to Houston."

"Where Joi and the kids?"

"Over her mama house." He answered in a nonchalant attitude. Lately he'd been acting like he was womanless and childless. I saw more of Supreme and Trinket than he did. He had the option of taking them with him and never did. I knew he loved his kids, but I don't think they knew it.

"Is everything set for Daytona and Cancún?" He asked, with the excitement in his voice that he should have had about Joi and his kids.

"Yeah, Money got one beach house in Daytona and he workin' on a mansion with Jay-Z for Cancún."

"That nigga just wanna see some hoes shake they ass." We discussed a few more details and ended the conversation.

Sap began to fall asleep, and I started getting lazy-eyed as well, so I shut down the computer and grabbed Sap. We got into my bed, snuggled, and were out for the count.

Lying there, I thought about all the women that had come in and out of my life, all the pussy I passed up, and wondered if waiting for the perfect woman was becoming a waste of time.

There was Tiona, twenty-six, with two B.A.'s and a Masters in physical therapy, bad-ass body, beautiful attitude, and could cook her ass off. But I felt she was becoming clingy and possessive. She definitely was not platinum—or maybe she was and I was just afraid of commitment.

Then there was Nina. Man, she was all prissy and too high-class for me. Shit! I got money, too, but I didn't let it rule my life or attitude. But I must admit she could suck a good dick.

And Wendi was a trip. Fun, carefree attitude, but definitely not the bullshit type. She demanded everything, my time, my attention, my whole life. She would ask, "Who is that on the phone? And what time did you say you'd be back?" She used to trip about me watching Howard Stern, saying it was nonsense and only exploited naked women. That nigga was a fool. I had to catch that every night. If someone tripped on him, then he or she was just as big an asshole as he was.

The one that brought back the fondest memories was Koshia. Shit! She had to have some fly shit between them legs, the way she walked and strutted around smelling good all through the day. She was a hundred percent platinum, but then she said, "Chinoe, if I get totally involved with you, I will lose myself. Right now, I need to find out who I really am—in terms of my career and what I want out of life. I'm sure we'll meet up again."

It had been almost four years, and that girl from the mall was still etched in my brain. Atlanta was not as big as people thought but I still hadn't seen her yet. I was sure I would see her again and prayed about it every night.

Chapter Seventeen

Chocolate

I looked at my watch, as I anxiously awaited Money's arrival scheduled for 1:45 p.m. Family and friends were waiting, too. His grandmother, my mother, Salone, Taeko, Joi and the kids, waited impatiently with Sap clinging to Money's grandmother. Mrs. Loane was so attached to her.

"This is the sweetest babe. Jesus! I swear she looks like Maynea. Just hope she don't grow up actin' like 'er."

Last I heard, Money's mother, Maynea, had gotten herself straight and was living in Tennessee.

By one-thirty the kids started getting antsy and hungry.

"We thirsty."

"I hungry."

"Y'all can't wait until we get to the restaurant?" I

asked, wishing we'd gone with the original plan of letting Precious keep the kids.

"Noooooo."

Me and Taeko let everyone know that we were going to get the kids something to drink.

Taeko gently pushed the kids ahead of us. "Chocolate, I need your opinion on something."

"Shoot."

"I'm not happy with my life."

Here we were again with that stupid shit. Taeko had what every man dreamed of, a long-term relationship with the same woman, two beautiful kids, and a career as a professional basketball player.

"What the hell can possibly not be going right to make you unhappy?"

"I want my freedom."

"What? A free agent or what?" I looked at him like he was stupid.

He looked disappointed and sad. "Man, stop playin'. I'm willin' to give all the cheese in the world to be apart from Joi."

I really didn't want to hear that shit. Joi was a good woman and had been there for Taeko through paternity tests, Enquirer scandals, and other woman suing for all types of shit. And most of all, she was there when his ass only had five dollars to his name.

"Man, Joi has been there for you when you didn't have shit or wasn't shit. Plus that's pussy at home that you know is disease-free."

"I know, but I feel like I haven't had a life for myself. Shit, we had Trey when we were in the eleventh grade; we've been together since the ninth grade. I need some time to myself."

"Man, please," I told him, dismissing him with

my hand. "Niggas dream of a relationship like yours. Well, you know I'm bias to this situation because that's what I long for."

Shit, Taeko just didn't know. I prayed for what he had. I needed that kind of companionship. I wanted someone to lie down with at night and wake up with in the morning.

We reached the store and began purchasing juices.

"I want the red one," Trinket yelled.

"I want the yellow one," Sap added.

A young lady with Chinese eyes and bob-length hair walked in the store. We both looked at her like a piece of meat. The flight attendant gear fit her to a T. She placed her purchase on the counter next to ours.

"Those are some beautiful girls."

In unison, "Thank you." I turned around because I didn't see Trey.

"Uncle Cha-late, Trey ran down there," Trinket told on her older brother.

"Damn! I'll go get him, Taeko."

Taeko

"Um, Taeko. That name sounds familiar. Are you Taeko of the hot Hawks?"

Taeko almost lost his smile. He wanted to get with a woman who didn't know that he played pro ball. He wanted a woman who wanted him for himself and not for the hype of his name or the size of his bank account.

"Yeah, that's me. Can I get that stuff for you?" Taeko asked, thinking what the hell, she looked like a nice piece of ass.

"Sure." She smiled.

"Can I write my number down, so that we can keep in touch?"

The girls were busy playing with their dolls.

"Yeah, but what's your name?"

"Sema."

"Well, maybe we can get together this weekend?"

"I have to fly out this weekend; I won't be back until next week, Thursday."

"Well, my boy is coming home today, so I will probably be hanging with the boys, anyway. So how about I give you my cell number, and when you get a chance, hit me up."

"Okay, Taeko. Nice meeting you." They shook hands, and Taeko watched her sashay out the store.

"That's what I miss in Joi," Taeko reflected. She was not sophisticated or elegant. She was homebody and ghetto-plain, still stuck in the blonde-hair phase, tight-ass pants, and long-ass nails. The woman I wanted standing next to me needed to have neatly done hair, flowing pant suits, some casual wear, with manicured nails.

"If Chocolate isn't going to support me, I know who will. It's one forty-two pm, and that nigga will be arriving in three minutes."

Chocolate

Everyone started screaming and waving signs, giving welcome home hugs and kisses. Even though they didn't win the Super Bowl, the city of Atlanta still considered them winners. Jamal Anderson, Jessie Tuggle, Gary Downs, Chris Chandler, Terrance Mathis, and Money Loane all walked behind each other like million-dollar men.

Sap took off running towards Money. Trey was giving all the Falcons dap.

"Hey, Baby Doll, look what I got for you." Money handed Sap a beautiful, black cheerleader baby doll with her name engraved on the front of the sweater and his number on the back. He handed another doll to Trinket and gave a football with all the players' signatures to Trey.

"Hey, Grandma." He kissed her on the cheek.

"Your grandfather is so proud of you. He's still in Italy. But he said be ready to tell him all about it when he get back."

He dapped me and Taeko as we congratulated him and made jokes. "That game was lame as hell, Dawg. Y'all did good, though. Just got a little overexcited about going to the big bowl."

"Yeah, that's all that mattered, I was there. Next year, Dawg, next year." Money laughed.

"I'm surprised y'all showed off with the little bit y'all did. Your boy, Tim Dwight, went off with that kick return; your boy Jamal had the slippery hands, though. But you made a pretty tight touchdown, that's all I was looking at."

Salone wiggled through us, "'Scuse me, I need to see my man too." She hugged Money tight around the neck, sliding his duffle bag onto her arm. "I'm so proud of you."

"Thank—" Money paused and replaced his joy with a blank stare. Everyone noticed and followed his eyes. We all ended our stare on Luvly.

"Oh, hell, naw. What the fuck she doin' here?"

"Salone!" my mother yelled.

"Tell 'er to leave, Money," Salone demanded,

standing face to face with Money. "Tell 'er to leave!" she screamed.

Money stood speechless, still looking into Luvly's eyes.

"Look, I don't want to cause no—"

"Bitch, you are trouble," Salone interrupted Luvly. "Get the fuck outta here."

"Salone, shut up! Don't you see my grandmother and Seal standing here? You so goddamn disrespectful. Damn!"

"Ooooh, Uncle Money said a bad word," Sap boasted. She jumped out of his arms and ran to her mother. "Look what Uncle Money bought me."

"That's very beautiful, Babe. Look, it has your name on it."

"Look, I'm gone take the kids home. They don't need to be around this mess. We'll meet ya'll at Spondivits." My mother said disappointed.

Salone stared at Money with disbelief. In a whisper, "How could you?" She dropped his duffle bag and walked towards the moving sidewalk.

"Hi, Money. Welcome home," Luvly said sweetly, looking like a movie star.

"Hey to you too." He hugged her, squeezing her hard. "Causing all this drama in here." They smiled at each other. "Ya'll ready to dip?"

"Well, I caught a ride up here, so I—"

"Ride with me. A limo is waiting outside," Money said. Luvly looked at me, asking for approval with her eyes.

I looked away. Her hesitation was only for a second as she let Money lead the way to the limo.

Chapter Eighteen

Luvly

Nervous, I didn't know what to say to Money. This man had always had my heart even though I chose to be with Diamond. *Every woman makes a bad relationship decision. That's what makes us wiser and able to decipher through the good and bad.*

I knew that Money loved me, always had. He had a weakness for me that Salone could never harden.

Now here we were discussing my life, his life, and, most importantly, Sap's life.

"What? You came today to make a show or what?" Money asked sarcastically.

"No."

"Oh, you came to see the same people you see everyday, or are you dating a football player I don't know about?"

"No."

He bit his bottom lip. "You still fuckin' wit' Diamond?"

"No."

"Say something besides no, dammit!" he yelled, hitting the window hard enough to break it. "I haven't talked to you in six months—and before that—barely. What the fuck is wrong with you?" Big teardrops started falling from his eyes.

"Money, I know you hate me, but I'm sorry. I don't have an excuse. Only thing I can say in my defense is that at the time, Diamond was a provider for me and Sap. Please forgive me." I got down on my knees, at his mercy and wiped the tears from his eyes.

"Luvly, you hurt me so bad when Sap was born. You had Diamond and me at your bedside about to kill each other." He looked into my eyes. "I would have killed him for you." He rubbed his fingers along the side my face; I, in turn, kissed the palm of his hand.

"I played along with this bullshit 'cause I was too young to know any better or maybe even because I was pussy-whipped. But there was never a time when money was an issue. I had two million dollars in the bank, and my grandparents would have taken care of you and Sap in a heartbeat. I would have married you, Luvly; I knew I was going pro in the tenth grade; but like I said, I already had money. I think you wanted to live the ghetto-fabulous lifestyle." He scooted back into his seat, hurt from reminiscing about our past.

"You never told me that you would always be in my life or that you wanted me forever. You played games yourself, always tellin' me that me or Salone could make you settle down. I knew that you loved her . . . maybe not as much as me . . . but you did. You didn't guarantee me anything. Money, it was always about what you wanted and what was best for you." Shaking my head in disgust, "We were just fuck friends."

Money jumped slightly off the seat and hitting his knees into my mine, "So that's all we did, Luvly? Fucked? Girl, I loved you the first time I saw you at the gym."

"I loved and still do love you, Money. But what am I s'pose to do about Diamond. Lately he has been at my throat more than ever before. I'm scared for my life. The only time he wants to come over is when he knows Sap is not there."

"Get a restraining order. I know I send you enough money to pay for everything, so why is he still around?"

Quietness wrapped around us like a warm blanket on a cold winter night.

When we pulled up to Taeko's house, Salone was standing outside talking with Joi.

"Damn." He sighed loudly, rubbing his hands over his head. "I really don't want to deal with her bullshit today."

"Well, Money, she loves you, and you've made her believe that y'all have a future."

He reached over, grabbed my face, and kissed me deeply. His warm tongue, tasted sweet.

"I love you, Luvly. I know that I don't tell you as much as I need to, but I do. We have a lot of things to talk about and get straight. I need you, Babe. I want you so much in my arms every night when I go to bed; and to look into your eyes every morning I wake up." He hopped out the car before I could say my piece. He gave the driver an extra bill and directions to take me home.

I put my hand to the window as if his was there. "We will have those nights and mornings, Babe."

Chapter Nineteen

Money

Fuck! I didn't want to deal with Salone. I don't understand how she could be so pissed when she already knew the deal with me and Luvly. I wish she would just disappear into thin air.

Before I could get into the driveway good, Salone let loose like a wild woman. Hitting me in the chest with balled up fists. "Money, how could you have that ho meet us—your family, at the airport?"

"I didn't know she was going to be there. But I, nor my family, had a problem with it." I bit into my bottom lip.

"Shit, Money, what is it! That bitch is so triflin'! She uses yo' good-heartedness as a spleen, and you so stupid . . . you can't even see it. Does she suck your dick that good? If I didn't know any better, I would say she puttin' some shit in yo' food."

I looked at Joi out the corner of my eye. She was

ready to vent on me, too. "Look, y'all come inside; the media and photographers are always hiding somewhere out here."

We entered the house still arguing. "Money, she has lied to you over and over again! And I know you know she still fuckin' Diamond."

"That makes two of you."

She backed away from me like she was trying to save me from a slap. "Believe that dirty bitch if you want to. She just tryin' to drive us apart.

"You sure?" I asked, knowing in my heart that she had been with him out of spite for me and Luvly.

Trying to change the subject she said, "That bitch won't even give you a blood test for Sapphire. She is just stringin' your ass along; and you steady climbin' that shaky rope."

"Why you have to bring up that subject? Sap is the innocent one in this, and I plan on keeping it that way. No matter what, I'm still going to love and take care of that little girl."

She rushed close up to me, looking into my eyes. "Love me, Money."

She was so lost to the fact that I couldn't do that. There was no room for her in my heart.

"I've been here through all your bullshit. Don't I get any say-so? Let Luvly live her life with her child and the man she has chosen over you a thousand times before. Stop playin' the pussy in y'all relationship."

Slapping the shit out of Salone would have only justified everything she was saying. She knew that Sap was a sticky, heart-felt situation. "You know that me and Luvly have things to discuss. I can't jus' leave her alone."

"Child support for a child you don't even know is yours? Payin' for that ho to live in a house in Alpharetta, buying her a truck and shit. What the fuck!"

Saliva flew from her mouth. I could almost see the steam coming out of her ears. "She's my friend," I said with a nonchalant attitude. "She's my friend before anything, and that includes you, too." I put my hands over my head and clamped tightly, wanting to squeeze all the bad shit out, and run back to my past, when me, Chocolate, and Taeko were thirteen years old, watching porno flicks, living the easy life.

Hugging my waist from the back, she whispered, "Money Loane, I love you so much . . . more than humanly possible. I never gave you grief about any of your extra relationships, but I'm beginning to fall in a place I've never been before. I've had other men, Money, but not one of them has ever been able to touch my heart and make me feel the way you do. The slight touch of your hand sends my body to another level. When you send me those e-mails telling me how you can't wait until we share each other again, I hold on to each and every word, hoping that will be the time you tell me you love me. I have to, because I don't know if you will walk out of my life like you have so many times before."

I knew she was telling the truth. I had walked out of her life every time I thought the grass was greener on the other side. But what was I supposed to do. I was torn.

Me and Luvly were perfect together. I loved that girl with a true heart. Even if Sapphire were Diamond's, I would still love her the same.

"Salone, I don't know what to tell you. I'm not going to make a rush decision to appease you. When, and if I'm ready, I'll let you know."

She looked at me, blew a kiss, and walked out the room.

I heard the front door slam. I felt a sigh of relief. At that point I didn't care if I saw Salone again or not.

Chapter Twenty

Chocolate

It was 6 p.m., and I was chillin' at Mama's house, trying to figure out what had taken place between Money and Luvly. I hoped they both came to their senses and decide to get married and raise their daughter.

On the day that Sap was born, I remembered being in the delivery room while Luvly was giving birth.

Shaking her head in a violent manner, she screamed, "Ahh . . . ahh . . . I can't push! I can't! It hurts!"

"Breathe, Babe, breathe. Hold my hand." Money held her hand while Mr. and Mrs. Mancini videotaped the birth.

"I . . . can't . . . do this! It hurtssss!" Luvly hit the

bed rails. "I need . . . drugsss, ahhhh!" She continued screaming, crying, and grunting.

"Come on, honey. You can do this. The baby will be here, and you will be a great mother," her mother said, holding a cold washcloth to her forehead, trying to comfort her.

Shit! I was never fond of blood, and was about to faint.

The doctors instructed us to each hold a leg, and hand. Her father held one leg while I held the other.

Money held her hand like a proud and concerned spouse. "Hey, Babe, just think about how good it felt when we were making this beautiful miracle. Give one last push," he encouraged as Luvly continued screaming.

Her father and mother looked at each other. I couldn't tell if the look was of surprise, shock, or joy because it was possibly not Diamond's.

The baby came out covered with blood. I stumbled and almost fell. The nurse had to take me back to the room and give me some juice and crackers.

Once Luvly was stable they brought the baby back in for a minute. She said that the baby had a high temperature and needed fluids and observation. But aside from that, she was gorgeous. Money and I both fell in love instantly with the baby.

Money stayed all three nights at that hospital. On the second day, Diamond decided to come back from a cruise that he was taking with one of his extras. Luvly and him were still living together at the time. He walked in with roses and a big teddy bear. Money was 'sleep in the pullout cot, and I was sleep in the chair. Diamond walked over to Luvly and stared down at Money.

He leaned down and kissed her on the forehead. "How you doin', Babe? How's the baby?"

"She's fine." Luvly looked disgusted and insecure.

"Was the delivery hard?"

"No, I had Money and my family by my side," Luvly said with courage in her voice.

"Umm hmm. Your comforter always here, huh?"

"You smell like Cool Water for women. Pila, huh? I know that's who you took to the Bahamas."

"Look, you just had our child. Calm down and take it easy. When can I take y'all home?"

Luvly looked uneasy. I knew she wanted to leave him. We had talked about it her whole pregnancy. "I don't know if you are taking us home."

"What!" His voice got loud and forceful. Luvly flinched at the tone of his voice. "You damn right! You better know y'all comin' home with me! Fuck that shit you talkin'!"

"Hey, Dawg, remember we in a hospital, again. I'm sure they can fit your ass in a room." I was on my feet ready to knock this nigga out again.

The nurse came in with the baby. "Here's your mommy, sweet baby. She's so beautiful. Have you thought of a name yet?"

Smiling nervously, Luvly received the baby in her arms. "No, Ma'am. I haven't thought of a most unique, beautiful name yet. Hi, there, Sweet Girl." She kissed the baby on her forehead.

"Well, if you think of the name before you leave let me know so we can get the birth certificate filled out." She smiled, spoke to everyone, and tapped Money on the leg. "Mr. Loane, your daughter is here."

Luvly covered her face, as Diamond's face got tight. At that point I knew we were going to have to wear his ass out.

"What the fuck did that white bitch just say?"

Money jumped out of his seat ready to stomp a new hole in that nigga ass. "Nigga, she said my daughter. The *only* man who has been here with her. The *first* man's arms she's been in."

"Look, Luvly, I'm not for no games. You better get this shit straight before you come home."

He dropped the roses on the floor and stood face to face with Money. "Nigga, you know I ain't got no love for your wanna-be-somebody ass. This is, always has been, and is always going to be, my woman. And this is my daughter. So whatever bullshit y'all done sat up here and concocted, flush that shit."

"Stop it! Just stop it." Luvly had pushed the nurse's button seconds before they stood face to face.

A nurse and nurse's aid came in, "Is everything okay? I could hear you all in the hallway.

"Can you ask him to leave, please?" Luvly pointed to Diamond, not looking him in the eye.

Ring . . . Ring . . . Ring.

"Starr residence." My mother caught it before I did.

"Yes, he's here . . . No, I need to know how you are? You and that nasty girl didn't get into a fight did you? Well, that's good to know . . . She's outside with Trinket. Are you coming to dinner? It will be a good idea. Luvly, you are family, and that's more important than anything. I am more than a babysitter; I am your surrogate mother. Hold on, sweetie . . . Chocolate, Luvly on the phone."

"I got it." I grabbed the portable phone and walked outside. "Luvly, what was that all about? I asked you, 'Did you want to come?' and what did you tell me? You still playin' games just like Salone."

"Don't you ever compare me to that tramp!" she screamed. "I didn't want to go to the airport at first, but the more I fought myself, the more I knew I needed to be there," she said in a softer tone.

"So did y'all come to an agreement about Sap?"

"Sort of; we suppose to talk some more."

"Are you going out to eat with us?"

She hesitated for a minute. "Do you think I should?"

"Yeah, bighead, I wouldn't want you to make another grand entrance."

Money and Taeko arrived at the house high and drunk.

"Man, y'all smell like a damn weed plant," I said to them, disgusted. They laughed, ignoring the fact that the girls were right inside the house.

"Chocolate, you need to puff on one. Maybe you'll relax enough to wanna poke on something."

There they go again wit' that crazy shit.

They dapped and laughed even louder.

"The kids in the house takin' a bath. And you know they notice every little thang."

"Chocolate, you always actin' like a bitch," Taeko responded, with anger in his voice.

"Man, y'all too old to be acting like this. Let's ride for about an hour until everyone is ready."

We jumped into my truck and rode out.

Chapter Twenty-One

Chocolate

I put in a mixed CD of Pac and Biggie, layed my seat back, relaxed, and headed up 85 North toward anywhere.

"Money, let me ask you a question," Taeko said.

"Shoot."

"Are you happy with your life as a professional football player? All the ass you want; Phat-ass gear and rides. Platinum everything. Are you happy with your freedom?"

"Yeah, I'm happy for the most part, but I'm missing the woman of my life. I wish I could do a lot of things different."

"Well, I ain't happy and I want out," Taeko said, as he leaned back against the soft leather.

"Out of what? All your money, your kids, your house, and most of all, your sanity?" Money asked with a frowned up face.

I could tell that they were sobering up. Reality of life was hitting them in the face. "I told Tae he got it good and he better sit his hot ass down," I enforced.

"Nigga, when you gon' get some cut up?" Taeko defended himself.

"Whenever I know her shit clean and she got that fire. My day is comin', and when it does, y'all niggas will be the first not to know." I wanted to see where these niggas mind was. "Money, you think about havin' kids?"

"Yeah, I do. I want a real family—a wife, and three or four kids to add to my two dogs and house on the hill."

"What about Sap?" I asked. I knew that was a touchy subject, but I had to know 'cause I'd taken on being her daddy; I loved her like she was mine.

"I hope she is mine. I love that little girl."

Taeko sat back like he wasn't part of the conversation.

"Taeko, you don't have anything to say?"

"Naw, I told you what I wanted. I feel it deep in my heart. I love my kids. I know I don't put my all into them, but they know I love and care about 'em."

"The way you treat their mother is an important part of how they act and feel," Money said, sounding like a therapist.

"Well, I want a family one day; I'm getting older," I said seriously.

"Boy, you only twenty-two; you got a whole life to plan for. That's why I'm battlin' with my youth, wantin' to party, hang out, screw broads, my maturity, and taking care of Joi, the woman who was there with me when I was eating nothing but bologna sandwiches. She had my baby boy when we could barely spell paternity and has stuck with me through sugar and shit. I know I need to be a man in the situation, but I can't get over being just a man. You betta slow down and take your time. Enjoy being you—free, with no kids. When you get all of the above it'll make you happy, but just be ready."

Nobody said anything for a minute. I was feelin' Tae, but I still wanted a wifey by my side. "I want a little girl. Brandy, that's what I'm going to name her. I'm gon' raise her to be a daddy's girl, keep her close to me and away from niggas like y'all." They laughed in agreement. "Speaking of sons and daughters, Mrs. Reese called earlier today about our Halo program. She said that we have three doctors to add to the program."

"Are they black?" Taeko asked.

"I don't know. As long as they take care of the little rug-rats, and treat them as they would kids with insurance, I don't care if they're green," I replied.

"Are they looking for hella cheese? Or are they going to ask for a grant or do it pro bono?"

"Either way is straight. I told her to make sure they understood that we use our money for housing, clothing, and food. Shit! They make well over the tax break; giving their time and skills for underprivileged children shouldn't hurt their pockets."

"*Essence* and *Ebony* called, asking if they can put us in their magazine, but I told 'em that we do this for the kids all over the world, not for press or publicity. They said they just wanted to give thanks. But I don't know, I told them we'll get back to them," Money added.

"But that could mean more sponsors. I mean I know we have the money, but more won't hurt a bit. Maybe we can build that apartment complex for low and no-income families."

"Yeah, yeah, you right. I'll have Mrs. Reese give them a call."

Mrs. Reese, our publicist, was a lifesaver. She was like an auntie. She helped us organize Halo, the name of our center for getting clothes, supplies, computers, and anything else needed for the kids and their families to succeed.

"Chocolate, you ever see that hopeless star you saw at the mall?" They both start laughing.

"Naw, but I'm keeping my eyes open. The situation is not hopeless."

"I don't see her nowhere around, and you keep talking our heads off about her. So it seems hopeless to me," Taeko said.

"He been hollin' at some li'l honey that he been hidin' from us," Money taunted.

"I ain't been hidin' Haven, just checking her out for myself first. She a flight attendant for Costal Airways. She got her own place, car, and no kids—just my cup of tea."

"Haven? Umm, I'm trying to think if she is one of those young flight attendants dat done served me more than first-class service," Taeko proudly said.

I knew Taeko was dead-ass serious. I hoped she escaped his wrath, for our sake. I ignored them discussing my life and listened to Outkast spit knowledge through the speakers. I liked them boys; they actually had meaning to their songs.

I couldn't help but think about my mystery woman. Was she single? What did she do for a living? Where in the hell did she get that beautiful face?

Chapter Twenty-Two

Chocolate

Dinner was going great. My mother and father, Money's grandmother and two aunts, Luvly and Sap, Taeko and his family, and my guest, Haven, were all there.

Haven was looking good in a sky-blue and cream pinstriped pants suit. The top was halter, showing off her smooth, broad shoulders and the pants flared out, leaving room to see the baby blue strapped sandals. Those types of sandals drove me crazy; they were so sexy. Her long streaked hair was pulled up in a bun with some dropping around her bright, full face.

"Are you okay? You want a drink?"

"No, Chinoe, I'm fine. I'm just enjoying all this celebrity status." Her voice so sweet and low, I knew she was impressed. A pro football player, an

Atlanta Hawk basketball player at her side, and an up-and-coming supermodel, she was in heaven.

"So, Haven, how do you like this big melting pot?" my mother asked, not really feeling Haven. I could tell by the look on her face.

"Oh, I love it here, Mrs. Starr. A little hotter than I'm used to, but Chinoe does a good job of keeping me cool." she said, smiling while looking into my eyes.

My mother gave me a tight, fake smile.

After ordering and eating everything on the menu, everyone was ready to go. After the waitress placed the check on the table, everyone jumped from a cold splash.

"Salone, what the hell is wrong with you?" Money jumped to his feet, wiping the beer from his face that she threw on him and Luvly.

She moved close to his face. "You are what's wrong. I'm tired of living for what you need and want. This tramp don't mean you no good. All she want is some dick on hold."

"Salone, watch your mouth, you see these kids here," Grandma Loane warned.

"Fuck these little bastards! Ain't none of 'em got no real daddies." Salone was three times D.U.I.

Wiping beer away from her eyes, Luvly stood up. "My child is far from being a bastard. You might want to look in the mirror for a bastard. My child has a father. Maybe the man who you want to be your husband and the future father of your kids doesn't want you." Luvly set off a time bomb.

Salone grabbed the pitcher that she just threw beer from and slammed it across Luvly's face. My mother and Grandma Loane rushed the children outside. Money's aunt helped rush everyone to the front of the restaurant.

Other patrons of the restaurant started pointing fingers and acknowledging that there was a famous basketball and football player in the restaurant.

Joi was trying to pull Salone back, but Luvly got a hold of her and started choking the shit out of her.

"Bitch, I'm . . . gone kill yo' ass."

Salone spit a big glob of saliva into Luvly's face, at the same time grabbing a handful of hair.

They tussled, getting the best of each other until Salone slipped on the same beer that she had thrown just seconds before. Luvly used all her force to slam Salone's head into the table.

"Moneyyyyyy . . . Monnnneyyyyyy," Salone called Money's name, for dear life.

While Luvly held Salone by the throat with one hand, she grabbed a fork off the table and stabbed her in the chest; blood went everywhere.

"Luvly, STOP! STOP!" Money tried to pull her off Salone, but pent up anger poured from her heart into her hands.

"Luvly, put the fork down! Let's go before the police come!" While I tried to talk her down, Money wrestled to get the fork out of her hand.

After a few minutes of struggling, she dropped the fork and looked Salone dead in the eyes. "Bitch, don't you ever disrespect my child." She spit on Salone's wound. "I'll kill you next time bitch."

I hurried Luvly out of the restaurant.

"I'm gon' kill that yellow bitch." Salone was still bleeding pretty bad, but still came after Luvly with more threats. "Ho, this ain't over! I will fuck your world till it's dry! I won't forget about this shit!"

"Why did you have to come up here, Salone?" Joi asked with a perturbed look on her face, tired of their shit, as was everyone else. "And, Money, you need to handle your business better than whatchu doin'."

Money's demeanor turned into fury. "Fuck that, Joi! Salone is a grown-ass woman! She can play crazy fah y'all, but I know she ain't crazy!" He lowered his voice, and looked around at the crowd that had formed, and realized that he was the one sounding crazy. "She already knows the deal, just like you and I. What am I suppose—?"

"You're supposed to be my man, Money. Take up for me, sometimes," Salone cried hysterically. "Why did you let that bitch do this to me?" The paper towels that she held to her chest were drenched in blood.

"Take her to Grady; I'll be there," Money ordered, heading out the door.

Salone fell into Joi's arms. "Joi, look at this shit. He goin' to see about her triflin' ass and I'm the one who's stabbed." Her loud cries and moans were not from her wounded chest, but her wounded heart.

The ride in the car was quiet, except for the smothered sound of crying. Luvly was sitting next to me, so I knew it wasn't her. I looked in the rearview mirror at Haven, and she looked spaced-out. Me and Luvly looked in the back at Money.

I pulled off on Aviation Boulevard where I usually go to think and watch the planes take off.

Maybe that would give Money the same peace of mind. "Money, man, what's up?" This nigga was crying so hard he was about to make me cry. "Dawg, talk to me."

"Luvly, why did you have to do that? I wouldn't have let her hurt you and you know that. Why don't you ever trust me to take care of you?"

"Money, she slapped me in the face with a glass pitcher. Have you taken a look at my jaw? She called Sap a bastard. I should have stabbed her to the heart."

"Babe, we need my career. You know this is going to be all over the news. And anyone who wants to make a dollar can sell the story to the Enquirer. I'm so tired of all of this shit! Every six months. Damn! What is it?"

Luvly climbed out of the front seat to sit with him. "Money, I'm sorry. I'm sorry if I've caused you any trouble, but I'm not sorry for whuppin' Salone's ass." Haven shifted in her seat. The look on her face was that of a scared, lost child.

"Haven, are you all right?" She nodded yes, but I knew she was ready to get to the other side of the planet.

After dropping Money and Luvly off at her place, we went home.

"Haven, I'm sorry that you had to witness that. That's been building up for some years now."

"I don't understand. Who was that girl with the short hair?"

"Girlfriend."

"One of them, I suppose?"

I snickered because I couldn't lie. "Yeah. He's

been seeing both of them for a pretty long time. Luvly has about three years over Salone, but if you break down the time she's been back and forth with Diamond, it's been about the same amount time."

"Diamond, that's Sapphire's father?"

"Well, see, that's another issue." I wasn't going to let her know how trifling my friends were.

"Diamond and Sapphire; that's cute. What's her middle name?"

"No, she named her that because that was the first stone that Money gave her. That's Money's favorite stone. Her middle name is Cashews."

"Like Money, huh?" She laughed in disbelief. "I thought I'd seen some drama on the plane, but this takes the cake."

We didn't discuss our business with anyone but each other. I had to be careful about who I discussed Money and Taeko's business with.

Like Money said, "Anyway to make a dollar, anybody will sell a story."

Me and Haven walked up to my condo, arm in arm. Could she be the one? She still had to pass a few more tests.

"You know I really enjoy being with you, Chinoe."

I just smiled and placed a kiss on her cheek. Releasing her from one arm, picking up a package that was left on my front doorstep, I said, "What's this?" I scooped up the package, and we headed inside.

"Would you like something to drink?"

"Yeah, a Sprite if you have it."

"Comin' right up."

As I fixed her drink I heard the Isley Brothers whispering softly from the living room. That's what I like about her; she was so mellow with no drama or complications in her life.

"Hey, sexy, you want to take a shower?" She whispered, laying on the floor stretched out like a cat at play. She smiled with a devilish grin. "Will you promise not to get my hair wet?"

I didn't respond because I couldn't promise that. Taking her by the hand we headed upstairs to my bedroom. Haven didn't know that I was a virgin. Actually, she thought I was screwing all of Atlanta. She thought I was taking my time with her; being a southern gentlemen.

Haven and the shower were steamy and hot. Before I could get in good, she was taking kisses, her hands roaming wildly over my body.

My dick rose to her invitation. She sat me down on the shower bench and filled her mouth with as much of me as she could take.

While I looked at her lick my dick from my balls to the tip of the head, my vision went blurry. Her face started to change; still the caramel complexion, but the eyes were brighter, lips fuller. Her hands softer, her mouth felt deeper. Her image always surfaced when I was at my highest sexual peak. *This is crazy! A girl that I don't even know takes me to higher levels, and I haven't even touched her.* As I opened my eyes I released in Haven's mouth.

With Haven lay exhausted from her tongue bath, I went to the kitchen to open my package:

Mr. Starr,

We are happy to welcome you into our family, Platinum Impressions. Your portfolio was very im-

pressionable. Clients have expressed great interest in your layouts.

We are hosting a welcome party in your honor. Please give us a call and inform us of the number of guests that will be attending.

Tracie Mills will be handling all of your contracting, scheduling, and contacts.

We will provide you with a vehicle of choice. A fund that shares the cost of housing is also available.

Credit cards ($500,000 limitation, unlimited wardrobe credit card, and unlimited flights) all provided by Platinum Impressions.

There are some terms that all our models must comply with:

1. No smoking cigarettes, cigars, or marijuana.

2. No contracts with outside agencies. Any video appearances must be approved by the agency. (Image is everything)

3. On the day before a shoot or show, you must be in your home or hotel at 9:00 p.m.

4. Dental cleanings or whitening are to be done one day before shoot. (A beautiful smile captures the camera's lens.)

If these terms are violated there will be fines starting at $15,000 and increasing with each infraction.

If you have any questions, please contact Tracie Mills.

Again, welcome, Mr. Starr.

Sharon Davon, President
Platinum Impressions

* * *

I almost fell out of my chair. "Ahh shit, I done made it!" I was about to ball 'til I fall. But my joy came to a halt; *I'm missing one thing—the woman of my dreams.*

Chapter Twenty-Three

Luvly

Why am I at the place where I've experienced my worse nightmares come true? Why can't I stay away from this clear and present danger?

He grabbed my hand, gesturing his head toward the house. "Come on, Luvly. Trust me." He held both hands up. "I won't try anything. Just come in for a minute. I can't see Sap outside in this truck, she's 'sleep."

A brand-new champagne-colored Jaguar trimmed in gold rested in the driveway. Something that expensive and gaudy belonged to only one person—the bitch that bore the heathen in front of me.

He looked back towards the house at his mother, Mrs. Ruby Shai, and his sister, Crystal, staring out the window. He smiled handsomely. "You know they want to see my baby."

I placed my hand onto my head. Why was I sitting there contemplating torture for myself, let alone my child, seeing Diamond—spun from hell, and his mother—the devil herself?

"Where is Russell?" I asked. Diamond's stepfather was the peacemaker and the only sensible one in their family, my savior any time Diamond decided he wanted a punching bag and his mother wanted to go off.

"Is that the only way I'm gon' get you out of this truck?"

I looked at him with questioning eyes.

"Naw, he don't get here until tomorrow night. Please, Luvly, let my mother and sister see their grandchild and niece. If it makes you feel any better, Jae is around back with the dogs."

Listen to your mind, Luvly. Listen to your mind. Take your ass home! But my heart was taking over. And damn, he was lookin' good! "Okay, but just for a minute."

A smile swept across his face as he opened my door and grabbed Sap, putting her on his shoulder. He grabbed my hand like we were the happy couple.

I walked slowly behind Diamond, letting him lead the way. My stomach tightened with every inch that I was closer to the door. I could see Ruby's blue-green eye shadow above her popped eyes, peeking through the curtains. Her ruby red lips were ready to spit poisonous venom. The heavy makeup made her look fake and hungry for the attention she so much cried out for. The long, bottled, red hair that sat just above her waist was the only thing that gave her softness and femininity.

And Crystal, the evil wench, waited like a hungry pit bull, ready to strike on her mother's command. She should've just been thankful that her Chinese-looking eyes, flawless skin, beautiful smile, and long legs were gifts from her deceased father, who was killed during a bad drug deal when they were little.

Word had it that Mrs. Ruby had him set up. She was tired of always fighting him and all the women he was running the streets with. Diamond told me that one time, after his mother had been fighting one of the women, the woman came to their house and cut Ruby from her ear, straight across her cheek to the corner of her mouth. That's why she wore all that heavy makeup.

After she had him killed, she started running shit like she was "the man," taking over the drug business and setting everything up for Diamond to take over when he turned thirteen. Diamond has an older brother Jewel, but I've never seen him. He knew of his mother's handiwork in their father's death and went to stay with his father's parents. Ruby cut him off just like the rest of the people in her life that she couldn't control.

They met us at the front door. "Oooooh, look at her, Mama, she so pretty. Looks just like us." Crystal gave me a dirty look then smiled at her mother and brother.

"She's not feeling too good. Please let her—"

In a thick Cuban accent, Ruby interrupted, "That why she should be livin' with us. Where she be wit' same people ever'day. Nailshop no place for baby with all dem chemicals." She pinched Sap's cheeks, which my baby hated. Sap tossed for a moment then settled back into her sleep.

"Ruby, I take good care of Sap," I let her know, rubbing Sap's red cheeks.

"She could use more fat on dese legs." She popped her hand on them. Then she rolled her eyes at me and motioned for Crystal to take Sap out of my arms. Before I could protest, Diamond pulled me down the foyer.

It had been a minute since I'd seen the place I used to call home. It was still as neat and sparkling as the day I left him. No one would ever be able to tell that my blood once lined this foyer like spilled mop water; that he threw me onto a glass table, my back busting it into pieces, or that the stairs hold the spirit of my second miscarried baby. The restored banister above the steps snatched strands of my hair when Diamond threw me into it. That landed me in the hospital, unconscious for weeks and not expected to make it.

My pictures still claimed the walls. The sunshine came through the big bay window illuminating my smile. To the unknown eye, I looked happy, but on the inside, I was quickly dying.

"What do you want to drink?"

"Oh, we won't be staying that long, so—"

"So what?" he asked, walking up on me.

His sweet dark skin, brown eyes, and soft hands rubbing my back was making me weak. When he was sweet, he dripped honey.

He picked me up, and my legs automatically wrapped around his waist. "Put me down, Diamond," I protested, not really wanting him to.

He walked us into the den.

"Come home, Luvly. I need you here with me," he pleaded, kissing my neck.

I was melting in his arms.

He layed me down on the sofa and wasted no time undoing his pants. "You wore this skirt for me, didn't you?" He roughly reached under my skirt and yanked off my panties with one hand.

I pushed his hand back gently. "Diamond, I don't want—"

He dug his mouth into my pussy. I couldn't fight it anymore. *Do I really miss Diamond, or do I miss the way he hungers for me?* I always got it confused at this point. "Damn! Ummm, yeah! Make me cum in your mouth!"

"Shhhhhh. Cum on, baby. Come home!"

I came all in his mouth.

Then he shoved himself into me. He was strong and passionate. "Is it good to you, baby?"

"Yes, Money!"

His eyes got big.

Smack!

"Noooo!" I pushed back on the sofa, tasting the blood on my lips.

"Bring yo' muthafuckin' ass here!"

I kicked and screamed, "Diamond, nooo! Don't!"

He punched my head until I rolled onto the floor.

Smack!

Kick!

He stomped me like a roach.

"Diamond, pleaseeeee!" I pleaded through a loud cry.

Through clenched teeth, he ordered, "Shut the fuck up," muffling my mouth with his hand. "Get cho ass up."

"I can't." The pain in my stomach was excruciating.

His mother and sister could have stopped this shit if they wanted to, but they hated me more than he did.

Smack!

Each hit was harder than the previous. How was I going to stay away from Money and my family until these bruises healed?

He pushed me onto my back. "I'm gon' get this pussy. I'm gon' nut all in this pussy! Give you something to take home to yo' nigga."

As I looked away from him to allow him to rape what was left of me, Sap was standing in the foyer, wide-eyed, with her finger in her mouth. I tried to fight harder so that my baby wouldn't have to see Diamond violating me, but he punched me in the chest, leaving me breathless. Grabbing my shirt, he shook me like a rag doll.

Sap screamed out, "Mommieeeeee!"

"You already disrespectin' me by livin' in that nigga house, then you gon' come in my house and call me that nigga name while I'm fuckin' you."

Smack!

He slapped me with full force. The left side of my face was flush with heat and became numb.

A rough Cuban accent yelled from the foyer, "Get outta dere, Sapphire."

Sap turned to look into the pleased face of her grandmother, pleased that her son—in front of her—was beating my ass into submission. The reasons why he abused me never mattered to her.

One night, me and Crystal got into a heated argument about Jordan, one of Diamonds baby mamas, and all hell broke loose. I cussed Crystal and Ruby out, and told them where they could stick it. Ruby said, "You got a smart, slick mouth. Don't know your place. Need your ass beat! You learn then!" She told Diamond that he was being stupid and acting like less than a man for a piece of ass, and that he'd better get rid of me before I ruined their family, but he wouldn't leave me alone.

Ruby asked the one question that I, myself, and so many others have. "What is it about that damn Luvly that's so special, got you runnin' round crazy in love? All the others know they place. That one piece of pussy gon' land you in hell, 'causin' you more trouble than it's worth."

Through hiccups and gasps, Sap pointed at me bleeding on the floor and said, "My mommie."

Ruby knelt down to face Sap. "She's been bad girl. Come wit' Mama." Sap pulled away from her, leaping toward me. Ruby whispered loud enough for me to hear, "That little bitch is just as defiant as 'er mother."

Jae was chilling in the kitchen when he heard me screaming and rushed into the den. "Damn, Diamond! Get off of 'er. Your daughter is right there." Jae wrestled him off me.

Out of breath, Diamond spoke from his heart. "I'ma kill dat bitch, man. I'ma kill dat bitch."

My crying was steady because I knew he meant every word of it. I slowly got off the floor, making sure Jae had Diamond in a stronghold.

"Get Sap and leave, Luvly; I can't hold him for long."

"Never shoulda let Sap come back 'ere from Cuba last time, but we will get 'er back, and for good. Be gone wit' your triflin' ass." Ruby sternly scolded me.

I grabbed Sap and ran for my life from that crazy-ass family, leaving behind my panties, Sap's sweater, and, once again, my blood.

Chapter Twenty-Four

Chocolate

My first professional photo shoot was on a Saturday afternoon with Phat Farm.

Russell Simmons had me greeted with VIP status; champagne, all type of exotic foods, and anything else I needed or wanted. Jay-Z also came to see who the new face on the runway was because he was looking for fresh faces for Roca Wear.

"Hey, Dawg, I'm giving a phat party tonight. Jus' hit me, and I'll send somebody to scoop you up." J shook my hand and left me to my shoot.

Ring . . . Ring . . . Ring.

"Holla at me."

"Well, I see you feel at home already."

"Mrs. Tracie Mills, how are you?"

"Wonderful. Thanks for the arrangement, they were beautiful."

"You're beautiful, and thank you for everything."

"You are going to make us a lot of money, sexy. If you need anything, give me a call."

"Chinoe, you ready to start?" Chaise, my photographer asked.

I nodded yes, "Just point me in the direction you want me."

She bit down on her bottom lip seductively, "Why don't you sit on the blue cube and let the ladies surround you. We'll start like that and you take it from there. Let's keep it sexy with a bit of gangsta."

It was going good; no pressure, no confusion. With Frankie Beverly and Maze pumping in the background, I felt right at home. Some of the most beautiful women surrounded me in compromising positions, in Baby Phat outfits.

If Haven had been there she woulda been flipping out. She was insecure and a little overprotective, but all in all, she was very supportive and excited about the whole idea. I'd become kind of used to her being around. When she wasn't flying, she was my assistant handling my finances and personal care.

"Chinoe, you really have a genuine love affair with the camera."

Flashing my thirty-two's, I assured her, "That's you, Chaise, letting your fingers make love to the camera, and looking at your pretty face made it a lot easier."

Twisting the cap onto her camera she asked, "Is

that why you picked me out of thousands of photographers?"

Naw, but that ass is phat and that's why I picked you.

"Nope, there aren't many black photographers—sistas at that—and you were close to my age. I think young black people need a chance at a great career. But truly, black people need a chance. Period."

She stood, staring at me like I'd made the Martin Luther King I HAVE A DREAM SPEECH. "You're not only fine as hell, you're also intelligent."

Packing up her camera equipment, she said, "Don't catch that too much anymore."

"Ahhh, you talk like we, black men, are hopeless and ignorant to education and fine grooming."

"Naw. Not saying that, but a man usually has one positive element versus the other ninety-nine negative."

My pager had been blowing up all session. My warning signal alerted that I had messages waiting.

"Well, Chaise, are we done?"

"Yeah, we're done. Be here at seven-thirty a.m. sharp."

"Yes, sir. You got it, boss."

"Naw, think of it more as a partnership. I love the camera, and the camera loves you."

I had five messages. Everyone used the emergency code. I called my mother first. The majority of the calls were from her

"Yeah, what's up, Ma?"

"Boy, I know I raised you with manners? You've gotten up to New York with those northern people and gone crazy."

"No. Hi, Mother dear, how are you? Do you need something?"

"I was just checking on my only child. Are you eating healthy, getting enough sleep? You know how grumpy you are if—"

"Yes, Mama. I'm doing fine. I've only been gone three days," I said, stopping her before she got herself worked up, and flew out here.

"Anything can happen in a matter of seconds."

"Hey, where is my baby? She been good?"

"That little pumpkin right here eating."

I'd missed little Sap. I hadn't seen her in three weeks. Luvly made up some lie about them going to New Jersey to see Diamond's family, but I knew that couldn't be true because they hated each other. And Joi said she saw Luvly getting take-out from some joint, wearing dark sunglasses and a hat. She said Luvly was rushing and holding her head down, trying not to be seen.

"Hey, Uncle Cha-late."

"Hey, Baby Girl. Whatchu been doin'? Being a good girl?"

"Where you at? Come see me at Grammy."

"I'll be there soon, Baby Girl. I have a surprise for you."

"Yeah, Yeah! Grammy, Uncle Cha-late got a 'prise fo' me!"

"Bye, Baby. Put Grammy back on the phone."

"Diamond hit Mommy and she cry."

"What?" She didn't repeat it. "What did you say, Baby Girl?"

"Diamond hit Mommy, and she fall down and cry. Mommy was crying loud."

I didn't understand Luvly. She was so strong, yet the weakest of all.

"Okay, put Grammy back on the phone."

"Luv you, Uncle Cha-late."

I knew those repeat pages had to be from either Luvly or Money.

"Chinoe, don't come home all upset and going after people. Luvly need to get her life straight. Y'all cannot make decisions for her. She runnin' her mother ragged."

"I know, Ma, but she done been through this ordeal too many times."

"Chocolate, listen to me. Luvly is a grown woman. She is a mother, a lover, and she's someone's daughter. And she is all those things before she is, last of all, your friend. She is like a daughter to me, but I let her business stay her business. She will never learn to make wise decisions if y'all keep bailing her out. Believe me, listen to me on this, Chocolate."

Silence choked my voice. I didn't have anything to say. I knew my mother was telling the God's honest truth.

"Kiss Sap for me. I'll be home Friday."

What in the hell was wrong with this girl? Money had moved her into her own place, set up an account for her and Sap, and she still actin' stupid. What is her reason for seeing Diamond? What the fuck was on Luvly's mind?

I couldn't even talk to her right then. I would hurt her feelings. *Let me call Money to see what's going on.*

"Talk to me."

"Aye, man, what's up?"

"Nothing, nigga. What's up with yo' pretty ass?"

I laughed. "Ha!Ha!Ha! Nigga, stop drinkin' that Haterade."

"Nigga, you been missin' all the Super Bowl parties."

"Y'all sorry niggas still celebratin'?"

"Ya know it."

I wanted to hold off on asking him about Luvly, but I knew he was the one to ask.

"I talked to Mama and Sap. Sap said Diamond jumped on Luvly."

He let out a long sigh. "Hmmm. Then she was at the 50-yard line two days ago waiting for me to get there, and he walked up on her and tried to make her leave. He started pushing on her and slapped her to the ground. She cut him with a broken glass. Some of the girls she was with took her home."

"You didn't kill that nigga?"

"For what, Chocolate? Luvly ain't through with that scene. She not gon' have my life and reputation fucked up because of her irresponsible ass. That nigga got fresh pussy on his breath. That's why he didn't beat her ass into a coma."

"Yeah, I feel ya."

"So how's cheesin' for cheese goin'?"

"Lovely. Better than I ever imagined. Jay was at the shoot this morning. He supposed to be giving a phat-ass party tonight. You need to fly up here."

"Naw, I got an interview tonight with ESPN. I'll let you hold them hoes down for me."

"Aye, Saturday we got to hand that food and clothes out to the homeless. Do you know if Salone is still down?"

"I'll be ready, but Salone crazy ass is on her own. She called here the other night playing that Brandy song, 'Almost Doesn't Count.' She still flaky, and I 'on't need any drama right now."

"Boy, that pussy got a hold on yo' ass."

"A'ight, I'm gon' show you, Grandma, and Tae."

"Just show yourself. I'll be home Friday. I think I wanna hit the Platinum Kat."

"Yeah, I need to see a little ass and titties shakin'; go pay these hoes to spread it wide."

"Yeah, out."

"Late'a."

I was exhausted as hell. Never thought smiling and looking good all day could make a person as tired as I was. *A long, hot shower and a glass of Brandy will do me jus' fine.*

My message light on the hotel phone was beeping when I arrived at the hotel.

Beep: *Hi, Babe. Where are you? I thought your shoot was early this morning. I know you probably out smiling up in all those beautiful women's faces—just playing.*

"Yeah, right."

She hesitated. *I hope you are having fun, not too much, though. I'll be waiting to hear from you, Babe.*

Beep: *Chinoe, I was just calling to see if you wanted to go get something to eat. I know this great soul food place named Plenty. I figure we have a lot in common and can share some good ideas. I'm at the Grand Hotel. My room number is 2325. I have to stop off at the lab first. I'll bring you some of the prints from earlier so you can see your work. That's if you accept my invitation. Everything's on me. Talk to you sooner than later, Chinoe Chocolate Starr. Hmmm.*

Beep: *Hey, nigga, give me a call. Some shit done went down.*

Beep: *Chocolate, how you doin'? Hope your shoot is going well. Look cute when the camera shines on you. Chocolate, I hate to hit you with bad news, but it wasn't* *my fault. Diamond started harassing me at the 50-yard line. I was waiting on Money to get there, and he started popping off at the mouth talking 'bout, 'Take yo' ass home . . . in here looking like a prostitute, looking for a sugar daddy, a date.*

Chocolate, I was so embarrassed. I threw my drink in his face, so he started pushing me. Then he slapped the shit out of me. I fell and my glass broke. I was fearing for my life, so I just started swinging, cutting his arm and neck. I don't think I did any serious damage, but I'm alive. That's all that matters.

Well, Sap misses you, and so do I. Chocolate, I can't help but think about that night we . . . never mind . . . it's done and over wit'. But sometimes I wonder if everything would be different?

Call me. Hurry home, and don't get caught up with them northern hoes. **Beep.**

Chapter Twenty-Five

Chocolate

"This a nice li'l place. The food is good."

"Yeah, I found out about it last year. My ex brought me here." She said ex like it was a disease.

"How long an ex?" I inquired, just in case I wanted to take a chance.

"Six months."

"That's not an ex, Chaise. That's an argument waiting for some bumping and grinding, then everything is back rolling."

"Man, please. I'm not about to read that book twice. If I read it twice, somebody gon' have to shoot the shit out of me."

We both laughed about the situation.

"So, Chinoe, how did you get the name Chocolate? You're not dark."

"My mom wanted a chocolate, dark-skinned boy. She thinks dark skin is the most beautiful thing."

"What's her complexion?"

"She's high yellow. And I have to agree with my mom— dark skinned sisters are some of the most beautiful women in the world. I wish someone would tell me why we are so crazy about yellow, red-skin complexions. Don't get me wrong, all shades of black are beautiful."

"Umm, I guess that means I fit the bill, huh?"

I just smiled. I really didn't want to get into that kind of conversation.

"So, Chaise, tell me about how you started taking pictures."

"Well, I use to model when I was younger, but the industry seemed like it was taking control of my life. I never slept, hardly ate, and I was always fighting to keep my panties up and my dress down."

"Ha! Ha! Ha! Bet that was hard, huh?"

She hit my arm like we were old buddies. "So how did you get started modeling?"

"Why you gettin' off the subject? Finish telling me about your dress being up and your panties being down."

"I am safest on the other side of the camera. I don't have to sell myself, just some one else."

"Oh, so what you tryin' to say? You think I'm selling myself?"

"You are. Women and men aren't looking at the outfits in these magazines. The first thing they see is body shapes and faces, all mirages of fake tales— fake hair, overly used makeup, and computerized tummy tucks. And that's what makes consumers buy the clothes, hoping they'll make them look like you guys."

"Hmmm. You have done your homework."

"No, Chinoe, I lived it. Just be careful and don't let this game pimp or play you; you make the first move."

After we ate, she took me to some shops so that I could buy gifts. I saw a black Barbie with a New York T-shirt on. Sap loved dolls so I knew that would be a perfect gift for her. I also picked up a pink sweatshirt for her with New York written in glitter and her name printed on the back.

"Chinoe, you have kids?"

"Oh, naw. This is for my goddaughter."

"What's her name?"

"Sap. Sapphire."

"How old is she?"

"Grown," I said laughing. "She's three. Ahhh . . . she'll be four in May."

"So you and her father are like brothers?"

She's trying to pick me, figure me out. I don't like to be picked. "No, her mother and I are like sister and brother."

"Oh, okay." She didn't look convinced, not that I cared. "Your girlfriend doesn't mind?"

"Mind? She doesn't have a choice. Luvly has been there since I was in the ninth grade. She's going to be there no matter what."

"Sorry. I didn't mean to make you get on the defensive."

"You cool. Lots of women seem to have a problem wit' men and women being best friends. She's good-looking, but I don't look at her like that."

"Have you ever?"

"For a hot second."

She got quiet. *Did she get offended by my answer?*

I put my arm around her. "Ahh, girl, lighten up."

She gave me a fake-ass smile.

We ended up at a jewelry store. There was a diamond and sapphire bracelet for two thousand dollars—not bad, and it was sizeable. Sap could wear it now and add to it later. Perfect birthday gift.

I bought my mom and Haven coach bags, T-shirts, and Luvly some Prada boots and matching purse.

Chaise had a distant look on her face. "You straight?" I asked her.

"Yeah, I'm okay. I was tryin'a get all up in yo' business without an invitation. Sorry."

"No problem."

By this time it was 9:30 p.m., and I was exhausted. We had an early shoot the next morning and her hotel was on the other side of the city.

"Chaise, I'm not trying to get in your drawers or nothing, but would you like to stay with me? I mean in my room tonight. I know you tired, and my room is just up the block."

She smiled and put her arm around my neck. "Sure. But don't be tryin' to sneak a peek."

"Ha!Ha!Ha! Naw, it ain't even like that." Even though I wasn't looking to get involved, I couldn't help looking at that fat ass of hers.

"Let me run in this shop and buy me a nightgown and an outfit for tomorrow."

After she got the necessities for the night we went to my suite.

"Chinoe, this is nicer than mine."

"Yeah, right. You probably got a condo."

"No, really. You have a bedroom and a living room; a Jacuzzi in the middle of the floor and all. They must be giving you the platinum package."

"The shower's in there. I'll call us up some food."

She went into the bathroom and turned on the shower.

"What do you want?"

I could barely hear her. "A cheese steak and fries, honey mustard sauce for my fries, extra cheese and onions, and a pickle."

"And to drink?" I walked closer to the door so I could hear her. She opened the door so fast I couldn't look away. *She's fine as hell!* Her hips were like Jessica Rabbit's. Her breasts were average, but full. And the natural sag made them beautiful. Her thighs plump and juicy, I wanted to make a move, but I promised myself that I would be good and try to get into Haven, try to make her the one.

"My bad, Chaise." I said, still staring at her, trying to act like it was okay. "I just couldn't hear you over the water."

"I'm not asking for an apology. I'll have grapefruit juice."

She closed the door, and I closed my eyes. I wanted to see that body again. I wanted her to walk out and pose for my eyes.

Ring . . . Ring . . . Ring.

"Hello."

"What's up, nigga?"

"Just chillin'. About to turn in so I can do this shoot in the morning. How your interview go with Al Michaels?"

"It went smooth. I'm jus' tired of all the same questions. Can't they watch one interview and not ask the same shit—like my answer is going to change?"

Chaise cut the shower off, singing a Rachel Ferrell song.

"Who is that with the sweet voice?"

"It ain't what you think, boy; she's my photographer."

"Umm hmm, nigga, I bet she is taking pictures. Nude pictures?"

"Man, she about twenty minutes from her hotel, and it was gettin' late." *Why was I explaining to this fool about something that's nothing?*

"Late, my ass. Chocolate, I knew you was lyin', nigga. You about to screw that girl."

"She fine, but she ain't that gold."

"You ain't gon' ever find no pot of gold if you don't test it out first. Nigga, I swear you get the baddest dimes and don't do shit with 'em. But anyway, I called to tell you to get me some of that new Phat Farm, and Mecca, that ain't on the street yet. Jeans and sweats."

"Nigga, I ain't y'all personal shopper." I laughed at my own joke. "I'm already on it, though. Hopefully, after my shoot in the morning I can get 'em and be out."

"I thought you weren't coming back until Monday afternoon."

"Chaise said she works fast."

"I bet Chaise do." We both laughed.

"Chocolate, do you have some lotion?" She asked, massaging her thighs like they were already full of lubricant.

"Nigga, you crazy. Chaise, my boy Money said hello."

"Tell him I said hello." She found the lotion but was interrupted by the thought of who Money was. "Money Loane? Falcon player?"

"Yeah."

"Damn, he fine as hell! Um um um."

"Man, I 'on't wanna hear all that."

"Tell shawty I'm feelin' 'er."

"Late'a."

"Late'a."

"I didn't know you and Money Loane were best friends."

"Yeah, since fourth grade."

"Did you order the food?"

"Oh, naw. Damn! Money called and threw me off track."

After I ordered the food Chaise took me by surprise. "Chinoe, will you rub some lotion on my back?" *Is she trying to give me a heart attack or what?*

Ring . . . Ring . . . Ring.

The phone interrupted, saving me from cheating on Haven.

"Chaise, be quiet . . . please. It might be my girlfriend, and I don't want her to get the wrong idea."

She nodded her head in agreement, and then pointed at her legs, motioning for me to rub lotion on them.

"Chinoe, speaking."

"Hey, Babe, what's up?"

"Nothing, lovely lady. What's up with you?"

"Just chillin'. How's your trip going?"

My lips started watering from my fingers touching Chaise's thighs. The way she was staring at me told me that she was enjoying it more than I was.

"Chocolate?" Luvly detected the distraction in my voice.

"Oh, yeah. Yeah, it's cool."

"Are you busy?"

"Naw." Chaise turned over so that her healthy ass lay open in my face. I wanted to just stick my face all in it and smell it—*I'm trippin'!*

"So you gon' get my Via Spiegel boots and purse?"

"Are you staying alive?"

"Yeah, I think I'm going to have to get a restraining order."

"I've heard that 'restraining order' story too many times."

"Chocolate, will you please get me my boots and purse. And don't forget something for my baby. She been buggin' me about when you comin' back and what you gonna bring her."

"You would forget her before I would." She hesitated like she wanted to say something else but didn't.

"Bye, Babe."

"Bye, Babe."

Chaise looked back at me with an inquisitive look on her face. She slid her legs away from me. "Was that your girlfriend?"

"No, Luvly. But let me call her though, since you are being a good girl." I patted her on the ass.

Talking to Chaise was kinda like talking to Luvly—a sister. Except Luvly wasn't trying to get at me romantically.

It was 12:27 a.m. and I wanted to talk to my baby.

Ring . . . Ring . . . Ring.

Haven's phone rang about five times before it was answered.

"Hello." A male voice answered sounding sleep.

What the fuck? Who the fuck? I looked over at the clock again, 12:29 a.m.

"Hello?" The male said, clearing his throat.

I was debating, if I said something, would he hang up or give Haven the phone. Nine times out of ten, we would have exchanged some nasty words and then Haven would have some lame excuse to throw at me.

I heard Haven lazily say, "Who is it?"

"Hello," he said again. "Muthafucka's playing on the phone."

"Hang up, Baby." And he hung up.

"Ain't that 'bout a bitch."

"Huh?" Chaise asked me.

"Nothing. Talkin' to myself."

"Do you want a massage?"

I did need one, but right then I was too tense to be relieved. "No, thank you. Let me ask you a question."

"Shoot."

"If your man was good to you—bought you everything, took you anywhere, gave all the money necessary, no kids and was a virgin, would you cheat?"

She stared at me for a few minutes, trying to figure out if the scenario was mine, but I could tell the virgin part had her stuck.

"Virgin? He's all that and still fresh? Pure? Hell, I might lock his ass away on an island and have twenty babies from his ass."

"Yeah, that's what I would think." I smiled because as much as she was joking it sounded like a nice invite.

"But the real question would be, does he love me? Truly. Not just being in a relationship until the real thing comes along."

Damn! She read right through me.

"Chinoe, you a virgin?" She sat up and had the same look on her face as when she found out I was on the phone with Money.

In a cocky 'tude, I said, "If I am?"

"Can I be your first?" She looked at me dead serious, and after a few seconds, busted out laughing. "I'm just playin'. Lighten up; I ain't gon' take your goods."

"I think Haven got a nigga over there." All this ass was in my face, and I was stressing out over a piece of ass I hadn't had.

"That's your girlfriend, right?"

"Yeah."

"Well, you're here and she's there. Sooooo . . . you won't know unless someone can go over and knock on the door right now." Chaise had a mischievous grin on her face. "Or I can call and pretend to ask for someone and play her into telling."

Man, I was too old for these games. I'd never done no bitch shit like that. I always had women doing that type shit to me. But my gut feelings were telling me that she had some lame dude over. But I didn't even care about this girl, so why was I trippin? *This girl was handling my money, about to live in my house. Shidd.*

"Hell, yeah. Do yo' thang, Chaise. You know how connivin' y'all women can be."

"Don't hate the Player, hate the game. And ya'll men aren't far behind; y'all just don't like to let a woman know how far-whipped or strung out y'all are."

"Not me."

She looked at me with a smirk on her face. "Look at what you are about to do."

"Feelings are not the factor here. This girl is handling a lot of my money and my house. I need to know whether this a business or pleasure relationship."

She smacked her lips. "What's the little heifer's number?"

"Call from your cell phone. She got all that ID shit on her phone."

Haven picked up on the second ring.

"May I speak to Haven?"

"This is she; who's speaking?"

"This is Lauren. I'm calling from Platinum Impressions Agency. I need to know if Chinoe Starr is available."

Haven hesitated for a moment. Then whispering into the phone, "This isn't his number."

"He had your number down for an emergency contact."

"Oh . . . what do you need me to tell him?"

"Can you write down a message and number for him?"

"Sure. Kal, give me a pencil and piece of paper."

Chaise's eyes got big, and she put her finger over the receiver and whispered, "Kal?"

"Who?" I said out loud, unable to control my anger.

Chaise motioned for me to be quiet. "Hello, Lauren. Go ahead."

"Yes, we need him Tuesday for a shoot."

"Ok. Thank you."

Chaise put the phone down. My heart was in my stomach, thinking that this ho could run off with all my money. How could I have been so stupid?

"Come on, Chinoe," Chaise motioned. "Lay down right here." Chaise pulled my head down into her lap. My head felt good on her cushiony thighs. "Chinoe, maybe it was her family or something."

"Ain't no nigga gon' be at no woman house at

one in the morning and nothing be goin' on! And it ain't no damn family. I heard her call him baby. They were in the bed."

"So what are you going to do?"

"Bust her ass."

"You just started your career. Think this thing through. Pop up. You leaving early. She thinks you coming back Monday night."

Bam there it was. Women were always scheming.

"Can I just say that she's losing out on the most beautiful brother I've ever met?"

When the food arrived, we ate with the Evans family. Silence was caught in both our throats. We watched J.J. do his Dyn-O-Mite routine, and Thelma's fine ass parade back and forth.

It was almost 2 a.m. and I was tired, frustrated, and horny. And Chaise, was lying next to me with next to nothing on, and her butt cheeks playing peek-a-boo me.

Chapter Twenty-Six

Chocolate

When I pulled up in front of the ESPN Zone at 7:45 Sunday night, Money was already macking. Women were lined up along his Lexus oohing and ahhing.

"What's up, Cash Money?" We dapped each other, and the girls lit up.

"Ooh, you play ball, too?" a tall, statuesque woman asked.

"Who do you play for?" a short, stout girl with weave down to her butt wanted to know.

"You married?" another attractive young lady inquired.

One girl was just plain bold; "Hey, you wanna fuck? I live right up the street."

"Naw, boo, I'm straight."

She licked her big bubble-lips, "All right, but my

name is Tootsie—whenever you ready," then she stuck out her long lizard-tongue to top it off.

"Man, get outta this gold-digga magnet and bring yo' ass."

Money parked and got out smiling. "This is the land of opportunity," he laughed. "So what's going on with Miss Haven?"

"Man, fuck her! She dead to me."

Taeko pulled up and jumped out the car all hyped. "Hey, Dawg, when you get back?"

We dapped each other up and gave each other love.

"Tonight."

"I thought you were coming back late tomorrow?"

"People change, plans change."

Dapping Money, Taeko sensed anger. "This nigga on some trip shit or what, Dawg? I feel ya; need some pussy, huh?" He laughed heartily.

Anger was runnin' hot through my veins. I had no time for jokes. "I need you to ride by Haven's house."

A funny look took the place of his grin . . . like he knew something I didn't. "Aye, Joi said she saw Haven at Red Lobster last night with some dude."

"Where is Joi?"

"At her mom's house."

"Call her up."

When Joi answered the phone, she sounded excited to hear from me, "Hey-y-y, Chocolate. I saw your layout in *Vibe*. You really look good!"

My frown almost disappeared. Joi wasn't a real nice woman. She was very nonchalant and coldhearted, so any compliment she gave wasn't to be taken lightly. "Thank you, Miss Lady. That means a lot coming from you. Taeko told me that you seen Haven yesterday."

"You know I don't like gettin' in y'all business, but she was wit' a dude. He was tall, kind of thick, wit' dreads."

"He didn't look familiar?"

"Up North-sounding guy," she said, trying to sound like she was from up North.

"Yeah, she from up North."

"Y'all having problems?"

"Not yet—not until I reach her neck."

"I didn't wanna say nothin' earlier 'cause I saw how crazy you were about her, but she seemed sneaky from the get-go."

"All right then. Thank you, Joi."

"No problem." Joi hung up the phone.

"Why everybody always tryin' to save face. Shit, if y'all feel or see something, tell a brother early in the game . . . so I won't be stuck stupid later on," I told my boys.

I wanted to choke the shit out of her for embarrassing me, and about my goddamn money!

"Aye, Chocolate, man, maybe you over-reactin'."

"Naw, Taeko. She low-down just like yo' ho ass. A ho takin' up for a ho," Money said in a serious tone.

"Fuck you, man," Taeko defended himself.

Money confirmed the rumors that I was hearing in the street. "Chocolate, you know this nigga fuckin' that stewardess?"

"Aaahh, Taeko." I rubbed my head. "I thought you were over that shit, nigga."

He looked down at the ground. "Aye, the pussy good, and she don't want shit but some good dick."

"Yeah, that's in the beginning. They all willing to keep their mouth shut for some dick, but after a few months the price goes up."

"Well, she cool, and she know I'm not gon' mess up my home for some ass."

Me and Money both looked at him. That nigga was hot in the drawers and screwing everything walking—and doing the shit right out in the open. I knew he wanted out of being with Joi, but his shit was gon' catch up with him sooner than later.

By eight forty-five we'd made a plan and were riding in a borrowed black Chevy, like criminals staking out a house to rob. We pulled up two houses down from Haven's house. A gold Tahoe was sitting pretty at the front door, blocking in Haven's Volvo.

"Damn, that shit sittin' tight," Taeko's punk ass said to aggravate me even more.

"Mann, fuck you and dat slimy bitch."

"Damn, nigga, you on some blow or sumthin'? Or you in love?" Money asked with real concern.

"Love? Hell, yeah, wit' my money! Let's get this shit over with."

"You sure you wanna do this?" Taeko asked as he cocked his glock.

"Damn right, I'm sure," I answered as I pulled the black ski mask down, over my face.

Money drove down the street, passing a few houses, and parked behind some trees.

We went through the side door because it wasn't hooked up to the alarm. We creeped in like thieves in the night. But I wasn't looking to steal anything that didn't already belong to me.

We heard moaning and a thud from upstairs. "Sound like they in the bedroom," I whispered to my boys.

"I'm gon' wait by this door. Taeko, go to the front door. All right, boy, go handle yo' business," Money whispered.

I took off toward the steps. "Pssst," Money hissed. "Don't let your trigger finger slip. It ain't that serious."

I waved him off. I had no intension on hurting anybody physically. But mentally was another story.

I crept into the dark room. The moonlight shining through the blinds was my only guide. BACK THAT ASS UP by Juvenile was pumping from the stereo.

"Yesssss, daddy. Fuck me harder, harder!"

"You like this dick . . . it's good to you, huh?"

"Ssssss, ooooh, hell, yeah!"

The nigga was stroking Haven so hard in the ass it looked like he was trying to create a new opening.

In mid stroke, I stuck my gun between his ass cheeks. "What the fu—" He yelled, surprised to see me there.

"Shut the fuck up, nigga!"

"Ahhhh." Haven screamed, jumping up like her ass was on fire.

I pointed my Smith and Wesson dead at her face. "Bitch, lay yo' ass down."

"Please, please don't hurt me!" she cried.

Through clenched teeth I told her, "Lay yo' goddamn ass down!"

"Ahh, man, my wallet . . . my wallet in my pants over there."

"Bitch, nigga. I ain't ask you for yo' money." I hit

him in the back of the head with the gun I'd just taken from between his ass cheeks.

Holding his head, he said, "Damn, man! You ain't have to do that," he yelled out in pain.

"Didn't I tell yo' pussy ass to shut the fuck up!" I turned my full attention to dude and shoved the same gun full of ass, down his throat. Haven took off running. I didn't flinch because I knew my boys would handle her.

He began to gag, but I wasn't letting up, I kept a steady pressure. "I hope that ass is worth yo' death."

He shook his head back and forth, shedding tears and gagging even more.

In a split second, he vomited all over the gun, my glove, and himself. "Son-of-a-bitch!"

"Plea . . . Dawg, don't . . . kill me," he pleaded.

"Get up," I demanded, shaking the vomit from my hand. He reached for his pants.

"Naw, naw, leave 'em. Get moving." I grabbed Haven a shirt that was lying on the floor by the door. I could hear Haven pleading for her life. I smiled hard under the hot ski mask.

When we got downstairs, I pushed buddy onto the floor.

"Kal, are you okay?" Haven asked through sniffles. I could see the love she had for this nigga all over her face, and in her voice.

I threw the shirt into her face. "Put that god-damn shirt on." She looked up into my eyes, back and forth to Taeko, to Money, back to me, like she knew something was familiar about all of us.

"Put the muthafucka on!" I screamed getting frustrated at her unwillingness to obey my command. She quickly jumped to her knees and buttoned the shirt.

Taeko walked over to Kal. "Get cho bitch ass up."

"Mannn, I'll gi-gi-give ya'll—" Kal stayed seated, butt naked, on the floor trying to plead for his life.

Smack! Taeko slapped the shit outta him, grabbing him by his dreds. "Come on."

Money stood back, shaking his head at me and Taeko. He thought we were taking it to far.

Taeko and Money marched Kal outside. Taeko was laughing all the way to the street.

I pushed Haven up to the door so she could see the nigga she had chose over me.

"Hopscotch, nigga." Money finally decided to join in on the festivities.

"What?" Kal asked, shaking, scared to death.

"Hop, nigga—like a frog!" He hesitated, putting his hand over his dick. Taeko rushed him with the gun pointed straight to his forehead, "Take yo' hand down. You wasn't so shy when you was up in my man's girl." Kal started jumping around like a frog, dick swinging, and snot falling from his nose.

"Sing, nigga." Money demanded.

"Sing . . . what? Man, I don't care 'bout that bitch. I was just using her for money and ass." Still sniffing, he pleaded, "Please, let me go."

Taeko and Money looked back at the door, satisfied with their job.

"What!" Haven screamed. "I was using yo' ass. I got a man, bitch."

"Naw, baby girl, you use to have a man." I pulled the ski-mask off. She gasped, becoming big eyed, "Chinoe, I can explain."

"Just go get all my paperwork." I was unbelievably calm.

She ran to her home office and returned with three thick folders. "It's all there. Baby, listen—"

"Baby? Fuck you!" As I attempted to leave, she was fast on my heels, pulling on my shirt, pleading with me to stay.

She tripped and fell, crying, and I kept walking. "I'm sorry, I'm sorry." She jumped up, catching up to me, grabbing my shirt again.

"I'm done!" I shouted. "You can't explain yo' naked ass in the air." I snatched away from her, pushing her down hard onto the sidewalk. "Stay the fuck away from me!" Women always say if you play with pussy, you get fucked. Don't they know if you play with a real nigga, you get fucked harder?

The next evening after a restless night of sleep, I went to Mama's house. I knew Sap would be there. I needed to see her pretty, innocent, little face. She was always a breath of fresh air.

When I pulled in the driveway my mother, father, Papa Loane, Sap and Trinket were sitting on the front porch.

I tooted the horn. Sap and Trinket ran to the car.

"Get your butts back up here. Chocolate's coming," my mother yelled, getting after them as usual.

"Hey, Babe, how was your session?" She greeted me with a kiss and a hug.

My dad gave me a handshake and hug. He'd been out of town four months scouting new cars for the new millennium. He looked thinner. "Hey, dah, boy. How you been? You still playin' the pretty-boy role?" We laughed as he stole a punch to my chest. "You ain't too pretty to fight now, are you?"

I put my fist up. "Naw, old man. All this yard to whoop you in, you better be careful. You look a little underfed without your woman's cooking. Don't let this pretty face fool ya."

"Oh, boy, come over here and let Grandma Loane see you." Mama Loane hugged me and rubbed my face. "I'm so proud of you boys. Y'all keep on moving on up in this mean ol' world—and leave them white women 'lone."

"Grandpa Loane, what she yelling about?"

He gave me a hug and patted me on the back. "We hear Tae runnin' wit' white women."

"I don't know how he could risk the life he's made with Joi for some trash in the streets whether she's black, white . . . or any race. Black men always think black women want them for their money. Shoot, y'all better start thinking about whose going to stay down with you when y'all broke and don't have a pot to piss in, or a window to throw it out of. These white women see big penises, dollar bills, and no brains or common sense."

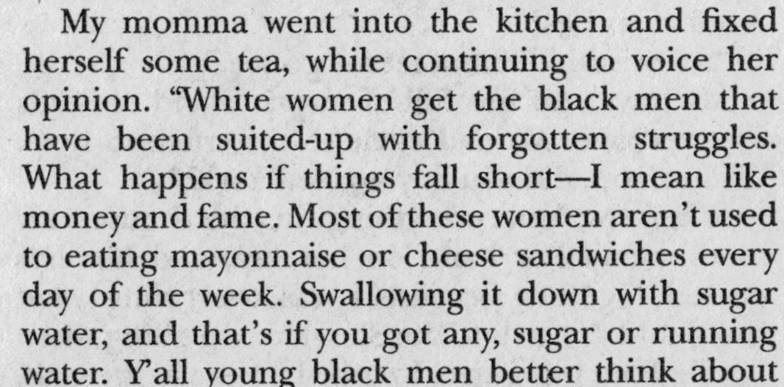

My momma went into the kitchen and fixed herself some tea, while continuing to voice her opinion. "White women get the black men that have been suited-up with forgotten struggles. What happens if things fall short—I mean like money and fame. Most of these women aren't used to eating mayonnaise or cheese sandwiches every day of the week. Swallowing it down with sugar water, and that's if you got any, sugar or running water. Y'all young black men better think about it—is all I'm saying." She sipped her tea, shaking her head. Probably remembering when she was a young girl and had no water or lights for weeks at a time.

"I haven't heard anything yet, Ma."

"I'm sure you will soon. If not from him, then from the news. They love to broadcast when one of their own has snatched up a young, dumb nigga that got a lot of new money with the same old mentality."

It was going on 6 p.m. and it was time for Sap to take her bath. This would give me time to see what my dad and Grandpa Loane thought of my situation.

"Sapphire and Trinket, come on and eat so you can take your baths," my mom yelled from the kitchen.

"Do we have to, Grammy?" Sap pouted.

My mom made her way from the kitchen quickly. "What have I told you about asking me questions after I have told you what to do young lady? Now pull those lips in and hop to it."

She blinked her big eyes and ran over to me. "Love you, Uncle Cha-late."

Trinket gave me a hug and sneaked in, "Where is our surprises?"

"Surprises? Ummm, let me go see."

My Navigator was full of surprises and presents for everyone. My dad came to the truck to help. "Damn, son, did you buy up New York?"

When we got everything in the house, my mother had her hand on her hip, and her lips pursed together because I was overruling what she'd told the girls to do. She started smiling when I pulled out her purse. I winked my eye at the girls.

Mama Loane started modeling her purse. Grandpa Loane sported his brown, leather Avirex bomber. I got my dad the same one in Black and a designer traveling briefcase.

The girls were jumping all over me. "Uncle Chalate, give me mine!"

"Yeah, Uncle Chocolate, give me mine, too!"

"I don't know if I have anything for two little girls."

"YES, YES, YES!" they sing.

I pulled out their dolls and sweat suits. They grabbed them, hugged me, and ran to Sap's playroom.

My mom clapped her hands. "Un, un, girls, bath's first." They headed to the bathroom, dropping their smiles and happiness before they begin.

That little girl was my life. Sap always had a home with my mom and me, forever. We had built our lives around her. Our schedules, money, and hearts are hers for life.

Trinket was just as special to us, but she had a mother and father that provided a stable home for her—thus far.

After I finished playing Santa Claus, I motioned for the men to come into the great room. I poured my dad a glass of Absolute and orange juice, and Grandpa Loane some Christians Brothers, as I mentally prepared to rack their minds for answers to some overdue questions.

"Aye, I got a question for y'all old heads."

"Boy, I might be a few years older than you, but I'm still young in some places that you still got to grow up." My dad winked.

"Don't be so sure about that." I winked back at my dad. Taking on a more serious demeanor, I said, "It's been a long time since we've sat down and had a talk about life, you know, like what's been going on since all this fame."

"Y'all boys don't sit still long enough to bat a eyelash." Grandpa Loane joked.

"Well, what's on your mind, Chocolate? Sounds like something bothering you." Grandpa Loan got straight to the point.

"Is there ever a time for a man to get tired of going from woman to woman and it be all right? I mean want to settle down and be with one special person."

They both looked at each other and then at me. My dad went first. "Son, if you have to ask yourself or anyone that question, you already know the answer."

"I mean, yeah, I know what I think, but I want another opinion."

"Your opinion is all that matters, Chocolate. Other people's opinions are for themselves, or a jealous venture to keep you away from what you really want."

"But I will tell you one thang, sex don't make the man, the man makes the sex. And sex ain't the only thing that's gon' make that special woman wanna stay wit' cha." My dad broke it down.

After everyone was gone, I decided to stay at my mom's for the night. Before retiring to the guestroom I went to my old room. It'd been turned into Sap's room. I stood in the doorway and reminisced.

It seemed like yesterday when me and Caymin were about to make history in that room. I really dug that girl. I wondered what she was doing now. Probably married with four or five kids.

Sometimes I wish I had made love to her that

night. I could still smell her; feel her soft body rubbing up and down on mine. The look on her face as she sat on top of me would forever be imprinted in my memory.

It was a shame that we lived in the same city for all these years and hadn't bumped into each other.

Sap came up behind me and grabbed my leg, hugging it tight.

"What's up, pumpkin?" I picked her up squeezing her tight, giving her a big kiss. "Love you, Sap."

She hugged her short little arms around my neck then put her little hands on my face. "Love you, Uncle Cha-late."

"Where is Trinket?"

"Sleeping wit' Grammy."

Kissing the tip of her nose, I told her, "You should be 'sleep, too."

She nodded her head yes, not really meaning it.

I walked into the great room and lay back in my favorite chair with Sap cuddled up under my arm. I felt like she was mine, my child, my responsibility, my life. Sometimes I wish it were me that Luvly got involved with. She and Sap would have had the best of everything.

I called Money to see if it was still on for tomorrow night.

"Talk to me."

"What's up?"

"Nothing, just chillin' with these honeys."

"Who?"

"Nigga, you don't know 'em, but they got a couple of friends. And they dancers, too, thick as hell!"

"Oh, yeah?"

"Oh, yeah."

"What 'er home girls lookin' like?"

"It's this one that's cute as hell. She got that long hair like you like, a white smile, and not to mention thick as hell. But she quiet as hell, keeping her clothes on, staying to herself."

"Sounds good. Sounds good. Where she at?"

"They all downstairs in the basement."

"Damn, Money, you got all of them in the Jacuzzi?"

"That's what they asked for. You need to come on over."

"Yeah, I will. I need to do something to take my mind off this shit." I forgot all about Sap being under me.

"Ooh, Uncle Cha-late say bad word."

"That Sap?" His enthusiasm changed drastically.

"Yeah, that's her big head."

"Who dat?" Sap asked.

"Who is that?" I corrected her, "It's Uncle Money."

Money spent time with her, but not enough. She thought that every time Money came around she was supposed to get gifts and presents. Love, she expected from my mom and me, but she needed to know love from him, too.

"Let me holla at her."

"Hel-lo."

"Big girl, I thought it was your bedtime."

She giggled. "When you coming here?"

"I'll see you tomorrow, okay?"

"Okay."

"I'll pick you up from school."

"Tomorrow?"

"Tomorrow, Babe. Now get some sleep. I love you."

"Everybody loves Sap."

"Yes, Babe. Everybody does love you."

"Man, she getting so grown. I got to get this shit straight before she get too old. She needs to be calling me daddy."

"You don't even know if she yours or not."

"Nigga, we both know the truth. Look at her. She looks just like Maynea." Money sighed, not wanting to continue the serious conversation. "So you comin' or what?"

"Nigga, them girls ain't goin' nowhere. They at Money Loane's house. You might have to kick 'em out."

"Tell Ma I'ma pick Sap up tomorrow."

"Luvly will have her tomorrow," I said, not really thinking about it.

He sighed. "Well, call her and tell 'er that I'll pick Sap up."

"No can do, baby daddy; that's all on you."

"Whatever, pretty nigga. I'll do it myself."

"Later."

"Later."

Sap was already asleep. I took her to her bed. Scooting Trinket over, I lay Sap at the opposite end and kissed them both on the cheek.

About to walk out the door I turned around and looked at them. Those little girls had everything a child could possibly need or want, but in actuality they were the poorest children because their parents were shaky and becoming more unstable by the day.

They didn't and would never have privacy. They could never lead normal lives. Everything they did would be exploited and scrutinized by a newspaper or magazine. The only thing they would probably have was each other.

My mother walked up behind me, putting her hand on my shoulder.

"Short lady, what you doin' sneakin' up behind me?"

"Just remembering when me and your dad would stand at this doorway and look down on you when you were their age, worrying about your future and if we were raising you right. Seems like yesterday I could protect you from everything and anyone, but now you're grown and you have to protect yourself. You have celebrity status now and vulnerability to the world. I just want you to know that your father and I will always provide a safe haven for you."

Turning around to face her, I said, "Thanks, Ma. I needed that. I'm just looking at them thinking the same thing. They're never going to be protected from everything or everyone."

"They'll be all right. They have a lot of loving people in their life."

I hated involving my mother in my personal business. She was so protective of me. Sometimes she flew off the handle, without understanding the whole situation.

So I didn't tell her about Haven. I guess that's why Luvly didn't like telling us about her and Diamond.

Chapter Twenty-Seven

Luvly

My life had not turned out how my parents or I wanted it to. I was the first to admit that I had made too many mistakes, some of them unforgivable. The biggest mistake of all—Diamond. I don't know why I couldn't let his doggish ass go. The crazy thing was, it had nothing to do with love; maybe it was obligation or the pity sermons he used on me. He made me damaged goods mentally, emotionally, and physically, took me to levels worse than I'd imagined.

The only man that understood where I'd been and what I was going through was about to walk out of my life. I knew he was tired of me being wishy-washy, but I needed Money to survive.

If it weren't for Money and Chocolate and their parents, I would have been in an insane asylum. I knew my parents were tired of the mess I went through and involved them in. And being strongly religious, they didn't believe in having a baby without being married. With them it was "until death do you part."

I wanted my daughter to grow up and become a strong successful, black woman with charisma, substance, and goals, something her mother did not possess.

Sure, my nail shop was doing well but I wanted to be a professional and have a sense of security. I wanted to go back to school for nursing or teaching. When I told Money about my plan, I thought maybe he would see that I was serious about us getting married and raising Sapphire as a family.

That beautiful house was a shock. I thought Money was so far up those hoes asses that he would sweep me to the side like he had done Salone for so many years.

The day that Money showed me the house, I was so depressed.

"Money, where are we going? I just wanna stay in your bed and sleep away my entire past so I can start fresh."

"Even me and Sap?"

"No, just the bad things."

"Well, I have a surprise for you."

"I'm in a sweatshirt and jogging pants, with a baseball cap and the smell of sex on me! I'm not going into public!"

"You're going to be in the privacy of your own home."

"What?"

We pulled into a circular driveway of a pale pink house. It was gorgeous.

"Money, I don't want to meet any famous people right now. Please take me back to your place."

He got out of the car and opened my door. "Come on, lovely."

I smiled because I knew he was calling me lovely and not by my name. He was so sweet sometimes, I guess when I wasn't bullshitting him.

"Whose house is this?"

"You like it?"

"Yeah." He opened the door and motioned me to go inside. "Boy, is you crazy? These people are going to call the police on me. Shit, you famous, they'll just ask you for your autograph.

He leaned over and kissed me passionately. "Luvly, get yo' ass in this house."

When I walked in the front door it had cathedral ceilings but no furniture. A five-step bridge lead into a sunken den.

There were two bedrooms side by side connected by a huge bathroom with a Jacuzzi in the middle of the floor. There were circular steps in the middle of the foyer that led up to the kitchen and an outside balcony.

"This house is the shit! I love the way it's designed. Matter of fact, I told you about this when I was sixteen."

He laughed. "Would you like to live here? Raise Sap here?"

"Hell, yeah."

"Come this way." He led me to a circular part of the house that turned into a huge round bedroom. An oatmeal-cream canopy with thick tall spiral poles and a dresser and armoire to match decorated the bedroom.

"Money, somebody lives here!"

He just smiled and stood in the doorway with his hands on the ledge of the door. "This bedroom is for a princess, no, a queen!"

I fell back on the bed. It was so soft and fluffy.

"Look under the pillow."

I looked at him like he was crazy. "What?"

"Girl, just look under the pillow."

There was a pink envelope. When I opened it, it read:

> This is a precious gift for the two precious women in my life. I love you, Luvly. Please accept this house as a home of love and care for you and Sapphire.
>
> Love You
> Money

I started rolling around in the beautiful bed.

When I looked up he was standing above me. "Luvly, I love you, girl. Just promise me something."

"Anything, Money."

He lay down on top of me and held my face. "Diamond is not to come on this property at anytime. If he wanna see Sap, take her to him, but under no circumstances is he to be in this house."

"You got it baby." We sealed the deal with a kiss.

Chapter Twenty-Eight

Chocolate

As I looked through the glass door, I noticed Joi's hands waving wildly, her lips moving tightly together, but still letting fierce words roll off her tongue.

"Fuck you, you bastard! I don't want to hear that same lame-ass shit you been talking for years! I'm so tired of yo' lyin', triflin' ass. You ain't shit!"

Taeko had guilt written all over his face. While he stood looking defenseless with his hands tucked into his pockets and shook his head from side to side. "I ain't lyin' to—"

"Muthafucka, we gon' see who lyin'!" She pointed her finger to the tip of his nose, her five foot three frame looking the same height as his.

"Look, don't bother Chocolate with dis right now," he pleaded. "He already goin' through some thangs."

I opened the door. "What's up now?"

Taeko gave me some dap without looking me in the eyes. He swiftly walked past me, and down the hall to get Trinket.

Joi stood in front of me with a glazed stare. "Chocolate, tell me what I'm hearin' in the street ain't true."

I couldn't look her in the eye. I hadn't asked Taeko about all the stuff in the tabloids, but I knew him, I knew it was true. "I don't know, Joi. I just got back in town."

"He told me that he spent two days in New York with you, but when I called your hotel room they said you weren't in and that I'd just missed you."

That could have been true. So what was she bugged about? "And?"

"I had just hung up the phone with Tae and he said that you were layed out, 'sleep." Her eyes began to water.

Damn, Taeko! What was you doing, man?

With pleading eyes, she said, "Chocolate, I've never asked you anything or involved you in my home life, but I'm in a tough situation." She wiped her eyes and clenched her teeth. "But if I find out that baby is his, I'm gone."

"What baby?"

"Some white flight attendant is claiming to be pregnant. I'll take his ass through the ringer! We not playin' house no more. This is the real deal, no matter how much y'all don't want to grow up."

Taeko came out with Trinket over his shoulder before I could defend myself.

In an innocent voice, Taeko said, "Ba', you ready?"

She turned toward me giving me a sharp look that said don't discuss what we'd just talked about.

"Let me walk them to the car, and then I'll be ready."

Always the hyper, energetic, joking one, Taeko's spirit seemed broke.

On the way to Money's house, it was quiet, but I had to ask Taeko about all these accusations multiple women and too many babies. Joi only mentioned one baby, but from my reliable sources there is one baby already born and two with paternity suits waiting. "Hey, man, you screwin' white girls?"

He looked at me then back at the road. "One or two."

"What!" I almost lost control of the car. "All we go through as black men, with black mothers, sisters, and daughters, and you go and screw some funky, nasty, white pussy. What do you think Trinket is going to think about herself, her father choosing a white woman over her black mother? If you were already with a white woman from jump and had kids with her, then I wouldn't be trippin'."

"Man, don't you think I think about that? I try to keep my affairs out of Georgia."

"Nigga, the media is everywhere you are! I thought you were smarter than that."

"Yeah, I thought I was, too."

Usually I would be dapping him telling him to go for what he know, but now he had kids, a home, and a very high-profile career, not to mention he was black and always being watched for that reason alone.

"What about this baby thing?"

"Babies?"

"Nigga, what was you thinkin' about?"

Sounding real hopeful, he said, "Renae is pregnant, but it might not be mine. This one girl I met in Philly who moved down here two months ago—she's about three months. She swears it's mine, but I 'on't know. I'm just gon' pay they ass to shut up."

"When you go for the blood test somebody is going to see your name on those papers and sell that story fo' sho. So payin' they ass is just what they hopin' for."

"Joi talkin' 'bout leavin' me. I thought that's what I wanted, but now that it's front and center, I'm about to break. I can't lose her or my babies. They keep me sane."

"Stay at home sometimes, and keep yo' dick out of everything movin'."

As we pulled into Money's castle, Maxwell's "Fortunate" serenaded us. We could hear the water splashing from around back. All styles of cars were sittin' pretty, parked every which way to fit in. As I passed a Tahoe, a sexy fragrance hit my nose.

"Damn, some girl was so cheeked up she forgot to roll up the window." I took another deep breathe of the sweet fragrance.

"Money, got this thang hot, don't he?"

"Probably got every stripper under the Atlanta moon in here." We both laughed.

I was glad that the mood had lightened. I put in my code, and we entered Money's pussy playground. Girls were running around in dental floss bikinis with titties flapping, and asses bouncing.

"Hey, chic, where's Money?" I asked a redbone with too much ass for her bathing suit.

"He's downstairs handing it out." She said excited.

When we got to the basement, he was sitting in his big-boy lounge chair with three girls dancing on and around his face. One girl was standing on the arms of the chair, facing us, with Money's face between her ass cheeks; the other two girls were shaking it up on the sides of the chair.

"Ooh, more football players!" A variety of women screamed.

"Naw, stupid. That's Taeko Hill; he plays for the Hawks." A sexy, chocolate sister with deep dimples confirmed.

"Ooh, that's even better." Someone from the crowd of women yelled.

One girl stopped dancing and walked up to me. "And you that model everyone is hollerin' about." She was high as a kite. Fine, but not my type.

Money finally came up for air. "Dah go my dawgs. What's up, Tae? Get at it, nigga."

The biggest grin covered his face, like a kid in a candy store. Two of Money's teammates and two Atlanta rappers were in the backyard, under the waterfall.

"Jazzy Hoes" by Jermaine Dupree came on outside, and the girls went wild. They start stripping and shaking their asses wildly.

"Why you and Chocolate standing there like y'all scared of pussy?"

One of the girls, slim and with some big-ass titties, came in wet from the pool, smiling from ear to ear. "I need a towel or a tongue to dry me off!"

Taeko's eyebrows raised, and Money licked his lips.

"Well," she said, cupping her large breast and waiting for a response.

The girl with the long red ponytail that was dancing on Money, took a towel and layed it on the couch for the big-titty girl to laid down. Ponytail started licking up her leg like it was a chicken bone. Me and Taeko looked at each other then back at them. She was sucking the hell out of her thighs.

The girl laying on the couch moaned as she stuck two of her own fingers inside herself, "Ummm, taste it, baby girl." She stuck her wet fingers into the other girl's mouth. The girl with the red ponytail licked and sucked on the moist fingers. She must have loved the taste of the girl's juices because she dug her face deep into the girl's pussy. Smacking and slurping like she was eating finger food.

"Man . . . these hoes wild as hell!"

"Just the way I like 'em." Taeko walked over to the girls and started rubbing on redhead's ass.

She started shaking and gyrating, motioning for him to enter her. I walked back upstairs. All that ass, smoke, and music was giving me a headache.

I decided to go to my custom designed guestroom, which Money had built for me. Right then I wished, I was at my new home wrapped up with my mysterious woman. That was a lost cause.

I checked my messages.

Beep: *Chinoe, I'll be in Atlanta in two weeks. Do you think you can spare up some time for me? I know Atlanta's my home, but since I'm never there it seems so unfamiliar. Give me a call on my c-phone. I had a nice time last night. This Chaise; of course you probably already know that. Call me.*

She's tryin' so hard, but this is the wrong time in my life.

Beep: *Chinoe . . . I don't know where to start. I'm so* *sorry for trying. I mean I know that I've messed up, but tell me how I can make it up to you.* She was crying and sniffing. *Please call me.*

She done lost her goddamn mind. Fuck her!

I layed across my old waterbed from my mother's house and tried to clear my mind. I was engulfed in darkness. I requested no windows be built into the walls.

The music sounded like it was gettin' louder and the girls wilder.

"Damn!" It was almost eleven thirty. I knew exactly what I wanted to be doing.

Ring . . . Ring . . . Ring.

"Hello."

Silence.

"Hello," I said with aggravation in my voice.

"Chinoe . . . it's me."

Man, this broad was not understanding that I was done wit' this episode. "Man, da hell you want?"

"You."

"After that shit you pulled? Hell naw."

"Chinoe, tell me what to do."

In the calmest voice I could render, I told her, "Kiss my ass."

She let go of a hopeful breathe, "Chinoe, please—"

"Please what, Haven? You want me to keep walking out the front door, while he comes in the back?"

"No, no, it's not like that at all."

"I'm hangin' up since you don't want to fess up."

"No, Chinoe, wait!" She was playin' right into my hands, sounding desperate. "I thought you were seeing other people. You are always gone. The only way to get in touch with you is that damn cell phone. Look at your buddies. They are all hoes and sluts. Money screwing anybody and your, supposedly, best friend. She fuckin' him and her boyfriend and don't know who her baby daddy is. And Taeko got babies floating everywhere. What am I to think?"

"Whatever you want about my friends. 'Cause I'm not them, so you are dead wrong for stereotyping me."

"Chinoe, why do we have to end like this?" I could hear her crying uncontrollably.

"All right, come on over here and fuck something. No talking, no nothing, just fuckin'. You act like a trick, so I'm gon' treat you like a trick. Fuck or get cut." *Click.*

I'm tired of playing the nice guy and looking for something that doesn't exist.

BAM!! The door swung open and slammed shut fast.

"What the hell!" I couldn't see who it was, but I knew it was a female from the sweet scent in the air, the same scent coming from the truck outside.

"If Taeko or Money sent you up here, I'll pay you double to leave."

"Oh, I'm sorry. I didn't think anyone was in here, and furthermore, I'm not a prostitute."

"Whatchu wearin'?" I asked sniffing the air again.

"My skin." She said with a smart attitude.

Oh, she got jokes. "Damn, Miss Lady, I was just complimenting you on how good you smell."

"Well, you better be specific about what you want. It's called Ocean Dream. And I'm sorry I barged in on you. I didn't think anyone was in here. I figured I could pick a door and hide behind it."

"Hold on. If you dodging bullets you got to get the hell outta here."

She laughed. Her voice sounded familiar, a little rough and hoarse all intertwined to equal soft and sexy.

"Do I know you from somewhere?"

I tried scooting closer to her voice. I wanted to fill my nostrils with this Ocean Dream. Maybe it could take my mind off of reality.

"I don't know. Do I look familiar?"

"I don't have x-ray vision."

"Oh, shit, it is dark, huh?" She laughed with that beautiful sound again. "My room is like this, too, but I have windows. I had to put dark blinds and drapes over them. I love the darkness; it feels calm and relaxing."

"My boyz say I'm crazy for wanting to be closed in all the time."

"Safest place," we both said at the same time.

"So why are you up here hidin'?"

"First of all, I don't smoke weed. the smell clings to my hair and clothes. And I'm not a ho, so there was no use in me teasin' if I'm not pleasin'."

"So why come? You know what these parties be like."

"Brought some friends. But I think I'm about to go home so I can listen to some Frankie Beverly and Maze or, better yet, some Anita Baker.

"Girl, you don't know 'bout dem Maze boys or Ms. Baker."

"I might be young, but I love all the oldies."

"Those are two of my favorite artists."

"So that means you have them in here."

"Yep."

"Well, before you get it crunk in here will you help me to the bathroom?"

"Here," reaching through the dark to meet her hand, I led her to the bathroom door. Then I hurried to turn on the light so that I could see her and find the CD's.

Not moving fast enough, I missed seeing her face, but I got a glimpse at a nice ass.

Damn she sounds familiar. I know I've heard that voice somewhere. I know I have.

I found Maze, THIN LINE BETWEEN LOVE AND HATE soundtrack, Anita Baker, Isley Brothers, Al Green, the Chi-lites, the Gap band, and to top it off Prince, just in case she wanted to get freaky.

Cameo was already in, so I played CANDY and put it on shuffle.

As soon as I cut the light off, she came out of the bathroom.

"That tub is nice. Platinum, I love it. It's the new color signifying wealth. You aren't going to believe it, but my bathroom color's the same. I guess it caught your eye, too."

"Are you me in a female essence?"

"Naw you just have good taste."

She felt around and sat down in the chair in front of the bed. "That's my jam. I always dance off of that."

"Oh, yeah, well, if you shy this is your chance to dance; I can't see anything."

She got up and walked toward the bed. "Ouch."

"Be careful."

She grabbed my head.

"Sorry. Give me your damn hand," she said, trying not to laugh.

"Sure thang. You know you have a sexy-ass voice." She smiled. I couldn't see it, but I could feel it. We started dancing. She put my hands on her hips. "Nice."

"Huh?"

"Nothing."

Her hips felt so full and soft. *Damn, she feels good!*

My hands took control, rubbing up and down her sides, feeling every curve her body owned. She smelled like a dream.

"What did you say that perfume was called?"

"Not telling."

"You already told me once."

"Right, already told you once. You got to learn how to be sharper; women love that stuff." She got right up on me. Even her breath smelled good.

"Are you wearing lipstick?"

"No, I hate makeup." I squeezed her closer. She lifted her head quickly, bumping me in the lip.

"Ooh, sorry."

"Do you want me to turn on the light so you don't kill me?" I asked, mocking a serious tone.

"No, I'm sorry. If you turn on the light, I'm leaving."

"Wouldn't want you to do that." She was moving so sexually. Her body felt like it was meant for mine. It felt like a bale of cotton spun with pure silk. "Mmmmm, your skin is so soft."

"Are you trying to seduce me?"

"No, no, just giving you your props. Don't let it blow up your head."

The girl had a jazzy mouth. She was probably ugly, but her conversation and company were soothing.

Anita Baker's ANGEL came on. "Ooh, that song

is sooo beautiful. It makes me feel sexy." She came close to me again. We started slow dancing, and her body melted into mine. "You feel pretty good yourself. I'm in love with strong arms and big hands."

"Better to hold you with my dear," I said, squeezing her. "And better to touch you with."

She rubbed her hands across my face slow and sensual. "You have smoother skin than I do."

"Not possible. I'ma have to call you silk." I could tell she was blushing.

"Thanks."

We continued to slow grind and I started to get aroused. But this wasn't a feeling like I had to fuck, it felt stronger, mentally stimulating.

"What time is it?"

Damn! Is she trying to leave already?

"It's, I can't see the clock or my watch, and you told me that if I turned on the light you were leaving."

She smacked her lips. "You're good, real good. Listening." As the music continued we slowed down our pace. "I'm getting tired. I've been on my feet all day. Can I take off my shoes?"

"Yeah, take off whatever you want."

"Umm hum. Don't get fresh."

I'm serious. Her body felt too good. I wanted to squeeze her soft breast with my bare hands, no clothes.

"I'm thirsty."

"You want me to get you something to drink?"

"Yes, please."

"Soda, beer, mixed drink?"

"I would like an Amaretto sour, but I don't really drink. Some cranberry juice and Sprite would be nice."

"Mixed?"

"Yeah, mixed. It has a tangy taste to it."

"Okay, if you say so." I ran downstairs to get this unknown lady a drink. The party was still bumping. I got her the nasty shit she requested and got myself some Hennessy and Coke.

Before going back upstairs, I went to the basement to see what them niggas was doing. Taeko was layed back, getting head. "Damn Tae, you still at it?"

"Hell, yeah . . . these hoes—sssttt—givin' brains like crazy."

"Where Money?"

"Fuckin'."

I waved Taeko off and went to Money's room. I opened the door to him bonin' some girl with a fat, round, jiggly ass.

"My bad Dawg." I turned my head. "Just lettin' you know I'm in my room."

He waved his hand. That nigga was high as a kite and jimmyless. Them niggas wasn't never gon' learn.

Back in my room, an alluring scent pulled me in—bubble bath. "Hey, where you at?"

"Hey is for horses; I'm in here."

I walked into my bathroom to find her in the Jacuzzi. I couldn't see her, but I heard her. "You just takin' over, aren't you?"

"I just thought a bath would be relaxing. This tub is big enough for five, so why don't you fill the other end."

What the hell. Maybe it would relax me, too.

"I know you had to turn on the lights to do all this."

"Maybe, maybe not. I could just be good with my hands."

"I can believe that." As I began to take off my clothes, I felt a wet hand helping me unbutton my shirt. She got it off in seconds. "Pro, huh?" She didn't respond.

Did she do this all the time?

Then she unbuttoned my jeans, letting them fall to the floor. "Umm . . . boxers. What color?"

"Purple."

"Wha'dddd? That's my favorite color."

"I thought it was silver?"

"I didn't tell you that; I said my bathroom was that color. Listen."

"Damn! Your mouth jazzy."

"Yeah, got a Masters in it."

"Oh, you not gon' finish undressin' me?"

"You seem like a big boy." She patted my chest. "You can handle it."

I grabbed some towels and gave her the drink she requested.

"Umm mmm!"

"Does it taste good mixed?"

"Yeah, the drink and the feeling of this water."

I stepped into the tub. It was hot as hell. "You like your water a little hot, don't you?"

"Sorry. Do you want me to run some cold water?"

I slid down slowly into the water, "No, don't worry bout it, I guess my nuts won't turn into raisins."

We sat quietly for a while, the music playing softly, my mind wanderin' aimlessly. But my curiosity quickly took over.

"Is your hair long? Or do you have a horse's tail?"

"Yes, it comes mid-back, and it's all mine."

"What color?"

"Jet black."

"Do you wear makeup?"

"No, just a little lipgloss and maybe a little eye shadow. I think makeup is so superficial; it makes a woman look fake. When you lay down with her at night she's beautiful, but when y'all wake up in the morning she look like boo-boo."

We laughed together.

"I don't like women that wear makeup. It's messy and fake. But I do think that shiny stuff on the lips is sexy. A little eye makeup to match the outfit is sexy, too, but not that black-liner stuff under the eye and around the lips. Makes y'all look like witches."

She reached up and touched my face with her wet hands. "You have a goatee. It's sexy on the ugliest man." She passed her hand through my hair. "You have beautiful hair, too. It's so curly and soft."

"Thanks to my dad."

"A young black man with a true father is rare."

I almost took offense to her comment, but she was absolutely right, too many sperm donors and not enough hardhats to stick around. "You right. A lot of young men, and men in general, couldn't say my dad or even knew their dad." Money came to mind as I said that.

"Where you from?" she asked.

"I was born in Michigan, then we moved to Columbus, Georgia because my father was in the military. After he completed his service, my mother wanted to move to Atlanta, so when I was in the fourth grade we moved here. And here I am. What's your story?"

"You're not going to believe this, but I was born in Minnesota. Then my father moved my mother to Atlanta. My mother then moved to Columbus for some reason or another. And then back here."

"Yeah, right. Stop telling jokes," I said.

"No joke. I grew up between Columbus and Atlanta. I moved to Columbus in the fourth grade then came back to Atlanta my eleventh grade year."

"So we missed each other?"

"I guess so."

"What school did you graduate from?"

"I went to homebound school for three years. My mother thought it would be less distracting and more advanced."

"My mother teaches homebound school. Her name is Seal Starr."

"Mrs. Starr is your mother?"

"Yeah, you know her? Had her as a teacher?"

"Yes, and she was my advisor. What school did you graduate from?" She asked excited and truly interested in my world.

"Banneker High."

"You have a beautiful mother inside and out. She used to talk about you all the time. Most of her classes were subjected Chinoe Starr. I could never forget that name."

"So how often do you go to Columbus?"

"Once a month. My father, grandmother, and cousins live there."

"Do you ever go out to the clubs?" I asked.

"The F&W sometimes, and Tucks when I'm down there on a Thursday. Do you ever go?"

"Not hardly, just to see my family on occassion." My foot accidentally touched her pussy. "My bad. I'm sorry."

"I didn't complain."

I'm really feeling this girl. It's just that I don't know what I'm facing, literally.

"I wonder what time it is?"

"Why are you so concerned with time? My company not intriguing enough for you?"

"No, that's not it. I have to go to school at seven-thirty in the morning."

"Oh, I'm sorry. Thought you had a date."

"I do, with my professor."

"What are you taking up?"

"Law. "

"What type of law?"

"Entertainment law."

I was ready to ask this girl to marry me. "I know you goin' to think I'm gamin' you, but that's what I started going to school for. I got sidetracked and stuck with computer programming."

"If everything we are telling each other is true, we better elope right now." She laughed sweetly.

"What's your classification?'

"Junior."

"What school?"

"Clayton State University. I'm doing the integrated studies program."

"I went to Clayton too"

"I told you, you had good taste.

Shit! My mind was going in a thousand directions, this woman could have been a murderer; a crazy person that did this all the time. Or she could have been someone's wife or mother—two drama areas I wasn't willing to deal with.

"Ahh—" I paused because I didn't know her name.

"Brandie."

I grabbed my dick because she said it so sexy and powerful.

"Intoxicating?"

"Yeah, to those who dare take a sip."

I wasn't going to tell her that I planned to name my first-born girl Brandy; she was already high on her horse.

"You got any tat's?"

"Yeah, on my lower back. It says Caramel with drips, dripping all over it."

"Ummmm."

"And you?"

"Nope. Not yet." I cleared my throat, ready for the serious questions. "So, Brandie, are you married? Boyfriend? Booty partner?"

"Well, I am seeing some people right now, but nothing concrete. School and work take up all my time. I work at PNC Bank for a couple of hours after school."

"Some people? Hmm."

"What? I know you probably got women crawling all over Atlanta."

"Nope, I'm single to mingle."

The water started cooling off, and I wondered if my conversation was headed in the same direction.

"Since we don't know each other, is it okay to ask personal questions?"

"Shoot."

"When I was at work yesterday these girls were

talking about how many guys they had slept with. How many do you think is too many?"

"Any."

"Huh?"

"One is too many, if you ask me."

"Oh, y'all kill me wantin' a virgin and ain't one yourself."

I just let her have that li'l bit. Figured the best thing for me to do was change the subject, so if something popped off she wouldn't think I was inexperienced. But she piqued my interest so I wanted to know more. "Have you ever had a one-night stand?"

"No, but that's on my to do list before I settle down."

"Umm. Have you ever been with a virgin?"

"I'd probably take his mind along with his dick."

"Meaning?"

"I'm not one to toot my own horn, but I know what I'm doing. I do it well."

I bet she did, as fine as she felt and moved in my hands. I knew it would feel even better on my dick!

"I like to do all types of things," she added. "But only if I like a person. You know how hard it is to do anything good if you don't really like the person you're doing it to or with."

She had a valid point.

"Do you like to give head?"

Brandie laughed so hard, bubbles fly into my face. She felt them blow. "Oh, I'm sorry."

She raised up on her knees trying to find her way to my face. Instead she grabbed my bicep. "Umm, that's not it." She slipped and her hand fell on my dick. Already turned on by her sexy voice and soft skin, I instantly became hard.

She didn't move her hand. "Yes, I do like to give head—" I'm breathing her breath, she's so close. "If I like the person."

"Do you like me?"

Brandie had my emotions running high. I wanted her physically, mentally, emotionally, and forever. She must have felt the same breath exchange because she started kissing me. "Umm," she kissed me. "Umm," she kissed me even more deeply. "Ummmm."

ADORE by Prince began serenading us into ecstasy. Her lips were as soft as her body. Our tongues met, slipping in out of each other's mouth. The taste of sweet cranberries was still lingering on her tongue. I pulled her onto my lap as she gracefully wrapped her thick legs around my waist. I wished I could see her face, attractive or not. I loved to see a woman at a higher view. They looked so sexy and in control. To make it even better, I envisioned my mystery star.

Chapter Twenty-Nine

Brandie

"Chinoe, you feel so good. It feels like we can melt into each other." He felt like the man of my dreams, the way his strong hands gripped my hips, the way he talked, and he liked everything about my look, even though he couldn't see me.

I didn't know why I didn't tell him I was a dancer. It seemed like he had his life under control, and I didn't want to stir things up with my wild lifestyle.

He looked so damn good! I cheated. When he went downstairs to get my drink, I saw the big poster of him on the wall.

I put my hand on his dick on purpose. I needed to feel what he was working wit' so that I wouldn't be disappointed in case we got overheated.

I'd never had a one-night stand, but at that

point never was about to be thrown away. I knew he was puzzled about what I looked like, but without being conceited, I could promise him that I was worth it. Just repeating what I'd heard about my thick, five-six frame, and caramel complexion.

People were always asking me if I was mixed with Hawaiian, Indian, or Samoan. I guess my long jet-black hair and thickness were all in the right places, including the stomach area, but it was tight.

We were getting hot in everyway possible. The water started to cool off, so I turned the Jacuzzi jets back on. There was no more talking going on. FREAK TONIGHT by R. Kelly from the THIN LINE BETWEEN LOVE AND HATE soundtrack set the mood just right.

He pulled me onto his lap. I loved this position; it made me feel like I was in control. Like I was 'the mommy.'

All my natural toys were at his disposal; I grabbed his hands and placed them on my breast. He pushed them together, sucking both my nipples, rolling them between his tongue and lips. "Ummmm, sssssss, suck em' harder," I whispered through the pleasure I was experiencing. I leaned back as he kept a strong grip, keeping them both in his mouth.

Using one of his hands, he pushed my arched back closer to his mouth. "Damn, Chinoe!"

He began shaking his head, making my breast dance to his rhythm. He licked from my chin down to the top of my hairline. I wanted him bad, but I wasn't in control; he had my body under a spell.

Sitting me back on the seat, he raised my body just above the water. He slowly sucked my toes, licking the top part of my foot, then sinking his teeth into my arch. "Umm, Chinoe, you making me wanna fuck!"

Coming close to my face and kissing my lips, he whispered, "If that's what you want, then that's what you can have."

He moved back to my legs, licking me from my ankles to my calves then to the back of my knees. My pussy got wetter than the water we occupied.

"Stand up, Brandie."

I did as my king said.

"Turn around."

Before I could turn all the way around, he started sucking my left hip, then around to the dip above my ass, grabbing aggressively on one of my ass cheeks. He bent me over, placing his warm, wet mouth on my lower lips. I reached around and pushed his mouth deeper. I lost all my self-control in the pleasure he was giving. I stopped him before I was about to cum. I didn't want to become weak and lazy. I gently moved away and pulled him into the seat I just occupied.

Chapter Thirty

Chocolate

That girl was bad. She had me trippin'. Her body was amazing, and the pussy tasted perfect. Her feet weren't rusty either. I knew she had to be a dime piece!

As I sat in the chair as my queen requested, she kissed my lips and whispered, "Yes, I do like you." Then her wet kisses meet my forehead. She licked my eyebrows down to my nose and on to my cheeks and ears.

She aroused every erotic part of my senses by sucking the hair on my chin, slightly pulling it with her teeth and lips.

She seductively licked all over my stomach, deep tonguing my navel. I knew exactly where she was headed, so I stretched out, making my body go straight as possible.

I got more aroused smelling my lips—the sweet

smell from her pussy. It smelled like something I could eat on a regular basis.

She took my dick in her hand and began licking the tip in a circular motion, sucking strongly on the head, making a popping noise.

"Umm, girl, you tryin' to make me nut already?"

"No, wouldn't want you to do that. I thought I could sit on you for that."

She licked my nuts up the strong thick vein on the back of my dick, down again and back up to the tip of the head, engulfing my whole dick. I felt like she was about to swallow me whole, her throat was so deep. She took me back to my dreams of my mystery woman. I didn't know if it was because I was trying to put her face to this body or what.

She was about to make me cum, but she pulled her lips away just in time and put her pussy in my face. I grabbed her hip and kissed it. As she sat down on my lap, I took in a deep breath and prayed to God that this was the one, hoping that I wouldn't cum too fast.

I sat up straight as I could. As I tried to slide my dick into her, the tightness of her pussy rejected me. She moved her hips in a circular, back and forth, until she worked me into her pussy. Almost nuttin' off initial contact, I groaned, "Goddammit, muthafucka!" Then I tried to focus on the game of golf, to repress my soldiers. But I kept thinking about deep holes and balls!

She moved her soft tightness in a slow, circular motion, her muscles closing and opening rhythmically. "If you keep doing that I am goin' to cum." I said seriously.

"Sorry, but you got me so excited." We both requested kisses at the same time.

"Damn! Yo' pussy is . . . so good!" Suddenly, I gained strength and control from somewhere. "Work this dick to yo' satisfaction."

"Chinoe, you so big!" she whispered.

I had that pussy at my command. It felt better than I expected, like wet, thick, heated cotton squeezing my dick. I could stay in this position forever with her ass covering my lap, my hands on her hips, and her lips stuck to mine. She started bouncing her ass up and down as I held on strong and proud, making the feeling more intense.

"Ssssst, Brandie, you about to make me cum!"

We were fucking so hard we fell back into the water. She kept her ass playing pitty-pat with the water. *Slap, Smack, Spat.* I grabbed her ass and lift her up, "Damn, Brandie!"

She quickly jumped up, grabbed my dick in her soft hand, and sucked me until my soldiers released.

When I finished, I realized that I was squeezing the shit out of her head. "Sorry. Sorry. I'm sorry, Brandie."

"That's okay; I understand that it was your first time."

I pulled her close to me. "How you know?"

"By the question you asked me earlier."

I held her close to me. I couldn't stop kissing on her. It was like she was made for me. "You . . . umm . . . felt kind of tight yourself. You sure you wasn't a virgin?"

"Positive," she said, grabbing my face. "Not that it would have been a bad thing. It's just my stuff stays tight like that."

"Ummm hmmm. Can I turn on the light now?"

I had secretly fallen in love. And it happened before the sex—after our life introductions.

"Nope, I like it like this."

I grabbed two towels and wrapped one around Brandie and the other around my waist. When we made it to the bed I dried her off and layed her down. I went to the bathroom and turned on the light.

My initial thought was to see what she looked like, but I didn't want to ruin the feeling if she turned out to be unattractive. Instead I focused on the tub where I'd just made love for the first time. I wanted to bottle up the water and frame it.

I grabbed some lotion, ran hot water over the bottle, and returned to Brandie. Starting with her feet, I put lotion on them and massaged until I heard her moan. Then I poured it on her entire body and some on that smooth, round face. I massaged her entire body, releasing any tension she had.

We made a second go-'round and then layed exhausted. It had to be around three or four in the morning.

Chapter Thirty-One

Brandie

Nervous, excited, and scared, all at the same time, I entered my home at 4:50 a.m. I knew I was going to be sluggish in class. I had about three and a half hours to get a catnap. I lied to Chinoe about my class because at the time I was ready to go, but my stay was well worth it.

I walked into the bathroom and looked at myself in the mirror. "Brandie, did you just sleep with a stranger?" I asked my reflection.

I turned my stereo on, pressed number five and let Anita Baker sing 'Angel' to me as I thought about what I had just done. As I held the phone in my hand, about to check my messages, the phone rang, "Who in the hell?" I glanced at the caller ID, no data. "Hello."

"Where the fuck you been? I been callin' you all

day, leavin' messages on your cell phone. Why haven't you called me?"

Damn, excuse me for being grown! "Calm your nerves. I had a show to do."

"Brandie, not all damn day and night. Why was your damn cell phone off?

"Look, I'm tired and I have class in the morning."

"Bullshit, Brandie!" He kept saying my name and he knew that bugged the shit out of me. It made me feel like I was in trouble or being a nuisance.

"Sean, I'm going to bed. I'll talk to you tomorrow . . . later on today . . . whenever," I said, looking at the clock.

"That's yo' ass, B—!" *Click.* I didn't know if he called me Brandie or Bitch. Either way, he was irate and I was tired.

I hated arguing with Sean. In the beginning, I thought we could have lasted forever. But truth be told, his life had no room for a committed relationship, on his part. I was supposed to be faithful and wait for him to finish fucking as many women as he could. I couldn't get with that. I wasn't hatin' on the player, just hating the game.

I layed back on my bed, staring up at the stars, it felt so peaceful. The moon seems to always find my bed.

Dear God, Please help me to be all that I'm capable of being. Thank you for helping me walk through this world with my head held high. Continue blessing me with guidance, protection, and knowledge. Amen.

Chapter Thirty-Two

Money

What day is it? And who is this laying in my bed? Who is that at the foot of my bed?

Man, my head was throbbing. I needed some aspirin. I slipped on my boxers and headed downstairs.

I could see that my house was a wreck. "Damn, niggas don't know how to act! Always tearin' folks' shit up. Never again at my shit!" I knew I needed to change my lifestyle. I wanted to settle down and have a house full of kids.

Ring . . . Ring . . . Ring.

"Ahhh, shut the hell up!" The phone sounded like it was inside my brain.

Ring . . . Ring . . . Ring.

"Hello, goddamit!"

"Sorry. Do you want me to call back later?"

"Naw, what's up?" I calmed down when I recognized Luvly's voice.

"Someone wants to talk to you."

"Hold on. What time is it?"

"Eight a.m."

"Damn!"

"Hel-lo, Uncle Money." Her voice sounded so sweet and innocent.

"Hey, baby doll, what are you doing?"

"Going to school."

"It is that time, isn't it, baby doll?"

"Yes, yes, yes."

"Daddy will be there to pick you up after school, okay." *Oh shit! What did I just say?*

"Dad-die?"

"What! Sap, give me the phone."

"Money, are you crazy? What did you just say to her?"

"I told her Daddy will be there to get her from school. I'm sorry. I wasn't thinking. I got a hangover."

"That's fucked up. Don't confuse her like that."

She was about to make me snap on her ass in one point two seconds. "Luvly, my head is throbbing. I said I'm sorry."

"Let me tell her the difference between you and Diamond."

"Fuck Diamond and what he feels or think! What about me, Luvly, what am I suppose to do? You are the one confusing her. You are the fuckin' mother! Get this shit straight, Luvly, or I'ma take yo' ass to court!"

I hung up the phone on her ass. "Talkin' that shit to me. Is she muthafuckin' crazy?" She had me talking out loud to myself. *Damn, my head hurt.* Before I knew what was happening a glass was busting against my brick fireplace.

I heard footsteps running fast down the steps.

"What the hell is going on?" Chocolate asked, scaring the shit out of me.

"Man, Luvly callin' here early this morning with some bullshit."

"So you gon' break yo' shit?" He made his way down the stairs and sat at the bar.

"I made a mistake and told Sap that Daddy was going to pick her up, and Luvly started snapping."

"Why you do that? You claiming her now?"

"Man, I wasn't thinking. I told her I was sorry and she gon' say some shit about that nigga, Diamond."

"Y'all need to get that shit straight anyway," Chocolate said, picking up some of the mess on the floor.

As we cleaned up I passed Chocolate. I walked by him again, then right up in his face. "Who pussy you been eatin'?" I asked, smiling.

"Nigga, what?" He pushed me out of his face.

But I ran back up on him, looking at him dead in his eyes. "Nigga, you got some pussy last night!"

"What? Man, cut that shit short."

"Chocolate done cut some broad," I yelled, jumping around slapping him on the top of his head. "That nigga done got some ass. Who was it, Dawg?" I knew he didn't want to tell me with his ol' secretive ass, but I had to know what she looked like.

"Brandie," he said smiling like he was still in the pussy.

"Brandie? Brandie? Did she graduate with us?"

"Naw, she went to Mom's school."

"Smart girl, okay. Is she packin'?"

"Hell, yeah, she packin'. Full and fat. She fine as hell." Please don't let him ask me how she look.

"So what about above her neck?"

"Look, I don't know. She came in my room last night tryin' to get away from y'all wild-ass niggas. And you know it's dark in my room. So we just talked and got in the Jacuzzi, and everything went from there."

"Whaaaaa?"

"We talked from about eleven forty-five to two-thirty this morning, then it just happened. After we got out, it happened again. The shit was good, wet, warm, and tight as hell. Her ass was plump, her pussy tasted brand-new, and that's that."

"So her shit was that platinum?"

"Yes, sir. I fucked her mentally before I fucked her physically."

"Umm hmm. You didn't get her number? She didn't get yours? Man, you wildin' out." My nigga had got his first piece. Never thought I'd see the day. Smiling, shaking my head back and forth, I added, "I got to find out who the hell them hoes is in my damn bed."

We both walked up to my room. "Man, that red bone tight."

"Shit, the other one is tighter," Chocolate said, looking at the other strange honey-colored ass, with his head cocked to the side.

"We got different opinions on women anyway," I said, remembering how good they both performed last night.

"That's the girl that was sittin' on your face last night when me and Tae came in."

"On my face? I don't eat no strange pussy."

"That weed had you blasted."

"Where Tae at, anyway?"

"He better be at home with Joi. She was trippin' last night when they came and got Trinket."

"What was she trippin' about?"

"She was asking me about paternity test and other women. I didn't want to be in the middle of that shit."

"Tae need to get his shit together. Dat nigga thinks the sun rises and sets with his ass." I glanced at the two exposed asses in my bed. "Shidd, let me get these ho's outta my bed."

Chapter Thirty-Three

Luvly

I couldn't believe Money. Why would he do that to her? He knew she repeated everything.

"Sap, stop throwing cereal around this car!"

She was my baby girl and I didn't want any static in her life.

I knew she needed a father. But I was too scared to do the right thing. It could have costed my life.

Ring . . . Ring . . . Ring.

"Hello."

"Hey, I apologize about earlier . . . can I ahhhh . . . come by the shop before or after I get Sap?"

I loved him so much and wanted us to be a normal, happy family. "Yes, Money. I would love that."

"I know we aren't together yet . . . but . . . Luvly, I'm working on it. Please do your part. That's all I ask of you." *Click.*

I looked through the rearview mirror at our

beautiful daughter. In my heart I knew she was Money's.

Ring . . . Ring . . . Ring.

"Yes, Babe."

"Oh, so I'm your babe now?"

"No, I thought you were someone else." I said, annoyed by the familiar voice.

"Better not be nobody else."

"Whatever. What do you want at eight-thirty in the morning?"

"You."

"I'm not available."

"Yes, you are. Why you actin' like that, Luvly? You know I love you, girl. Where's my other girl?"

"She's in the backseat about to get a beat down." I popped the shit out of her, throwing that damn cookie crisp cereal everywhere.

"Ahhhh!" she cried out. "I want my Uncle Money."

"What the fuck did she say?"

"Mommie."

"Naw, sound like she cryin' for that bitch-ass nigga."

"Diamond, please. Stop your drama. Go fuck wit' Pila or that new young bitch that I heard is pregnant."

"Man, fuck Pila! Fuck all dem hoes! I want you and Sapphire. Y'all are where my heart's at."

I did not want to hear the same sob story that I'd heard so many times before.

"Fuck her? But you livin' with her, Diamond. You havin' ménage à trois with her and Jordan. Why must we keep reliving this nightmare? Ain't you tired of whuppin' my ass and tellin' the horror stories to your other baby mamas to keep them in line?"

"You gon' make me beat cho ass!" he said, getting loud.

"I can't believe you. You started that shit when I was young, tryin' to train me, beat me into submission! And you still bullying me."

"It didn't work; you still think you grown as hell. Hot in the ass."

"Diamond, the world wasn't built with your master mind. I wasn't made for you. You are triflin', abusive, and miserable. Just stay away from me."

"You use to love me. What happened to all of that?"

"I loved you when you weren't puttin' a foot in my ass or mouth. I liked the lifestyle, all the power you possessed, but I'm over that now. I'm finished paying the price for being with you, Diamond."

"Man, you livin' in another nigga's house."

"Excuse me. My name is on that house."

"That nigga paid for it. You drivin' a Range Rover that I ain't buy for you. So you tell me?"

"Diamond, my nail shop is number one in Atlanta and I'm working on it being number one worldwide."

"I know Money bought that shit. But all I'm gon' say is I'm gone fuck yo' world up if you don't come home. I'm gone see about you." He said calmly.

"I'm at the grocery store. I got to run in here and get Sap some snacks for school."

"Luvly, please . . . I'm going insane," he said, sounding like a sincere gentleman.

"Pila and Jordan and the rest of your baby mamas are there to pick up the pieces."

"Luvly, you are mine!" He screamed. "I raised you from shit to sug—"

I just hung up and turned the phone off. I wished I could turn him off. Lord knows I didn't want to be involved with him, all the shit I had to put up with.

And on top of all of that, his baby mama, Jordan, had the nerve to name her kids Diamond and Sapphire; that was the kind of shit I was dealing with everyday.

I just wanted Money, my daughter, and my surrogate family. My mother and father would always be there for me. I just hoped that I would make it to see all of this happen.

"Come on, Sap, let's get your snacks."

"Yeah, yeah."

"What do you want Mommy to get for you?" I asked, kissing her on the hand.

"Pizza, Mommie."

"No, you need some healthy snacks, not pizza."

"You need to get a whole new life," a voiced screamed from behind me.

"What?" I turned around and was greeted by part of the problem I was running from.

She ranted, with a mean look on her face, "Bitch, you know what I'm talkin' 'bout! I'm tired of your lame ass stopping my happiness!"

"Look, Pila, I'm shopping with my daughter. I don't want her around ignorance."

I tried to push my cart around her, but she blocked me off, walking up on me. Pila was Diamond's youngest baby's mother. He had four others, but Pila was the worst. She had two boys by him and thought that made her the shit. Everyone said that we could pass for sisters.

"Ho, please! Don't give me that good-mother shit. Diamond told me how he beat your ass in front of her. She lives around ignorance everyday if she always with yo' triflin' ass."

"Tri-fling ass," Sap repeated.

"No, Sap, don't say that."

"If she wasn't with you, I'd whup yo' ass up and down Kroger."

I was getting pissed now, but I laughed at her to piss her off even more. "See me in the streets, Pila . . . like a real woman, not like the little girl that lets her baby's daddy other baby mama tell her when and how high to jump. Don't you have to go lick her cat or something?" I'd heard that Pila and Jordan were sleeping together with and without Diamond.

"Why don't you just tell Diamond that that little bitch isn't his and we can all get on with our lives?"

"Why does it worry you so much? You scared that in the end I'll be the one he chooses?"

She smirked and I knew that I'd hit a nerve. "Look, Luvly, I know you been hanging in there the longest with Diamond, but he don't love you. How could he? He has had seven kids on you. And you know he's still seeing Brittanie. I heard she pregnant again. So why hang on to him? Get a blood test and prove that Money Loane is her daddy and go be happy."

I'd heard all the rumors and knew that they were true, but I was not gon' let no little young girl think she was gone run me out of my post.

"Well, I heard you were pregnant again, too. Why you keep playin' baby-maker?"

"I've come from nothing. Diamond bought me a house, car, and has me a full bank account at all times."

"And that's worth your dignity?" I covered Sap's

ears. "You and all those other women are using your children and pussy as commodity. I give my child love and love her because she comes from me, not to make him love me. And Diamond don't touch this good pussy, but he still takin' care of this ass."

"Diamond will believe anything about that little bastard if it means he can have you," Pila said, gritting her teeth. "But I'm asking you as a woman. Go be with Money and leave Diamond alone."

I couldn't believe this bitch was degrading herself and calling my baby a bastard. "Your kids are the real bastards. I asked Diamond about his sons' birthdays. He flat out told me that he really didn't know when it was. The day I asked, it was your sons' birthday party. How could he not know? They were born on the same day, a year apart. He layed up with me and Sap all day. He doesn't even claim your boys."

Then at the top of her lungs, she yelled, "Fuck you, ol', mixed-up bitch, you and your mut. Diamond ain't gone never leave me. He gon' kill yo' ass one day, and I'm gon' be there to throw salt on your wounds and spit on your grave. Salone should have killed that little bitch in the womb."

"Come on, Sap. Get out of the buggy. Mommy is going to count, so you can run."

"Coun, Mommie! Coun!"

"One, two, three, run." There was no time to correct her; I had an ass to whup. As soon as her little back was turned, I ram the buggy into Pila. It pushed her into the shelf, and a small jar of pickles fell on her head.

"Bitchhhh! Aaaahhhh," she screamed, falling to the floor.

I placed my foot on her chest, tried to press my heel through her heart. "Bitch, don't ever fuck with me when my daughter is around. I don't want Diamond's sorry ass. I wish all y'all would leave me the fuck alone. Ain't none of y'all gon' be shit but a dope man's bitch. Look at chu. He got you eatin' Jordan's pussy and suckin' his best friend dick." Pushing my heel deeper into her chest, "You talk that shit about spittin' on my grave, but you're already dead on the inside. I'm just beginnin' to breathe again." I could hear Sap's little shoes tapping around the aisle. "So I guess it's appropriate to spit on your grave." I spit in her face.

I met Sap coming around the corner. I kneeled down, and she ran into my arms. "I make it, Mommie! I do it!"

"We both did it today, baby."

Chapter Thirty-Four

Brandie

Antsy in my seat, my attention was on what I did last night. "Miss Wine?" Professor Arendril called.

Wondering if Chinoe's mother would still remember . . .

Professor Arendril stood in front of my seat. "Miss Wine, are you with us?"

Squirming in my seat, I said, "Yes, Professor Arendril. I was just thinking about the philosophy behind that situation." *Yeah, my situation.*

I was not regretful; I just felt guilty. I didn't even know Chinoe and I let him slip his love all up inside and out of me. *Oooohhh Weee!* Last night was off the chain. I enjoyed talking to him too. I couldn't believe we had so much in common. I just hoped and prayed that I didn't get a disease. But, he was a virgin. What if I gave him something that I didn't know I had? I'm not nasty or trifling, but some diseases don't surface, like herpes and other heebie-jeebies that hide.

"Brandie. Brandie, class is over," Mesia yelled as she tapped a hole in my shoulder.

"Oh, oh girl, I'm in another world."

"Are you going to IHOP with me and my girl Caymin?"

"Yeah, where she at?"

"She should be out of class in ten minutes."

"I'll be outside in my truck. I need to make a phone call."

"I'm ridin' with you."

"Yeah, okay."

Hoes always wanted to flex and ride in my shit. My Yukon was not a taxi. I think they were more impressed with who bought it.

I wondered how I could get in touch with Chinoe? I didn't want to go back over to Money's house; *he might think I'm a stalker or a groupie. I know some girls who mess around with Money, so I'll put an APB out on Chinoe.*

I really didn't want to be bothered with Mesia, but a girl always needed to keep a down partner on hand, willing to do whatever, whenever. Just like a girl needed to keep more than one pair of strong arms to hang on.

Ring . . . Ring . . . Ring.

"Yeah." Hunt sounded so confident and business, just downright fuckable.

"Yeah, is that how you speak to your princess?"

"Sorry, Ma. Where you at?"

"Just gettin' out of class."

"That's my girl—fine as hell and loaded with brains."

In a girlish voice, I asked, "When am I going to see you, Hunt?"

"Now. Can I pick you up for lunch?"

"Am I lunch?"

"You know it."

I was just juicin' his head up. He definitely wasn't gon' get this today. I just needed to keep him fiending. "Well, I have Mesia riding with me, and this other girl is suppose to meet us there."

"That's cool. I'll bring Robert with me."

"Okay, I'll see you."

"Hey, where you goin'?"

"IHOP, off Highway 85."

"On my way, Ma." Hunt was handsome, and he had old money that ran long. But he also had other women, and I wasn't with being number two or getting lost in the shuffle. I didn't want a man that belonged to other women and the streets.

He was no Chinoe—sweet, sexy, honest and possible baby daddy. "What am I talking about I don't even know his damn phone number."

"Know whose number?"

"Oooh, shit! Mesia, you scared the shit out of me." Mesia was leaned over in the window of my truck.

"Caymin, you remember Brandie? Brandie, you remember Caymin?"

"Hi."

"Hi."

Eyeing Caymin out the corner of my eye, I said, "Oh, this guy, I met last night." I said with a slight 'tude.

See, Mesia was about to make me snap. I didn't say this girl could ride with me; I didn't like too many people in my shit or my business. My truck only pimped one pussy.

"Damn, I should have left with y'all. I know they were paid."

I gave Mesia the evil eye. I didn't know Caymin that well for her to be putting her all up in my business. I turned up Erykah Badu.

"So tell me how last night was." She turned the music down. "Who was there?"

She must not have understood me giving her the damn evil eye. Flossing was her style, not mine. "It was cool, but everybody got wild. So I went upstairs to one of the rooms and chilled until everybody was ready to go."

"You didn't dance for Money Loane?"

"No, he was occupied with Red and Peaches."

"Money Loane?" Caymin asked excitedly. "I went to school with him."

See, there she go all in my conversation where she wasn't invited.

"Oh, really? Ya'll still see each other?" Maybe I could use her ass to get to Chinoe.

"Naw, we didn't have a relationship. He used to date my girl Luvly; I think they still messin' around."

"Umm um, I wanna get some of Money . . . and some of that money." Mesia licked her lips.

"Mesia, you so crazy. He is freehearted with his money. Even when we all use to go out, he would pay for everything."

"Maybe he is willing to pay for any and everything," Mesia said seductively. She was the gold digger from hell that would screw my daddy if he flashed the right amount of money. She could dance her ass off, but she was still a ho. And I hated hoes, and hoes hated me. But like I said, she was a true road dawg, willing to do dirt.

A truck driver tooted his horn at us. "Girl, blow back! He cute." Mesia jumped up and down in her seat, waving wildly out of the window.

"Mesia, you gon' get killed one day messin' wit' these niggas."

"Niggas love it when you a naughty girl." Mesia clucked her tongue, jumped onto her knees and reached around her back.

"Girl, unhn, I know you ain't finna do—"

Mesia pulled up her shirt and shook her titties at the truck driver.

"Girl, you need to let me suck them big thangs at the same time. Or put my dick between 'em," the truck driver yelled, tooting his loud horn again.

I sped away. We laughed and high-fived each other.

Pullin' into IHOP, I scanned the parking lot to see if Hunt's Tahoe was present. It was so damn noticeable, twenty-two inch chrome rims.

Once inside, heads instantly turned. I knew Mesia's loud ass would let them know we didn't appreciate the stares. "Damn, can a sister eat without everyone knowing what color drawers she has on!" They all did their ums and ahs and cut their eyes. "I don't know why women be starin' anyway unless they gay or payin'."

I guess three attractive women would cause a little ruckus. I had to admit, Caymin was a pretty girl. She didn't have anything on me, but she was cute.

Her long hair was the same color as mine; it was just cut a little different. It complemented her face. And the girl could dress her butt off. I'd seen her a few times around campus and wondered where she got her shoes and purses.

As soon as we got our table, Hunt walked in.

"Ooh, look at that. He is fine." Caymin let loose. She looked outside to see what new cars had pulled up. "I wonder if that is his Tahoe? Damn!!"

I let him stand at the door and look for me, to show them hoes what my name truly was.

Mesia was already pushing her breast in the air to catch anybody's slob. And the look on Caymin's face said she'd struck gold. Right then I knew she had to go if she liked the same type of men I did.

Hunt spotted me and walked over to the table. "Hey, Ma." He reached for my hand to kiss it.

"Hellooooooo." I smiled from ear to ear. Sitting on the end of the booth made it easy for him to place warm sweet kisses on my neck.

I guess that wasn't enough for him so he pulled me out of my seat and into his arms.

"You smell so damn delicious." His smooth skin brushed my cheek.

Hunt continued to be the gentleman that he was. "What's up ladies?"

Caymin's Cheshire cat grin dropped to a mere smirk.

"Mesia, this is Robert. Robert, this is Mesia." They both smiled at each other. But his eyes were full of Caymin. "Oh, I'm sorry. Caymin, this is my very special friend, Hunt, and this is his friend, Robert."

Robert pulled up a chair and placed it across

the table from Mesia and Caymin, trying not to be bias.

Caymin had something about her I just didn't like. She looked at me through jealous eyes when Hunt kissed me on my neck.

All I knew was that she had better get at Robert before Mesia gobbled him up.

Robert was an all right looking dude, tall and kind of on the stout side, with an acne problem. But what he lacked, his beautiful mane of hair made up for. He was a successful producer from Ohio.

"Caymin? I like that name. Is it Hawaiian?" Robert asked with lust in his eyes.

"No, American ghetto," she answered cutely.

Everyone laughed but me. I just couldn't get comfortable with her. I wasn't jealous, but like I said, I didn't like new problems—female friends.

"Brandie, y'all cousins? Y'all look alike," Robert asked, still noticeably admiring Caymin. We both smiled uneasily at each other, shaking our heads no.

"So, baby, are we on for tonight or what?" Hunt playfully squeezed my waist.

"I work tonight. You know that."

"What club is it that you work at Brandie?" Robert asked as he looked around the room for the missing waitress.

"We work at Platinum Kat," Mesia answered, feeling left out.

"Aye, Dawg, let's check that out tonight," Robert suggested, his eyes still glued to Caymin.

"You know I'm game to see my Boo any time." Hunt winked.

"Caymin, you work there, too?" Robert asked hopefully.

"Nooo!" she said, like dancing was beyond her or something. "I work at Wachovia."

"Why you say it like something wrong with dancin'?" I asked, irritated.

"I didn't say anything was wrong with it, but I do think it's a little bit degrading."

"What's degrading about dancin'? I make my money and go home. I don't trick . . . so—" I tried to explain, defensively.

"Brandie, don't take offense to what my opinion is; I didn't mean to offend y'all." Caymin defended herself, sounding like a child.

"Naw, I'm not offended. I got my own house. My own nice ride and can buy whatever the hell I want, which I couldn't get by working at a damn bank!" Everyone got quiet.

Caymin took my answer like a shot to the gut. She lived at home with her mom and two sisters and their kids, and she didn't have a car. The only thing she had was some sharp clothes, shoes, and purses. Mesia told me how her family struggled, so I knew she wished she could dance for the cheese I made.

"Y'all trippin'. All you young ladies are doing well, so what's the problem?"

"There isn't one. So what time will I see you tonight?" I asked, rolling my eyes at Caymin.

"About twelve a.m. I got some errands to run."

After we ate, the ride back to school was full of Eric Benet. I wanted that bitch out of my shit! Degrading? That ho musta had a complex problem.

Shiddd, don't hate me, cuz; you ain't me. I needed to get a drink, for real. She had my nerves jumping.

"I'll call you tonight, Brandie," Mesia yelled.

"Yeah, and don't forget to pick my suit up when you get yours."

"All right, girl."

Caymin got out of my truck with an attitude and without saying a word.

Wait, I'm not that childish. I drove around to where she was walking to her car. "Look, no hard feelings. I was just bugging."

She looked relieved. "Yeah, I'm sorry about what I said. I didn't know how to apologize; my foot was already in my mouth."

"Looks like Robert took a liking to you. So if you take the bait I guess we'll be seeing a lot of each other."

I could see Mesia looking at us through my rearview mirror. I knew she got a kick out of what happened at IHOP. That was the type of female she was, but she was probably flaming now that we were conversating and laughing without her.

Caymin and I exchanged numbers. Maybe a new friendship was what I needed. She wasn't a dancer, loose in the streets, and we favored each other in more ways than one.

Lord, please give me strength and guidance in my time of need. Surround my life with people who are strong and good. People that need appeasement from your hands.

Amen

Chapter Thirty-Five

Chocolate

"Luvly shop is off the chain."

"Shit, it's Friday. These freaks got to look hot tonight."

As we walked through the doors, everything shut down; machines cut off; conversations stopped mid-sentence. All eyes were on us.

Sap layed sound asleep over my shoulder.

One of Luvly's assistants took Sap. "I'll lay her down on the cot in the back."

"Thank you."

"Hey, Money. Heyyyy, Chocolate!"

" 'Sup, Precious," we said in unison.

Precious was capital G-H-E-T-T-O and not all that cute. Her speaking to me was like someone running their nails down a blackboard.

Luvly came from the back. "Hey, y'all. What's happenin'? Have a seat."

Both Money and I looked like, "Where?" We just continued to stand in the middle of the floor with eyes glued to us.

"Thank you for picking up Sap." She walked close up on Money.

"No thanks needed." He almost kissed her because of their closeness, barely catching himself.

"Can I get your autograph, Mr. Loane? For my son," the young mother asked, looking hopefully into Money's eyes for an introduction for herself as well.

"Sure. Whom do I make it out to?"

"And can I get your autograph for my daughter and sister, Chinoe?"

I signed my autograph and let Money play movie star. I needed to talk to Luvly about my little escapade.

I pulled up a chair next to her so I could see why women pay so much money to get their nails done. "I want to ask you a question."

"Shoot."

"If you slept with someone and you didn't know them, but before y'all did it y'all told each other everything about each other, would you feel guilty?"

Bucking her eyes looking at me, she made a mistake and filed the woman's finger.

"Ouch!"

"Sorry, Mrs. Hines." In a low hurt tone, she asked, "Chinoe, you slept with somebody?"

I looked at the expression on the older woman's face. "Babe, everybody got a little freak in 'em. One time is all right." She was so tickled.

"Chinoe, you finally did it? With who?"

I scratched my head not realizing what she would feel. "Ahm . . . I don't know."

"Don't know what? If you did it, or who you did it with?"

"She came upstairs last night at Money's."

"Money's?"

I ignored her nosy question. "The lights were off and it was comfortable. So we left them off. We started talking about everything from A to Z. I went and got her something to drink. When I got back she was in the Jacuzzi.

"I told you y'all was up to no good. I knew hoes were there, excuse me Mrs. Hines."

The older woman was still listening, taking it all in.

"We got in the Jacuzzi."

"Naked?"

"Yeah." What we did was so long ago—Luvly and me—that I never thought this would affect her.

"Get it, Chinoe," the older lady put her two cents in again. I smiled at her because she sounded so funny saying it.

"Then we started moving around, and her hand slipped onto my . . . well, you know the rest."

"She did that on purpose, baby. I bet she pulled back real slow, too didn't she? She was just trying to size you up." I shook my head at the freaky old lady that was getting off on my life.

"Well, after that we started bangin'—"

"Where is the condom?"

This was the part I didn't want to tell her. "No condom."

She dropped the woman's hand. "What?" She was so loud that everyone's attention was diverted from Money. "Sorry, y'all go back to jockin' my man," she said, smiling.

"Chinoe, what were you thinking? Boy all these diseases and crabs, I thought you had better sense then that."

"She made me feel just that special." Her warnings couldn't wash away my happiness.

"So how was it?"

I held my head down with my hands on the top of it. "It was tight as hell, literally and figuratively."

"So she was a virgin, too?"

"No, she just had that fit. She was the platinum I've been waiting for."

"Chinoe, if it felt right to you, then I guess it was right," Luvly said, calming my nerves about the situation.

"Babe, everyone has to live for the moment, for we don't know how long we have. You just gotta be safe nowadays. God didn't leave us with instructions, just brains."

"Thank you, Mrs. Hines."

After Money finished playing superstar he sat down next to us.

"So what are y'all doin' tonight?"

"Goin' to Platinum Kat," Money answered in a low voice.

"I wanna go!"

"Why, Luvly? So you can get mad and get into your third fight at that club?" Money asked.

"No, I just want to be with you. We don't go out very much," Luvly said with a pout, to see how far she could get with Money.

The whole time they were talking, I noticed an attractive girl with a Halle Berry haircut sitting in the corner of the shop, like she was trying to go unnoticed. She was talking on her cell phone, covering her mouth.

"So can I go with y'all? I use to hang like one of the boys," Luvly begged like a little girl.

"Until you became a mother," I added.

"That ain't got anything to do with it. And anyway, Chinoe, from what you said you did last night you might be somebody daddy."

"Man, you trippin'." I went outside to get a breath of fresh air from the chemicals in the shop. As I leaned against the car my two-way went off with a 911 message from Joi. It said that we needed to get to the house ASAP.

A couple of minutes later they came outside hugging and kissing.

"Man, bring yo' ass!"

Two minutes later, a familiar Suburban pulled up in front of the shop. We all knew who it was. And that nigga Diamond was known for shooting, so I went into to the car and grabbed my pistol.

"Why now?" Luvly asked, with fear all over her face.

"It's all right, Babe. Just hold tight," Money said, hugging her before he pushed her behind him.

The driver side of the truck opened and one of Diamond's baby mamas, Jordan, got out. "Heyyyy, bitch. Hi, Money." She blew a kiss to him. All the while keeping the door open for a quick getaway. "Yo' sexy ass still fucking wit' that stanking pussy ho?"

Luvly had whup-ass all over her face. "I got yo' ho', jealous-ass bitch." Luvly took off for her but Money was holding on to her arm.

"When you ready to fuck a real woman, come see me."

Out of nowhere, the same cutie pie with the Halle Berry haircut came charging at Luvly. She swung a left blow to Luvly's back because Luvly had gotten loose from Money and was on her way to beat down Jordan.

I grabbed the girl by the waist to restrain her, but Luvly started beating her in the face. Jordan snuck up on all of us and grabbed a handful of Luvly's hair, pulling it out by the root.

I threw the girl into Jordan and they fell to the ground. I pointed the gun at them both, "Get ya'll stupid asses up outta here."

"Let me go, Money, unh unhhhh, let me go." Luvly tussled with Money.

"Yeah let that bitch go," Jordan screamed, waving a hand full of Luvly's hair around in the air.

"Ho', take yo' slum-ass back to that fuckin' nigga."

"It's me and you, bitch, me and you," Luvly warned Jordan, as Money dragged her back into the shop.

They jumped in the truck and screeched out of the parking lot.

"Them hoe's crazy," I said shaking my head. My two-way went off again with Joi 911-ing me.

Money came out of the shop shaking his head, "We moving the fuck away from here."

"She all right?"

"She cool. She going to my house."

"We need to take a ride to Tae's. They been 911-ing me."

"Let's ride."

Chapter Thirty-Six

Chocolate

As we pulled into Taeko's yard, Joi was outside with her mother and sister. Her voice met us before our feet hit the concrete. "I knew y'all would be coming around here trying to take up for 'im. I'm through wit' dis shit, though."

Both of her eyes were black, lip busted, and cheeks, neck, arms, and chest scratched up, Joi looked bad.

"Where is Taeko, Joi?"

"He probably layed up with some bitch that all y'all was fuckin' last night."

"What the hell happened to your face?" I asked, cringing at the sight of her face.

"Taeko going to jail!"

"Hold on, Joi. Take it easy." Money tried to touch her shoulder, and she went nuts.

Her clothes were torn and hanging off her body, hair standing on top of her head, and face wet like someone threw a bucket of water on it.

"Don't tell me to calm down," she screamed. "That nigga jumped on me because he brought me a disease from some nasty slut in the street. I been that sorry-ass nigga's backbone and bore his goddamn children. Shit, when I got pregnant with Trey, I was headed to the clinic, but no . . . Taeko wanted it. He said he would be a good daddy 'cause his wasn't shit. I dropped out of school because of all his promises.

"When I was nine months pregnant, I worked so that he could have the latest sneakers and outfits to fit in with y'all clique. Money, I wore tore-up, too-small Puma's with swollen feet and didn't complain. And after all that he gives me other women's babies, all different types of perfumes on his body, panties in my goddamn bed and pussy on his breath . . . and now some kind of disease. That's the reward I get for all that I have done and been to him. Fuck money and living this basketball lifestyle. I haven't forgot where I came from."

She looked tired and worn out. I wanted to hug her and tell her everything would be all right, but right then she saw us as the enemy.

"Boys, I know that y'all aren't Taeko, but you his friends. Talk to him. Joi ain't gon' call da police on 'im. She just want thangs right for 'em."

"We understand, Mrs. Park, but what we don't understand is Taeko."

Money got on his phone, trying to find out where Taeko was.

"He has a beautiful family and home. I don't understand why he would risk his reputation and career for this type of misbehaving," Mrs. Park said.

Joi had a lot of rage in her. She was venting from years back. "Don't talk that intelligent shit to my mama. She know 'bout y'all triflin' asses!"

"Joi!"

"Naw, Mama. Hell, he was with them screwin' dem bitches. He always tryin' to fit in with Chocolate and Money, makin' babies and buyin' other women houses!" She fell to the pavement. I reached over to catch her, but she fell fast.

I kneeled down in front of her and looked her dead in the face. "Look at me, Joi." I lifted her heavy head with my fingers. "Joi, Taeko loves you." She shook her head slowly from side to side in disbelief. "He does love you; he's just confused right now. You are right. You did sacrifice a lot for him, your whole damn life. He knows this. But he feels like he has grown up too fast, and this lifestyle has been his anchor. I know that's no excuse, but this is only going to make you stronger, Joi. You have been our backbone since high school, the loudest cheerleader. We love you, girl." She reached up and hugged me.

Joi's sister broke the moment with her loud-ass mouth. "Joi, come on, girl. Get cho ass up. Fuck dese trifling-ass niggas, 'cuz dey 'on't give a shit about you. Never have. You gon' get dis house and a nice check every month. Trey and Trinket know dey sorry-ass daddy. Fuck 'em!"

I closed my eyes and exhaled all the bad energy. "Toiya, please don't get her excited again. Why not try and comfort your sister."

"Why lie to 'er? Taeko ain't 'bout shit; all he got is

a basketball career. He ain't shit, just like Money ain't."

"Now why you goin' there, Toiya? We were years ago."

"You damn right. And I'm glad I got an abortion. I would probably be dealing with dis shit my sister going through. Probably worse."

"Naw. Like you said, a house and a nice, fat-ass check every month," Money taunted Toiya.

"Y'all, stop it! Stop it! This here is nonsense. Now find that boy! Send him home. Send him home." Mrs. Park got Joi off the ground and took her into the house.

Toiya stayed to finish her venting. "Fuck you, Money Loane. I knew your stupid, half-raised ass when you weren't wearing no Armani and Versace. Tell that low-down-ass nigga I'ma make sho my sister press charges and make him pay. Fuck y'all." Then she walked away, waiting for no answers or questions.

"Man, that bitch is sick."

We got in the car to leave, when an unfamiliar black Acura pulled in behind us.

"Ahh, shit! Man, not today," Money groaned with a look of disgust.

"Who is that?" I asked.

Salone stepped out the car. The expression on her face was nasty.

"Miss Lady, can you move your car please." Money tried to ask pleasantly.

"Drive around the driveway," she said in a mean, pissed-off voice.

"Girl, you see those other cars blockin' the damn driveway."

"And? Hit 'em and drive away like you do me."

I could see anger brewing in Money's eyes. "Salone, can you please move your damn car so we can find this boy and solve the problems in this house."

"Were y'all that worried about me when your baby mama stabbed me? Ha! Nope. Y'all left Joi and Taeko to take me to the hospital."

"Salone, I stayed with you that night."

"For pity's sake."

"Move ya goddamn car!" Money screamed, ramming the engine, making the car jump.

She quickly got back in her car and moved it, a middle finger hanging out the window.

Money hit the steering wheel. "I'm tired of all this shit! All these hoes in Atlanta on some shit. Man, when I get everything straight I'm moving my family away from here.

"Did you find out where Tae is?" I asked.

"At my shit."

They lived down the street from each other, so it took just a few minutes to get to Money's house.

When we got in the house, Tae was sitting at the bar between some young broad's legs.

"I know this nigga better tell me he on crack or snorting powder."

He heard us come in but didn't acknowledge us. "Taeko, what the fuck is goin' on?" He said nothing. "Taeko, man, you hear me talkin' to you, Dawg."

He said nothing, still sitting, facing the bar. Money picked up a glass ashtray and threw it next to his head. The girl jumped down off the bar as the glass splattered over Tae.

"No offense to you, young lady, but get yo' shit and get the fuck out of my house. And stay the fuck away from this man." With tears of fear in her eyes, she stood in front of Money. "Understood?"

She nodded and started gathering her things. "How am I supposed to get home?" She wiped her eyes trying not to seem like the vulnerable, young girl that she was.

"Call a cab, and I'll pay for it. Use the phone in the foyer and sit out there."

As soon as she walked out the room, Money ran over to Taeko and busted him dead in the jaw. "Get your punk ass up, sorry-ass nigga!"

"Taeko, man, what the fuck is wrong wit' chu? Say something, nigga. Joi about to call the folks," I pleaded with him before Money beat him to a pulp.

He stood his lifeless body up.

Money hit his ass again. "You wanna hit somebody, nigga? Hit me! Hit me, nigga!" Money started whaling on Taeko like he was a nigga in the street. Taeko took the first few body blows, and then tried to hold onto Money to stop the hits from coming.

"Money, this is not Diamond," I said, pulling him off Taeko. "Cool out, nigga. Chill."

Everybody was out of breath.

Taeko, rocking back and forth, holding the back of his head, "I didn't mean to hurt her." He started crying like a child. "She started talking about leaving me, taking my kids. I lost control. Is she hurt bad?" he asked with regret in his voice.

"Emotionally more than physically. Her face is fucked up. I can't believe you hit her like that. You better get yo' ass together. You goin' home and you gon' do whatever it takes to save your family and career," Money warned.

Taeko cleaned himself up, and Money drove him home.

I sat on the sofa and took in a deep breath. "What the hell is going on? What has happened to us?"

Ring . . . Ring . . . Ring.

My phone was ringing at the wrong time. Private number, too.

"Hello."

"Chinoe, can we talk?" Haven said quickly.

"You gon' fuck?" My attitude was nasty and hard. She deserved no chances.

"Yes."

"Bitch, I told you, you was triflin'." *Click.*

I walked to the bathroom to look at myself in the mirror, wondering if I was becoming everything I didn't want to be: chasing women, screwing meaninglessly, being a rude-ass nigga, and making money—forgetting where I came from.

Ring . . . Ring . . . Ring.

"Damn! Hello."

"Chinoe, hi. Did I catch you at a bad time? This is Chaise."

"What's up, Chaise. Can I get back with you later?"

"Yeah, but we have a shoot on the second of May."

"Where?"

"Atlanta."

Good. At least I don't have to leave home. Too

many problems that need my attention. "All right. Thanks."

"I'll be down a week earlier. Will I be able to see you?"

"Yeah, sure."

"Okay, see you then."

Man, damn, why I tell her that? Oh, well, what's done is done. Shit! I'm living the single life.

Chapter Thirty-Seven

Chocolate

'2000'

Springtime in Atlanta was gorgeous, but hot. The heat always announced that this was definitely the South.

My new house gave me peace and seclusion. I was chilling on my balcony that lead from my bedroom that included a Jacuzzi, two lounging love seats, a wet bar, and a fifty-inch plasma TV.

Everyone was trying to gather their senses and make amends. Luvly and Money have not made their union official, but they' were working on it. Tae and Joi were giving it another chance. Tae was still slipping, of course. They all needed to come sit on my balcony and think about life.

Sap's fifth birthday was in two weeks. And I needed to touch bases with Ma and Luvly to make sure everything was planned.

"So when am I going to meet this sweet, little girl I keep hearing about and seeing all over your walls?" Warm soft hands caressed the back of my head, down to my neck.

"Well, I'll go get her tomorrow or Thursday. Let's rest and get cozy for the next couple of days."

"That sounds good to me," Chaise said, sitting on my lap. She felt so warm and good. Her thighs were making me horny.

We'd been kicking it for about two months.

After Brandie, I got kind of wild, trying to replace her. There'd been five women since her. To most men that's nothing, but in my world that's more than too many. Too many diseases and scandalous women tryin' to catch a "money-nut."

I hadn't seen Brandie in a year. Damn! I missed her. I know I didn't see her face, but I missed her conversation, the perfect way she felt in my arms. I really wanted to get to know her. She put something on me that night. I tried not to think about it because it made me mad. The woman who took my virginity disappeared. My mystery star had fallen from the sky. What was a brother to do?

"What are you thinking about, Chinoe?" Chaise asked, searching my eyes, hoping I would say my thoughts were consumed with nothing but her. *Wrong.*

"Life."

"What about it?"

"Why are we put here on earth? Why do we suffer, cry, be hungry, kill each other for greed and power? What does all this really mean?"

She hugged me tight, rolling my head in her breast. "I told you when I first met you that you are unbelievable, always thinking of others, so giving, and fine as hell. You makin' me want some."

"It's all yours for the taking."

She jumped off me and ran into the bedroom. I chased her like a little kid. Sex was the only thing that kept me calm. But I had faith that Brandie would find me and tame what she had started.

Chapter Thirty-Eight

Brandie

"I'll do the party Thursday, but I'm working in the club Friday."

"Okay, Miss Delite. Understood."

I don't know why they thought I liked working outside of the club. It just wasn't safe. Just last week a girl got kidnapped, raped, beaten, and cut up.

I think the only reason I still danced at that club every night was because I was in search for Chinoe. I'd often seen Money and his buddies in the club. I guess Chinoe's been out of town working. His spread in Ebony was the shit. I kissed the page when I saw him layed out in that cream linen suit.

I've kept him in my heart and memory for a whole year. I wanted him so bad to be in my world. I was tired of street-niggas, hustlers, and dope dealers. I needed some stability in my life.

* * *

It was springtime, and I wanted to be in love like the birds and the bees. I was in that big ol' house all by myself, and all I did was work and go to school.

The only place I went was New York to see Sean. I was his on call booty. But I tried not to get caught up. With his record company and being a big-time rapper, I knew women were at his beck and call, even though he said we were so-called exclusive.

I admit, he did try to get me to go on tour with him and move to New York, but I wanted to have my practice here in the ATL.

I pressed the intercom. "Yes."

"What's up, girl? Let me in."

"All right." Caymin walked in all smiles. "Hey, I just saw my old girlfriend, Luvly. She invited me to her little girl's birthday party."

"And?"

"And her daughter's father is Money Loane, so you know it's going to be off the hook. All types of ballers."

Money Loane! Shit! I'm sure his road dawg will be hanging.

"So you goin'?" I asked, trying to sound unentertained by the idea.

"Yeah, we goin'," she said, reading my mind.

"So you talk to Sean?"

"You know he on tour. He called Sunday, but that was the last time I talked to him."

"You lucky as hell. You got a superstar on your hands."

"It's not as good as you makin' it sound. Shoot! You see I'm in this house all day. I go to sleep alone every night."

"Come on, Brandie. That's by choice. Shit! Sean bought you this big-ass house, and Hunt bought you that Yukon. So what else do you want? Shit! If I could have all that I would sleep alone, too."

"Robert takes care of that ass too. So what's the difference?"

"I have a small townhouse and a Honda Civic. That's a little short of what you have."

"It's coming, baby girl, it's coming." We slapped hands.

Me and Caymin had become very close. We went out all the time, to the malls, clubs, seminars, and plays. We seem to be well-made friends. No jealousy or envy.

Thank you, Lord, for sending me a friend that doesn't cast a shadow over me or me over her. We lift each other up simultaneously. Your blessings are truly in need.

Amen.

Chapter Thirty-Nine

Luvly

"Hello."

"Hello?"

"Hel-lo."

"Hi, is this . . . umm . . . Chas?"

"Chaise. Yes, this is she."

Damn! She was already answerin' Chocolate's phone. *Must be gettin' serious.*

"This is Luvly."

"Hi, Luvly! How are you? Chinoe's on a phone call with the agency. Do you want me to have him call you back?"

What is she? His damn secretary? Have him call me back?

"Can you please tell him that I'm about to take Sapphire to the hospital?"

"Is she all right?"

"I don't know. Tell him I'm going to Emory and

he can either come or call me on my cell phone." *Stupid bitch! If I knew, I wouldn't be taking her to the damn hospital. I already don't feel this Chaise chick.*

"Okay."

"Thanks."

I didn't know what was wrong with my baby. She was burning up and saying her legs and arms hurt.

"Sap, your legs and arms still hurtin'?"

"Yes, Mommie," she cried.

"Okay, baby girl. Mommy and your uncles are going to take you to the doctor."

"No! No! He is going to hurt me!"

"No, sweetheart, the doctor is there to make you better," I tried to convince her, wiping both of our tears, as she lay in my arms, defenseless.

"I want Uncle Chocolate and Uncle Money!"

"Okay, Babe."

Ring . . . Ring . . . Ring.

"Damn! Money, pick up the phone!"

"This Money. Sorry I missed—" *Damn it!* I didn't want that shit. *Where could he be? Oh, damn. Today is the day he helps at the Boys' Club.*

"I think your Uncle Money is helping at the Boys' club today, Sap." She lay limp in my lap.

Ring . . . Ring . . . Ring.

"Hello."

"Are you leaving now, or do I need to come get you? I'm down the street from you."

"Yes, Ma, please. Sap is doing bad, and I can't find Money. I think he's at the Boys' Club!"

"Calm down, baby. I'm on my way." My mother, Lord knows, was a strong woman. She had to be, to be able to deal with me and all my trouble. I envied her smooth, dark-brown skin since I was a child. I saw her big, light-brown eyes every time I looked at Sap.

"Come on, Sap. Let me put some clothes on you." *What can possibly be wrong with you, little girl?* She had never been this sick before, apart from the occasional ear infection, chicken pox, and slight colds.

Ring . . . Ring . . . Ring.

Looking at the caller ID, I saw "Babe."

"Hey, Babe, what's up?"

Relieved to hear Money's voice, I told him, "Sap is sick. She has a one hundred three-degree fever, and she said her legs and arms hurt."

"I'm on my way."

"No, just go to Emory. My mother is on her way over here. It'll take you too long to get here."

"All right. Love you."

"Love you, too."

Once at the hospital, doctors rushed her back because of her high fever and swollen arms. They asked me to stay out front because they had to ask her questions about someone possibly abusing her. The small dark, purplish spots on her swollen arms looked like bruises. They were overreacting if you ask me, but that was procedure.

Forty minutes later, "Miss Mancini, we are going to give her an cool bath to bring her fever down. Do you mind helping us? She won't let us undress her. Said her grandmother told her no one is to see her but her mom, and her grandmas, not even her uncles."

I gave him a slight smile, proud of her little self-righteous self, and that he didn't come out and say she was dying. I put my hands to my mouth, and let out a deep breath.

"Ma, when Money get here . . . tell them that he is her father so that he can come back."

"Okay, honey."

Maybe all of this was the stress of me and Diamond fighting. I had to change my life if I want Sap to have a better one.

"Sap, are you feeling better?"

"A little bit."

"We gave her a mild pain reliever. Her arms and legs are very tender."

"Thank you very much."

I looked into Sap's beautiful eyes, thinking about how vulnerable she was right then. I hadn't been a bad mother; I'd just made poor decisions for both of us.

"Uncle Money!" Sap jumped up.

"Girl, sit down. He's coming to you."

"Hey, Babe." He kissed Sap, then me. "You okay, big girl?"

"I feel a lit-tle better. I had to take some nas-ty stuff."

We both laughed at her.

"She still silly."

"Don't chu know it. That's your side coming out." I said, hoping he would catch on to the fact that I was telling him that she was his.

"So what did they say?" He sat down beside her and held her tiny hands.

"She has to stay in this tub at least an hour."

I sat back and stared at them. They looked just alike. She had everything from him, except his lips and eyes—those belonged to me and my mother.

"What are you staring at?"

"You and your daughter."

Sap was playing with toys, so she wasn't paying me attention.

Money looked at me with wide eyes. "Are you for real?"

"Yes, Money. I know she's yours, but I know I'm still going to have a blood test to confirm it and to make Diamond a final exit." He hugged me tight. I felt all the love we'd been missing out on. "I love you so much, Money. Please tell me you are ready to be in love with both of us. Tell me you are ready to love me as your wife, lover, and friend, and your child's mother."

He closed his eyes and breathed deeply. "Do you know how long I've waited to hear you say those things and mean it. I've always been in love with Sap and the idea of her being my child, but you have taken me through hell and back with Diamond. I'm scared to just give my all to you. We tried this once before, and you failed. I don't want to fail. I want everything you do, but you have to show me that you are ready."

Being with Diamond as recently as three months ago, I knew he was right, so I couldn't blame him for feeling the way he did. "I understand. When the time is right, we'll know."

Money pulled me close and rubbed my back, telling me he loved me, while we waited for the doctor to come back with the results of Sap's test.

"Mommie, do I have a daddy? I don't have one, do I? Karrey at school has a daddy; Trinket has a daddy, too."

I looked at Money for an answer to give her. She was getting older and more inquisitive. We had to tell her something.

"You do know what a daddy is, don't you, big girl?" Money asked with a loving voice.

"Yesssss, bu-t-t I do not have one," Sap said, shrugging her shoulders, and raising both of her palms up.

"Yes, you do." He took a deep breath and a long sigh. "I'm your daddy. Would you like that, big girl?"

She stopped splashing the water and looked up at him. "You my daddy? Ump umm, you my uncle Money."

"Who is always there when you hurt yourself? Who is there to pick you up from school?" Money asked, seeming kind of sad from the years of frustration. "Take care of you and put you to bed at night?"

"Uncle Chocolate, you, Mommie, and my two grandmas, and Papa!"

"That's right, and we all love you very much. And Daddies do all those things and more."

"But Daddies live in the house with Mommies and kids."

In a hush-hush voice, he said, "Damn! She's too smart for her own good. Maybe she'll be a lawyer or politician." He smiled. "Your daddy will be living with you soon, Sap. Very soon."

"Okay, Uncle Money." She stood up and held her arms out for a hug.

My daughter finally knew that Money was her father, even though she really didn't understand. That's all I ever wanted her to know.

"Miss Mancini, everything looks okay. The swelling in her arms and legs has gone down, and her fever has dropped to 99.6. We're thinking that maybe she had an allergic reaction to food or the environment. But we would like to do some extensive tests. We'll call you with that information. Just give her this prescription for pain twice a day, and this one if her fever comes back. If she gets any worse, bring her back. We also would like to do blood work on you and her father."

"Okay. Thank you, doctor."

The doctor remained with a silly grin on his face. "Oh, can I ask you, sir, for one thing?"

"Do you have a pen? And tell me who to make it out to," Money said.

The doctor laughed and thanked Money.

"You want my autograph, too, Miss?" Leaning his forehead on mine.

"Yeah, on my stuff tonight."

"I'll bring my special pen for that autograph."

Everything was looking up; I just hope it stayed this way.

Chapter Forty

Chocolate

"Why didn't you interrupt my call?"

"I . . . I didn't know what to do, Chinoe. The call you were on was important so—"

In a strong, hard voice, I said, "Sap is the most important of the two—or anything for that matter!"

The look on her face told me she got the message loud and clear. Walking up to me, she layed her head on my chest. "I apologize, Chinoe. I truly do understand that she comes before anything," she said before abruptly going downstairs.

I knew I hurt her feelings by talking to her like that. But my baby was sick and she came before work.

Ring . . . Ring . . . Ring.

"Starr residence."

"Ma, Luvly call you?"

"Yes, she's on her way back home now. Money is with her. Mrs. Mancini was there, too. And where were you? Why couldn't they get in touch with you?"

I didn't even answer my mother. She just wanted to act a fool about whatever Luvly had told her about Chaise.

"What did they say is wrong with her?"

"She had a high fever, and her arms and legs were hurting. They gave her some pain medicine and a cool bath. She's doing better. I talked to her little grown butt. Let's not start letting the new cat in the cage handle your business."

"Yeah, Ma, whatever. Well, that's good. They had me scared."

"Whenever you can escape from your master come by. A package came for you."

"What kind of package?"

"I don't know; I don't get in your business. Hold on. Someone wants to talk to you."

"Hey da, boy."

"What's up, old man?"

"Living. Making a living and trying to live right."

"I heard that. So when you get back?"

"Two days ago, but I'll be leaving again next week. After that I'll only have to fly out one weekend every two months to make sure everything is going as planned."

"Yeah, I got to go to Cancún in three weeks. Until then, I'll be doing local shoots and two shows at the Cobb Galleria and Lenox Mall."

"Get your old man some of them 'Sace suits. Ha! Ha! Ha! Them some sharp suits." My dad still thinks he is as young as he is cool.

"I hear you. Tell Ma I'll be by tomorrow. I'm going to rest."

"All right. Check you later."

My dad thought he was slick, hanging under my mother for her good food, and loving.

"Chaise."

"Yes?"

"Come here, sweetness." I needed to apologize to her. She needed to know that I did respect her. Even though I was using her to fill a void in my life.

"Yes?" She came halfway up the steps to the landing step.

"Our shoot is in three weeks in Cancún."

She shook her head yes and started walking back downstairs.

"Wait a minute." I walked up behind her, wrapped my arms around her waist and my lips around her ear. "Forgive me."

"Stop, Chinoe," she said in a lazy, but happy tone.

"I'm sorry about snapping earlier. Forgive me?"

"Maybe."

"Maybe?" She jerked away from my arms and ran toward the stairs, but I caught her before she took her first step. "Where you goin'?" She started squirming, trying to get away. "Feisty, huh? You gon' make us fall down all these steps and break my back. If I break that, all of this is gone to waste." I rotated my hips on her ass.

We fell onto the landing of the stairs, and Chaise ended up on top. Damn! She looked good sitting up there. Her silk robe barely closed, I slipped my finger through the opening.

"Stop!" she said, slapping my hand. "I'm still mad at you." I kept fingering her through the opening of the robe. She slapped my hand again. "For real, Chinoe. You hurt my feelings."

"Let me make it up to your feelings." I opened her robe and massaged her breast. "Damn, you look good up there!"

She looked at me through lusty eyes but said nothing.

"Give me a kiss."

"Are you truly sorry?" she asked, pouting.

"Let me show you." She leaned down thinking I wanted a kiss, but I flipped her over.

I licked slowly across her lips, down to her neck. She held my head close to her trying to control the heat that was rising between her legs.

I continued my tongue bath, licking and sucking her breast, hungrily pushing both nipples into my mouth. Using my tongue like the wave of an ocean.

"Ummm," she moaned as I licked her navel down to her hairline. "Sssttt, Chinoe."

Her thighs were next, sucking on them like they were succulent ribs. She started backing up, so I pulled her aggressively to the first step, opening her legs and putting each one on a banister.

Her breathing was becoming heavy, as she tried to keep control of herself. I began sucking on her panties, blowing hot heat to make her wetter. "Damn! Chinoe, I want you."

"Be patient. I want you dripping."

I stuck my finger inside her to see how bad she wanted me. She was just right. I pulled my finger out of her and licked it in her full view.

She layed her head back and arched her back so that her pussy was right at my mouth. I slipped her panties off and sucked the hell out of that pussy. "Ummm. Damn! Chinoe . . . ohhh . . . umm . . . mmm, ahhh, ooooo, it's so good! Eat it, Babe!"

I knew this wouldn't erase any hurt I'd caused her, but it would calm her down for the moment.

When I finished wiping my wrong away, she sat on my lap. She was so excited, riding my dick fast and hard. It felt good holding her hips as she let my entire dick all the way inside her. But they weren't as full and soft as Brandie's.

Damn! I wanted her. Thinking about her sex, Chaise became better by the second. "Damn, Brandie!" I came so hard it felt like I'd busted a vessel in my dick.

She stopped riding and pushed my head. "Who? What did you just call me?"

"Babe."

"Chinoe, you don't call me that."

"I did this time; it was so good." I pulled her to me and kissed her. I knew she heard me call her Brandie. But damn, if she only knew . . .

"Do you want to go with me over to Luvly's?"

Her eyes lit up. I'd never introduced her to any of them, so I figured this would dig me out of the hole.

"Yes, I would love that!"

Patting her on the butt, I said, "I have to go by the center to set up vouchers for the new kids."

"I still can't get over how successful the center is and how much y'all give to families. That is just so sweet and unselfish of you all."

"That's what we became famous for: to give back to the community. Let's take a shower."

I needed to be intoxicated right then and forever with some Brandie.

Chapter Forty-One

Brandie

"I know Mesia didn't steal my sky-blue outfit last week, that skanky heifer! I know I put it on top of everything in my locker."

"She hatin' like that?"

"Yeah . . . that jealous bitch! She was jockin' Sean before he really blew up, so you know that put a dent in our friendship from jump."

"I heard she was trying to get close to Hunt?"

"What? Not my sugar daddy. I know him better than that, though. He likes women with class, with something going for herself. That piece of trash is very much lacking all of the above." Neglecting my initial mission, I turned towards Caymin. "Caymin, why you just now tellin' me this?"

" 'Cause y'all work together. I don't want y'all fightin' over no man."

"She fightin' me over you and you a woman," I

told her, looking at her out the corner of my eye. "You sure you didn't give her any?"

"Whatever," she said, throwing a big pillow at me. "Y'all were closer than me and her," she added, with raised eyebrows.

While trying to act unconcerned about Mesia being up on Hunt, I started applying lip gloss, trying to change the subject. "So are we going to the mall?"

"You got it, chic."

Not knowing about Mesia and Hunt was eating me up. "So tell me how you know about Mesia trying to get with Hunt?"

"Promise me you won't get mad and start no shit with her."

I looked away since lately I had been having trouble keeping my promises.

"Promise?"

"Promise."

"Robert said when they were in the club, you know, when you were in New York?"

"Yeah."

"She stayed at their table the whole night. She was trying to turn these two other girls on to them at first, but then, when Hunt asked them to leave, she stayed. Robert said that Hunt paid her about a grand."

"For what?"

"Dancing, I guess."

"Naw. Fuck that dancin' shit! Fuck that!"

I got on the phone immediately. Robert was in love with Caymin and told her everything, so I knew he told her the whole story. She was just trying to keep me from kicking Mesia's ass.

Ring . . . Ring . . . Ring.

"Yeah."

"Yeah, my ass."

"What's going on, Ma?"

"Mesia." I said with much attitude. "Did I stay in New York too long?" I grunted, slapping my hand on my thigh.

"Ain't nobody messin' around with no Mesia. She just danced for us—"

"You."

"Us, Brandie. If Caymin gon' tell the story, tell her to tell it right."

Hunt's mellow tone was pissing me off—like he was unaffected by me or life itself. "So why five hundred, Hunt?"

"Mannn, why you coming at me wit' that bullshit."

"Oh so you admitting it?"

"Shiddd, I was DUI and—"

"And I'm GDT!"

"What?"

"God-damn-through!" I hung up on his dumb ass.

"Brandie, why you call him? Robert ain't gon' tell me nothin' no more."

"Ahh, girl, your pussy and looks are your security," I told her, recognizing she was just worried about losing his money.

Ring . . . Ring . . . Ring.

"Hello."

"Brandie, stop playin' games!"

"This is not a game! I find out you fuckin' her it's over; this whole package will be expire."

"You don't mean that."

"Hunt, I'm going to the mall. Talk to you later."

"You need some money?"

"What I tell you about askin' me about what I need. I don't need a damn thing but God and my family!"

"Sorry, Babe. Will a grand be enough?"

"Yep," I responded smacking my lips. Niggas needed to pay for their mistakes. Maybe they would stop being so damn sorry. But the sad part about it was niggas like Hunt could afford to be sorry all their lives.

"That's all?"

"I'm not greedy."

"I'll shoot it through there in a minute."

"Naw. Bring it to Lenox."

"I'm right here by your house."

"Lenox!"

"All right."

He was gone set me straight in front of her ass. We had to pick up those suits for the party at 6:30. She would be there, and so would he and I.

Lord, please guide me and lead me to the right things in life. Help me make the right choices and avoid the same misguided decisions.

Chapter Forty-Two

Chocolate

Ding, Dong. Ding, Dong.
Ding, Dong. Ding, Dong. Ding, Dong . . .

"They must be fuckin' cause damn—it don't take nobody that long to get down eight or twelve steps."

"Let them enjoy each other," Chaise said.

I saw Luvly standing at the top of the stairway with nothing but a t-shirt on.

"Open the damn door ol' crazy girl!"

I barely heard her say, "Hold on," through the thick glass.

Money finally opened the door. "Nigga, it ain't cold outside, and I'm sure ain't no bullets ridin' yo' ass."

Chaise's eyes danced with excitement at the sight of Money.

"You know I had to handle a little business. Had to whup that ass in Madden right quick."

"Man, y'all left me outside for the damn Play Station."

Luvly hopped down the stairs like a little child. "It was getting crucial. Hey, you must be Chaise," she said, pronouncing it slowly and correctly.

"Yes. Hi, how are you?"

"Fine. Have a seat."

"Where my baby at?"

"She is just waking up from that medicine; it made her drowsy."

Running from upstairs, Sap shouted, "Hey, Uncle Chocolate. Hey, Hey!" and jumped into my arms. "I feel better, Uncle Chocolate."

"That's what I want to hear."

Her face looked a little swollen.

Pointing at Money, Sap asked, "Who is that, Uncle Chocolate?"

"Uncle Money, you silly girl." Her giggle made Chaise smile.

"Daddy!" My eyes got big as I looked at the smile on Luvly's face.

"You are so beautiful. What's your name?" Chaise asked.

"What's your name?"

"Chaise."

I really didn't want Sap to know her all that well since I didn't expect Sap to be seeing Chaise on a regular.

"Hey, you guys thirsty?" Luvly asked, playing happy homemaker.

Chaise cleared her dry throat. "Yes, I'll have something to drink."

"Chocolate, get your woman a drink; you ain't no guest in this house, boy."

Cutting my eyes at Luvly, I went to the kitchen to get us something to drink. "Aye, Money, where the cranberry juice?"

Walking into the kitchen with a smile on his face, he said to me, "She tight, Dawg."

"Yeah, but she ain't the one."

"What? She tight. She got a good-ass job and she travel. That means good pussy, self-supported, and space."

"She ain't the one."

"Man, stop chasin' that dead-ass dream. Be happy that that type of women is hangin' around. The type of women like her," he said pointing toward the great room, "are high above their means. They are usually too professional and independent to know what they want, but she wants you—bad!"

"You right, but she just isn't the one. Trust me, Money." We walked back into the great room with me shaking my head no.

"I didn't know Chaise was your photographer," Luvly said. "She does some beautiful layouts."

"Naw, it's just my beautiful face and body."

Both of them put their hands in front of my face.

"No. Like I said, she got an eye for a good shot."

"Jealousy is an ugly thing," I said in a funny accent.

Sap began falling asleep. "She's still tired. She had a rough day. I'm going to put her in the bed and myself as a matter of fact. I'm tired, and I haven't had any drugs. Nice meetin' you, Chaise," Money joked as he took Sap upstairs.

"Well, Miss Luvly, I just came by to see my girl. I'm still tired from the session we had a few days ago."

"So what are you going to do about Sap's party? I know y'all comin'?"

"It's on; whatever you need I'll do it. But Chaise got a shoot that weekend," I answered without confirmation from her.

"Well, I don't know yet," said Chaise with an "I-can't-believe-you-didn't-ask-me tone."

Yes, she will, if I have anything to do with it. I don't want her mingling with everyone, trying to make something out of nothing.

"Taeko talkin' 'bout rentin' a big place."

"Naw. Why? She only four. Let's have it at Dave and Busters."

"Yeah, that'll be nice; that way the grown-ups can play, too."

"How many people comin'?"

"Over seventy-five kids I know, and probably eighty-five adults."

"Well, call me if you need anything else."

Chaise seemed bothered by the closeness as Luvly and I hugged. For all the right reasons we rode in silence. I was through explaining my relationship with Luvly to her and anyone else.

Chapter Forty-Three

Chocolate

I had to literally shove Chaise's out of control, jealous butt onto the plane. She tried to make up every excuse why she should and could stay to accompany me to Sap's party. I convinced her that no one single would be there, and if they were, they had kids. And she knew I wasn't too keen on dating women with children.

We paid the restaurant to shut down the game area for Sap's party. But they left the rest of the restaurant area open so that it could make more money off of people coming to see celebrities.

Being agitated and feverish put a halt on Sap's running around and playing. She was more interested in looking than participating.

Taeko and Money saw to it that all their teammates and their families were there. Each giving Sap a card with a hundred dollars, plus a gift.

"Chocolate, do you think we should bring the cake out now? She's getting tired and sluggish."

"Give 'em a little more time. Let everybody get here."

"My mother and father are riding with your mother and father."

"Is Mama Loane coming?"

"Yeah, he sent a limo to get her." Money's grandfather passed early last year. He died peacefully in his sleep one night while reading his bible. Now the only joy Mama Loane had was Money, Sap, and me. My mother took care of her twice a week. But her heart and strength died with Papa Loane.

Luvly's parents and my parents walked in with arms full of presents.

"Heeeey." Luvly hugged everyone. "Y'all give this girl too much all year round; she doesn't need all this stuff."

"This baby needs everything and can have anything she wants." My mother picked Sap up. "She's warm, Luvly."

"I know, but I wanted y'all to be here to see her blow out her candles."

My dad gave her a hug and kiss. "You gettin' to be a big girl now," he said, pulling at her legs. "Gonna have to buy you a car in a few years."

She laughed and hugged him back.

"Hey, Pops," I greeted my dad, embracing him. "Old man, you smellin' good."

"Yeahhh, my handsome son sent it to me from one of those European places he visited."

"He is handsome, huh?" I asked, rubbing my face.

"Boy, you crazy."

Mr. and Mrs. Mancini hugged Luvly and Sap. "How's granddaddy's baby?" he asked Luvly. It's like he could read the worry of her entire life, on her face.

"I'm fine."

"Why are you not playing with the other kids, little lady?" Mrs. Mancini asked, placing kisses on her forehead.

Sap shrugged her shoulders.

"Aahhhh, hey, girl. Glad you could make it!" Luvly greeted someone screaming like she hasn't seen them in forever. I couldn't see who it was due to the armful of presents I was carrying to the room.

Before the music started blasting, I heard my mother say, "Hello, dear. How are you? Oh, my goodness! I haven't seen you in so long. You still just as pretty as you were. How are you? Are you still in school?"

I couldn't hear the voice of the person that responded because of the loud music.

"I didn't know you knew Mrs. Starr, Brandie."

"How do you know her, Caymin? You didn't go to Homebound school?"

Mrs. Starr just smiled. "Well, girls, nice to see you. Let me go help get this ton-pound cake ready."

Luvly hugged Caymin again. "Girl, I'm so glad you came. I bet you can't even pick which little girl she is."

Caymin scanned the room. "Right there."

Brandie's eyes followed her finger. "Ooh, she is so pretty."

"Thank you. And what's your name?" Luvly

smiled and extended her hand, recognizing the almost identical resemblance between Brandie and Caymin.

"Brandie."

"Oh, I'm sorry. Brandie, Luvly. Luvly, Brandie." They shook hands and exchanged genuine smiles.

"Luvly, she looks just like you and . . ." Caymin stopped mid-sentence because she didn't want to tell Luvly's business.

"I know. Like her twin," Brandie completed the statement.

"Here's her present." Caymin gave the box to Luvly.

"And here's mine."

"Oh, Brandie, you don't even know her. That's sweet of you."

"Girl, please. I love kids."

"Y'all come on in and make yourself comfortable. Let me go help my mom and Seal."

Brandie went to the bar to get a drink while Caymin stood around to see if anyone looked familiar.

"What's up, girl?" Money said, tapping her on the shoulder. "Long time no see."

"Hey, big-time football player."

"What's happenin', girl? You seen Chinoe?"

Her facial expression changed; she didn't want to seem too hungry for the reunion, but Money knew different.

"No, and I really don't have to see him."

"Ahh, come on." Money pulled Caymin into the room where I was stacking the toys and clothing store, and nudged her to speak.

"Damn, I ain't gon' have to buy nothing for years," Money said, trying to break the ice.

"Yeah, you and Luvly gon' have a job cleanin' all this up."

I turned around, and no more words would leave my mouth. She looked the same, a little thicker, but the same fresh face, long black hair, and smooth caramel skin. And still hadn't grown no titties, but everything still looked sweet. If I didn't know any better, I'd say she favored my mystery star.

"Hi, Chinoe."

"What's up? How you been?"

"Fine. Just fine." She adjusted her purse strap.

"I was thinking about you the other day. Wondering how you were. Were you married? Had kids?"

"No, still single. I live in Cambridge townhouses. My sister had two more kids . . . soooooo I was kind of pushed out of the house. And I go to Clayton State University." She was nervous.

"You? In college? I thought you weren't interested."

"I don't want to be left behind."

I stared at her as she told me about the life that I should have been part of, but I didn't have any words to give her. No explanations for why I acted the way I did. I was young and unconcerned about my future, let alone anyone else's.

Taeko walked into the room tipsy. "Is this the lovely photographer I've been hearing about?" Caymin turned to face him. "Oh, snap! Caymin, what's up?" She gave him an endearing hug.

"Where's your girlfriend, Chinoe?" Takeo asked, never knowing when to shut up.

"She's not my girlfriend; she's just a friend."

"Oh, God, you still hollerin' that 'friends' crap?"

Caymin threw up her hands and smacked her lips, looking at me for an answer.

I wouldn't look Caymin in her eyes. I didn't feel like I owed her an explanation about who Chaise was.

"Chaise had a photo shoot to do." He noticed the tension in my voice.

"Oh, Joi wanted to meet her, but I guess at a later time. Later, Caymin." He elbowed me on his way out. "She still look damn good."

"Chaise? Chaise Kemp?"

"How do you know her name?" Damn!

"She is a top photographer. Young—with the best model ever under her belt—and black, may I add. She graduated from Fisk University."

"Yeah, she was modeling to put herself through school. Then she started taking pictures and shooting layouts . . ." I realized I was sounding like a real, proud boyfriend.

She flashed that cute smile that always drove me crazy. "I'm taking photography classes; that's how I know who she is. I'm almost finished."

"Umm, so you gonna make big money, huh?"

"Try. Maybe if I can get your beautiful face in front of my camera the dough will role in."

"Well, when you have to do your internship, come holla at me. It'll be on the house."

We laughed like we hadn't skipped almost five years of our lives and headed back out to the game room. Damn, maybe this was my chance to put my puzzle together and finish what I started with her.

"I saw your mom. She's still looking nice."

"Yeah, I try to do my best with her."

A tall stocky dude with braids walked up behind

her, grabbing her by the waist. "Hey, Babe, I've been looking for you."

"I've been right here," she informed him, looking annoyed by his aggressive claim.

His body language let me know that she was his woman or that he was definitely hittin' it. Caymin looked uncomfortable standing in front of me with her lover, but I bet money that if I was absent from the scene she would've been hangin' on his every word.

"Chinoe, this is my friend, Robert." Robert cut his eyes at Caymin, but never letting go of her waist.

Uh oh, she slipped. She might not be able to pay for that mistake.

"Robert, this is my friend from school." She sucked her teeth and batted her eyes at me. "She is the birthday girl's uncle/godfather."

"Nice to meet you, man."

"Same here, Dawg." We shook hands, but my eyes never left Caymin's.

"Where's B?"

"Why? Hunt here?"

"No, I thought she came with you."

"Well, nice seein' you again, Chinoe. Let me find my friend. I'm sure she's in good company, though."

"A'ight! Check you later."

I walked out into the game area where Luvly and Money were playing proud parents.

"Y'all low-down as hell. Why you didn't tell me you invited that girl?" I asked.

Money was laughing like a little kid.

"Chinoe, I didn't do it on purpose. Money, shut up! I invited her when I seen her at the store, but I didn't think she would really come."

Money was getting a kick out the whole thing.

Taeko walked over. "Hey, y'all see Caymin's friend? She fine to death. She got that long, pretty hair like Caymin. She thicker than Caymin, though, but they favor a lot. She look familiar, but I can't put my finger on it."

"I hope she got some breast."

"Stop it. She looks pretty. And anyway, Chocolate, I thought you didn't care about her." Luvly winked. "And Tae, you been through too much to even be out here lookin' at anyone's ass."

"Mannnn, Luvly, I was just lookin'. Just lookin'," he said, throwing his hands in the air.

"Yeah, her friend is nice looking," Luvly said, rolling her eyes at them both. "She's a pretty girl. She's our age, too, and jazzy as hell. She does put you in the mind of Caymin, but she's a little bigger. Not fat, just thick."

"Umm, Umm." I rubbed my hands together, mouth watering. I knew how good Caymin tasted, so if she was thicker, good Lawd!

"Where they at?"

"They over at the bar."

"I'm shocked ya boy ain't showed up acting a fool," Taeko said.

Luvly's happiness disappeared from her face at the mention of Diamond's name. "He thinks Sap birthday is next week. That's how much the asshole cares about her." Her eyes became watery.

Money grabbed Luvly from behind, around the waist, kissing her on the cheek, "Her daddy's here now. I wish that muthafucka would come off in here."

"Well, he ain't and we all here so let's enjoy our baby turning into a little lady," I intervened, trying to bring some joy back into our conversation.

Everyone was standing around just like the old days. I often wished we could go back in time, before the kids and the stress of being responsible. Just being young and careless, hangin' tight, I missed those days.

The photographer came up to us. "Would you all like a photo together?"

"Ayeeee, let me get one wit' just me and Luvly first, and then one wit' each one of my boys." I grabbed her playfully. I wanted a picture with her by myself. She meant so much to me, more than any one knew.

After taking my picture with her, then an individual with Money and Tae, everyone swapped. "CP—tight to death!" We all screamed for the group picture. All our smiles were bright. Usually men didn't cheese, but we had a lot to smile about, health, family, friends, and life. The only thing that was missing was my mystery star—wherever she was.

Chapter Forty-Four

Brandie

Robert and Caymin walked up to the bar fussing. He was holding onto her so tight, I thought he was pinching her. "Will you just leave that shit alone. You are my friend."

"Bullshit! I saw how you was looking at that nigga. Smiling all up in his face."

"Look this is not the time and place for this. Please." She begged him.

She was all smiles when she walked up to me. That's what I loved about her, always the mediator, "Where you been hidin', girl?"

"Right here. Tired of every married man trying to hit on me. Their wives are out in the game room with their kids. Do they think just because they play some type of ball that I'll float into their arms?"

"Yes," they both said as if I was crazy.

"Where's Hunt, Rob? Out paper chasin'? Or fuckin' Mesia?"

Caymin grabbed my cup and smelled it. "This doesn't smell like liquor, so you aren't drunk. Why you look so down and depressed?"

"Just thinking about the direction my life is headed in. I mean school is coming along, but I need another job. I'm tired of shaking my ass in different niggas faces every night. I need more substance in my life," I complained, wanting Robert to tell me the truth.

Caymin felt my head. "You don't have a fever. Maybe your head band is on too tight."

"Brandie, substance is that three to four grand you bring home a week. Do you know how many hoes would kill for your position in the club? In life?"

"Robert, what did you just call me?" I asked to make the point.

"Brandie."

"No, you called me a ho."

"Naw, I didn't call you that. I was just talking about these hoes in the street."

"But that's how you and the other billion men and women see me as a ho shakin' my ass for a dollar. I don't want to be referred to as a ho; I know I'm not one. I want to be looked at as a respectable woman, and shakin' my ass is not gon' get me that title. Maybe I just need to kick Hunt's ass."

"Well, there you go. Problem solved. Cheer up." Robert patted me on the back.

The problem was far from being solved. A real professional man wasn't going to take me home to his family and say, "This is my girlfriend; she's a stripper. Shakes her ass for cash," only to have his mom respond, "What? She's a shake-a-booty dancer? She takes money from a man that would rather spend his money on seeing her naked than to feed his kids or pay the light bill? Oh, no, not my son."

Especially not Mrs. Starr. She would say, "I didn't give you that expensive knowledge to get up on a stage and shake your ass for money, and I be damned if Chinoe's going to marry a slut."

I put my hand on my forehead. Why was I still thinking about him, I was never going to see Chinoe again anyway, so I needed to get over it. "Maybe things will look up soon."

"There's always tomorrow. Tomorrow will bring a brighter day," Caymin said, as she fingered her hair.

She was just happy-go-lucky because she had caught her one. Robert wasn't going anywhere and he gave Caymin everything: money, time, space, love, attention, respect, and admiration. He gave her no problems.

"Excuse me, are you Miss Delite?" asked a tall, muscular, well-dressed, good-looking, bald guy.

I didn't know what to say. What if he was a reporter and he wrote a story about a stripper at a four-year-old's birthday party?

But what if I said no and missed out on him telling me that he had seen my show at the club and loved the way I moved, and that I was beautiful, and he wanted to make me his wife, have lots of kids, and move away to a private island . . . Yeah, right!

"Who wants to know?"

"One of your biggest fans." He extended his hand and kissed mine softly.

Four men with the same buff body came over with big Kool-Aid smiles on their faces. Robert whispered in my ear, "They're football players."

I nudged him in the side with my elbow. I knew what they were, but the key was to keep runnin' game like I didn't know.

"We wanted to know if you would be interested in doing a party for us."

I looked at them like they were stupid. This was exactly what I was talking about—disrespect. "Why would you walk up to me at this little girl's party and ask me that?"

"They didn't mean to offend you, Miss Delite. No disrespect intended. They're just fans. Not to mention you are such a beautiful woman. I myself am a single brother that is interested in getting to know you outside of the club, but my teammates," he said, pointing to the group of guys, "want you to perform at a party. Big as they are, they are scared to approach you. By the way, my name is Cartel."

"Nice to meet you, Cartel." I was impressed. Clean cut and cleaned up his mistakes very nicely.

"May I have a moment of your precious time? To myself?"

"Sure. My name is Brandie."

"Sweeter than Caramel Delite."

"You are too much." I blushed.

"All that you need and want me to be. Is there a number I can get in touch with you; I'm about to leave."

I wrote my number down without hesitation.

"Nice meeting you, Miss Brandie. I'm looking forward to enjoying your company."

Mmmmhmmm, his ass was plump and tight.

"Damn, he fine as hell in that beautiful cream suit. Caymin, did you see those big-ass diamonds in his chocolate ears?"

Robert had walked over to some people he knew. "Yes, ma'am, he is fine. Tall, chocolate, and platinumed out."

"I'm ready to hit the door. I need some sleep before tonight. Excuse me, bartender, can I have a cranberry and Sprite to go?"

"A cranberry and a Sprite to go?"

"Mixed."

"Mixed?" He showed the look of disgust.

"Damn, there are some fine-ass men here!"

The bartender brought the drink back, and it was the bomb.

Luvly walked over to us. "We are about to sing Happy Birthday to Sapphire."

"We are about to leave, Luvly," said Caymin; "Brandie has to go to work."

"Ohh, Brandie, I wish you could stay to meet the guys."

"Guys?"

"Yeah, Sap's uncles."

"Maybe next time."

She looked around to see if she could spot the guys, but they were obviously not in sight. She gave Caymin a hug and shook my hand.

"Caymin, keep in touch with me. You know I don't have any friends, thanks to Diamond."

"Well, maybe we can all go out one night."

"I need to go out tonight and get a break. Sap hasn't been feeling good and she's not doing too hot tonight," said Luvly.

"Well, I'm going to the Platinum Kat tonight.

I'm not gay or anything. Brandie works there," Caymin gloated.

"Brandie, you work there?" I nodded yes. "Girl, I use to love going there before I had Sap. Do you mind if I come along? I truly need a break."

She seemed real cool; I didn't mind. "Sure, I'll put y'all in VIP." I grabbed my drink from the bar. "Okay, see you tonight." I waved goodbye to Cartel in hope that he would come see me at the club tonight; I needed a different kind of attention.

Lord, please send me a God-fearing man

Send him packaged with flesh of steel, black as night, handsome. Send him with a soul of passion, prosperity, individuality, and a touch of congeniality made from Your perfect hands

Send him to me as fast as You can. But only send him when You have conditioned me for the sender.

Amen

Chapter Forty-Five

Chocolate

I was getting thirsty as hell, but I held out, since the singing was about to start. Sap layed lazily in my arms.

Luvly rushed over to me. "Sap, you don't feel well, big girl?" She just nodded her head.

"Luvly, she does feel hot," I said, rubbing her back and neck.

"Okay, I'm about to sing Happy Birthday and let your mother or mine take her home," Luvly said with a worried look on her face.

"Where is Money?"

Just as I asked, he walked up with the Teletubbies. Sap popped her head up. "The Teletubbies are here!" Jumping down out of my arms, she runs up to them and hugs each one of them. The photographer snapped pictures.

"She looks so happy, but I know she doesn't feel

well. She tries to be so strong." For the first time in his life, Money had no control over the situation. He summoned for the cake to be brought out. "Everyone, let's all come around. Please, everybody, gather around to sing Happy Birthday to Sapphire."

"Happy Birthday to you,
Happy Birthday to you,
Happy Birthday, dear Sapphire,
Happy Birthday to you."

"Yeah! Yeah! Yeah!"

"Blow out your candles, baby girl."

She gave it all her wind and blew them out. It seemed like we were all making wishes, all for different reasons.

"Did you make a wish?" my mother asked. Sap nodded yes and rested her head on Money's shoulder.

"Hey, I'm going to get a drink," I told Money, pointing at the bar.

"I'll meet you at the bar," Money agreed.

I didn't see Caymin at the singing. I wondered if her boyfriend made her leave because of all the swarming men, 'cause she did look good. Well taken care of. Those karats on her arm and ears weren't lying.

"Excuse me, Dawg. Let me get a cranberry and Sprite."

"Mixed, right?" the bartender asked.

"Yeah."

"A good-looking sister just left here with one of these to go; I thought she was weird. But I made myself one, and it taste pretty damn good."

"You happen to catch her name?"

I started acting like I was on crack. Shit! I was. Brandie was my crack, the first piece that got me addicted. I was her fiend and I needed a hit of that.

"Yeah, some football player came over trying to push up on her, but home girl was too sassy for that shit. I think she said Brenda. Brittany?"

"Brandie?"

"Yeah, yeah, that sounds about right."

I jumped off the stool ready to race Marion Jones. "How long ago did she leave?"

"Just a few minutes."

Running full speed towards the door, I knocked a little girl down. "I'm so sorry." The little girl was crying loudly, so I picked her up, still looking in every direction. It was hopeless. She was gone—again. Damn! My luck was buzzard!

I took the little girl to her parents and returned to the bar disappointed. "So, man, was she tight?"

"Tight ain't even the word. She was beautiful. Her and her friend could go for sisters, but this girl was thicker, had a rounder face. Beautiful full face."

"Damn! Damn! Damn!"

"You messed up with her or something?" he asked, wiping the counter.

"Naw, I never had a chance."

Chapter Forty-Six

Money

"My baby had a beautiful birthday party. She is getting so big," Luvly said as she put on some Al Green.

"Yeah, everything turned out nice, but next year will be the bomb, the big five."

Stretching out on the sofa and laying her head down on my lap, Luvly said, "Sap is sick, Money. I don't know what's wrong with my baby."

"I'm going to make some phone calls tomorrow and get some specialist to look at her."

"I'm so glad that you are here with me. With us."

As I kissed her on the forehead, she looked up at me with sexy eyes.

"Kiss me again." I kissed her again. "Again." I kissed her longer. "Again." I kissed her more passionate this time. "Again."

"Ha! Ha! Ha! Just tell me you want some," I said, tickling her a little bit.

"Nope. Again."

I kissed her until my already hard dick began to pulsate. "Get up, Luvly," I said, pushing her off me. "I wanted this to be about us, not sex. It's time for us to get to know each other all over again."

"Why? He raisin' up for me," she said, smiling and trying to grab my dick.

We started wrestling.

"Hey, did you see the look on Chocolate's face when he saw Caymin?" I asked, patting her on the butt, trying to change the mood.

"Yeah, I thought inviting her would be good for him 'cause he don't seem to really be into Chaise. Don't get me wrong, she all right, but not for him. I always thought him and Caymin were good together. But I didn't know she had a man or that, if she did have one, she would bring him to the party."

"Why you always so concerned about Chocolate's love life?"

If I didn't know better I'd swear they messed around before Sap was born. One time I went out of town to football camp and came back a day early. I went straight to Chocolate's house, and Luvly's car was in the driveway. (Seal let me in.) Once I get to the basement, the door is locked. It took them too long to open it, but I didn't stress the situation.

"Are you jealous, Mr. Loane?" she asked, smacking her lips. "I just think he deserves to be happy with the right somebody."

"Yeah, but Chocolate still chasin' a dream, a piece of pussy from some chic he don't even know."

"It was special to him."

"Yeah, his first piece. You move on to the next one after that. Test the waters." I patted her ass again and kissed it. "Mine was special, too."

She pushed me away this time, changing the subject that I was ready to start. "Yeah, but look at how it happened. I think it's kind of romantic that he gave his virginity to someone he hasn't seen. He felt her and got to know her from eleven forty-five to four a.m. He didn't judge her for her looks."

"Yeah, yeah. Like I said, chasing a dream when he has a perfectly good woman who wants to be good to him."

"Where were you when all this was going on is my concern?"

Jumping on her, pinning her down, I said, "So many questions." I kissed her, pecking her here and there.

"Caymin invited me to go the Platinum Kat."

"Damn! Chinoe done turned 'er gay."

"No, her friend works there. She wants all of us to go to VIP."

"Like I can't get that on my own."

"Whatever. I'm going. I need a grown-up night out. Actually she invited me, but I thought all of us could go: you, me, Chocolate, and Taeko."

"I'll call them after you do me a favor."

"What?"

I picked her up and sat her on the sofa. She didn't hesitate or resist. She held on to my neck, kissing me. I gently pushed her back into the cushion as far as she would go, kissing her deep and strong.

Her short T-shirt exposed her upper thighs. My hungry lips couldn't resist kissing them; they smelled like enticing fruit.

My next victims were her legs. Picking up one of them, I kissed and sucked her calves and felt her wiggle with ecstasy. Hearing her moan turned me on even more. I started sucking each toe slowly. From her toes to her inner thigh, my tongue dispensed wetness. "Luvly, I want to love you for a lifetime."

Grabbing my face with both her hands, she kissed my forehead, cheeks, nose, chin, and then my lips. "I don't ever want to lose this feeling, or you."

Chapter Forty-Seven

Chocolate

"Yeah, it was nice. Sap wasn't feeling well, but she did good."

"Did you give her my present?" Chaise asked.

"Of course, I did. How is your session going?"

"Going. The models are not as genuine as you, and they aren't as gorgeous either."

"When are you coming back to Atlanta?" I asked, not really wanting her here.

"Whenever you ask me to."

"Well, let me go put Sap in the bed. Call me tomorrow."

"All right. Bye, I lo—"

Click

I didn't want her to love me. I knew that I would end up hurtin' her. Damn! It seemed like I couldn't get it right with her. I knew why; she wasn't 'the one.' Just like Nikki, Tab, Joslen, Bashea, Wendi,

Sam, or Haven weren't 'the one.'

Ring . . . Ring . . . Ring.

"Starr residence."

"What's up, boy? You down for the Kat tonight?"

"That's cool. I need to be in a stress-free atmosphere."

"Call Taeko and let him know."

"Man, yeah. Joi gon' be trippin', and you know it," I warned him.

"Man, stop being a pussy and call that man. He needs a break, too."

"Hold on."

Ring . . . Ring . . . Ring.

"Hello."

"What's up, Joi? Tae home?"

"Yeah, hold on." She dropped the phone to the floor, letting us catch the loud thump in our ears. "Taeko!" She yelled loudly.

"See, she already got an attitude," I reminded him.

"Man, she and her sister were born with attitudes."

"Yeah," Taeko answered, sounding just as bothered as Joi.

"What's up, Dawg?" we both greeted him.

"We headed to the Kat tonight." I was hoping he said no. Joi was good for bustin' up in strip clubs and pullin' rank on his ass and fighting with the dancers.

Tonight I wanted to get me a couple of drinks, listen to some tight music, and look at some beautiful, thick sisters shake it fast.

"Yeah, I'm down. What time y'all leavin'?"

"It's eight p. m. now, so about midnight." I said midnight so that Joi wouldn't let him out. Tae got wild in the strip club, touching dancers, and calling 'em out their name. He could go to the VIP room and fuck 'em, for all the club cared. But damn! He was a professional basketball player and father of two, he shouldn't be all out on the floor showin' his ass.

"That's tight. I'll be there. VIP?"

"Yeah, one of Caymin's friend dance there, and she already got a spot for us," said Money.

"What? Man, hell naw, you playin' a bitch role," I told him.

"Aw, man. She gotta, man; she ain't jockin' you no more."

"Man, please. Can't no woman leave this! Chocolate is addictive."

"Whatever, pretty nigga. Midnight, Tae," Money said.

"Midnight." Tae hung up.

"Man, why you didn't tell me she gon' be there?" I asked.

"I didn't say she was going to be there," said Money.

"Well, I'm assuming."

"Making an ass out of yourself."

"Whatever. Who is her friend?" I wanted to know.

"I don't know her name. She talked to Luvly."

"Oh, so Luvly goin'?" My good night was definitely over.

"Yeah."

"Man, you invitin' drama all the way around," I warned him. "You know Diamond has a personal seat in that joint. Luvly hate half dem bitches in there, and you know when she get full she act crazy as Tae. I promise naw, I bet all the money in my pocket Joi gon' come up in that bitch and start trippin'."

"Man, Joi might be chill tonight; he been treatin' her better lately."

"And Luvly?"

"That's an unpredictable story," Money admitted.

"I'm out. Late'a."

"Late'a."

Chapter Forty-Eight

Brandie

"It's off the chain in here," Caymin said, amazed at all the naked women.

"Some type of game was earlier today." I knew she wasn't used to this type of environment, but she would be all right.

"Caramel, who is this luscious lady?" One of my regular customers asked with hunger in his eyes for Caymin.

"Zae, she is not a dancer, just a guest."

"Hey, baby girl, you should think about working here. Those half karats in your ears could be five karats if you fuck wit' me."

"We waitin' on you, Miss Delite," Zae said, pinching my chin, winking at Caymin.

Caymin's facial expression changed from excitement to scared. "Girl, hurry up and get me upstairs to my room."

"I'll be doing my show at twelve-thirty. Do you want to stay here or go on up?"

"Can I still see and hear upstairs?"

"Yeah."

"Upstairs," she said nervously, walking toward the staircase.

On the way up the stairs men were pulling on Caymin, asking her to marry them, could they have a dance, what was up for a night. One man offered us three gees for a night with both of us. She saw how easy it was to make a grand in minutes.

"Brandie, if I didn't have Robert I would be your money-making partner. All this money for the shit we do for free-hump."

Caymin's hot-pink, strapless sundress truly complemented her figure. And with her hair curled and pulled up, she looked like a slimmer version of me.

"All right, girl, chill out. The intercom," I informed her, pointing to the arm of the chair, "is to order drinks, food, and . . . women." I winked at her.

She cut her eyes at me.

"Hey, to each it's own." I laughed.

Mesia had walked in the room without making a peep.

Caymin joked, "I'll order you with a side of—"

"Well, well, what do we have here? Caymin, you turnin' on me?" She winked her eye at Caymin, passing her tongue through two fingers. "You let me taste it, and I'll have yo' ass crawlin' up and down my walls; you'd swear you had dick up in ya."

Caymin attempted to smooth things over by hugging her, but Mesia's hands hung free.

"You might wanna stick wit' lickin' pussy 'cause

if you fuck wit' my dick again, you'll be gummin' pussy for the rest of your life."

"I know yo' lame, wanna-be-somebody ass ain't threatenin' me." Mesia chuckled and tried to walk up close to me, but got cut off by Caymin sliding in between us.

"Try me, ho." I jumped at her.

"Bitch, you don't know me." She held her hand in the air, like she was holding a knife, toward my face. "I'll slice you from yo' fo'head, across yo' eye, down your nose, lips, down to yo' left titty, pushin' it into yo' stanking-ass heart." She motioned her hand like she was digging into a frozen carton of ice cream. "And I'ma make sure it's wit' a dirty, rusty-ass blade."

She tried to inch closer, pushing her body up against Caymin, but Caymin's determination held her back.

"Y'all bitches are pitiful. What? You got Caymin in here to show her yo' musty ass cock that got yo' men running to me?" She stared at me with dead eyes. Letting me know that she and Hunt had been together.

At that very moment I knew she had no love for me and would take me out at any cost. "Brandie, don't step on my feet tonight," she warned as she headed for the door. "Stay in your position, bitch, and I just might stay in mine."

She cut her eyes at Caymin, flipping me the bird as she exited.

It was taking everything in my power not to knock her the fuck out. And I didn't want anything to blemish my record—stop me from becoming the lawyer I was working so hard to become.

"How do you put up with her?" Caymin asked.

"She usually works Friday and Sunday from six p.m. to twelve a.m., and I work twelve-thirty a.m. to five a.m. So we miss each other."

"She crazy."

"She high as hell."

Walking to the dressing room to get ready for my show, I scanned the room to see if all my regulars were there.

"Miss Caramel Delite, how are you?"

His smile was already taking me in and making me weak. "Hey," I greeted him with an intimate hug, "I didn't expect to see you so soon."

"But I had to see you. I come see you a lot, but I make it a point for you not to see me."

"Why don't you ask for me?"

"I don't be wantin' to make you feel cheap. I knew that one day I would get the nerves to ask you out, but I didn't want it to be in this scene. Whenever I see you, I want you to feel like a million bucks."

I blushed. That was a hard thing to get me to do; I was not easily impressed. "Well, will you promise to call me up tonight? I need that million-dollar attention."

He flashed his smile again. "I'm watching you. Give me a special dance on stage."

I winked at Cartel and went to get dressed. I put on my diamond suit with the mask to match: Showing a good ass with no face always drove 'em crazy.

I went to the bar to get my favorite drink.

"Looking good, Caramel."

"Thanks, Tony."

"Lots of professionals in the house tonight. Not that you have a problem making money, anyway."

Tony was the coolest bartender/owner. He was

always slipping me compliments and invitations to dinner and a movie. I always ran the game that I only worked for my employers, not worked them.

"What time you up?"

"It was twelve-thirty but GP had to go get her baby, so I let her go first. Then li'l mama on stage was short on cash so I let her get in so I'm going on at one-thirty."

"You got a little while to go. Are you going to hang out with me? Draw 'em to the bar for me?"

I turned to watch the new girl on stage that's already been turned out. Cute with a pretty bob haircut, she walked in the door frail. Then Mesia got her claws into her the second day she was here. Now she's getting high and drunk, eating pussy, and taking three dicks at a time. That's why I need to get the hell on out of this place! It's not that I feel vulnerable to my surroundings, but I know I'm capable of doing better.

I walked to the deejay booth to pick the music for my set. "What's up, Caramel? Whatchu makin' these niggas crazy off of tonight?"

"I 'on't know, Cappers. I feel like some Prince, Cameo, and I don't know . . . Whatchu think?"

Capper's was what I called the perfect package, smooth, dark skin, dimples, and the brightest smile and full lips; his chipped tooth added to his sex appeal.

"Why you always dance off that medium music?"

"Don't like to sweat."

"I feel you. You must know something 'bout music 'cause these men walk in hollerin', 'Miss Delight, we love you." He stared at me. "Damn, Brandie! Why you won't give me a chance?"

"Cappers, why would you want to be involved

with someone you work with . . . in this type of place? And then, too, you wouldn't be able to handle all these men on me. You need to be with a nice college girl that works at a bank or something."

"I'll do what it takes, to be with you, Brandie." He looked at me deeply through those big, brown eyes, batting those thick, long eyelashes, almost convincing me. "You're in school, you have your own car and house, and you take control of your life. I don't think I can find all of that twice over. It's not that you're beautiful . . . 'cause you are that—a blind man can see it, but you have a presence about yourself that draws a person to you. I don't plan to be in this club forever either; I'm going to open up my own club. That's why I go to Morehouse—for business."

Damn! That made me feel good. He saw ass all night and still took the time to find out about mine.

I gave him a hug and handed him my set. "Cappers, when I leave this place, you'll definitely be the first to get a call."

He flashed those bright whites. "I'll definitely be waiting.

Chapter Forty-Nine

Chocolate

"Damn! It's packed tonight. Everybody musta' knew I was gon' be in da hizzy. Ha! Ha!" Money laughed out loud as we finagled our way to our seats.

"Hell, yeah. Off the chain! What's up, nah?" I threw my head up to a couple of niggas we all went to school wit'.

"Aye Swat get at me nigga before you leave."

"Luvly, you 'bout to go on stage and make 'em holla fo' a couple of dolla's?" I teased her about the shirt that barley covered the roundness of her breast . . . and the entire back out. "How in the hell are you holdin' it on?"

"With your starin'-ass eyes," she snapped, popping her lips.

"You got it, you got it," I say backing off, licking my lips at how sexy she looks.

"Y'all go on up. I'ma sit down here for a while. I'll be up in a minute," Money said, catching the eye of a dancer he used to mess with.

"Well, we can all sit down here," Luvly said with a full-blown attitude, noticing Money's focus.

Looking around the club, I noticed the atmosphere was just what the doctor ordered: phat asses, thick thighs, long legs, and pretty faces.

A short, smooth, dark-skinned sistah with wide thick hips-winked at me, while table dancing for a nerdy looking dude. Damn, if I had a lady I wouldn't even be in a room full of pussy; I'd be at home under the covers with my face between my woman's legs. I give the table dancer a wink back, with no intentions of getting any closer.

We finally got through the crowded room, to a table of Money's choice.

"Chocolate, you want something to drink?"

"Yeah, cranberry and Sprite mixed."

I felt different that night. It had been about two years since I'd been in Platinum Kat, but it felt familiar. The one thing about the club that was different from a lot, it smelled good—not like pussy.

A very unattractive dancer approached the table. "Can I get a table dance, handsome?"

"No, thank you," I said, giving her a twenty to keep her ass away.

"I wonder where Caymin is?" Luvly asked, looking over her drink at me . . . like I knew.

"Man, don't come at me like that. I don't know and really could care less."

"At-ti-tude," Luvly said, jokingly.

I scanned the room again to see if there was a li'l sumthin' sumthin' to take into the VIP room.

"Speaking of the princess," I said sarcastically as Caymin walked down the stairs. I had to admit she still looked good, wearing a hot-pink, strapless sundress.

"Hey, y'all." She hugged Luvly. "The room is ready upstairs."

"Chocolate likes it down here with ass all in his face," Luvly chimed in.

Shooting her a middle finger, "Fuck you, Luvly. How you doin'?"

"Fine, and you?"

I nodded but continued giving Luvly the evil eye. "Join us down here for a while. The table and chairs are for anyone."

"I was down here earlier, but every man in here was asking for dances, marriage, babies and all," she answered confidently, to let me know she was not just anyone.

"Shiddd, these girls make hella cheese in here; you betta get on it," said Money with a Cheshire cat grin.

"Money should know. He's bought a few cars, jewelry and new body parts." Luvly winked at him.

"See, I knew I shoulda left you at home."

"Where's your friend Caymin?" Luvly asked, ignoring Money's comment.

"Oh, she's about to come out. What's her name again?"

Before I could hear her say her friend's name, the deejay announced the next dancer. The lights begin flashing. "Please, everyone, give your attention to the stage, grab you dollars, 'cause she'll make you wanna holla . . . Miss Caramel Delite!"

Half the club surrounded the stage, with money

already in hand and mouth; the other half came out of their VIP rooms to see the feature show. Prince's The Beautiful One lured her to the stage.

"Damn, her outfit is tight; Money, I want one."

"You gon' do what she doin'?"

"Sho' ya right," she said, winking her left eye.

Luvly wished she could move like that. The masked woman held her hands above her head making her body move like a wave. Her hips moving in and out, sexually. Something was familiar about the way she was dancing. The way that body was looking, her face had to be messed up.

The deejay mixed the songs and played 'Get It Wet' by Twista. The club went wild! "Look at these niggas goin' crazy."

Taeko walked closer to the stage with five one-hundred-dollar bills in his hand; she rolled a hip in his face to accept the money.

This girl was bad. The way she was moving, her size—all of it had me mesmerized. Her thick, juicy thighs, and full breasts were perfect. Damn! She needed to take off that mask!

She appeared to be looking at our table. The music changed to "Seems Like You Ready" by R. Kelly. She leaned against the pole moving her hips slowly and circular. "Damn!" My dick was getting hard and she wasn't going home with me.

"Woo wee, she bad!" Taeko came back to the table. "She'll make a man leave his family."

"Well, we don't have to worry about this man leavin'." Luvly attacked his ass. She used to always brag on Tae and Joi's relationship. Even though her and Joi ran with rival cliques they always gave each other respect.

"She got a tight music set." I was giving her compliments like she was a ballerina.

She started making her way off stage, hungry niggas right in her footsteps. As soon as she made it close to our table "Candy" by Cameo mixed in. She stopped in front of me moving sexually.

"He can't handle that ass." Money and Tae started hyping the situation. "Put that pussy down that nigga throat." They were jumping out of their seats waving money for her to do as they said, but she had her own agenda. I was under her spell, her essence eluding me.

I followed her face, trying to study it through the mask. Why was she dancing like this—one on one? For a minute, everything and everybody was a blur. I could only see her. She turned around and tapped her ass down on my lap. I almost grabbed her hips but I controlled my hands. CARAMEL with drips, drippin all over it was on her lower back. Oh, shit, this was Brandie!

"Money, this her! Nigga, this her!"

"What?"

"The girl I've been talking about. My mystery star."

Caymin, twenty questions written all over her face, expressed a confused look. "He knows Brandie?"

"Yeah, Chocolate, that's her name, Brandie," Luvly said, snapping her fingers with excitement.

"Brandie! Brandie! This is Brandie?" My blood started pumping overtime, making sweat bead up on my forehead. She turned around and the mask was gone. She was more beautiful up close than in my dreams.

I stood up and kissed her. I didn't know where

this kiss was going to lead to, but I had to touch her lips again.

"Dat's my Dawg!" Money shouted, sounding like DMX.

"Money, what the hell is he doin'?" Luvly asked, looking back for the bouncers.

"That's the girl from his one-night stand."

"Ooooh, okay, get it then, Chocolate. Claim your stuff, boy!"

I released Brandie to get a good look at her. She stood in front of me with the biggest, prettiest, whitest smile I'd ever seen. "You know they on their way to put you out right." She continued smiling.

"You comin' with me?" The smiles on our faces could power a nuclear explosion. She was so perfect! Everything I'd imagined and more.

"Look, I know ya'll so-called celebrities, but you can't be touching the dancers," the swollen bouncer said, tapping my shoulder.

"Ahh, man, we got a VIP room. We on our way up."

"All right, Taeko, but your boy can't be slobbing down the dancers."

"Let me finish this set, and I'll be up." I let her go without any fuss, but kept my eye on her all the way up the stairs.

When we got upstairs Luvly was all in my business. "So, Chocolate, that's your girl? She was at Sap's party. She's a pretty girl."

"I guess we've been missing each other," I joked.

"Damn, nigga! You been chasin' this girl for about five years."

"Five years? We were together five years ago," Caymin stated flatly.

"I didn't know that girl then. I just saw her in the mall after graduation and thought she was nice-looking, but I never touched or talked to her," I said with a nonchalant attitude, not really giving a damn about her right then.

"Cool out, Caymin. Y'all were way back; this is now." Money left the room to go to the bathroom. I caught up to him outside the door, so I didn't have to deal with Caymin questioning me.

"Damn, man! Your girl, Brandie, tight."

"Damn right, that's the woman I want for the rest of my life."

"Man, she probably got niggas runnin' all through this club, up and down 85.

"Maybe, but she gon' definitely get off on 285."

"Don't be no fool, boy. Strippers are all out for one thang, and your heart ain't one 'em. Besides don't be puttin' your all in some chic you don't know nothin' 'bout. Fuckin' is one thang; makin' her your main lady is another."

"Son, why you tryin' to school the principal?"

Money took a deep breath and exhaled. "Man, I'm trying to tell you something I know. I been fuckin' up, sleepin' with Salone."

"What? After she set your car on fire and told the tabloids all that shit on you?"

"It only happened a few times. I 'on't be knowin' when Luvly gon' sneak out to go be wit' Diamond. Nigga, I be listenin' when you be insultin' me about sleepin' around. I don't want my dick to fall off, so I been tryin' to stick to home. Besides, me and Luvly ain't made it official yet."

"You don't have to justify it to me. You just need to check that shit. That girl messin' with your livelihood by telling tabloids and magazines that you beat on her, got babies all over and all kind of lies. You the one need to think about your life; you have a daughter."

"Whateva! Just squash this shit! I'll deal with this later. Just go get the woman you've been chasin' for most of your life." He paused, looking down at his shoes. I knew him better than he knew himself. He wanted to tell me something important but didn't know how.

"What's up?"

"I'm gon' ask her to marry me."

I knew this nigga wasn't gon' marry Salone. "Why?"

He smirked like it was the dumbest question he'd ever heard. " 'Cause I love 'er. We need to take this step to make everything right, to wash all these haters away." He rubbed one hand over the other. "I'ma tell Luvly—"

"Tell me what?" Luvly asked, walking out of the VIP room wearing happiness on her face like I hadn't seen in a long time.

"That I love you." He grabbed her and gave her a hug, putting his hand up to his lips signaling not to say anything about what we were really talking about.

I couldn't look her in the eyes, she would know everything.

Brandie came upstairs and fell into my arms. "Hi, Chinoe."

"Hey, Babe."

"Hi, Luvly."

"Girl, you gon' have to show me some of dem moves. You look good up there."

"Thank you, but you already have a winner on

your arm; you don't have to dance sexy to get 'em."

Hugging her so tight, I couldn't let her go for fear that she would disappear again. She smelled just like she did that night in my room and felt even better.

She was actually real! "Will you marry me?"

"Yes, baby, I will." She hugged me tighter.

Even though we were playing with words, it felt real. "You know I'm not letting you go, right?"

"Please don't; I like being in your arms." Her warm breath on my ear was making me ready to bust.

"I'm already hard as hell; you better get away from my ear."

She grabbed me by the hand and walked us into a private VIP room. Damn! I finally had her in my life.

Chapter Fifty

Brandie

Chinoe was finally in my hands. And he liked me.

"Did you know who I was, coming here tonight?"

"No, I just thought I was coming to the club to relax."

We hugged some more. "I have to confess, Chinoe, I knew who you were when you told me your name. I remember seeing your picture on your mother's desk, and that night at Money's house when you went downstairs, I turned on the light and saw that poster on your wall."

"Girl, you just don't know how long I've been after you, since '94."

"'94? Where did you see me in '94?"

"I seen you in the mall one day. But these little boys spilled ice cream on my shoes and their mother tried to help me clean them off. By the time I got to where I saw you, you were gone."

"For real?" I asked, lost in his lips, hanging on to his every word. This was like a dream come true.

We just sat looking at each other, appreciating the connection between a man and a woman.

"Chinoe, you are very special to me. I've been thinking about you since that night at Money's house. It was the best experience I've ever had."

"Sex?"

"Noooooo. Experience—I mean the way we connected from the soul; I've never felt that way before. Even with long-term relationships I've not felt that way." I wanted to jump his bones again right then but I didn't want to be too aggressive.

"I've been thinking about you, too. You just don't know how hard it's been, dealing with other females all these years, trying to compare them to a ghost, to a woman I'd never met before."

"Well, I'm here now."

I requested FORTUNATE by Maxwell. I started dancing for him. I was relaxed and in an extremely sexy mood, feeling every word of the song.

He stretched his arms around the back of the lounge chair and nodded his head to the beat, licking his lips never taking his eyes off me. For the first time out of my dancing career, I felt a little nervous. Despite the nervousness, I moved closer to his face, turning my back to him.

Licking his finger, he ran it from the middle of my back down to the dip of my hips, and then he gently sucked on my lower back, sending chills up my spine. "Shake it fo' me," he demanded.

I shook my ass slowly as I felt his face pressing hard into me. "Umm, Chinoe, don't stop." I was getting wetter than usual; the excitement of being with him had my whole body working overtime. I stopped moving and let him take over. "Chinoe, you about to make me cum!"

"Cum on," he said as I released in his mouth. "That is the best orgasm I've ever had—next to the first night we shared."

"There are many more where that came from, sexy."

As I gave him a deep kiss and hugged him tight, he asked, "That means you goin' home with me?"

"Yeah. But first I have to stop by my house to get a few things"

Jumping up and grabbing my hand, he said, "Let's go."

"I have one more set to do."

"How much do you make on stage?"

"About three hundred."

Reaching into his pocket and pulling out five hundred dollars, he said, "I gotcha." He grabbed my hand and walked towards the door.

"No, it's not that easy," I told him, pulling away. "This is my job, and I can't just walk out. I have a contract with this club."

"A'ight," he sighed. "I'll be waiting for you in the other room with my folks."

I kissed him and got back to reality.

Dear God,

I hope that this gift you have sent me is genuine and sincere. I'll hold it close to my body and breath out of my soul. Thank you Lord for all the blessings given.

Amen

Chapter Fifty-One

Chocolate

Her house was tight, black and glass on the outside, well-manicured lawn and garden. The girl had it going on.

"Look around; I'll get us something to drink." She smiled sweetly.

I grabbed her and pulled her lips close to my face. "I don't need anything . . . but you."

She wiggled loose. "I'm thirsty, and I need to replace the fluid that you sucked out of me." She twisted away.

A huge, all-cream, bearskin rug lay in the middle of the crème marble floor. Pictures lined the entire den. She could be a model instead of shaking her ass for dollars. Pictures of her with D'Angelo, DMX, Eightball & MJG, and Outkast caught my eye, but those with Sean Parter, Chico Debarge, and R. Kelly made me look twice. Where were all the female entertainers?

A metal bookcase that reached across the entire wall was filled with nothing but books. Running my hands over the books, Donald Goines, Iceberg Slim, Omar Tyree, Eric Jerome Dickey, Carl Weber, Terry McMillan, Roy Glenn, Sista Souljah—Damn! Had she read all those books, or was she just runnin' game on people to make them think she was smart?

"Hey, you, cranberry and Sprite, okay?"

"Yeah, that's cool. So, who are all these people? Not the celebrities."

"Oh, that's my brother Brandon and his girlfriend; this is my brother William and his wife Tiffany. That's my gorgeous mother; and this good-looking man is my father."

"She looks like your twin." I pointed to the picture of her mother. "And him?" I pointed this time at the dude she's straddling half naked. I knew instantly from the look on her face that she was screwing him.

"A guy I've been dating, Hunt."

I started to leave out of her house, save myself from the hurt and pain I was guaranteed. I wanted her to myself, but I had to face the fact she had a life before me.

"Umm. Y'all serious?"

"No." She looked unsure. Her answer didn't sit well with me.

I walked up close to her. With her shoes off, she was rather short, but still in kissing reach. "No need to worry about another man; you mine now."

She reached up and looked me in the eyes. "Yes, I am yours."

"Do you want to look around?"

"Yeah." Anything but standing there looking at these niggas smiling wit' they arms around her hips, waist, and ass.

"You have a nice house. Platinum Kat payin' you like that?"

She leaned back onto the wall. "Does that bother you?"

"You dancin'? Yeah, but that was your means before me, so I can't be mad at that." I pulled her close to me. "But I'm sure I'll make you so happy and take care of you so good you'll leave on your own."

We moved on to her bedroom, a place I wanted to stay in with her forever. The silver, king-size canopy bed, accentuated with lavender and silver throw pillows, looked like a bed for a flaming sissy. But as long as I've waited for Brandie, I'd be a sissy. And the whole ceiling was made of glass, off the chain.

"It's beautiful, isn't it?" She asked following my eyes across the ceiling.

"Do you open it?"

"Sometimes, at night when it's clear."

"Come here." She walked over to me with a little hesitation.

"What's wrong, beautiful?" I asked, pinching her chin.

"It's just that I've been waiting for you so long, but I don't think that you're ready for me."

"I am, Brandie," I insisted, grabbing her face with both hands. "I asked God to send you to me. The first time I saw you in the mall, I didn't know your name, how you felt, or that you were a dancer. I don't care if you were a bum or a prostitute, no hair on your head or soles on your feet; I want to be with you and only you. So stop worrying."

She looked at me, speechless. "Oh, you are too good to be true. Okay, but just tell me that you won't try to make me change my lifestyle."

Without saying a word, I pulled her on top of me and made love to her with the lights on.

Chapter Fifty-Two

Chocolate

The crowd was crunk, but our clique, sitting on the third row—my mom, dad, Joi, Trinket, Trey, Sap, Luvly, Money, me, and Brandie was more hyped. It was the second-to-last championship game between the Hawks and Sixers, Hawks trailing 47-50.

Taeko had been crossin' 'em up, puttin' that thang on 'em but seemed sluggish and tired. Probably stayed out all night wit' some chickenhead.

"Give dat nigga a facial, Shawty! Take us over the top before half time," I screamed.

Iverson ran the ball but missed the shot. Tae got the ball and started bullshitting.

"Break dat nigga ankles, Tae!" Money yelled, getting overexcited.

"Go, Daddy, go."

"Go, Uncle Tae."

The kids jumped out of their seats, screaming with us.

Buzzzzzzzzzzzzzzzzzzzzzzzzzzzz! *Half-time.*

"Y'all want something from the concession stand?" I asked.

"I don't know why y'all insist that we sit down here instead of at the top, anyway. We could be getting first-class service," Luvly complained.

"Man, stop bein' so damn spoiled. Whatchu want?" Money snapped.

"Daddy, I want some chips and cheese." Sap told Money.

"Me too, Uncle Money," Trinket added.

After taking an order for a million things, me and Money headed to the concession stand by the entrance for family of players.

"I'ma marry Brandie. She the one, Dawg."

"I know, nigga. She all you talked our heads off about. You betta marry her . . . and stay married. We gettin' older. Too much shit goin' on in this world to not have someone that is genuine and true that you really love to be by your side."

We heard commotion as we walked past the entrance. "Ma'am, you have to calm down."

"I will not calm down. I wanna see him right now! It's half time, so I know that he can bring his triflin' ass out here to see me!"

"It doesn't work like that ma'am. Please lower your voice." The officer pleaded.

Pushing the officer, "Let me in, goddammit!" the young woman screamed.

"If you don't calm down, you are going to jail."

"Groupies never learn, that's why I don't fuck wit' nobody but ol' souls. These new girls get too crazy," Money assured me.

"That's why I'm getting married," I agreed.

We could see a woman with streaked hair jumping up and down. "Look, I'm pregnant and I need to see him . . . or I'm going outside to the media and let them tell 'im."

"Damn, some nigga gon' get his shit blown out the water," I said, glad it wasn't me or my boys.

The officer looked concerned but probably more about the player's reputation than the woman's condition.

He announced into his mic, "Hey, Neal, you need to get Taeko out here or tell him to give Miss—what's your name?"

"Taeko's baby mama!"

"Look now, I'm trying to help you out. Chill out and tell me your name."

We stopped in our tracks. "Ahh, hell, naw. Money, what dis fool done went and done?"

The girl came in full view. Money looked as if he'd seen a ghost. "Man, I can't believe Taeko fucked that little girl."

"My name is Morgan. Morgan Fresh," she said, sucking her teeth and popping her lips.

"Who is that?" I asked, not recognizing her face.

"I hope legal now." Money headed over to the officer. He read the badge. "I got this, Officer Sol."

"Money Loane, how you doin'? Do you know this young lady?"

"Yes." The young cutie looked at Money like he'd saved her from a burning building. "She cool. She wit' me. Come on, Morgan."

She stuck her tongue out at the officer, "I tried to tell this toy cop—"

"Shhhh, let's go, come on."

"Thank you, Money. I've been trying to call him and talk to him, but he won't return my calls."

As they get closer to me I recognized the young face. She was one of the girls from the center. *I'ma kick his ass myself.*

She used to wear one long ponytail and was a little tomboyish, but was well-endowed for someone so young.

All of us were assigned families to see about. The Fresh family was assigned to Money, but Taeko took over one day when Sap got sick.

She looked down at the ground. "What's goin' on, Morgan? Why you get caught up like this? How you gon' take care of a baby when you and your family can't take care of yourself?"

She got defensive. "How you think we gon' take care of it?"

Money had anger and sympathy on his face. "This nigga is really fuckin' up. She only sixteen."

"Yep," she smiled, "a rich sixteen-year-old. Now, where that nigga at?"

I could see Taeko had been taking good care of her. The big diamonds in her ears and around her wrist explained a lot . . . but the rowdy attitude, Gucci backpack, and tennis shoes told the whole, young story. As we walked back to the dressing room she told us how it started.

"I just want to say thank you to y'all for everything that y'all have done for my family. Money, when you stop sponsoring us that's when it started. He came to the house and gave my mom our monthly check and food. 'Anything else you need, Mrs. Fresh, here's my number,' he said, staring at me the whole time. 'Call me.'

I took the card out of the drawer and put it in my purse. A week later I was stranded at school and needed a way home. I called Taeko. He picked me up in a big-boy Lexus, with the biggest rims I've ever seen.

"Thanks for picking me up. I had no other choice, but to call you."

"That's why you have my number."

"On the way to my house, can we swing by the mall?"

"Yeah."

"One store that we went into . . . I tried on sexy dresses for him. He told me that he would buy me some extra things if I didn't tell my mother or other people at the center. I have to admit I knew what I was doing. He's a star and I wanted to be a star or at least with one."

"Why didn't you call me, Morgan, and tell me he was pushing up on you?"

"I started this thing," she said apologetically; "I just didn't know it would go this far. When he dropped me off with over eight hundred dollars worth of stuff, I leaned over and kissed him before he had time to think about it. The next week I did it again, but this time I was dressed to impress with a new haircut and makeup.

"From then on, we did everything together. He told me about how his wife be trippin' on him and don't be givin' him none, so I saw my opening and stepped in. He flew me to L.A., New York, Houston, to go shopping.

"Then my body started actin' crazy. I thought it was because of my birth control pills, but I found out I was pregnant last month. I tried calling

Taeko. He said I was starting to act crazy and possessive and hung up on me before I had a chance to tell him."

"How far are you?"

"Four months."

My eyes landed on her flat stomach.

"Are you sure Taeko the father?" Money asked, reading my mind.

"Money, I was a virgin; he is the only daddy." Her soft, hazel eyes welled with tears.

Money went to get Taeko.

She started crying harder. "I'm sorry, I'm so sorry."

"Come here." I pulled her into my arms and comforted her. "Everybody makes mistakes. Even the greatest chef in the world burns food."

She wiped her face. "Thank you, Chocolate. That is what they call you at the center, right? I just don't understand why he been treatin' me like this lately. I haven't even told him I was pregnant."

"Every man has a conscience. And every once in a while they wake up and start to use it."

Taeko and Money walked through the double doors. Taeko was talking and smiling until he made eye contact with Morgan. "What she doin' here?" Sweat instantly formed on his forehead. "Whatchu doin' here?"

"Why haven't you called me back, Taeko?" Morgan said, looking hurt and confused.

"I gave your moms all the stuff y'all needed for the month."

I couldn't believe this nigga was gon' act like he hadn't been wit' this girl.

Squinting her eyes in disbelief, she yelled, "My

mama? I'm talkin' 'bout us—me and you." She pointed her finger at him then to herself.

"Man, she trippin'. You know how young girls act when you show them a little attention."

Smack! She slapped the shit out of Tae. "Attention? Fuckin' is not attention. Fuck you!" She spit at his face, missing she started swinging wildly. "Fuck you, bitch! You gon' take care of this baby."

Money grabbed her loosely by the waist, dragging her back to the exit.

"Baby?" Taeko acted surprised.

"Yeah, baby twice over; she only sixteen, Tae. You betta hope she fucked somebody else or she lyin' . . . or you up shit creek. You can kiss yo' family goodbye, as well as yo' career."

I walked away disgusted, leaving him looking dumbfounded. Why do million-dollar niggas purposely mess they life up?

Money met me at the concession stand. "If Joi didn't leave him before, she is definitely gone now if she find out."

"You think she tellin' the truth?"

"I don't know. When I sponsored them she tried to tell me she was eighteen, but of course, I had all their information. I ain't gon' lie, another time, career, and situation . . . I probably would'a hollered at her—look at her. But we got to do some interrogating with her mother and brothers to see if there are any other boys she been seein'. I'ma get her to the doctor to see if she really pregnant."

"I'm so tired of babysitting that nigga."

"She already has a soccer scholarship waiting for her," Money disappointingly told me.

"And she can't go pregnant or with a baby."

"Nope. When I mentioned abortion to her, she got uneasy. I know what she thinkin' about, though—taking care of her six brothers and crack-head mother."

Money gave Morgan his number and told her all of us would figure out what to do.

We got the food and returned to our seats as if nothing happened. Naturally, Luvly and Brandie were looking at us out the corner of their eyes.

Chapter Fifty-Three

Brandie

Sade sung loudly about her man's love being king as a dozen lavender and cinnamon candles burned strong and bright.

Ding, Dong. Ding, Dong

"No, no, no. I want to rest, with no company." I've been under Chinoe's arms every momemt since the day we laid eyes on each other at the club, and now he's in Cali for a shoot. True enough, I would be with him if I didn't have a test, but I'm thankful for this break.

Now who could this be at my front door?

I opened the door without looking to see who it is. "Why haven't I seen that beautiful, sweet face and sexy body of yours in months?"

"Sean . . . I've been busy with school. You know that."

"You've been in school since I met you, and it's never been a problem before."

"But I'm about to graduate soon, and there's a lot that goes along with that." He gently pushed me by the stomach away from the door, walking into the house, without an invitation. "And I thought you were on tour?"

He closed and locked door. "Yeah, I am, but I had to come home to see if my baby girl was all right." He exhaled loudly. "So whatchu been doin', Brandie?" He greeted me with a harsh tone.

I stopped in my tracks, noticing him holding something behind his back. "Excuse me?"

"Just because I'm traveling all over the world . . . I still have a phone."

"I've called Sean. Your assistant must be jealous or something 'cause I leave messages."

"No hug or kiss, Brandie?" Something in the way he said my name let me know that being far away as possible from him is the safest route.

"I've been working out; I'm all sweaty," I tried to convince him, pulling my short robe tighter.

We walked over the bridge down into the den he stopped at all the pictures. He picked up the picture of him and me that had been laid on its face.

Damn! I forgot to put that back up after Chinoe put it down, but I hadn't been home. I seen his eyes focus on the pictures of Chinoe and me.

"Um, um, um, you are so goddamn beautiful, girl." He placed the magazine that was behind his back next to the picture of Chinoe and me. My heart started pumping double time. I took a closer look and it was a picture from the lake. *Where did that come from?*

"There's more inside all about how you and Chinoe are the hottest new couple." He wiped his hand slowly over the long table, knocking all the pictures down one by one. "I thought I had found someone special when I saw you; I had to have you, no matter the cost. Do you think I'm one of these little, fly-by-night rappers—a nobody?" He screamed, "Shit! I am the greatest; I am the smell on the shit." Walking up closer to me, I could smell his cologne, what he ate for breakfast, and the anger that lingered on his words. "The question is, who the fuck do you think you are?" he asked, pointing his index finger in my forehead.

For someone that prided herself on never getting caught off guard, always being on time with a response, I was speechless.

His fists were tight and his arms jerked with every word he spoke, "Tell me, Brandie, I give you everything short of the blood running through my veins, and you repay me like this?"

He was right. I had him believing that we were an item. "I don't know . . . what do you want me to say?"

"You betta tell a nigga somethin'."

Getting full of myself, I reminded him, "Look, everything that you've given me is in my name, so what?"

Running his finger up my thigh, between my legs, he said, "Oh, I know this still got my name on it."

I pushed his hand away, looking at his mean expression, one that I'd never seen before. It seemed like eternity for us staring each other down, then the battle begin. He snatched my robe from my body, leaving me naked, and I tried to run to the back door. But Sean tackled me, and we landed on the kitchen floor.

His strong body locked me down at the waist. "Please, Sean, don't do this."

While pinning my head to the cold floor, he rammed his dick into me hard and dry. "Noooo-ooooooo!" My screams were buried with each thrust he shoved into me, tearing my vagina. "I'm sorry, Sean . . . please, stop," I screamed, crying hysterically.

With no words, he continued to violate my body while Sade's sexy melodies continued to play, like we were lovers playing a game of rough sex. My every thought was why is this happening to me? Maybe because I caught an attitude with the sales-girl at Wild Pair, cussed her out, threw a drink on her, and got her fired. What about last year when I wouldn't sleep with a married police officer, but let him eat my pussy, pay a couple of bills, and keep my reckless driving record clean? Or was it about that tootsie-roll and fat pencil with the big eraser that I stole from the corner when I was nine. Naw, naw, naw, I know the answer, being self-ish, a brat, not caring about nobody but my greedy self.

Ding, Dong. Ding, Dong.

"Girl, Whatchu doin'? Open up!" Caymin screamed through the intercom.

Sean released inside of me. "Goddamn, this pussy is so . . . ummmm. You still got it," he said and slapped my ass. "Too bad I couldn't taste dat thang."

I scrambled away from him grabbing my robe and some paper towels, wetting them, wiping my-self off. "Get out!" I screamed.

"Nooo, baby, I'm here for the weekend. Invite your friend in," he said as he buckled up his pants.

Ding, Dong.

"Brandie, girl, what are you doing? Open up."

"Sean, fuck you! It's over." I ran to the door.

"What's up, honey? I thought I was gon' have to call the fire department."

"Naw I was working out in the basement and I couldn't hear you."

Caymin's eyes looked past me, taking in a full view of Sean.

He walked up behind me, kissing me on the neck, "What's up? And your name is?" Extending his hand.

"Caymin." She looked at me with question in her face.

"Sean was just leaving. Thanks for everything." I excused him without looking in his eyes.

He laughed. "I'll see you later, baby girl."

"Never will be too soon." I said under my breath.

"That was Sean Parter, the rapper?" She asked, smiling from ear to ear.

"Yep." I said not interested in explaining how I knew him or anything about him. "So tell me about your cruise?" I asked trying to get her mind off of Sean.

"Wonderful, girl we went to the Bahamas." I looked interested, but my mind was on what had just taken place.

Lord, have mercy on me.

Chapter Fifty-Four

Chocolate

Ding, Dong. Ding, Dong.

"Hold yo' damn horses; I'm comin'," Miss Fresh hollered through the door. She cracked the door and buttoning her robe. "Oh, oh, come on in, Money and—?"

"Chinoe."

Smoothing her wild, uncombed hair with her hand, she said, "That's right. How y'all?"

"Good. Good."

"Thanks for all y'all have been doing for us and for getting me in this program," a thin Miss Fresh said, lighting a cigarette.

Morgan, a sixteen-year-old-used-to-be-virgin-before-Taeko, walked slowly down the stairs looking heartbroken and took a seat on the couch across from her mother.

"Miss Fresh," Money cleared his throat, "Morgan went to the clinic today, and she's four months pregnant."

Miss Fresh looked at Morgan. "Mo, why you didn't tell me?"

Morgan fiddled with her fingers, looking like the true little girl she was.

"Tell me, Mo. How we gon' take care of a baby when we got all these babies in here now?" She started scratching profusely.

"It's Taeko's, Mama," Morgan shouted wide-eyed, as if they'd won the lottery.

"What?" Miss Fresh still scratching looked confused and not nearly as excited as Morgan anticipated. She looked back at us. "Basketball player?"

I two-wayed him and told him to come in the house.

His six-eight, dark frame, sporting braids, expensive clothes, and twenty-karat earrings looked like a million dollars, and felt like shit.

Taeko walked in slow and cautious, standing at the door speechless.

"Why my baby, Taeko? She only sixteen, the one that was gon' make something out of her life. Your money don't mean shit to me . . . when you come in here taking advantage of my child. She has three meetings over the next six months with them scholarship people. How she gon' talk 'bout playin' soccer wit' a potbelly? Whatchu gon' do, Mo? Let all that go to waste over a man who probably don't want chu, anyway? Ain't chu married wit' two babies of yo' own?"

"Yes, ma'am."

"Don't ma'am me. What? Yo' life jus' s'pose to go on and hers stop for a damn baby and a couple of dollars." Then she turned toward Morgan. "Is that whatchu want, Mo? Money? Ain't they gave enough?"

"If it's mine," said Takeo, "I gone to take care of it, but I'm going to sign my parental rights over."

My hand was itching to slap this muthafucka, right then and there, for old and new.

Miss Fresh placed her hands on her hips. "Oh, you think that's gon' make the problem go away? She stuck with takin' care of it while you play ball and travel the world with yo' family? Livin' the good life?" she said sarcastically, beginning to scratch again. " Naw, yo' wife gon' know 'bout dis."

Money tried to reason with her. "Miss Fresh, I promise you, Taeko will be dealt with, but let's not get innocent people involved. We just need to calm down and figure this thang out."

"I want five thousand dollars a month until this thang is over."

"Hell, naw, I ain't payin' this crackhead ho no five thousand dollars a month!"

"You gon' pay worse than that in hell!" Miss Fresh jumped up and ran toward Taeko, but I grabbed her, taking her into the kitchen of her new house, that Money had just bought five months ago.

Morgan was still sitting in the same spot. "Taeko, I love you. I want to be with you."

For the first time in a long time he put someone else first besides himself. He pulled Morgan to her feet and hugged her.

They both sat down on the sofa. "Morgan, you are a special to me, but I can't be with you. I don't love you, but I like you a lot," he said, sounding like a grade school boy. "You are too young right now. I got caught up, but you have to go on with your life. I'm really fucked up right now. I don't know what's good for me, let alone someone else. I don't even take time up with my kids for runnin' the streets. I'm sorry, but this is it."

"See, what I tell ya! He don't want chu—none of 'em do. Done got yo' li'l pussy and gone," Miss Fresh said, rolling her neck, as I blocked her from going into the den.

"I'm getting an abortion," Morgan said with sadness, her head held down. "I want to go to school and play soccer." She swiftly turned to Money. "Money, please tell me this won't stop you from sponsoring us; we need it to survive. Don't put us back on the street."

Such a young, vibrant, beautiful young lady, with so much potential. Attention from a baller, older man, money, designer clothes and now a baby, a meal ticket for the rest of her life. Could anyone blame the impressionable young girl?

She hugged Money and Taeko.

We left the house in silence and got in the truck. Then all hell broke loose. "Muthafucka, I should take yo' ass out to a field, twist two wire hangers together, and whoop yo' ass like a slave." Waving my gun around in my right hand, "That young girl ain't got a daddy, but I'll take his place."

"Chocolate, I'm tired of this shit. Who the fuck you think you are? You done got a little pussy and think you the shit! Nigga, you still ain't shit!"

I stomped on the brakes in the middle of the street, grabbed my gun from my waistband, jumped out of the truck, and opened his door. "Get cho muthafuckin' ass out." I said calmly.

"Chocolate, throw me the gun," Money said, noticing my nasty attitude.

"Taeko will die tonight if he fucks with me." He

towered my six-foot frame, but I didn't give a fuck. "Talk that shit now, nigga."

"Look, take me to my shit so I can ride out."

I cocked the gun. "The only way you gettin' to yo' shit is if you whup my ass and take my keys."

Money was laughing in the truck, thinking I was just fuckin' wit' him, but I was dead serious.

The first punch came fast and stiff, knocking me to the ground; my gun fell to my feet. "Now, take me to my shit!"

Before he turned around I was on my feet and into his stomach, hitting his back into the open truck door. His arm flew between the door, so I slammed it on his arm.

"CHOCOLATE!" Money screamed, running around to the side of the truck we were on. "What the fuck you doin'?" He opened the door.

"Teach him to stop touchin' shit all the time. I know you fucked Haven. She told me 'bout that shit once she knew I wasn't gon' let her back in. That slimy bitch thought that shit was hurting me. I'm glad I ain't fuck 'er stanking-ass pussy—especially after yo' slimy ass. You act like a jealous bitch, always eatin' somebody else leftovers, but I got something fo' that ass if you ever try Brandie." I grabbed my gun and pointed it to his head. "Now get cho punk ass in the truck so I can take you to the hospital."

He had no breaks or fractures, just a swollen hand and a hurt heart. He got off easy, twice . . . in one night. *That nigga better pray about his life before his blessings run out.*

Chapter Fifty-Five

The Session

Luvly, Brandie & Caymin

"Robert got you sittin phat," Luvly told Caymin, as her and Brandie dragged bags of clothing into the house.

"I told her this Condo is tight," Brandie said, pushing Caymin playfully.

The marble floors in the foyer led into a round sunken den. Layered with fur rugs, and throw blankets—brown and crème. The Isley brothers serenaded us as we walked through.

"Ya'll the one with mansions laid. Come on in. I made some tea lemonade anddddd," waving a bottle of green liquid, "apple martinis."

"Where is the wine?" Brandie asked.

Smiling, Caymin went behind the bar. "I'm not gone play dress up, hostess and be a bartender. Here is everything you could possibly want."

Luvly and Brandie filled up two glasses a piece,

one of the pre mixed apple martinis and the other with wine.

"I don't drink, but I've been needing and wanting one of these." Brandie said as she took a big gulp of her drink.

"Where is Sap?" Caymin asked, getting comfortable on the sofa.

"With Joi," Luvly answered through sips of the tart, but strong drink.

"I can't get over how everything has changed with you and Joi becoming close."

"Not close, cordial, for the kids. Our daughters are the same age, you know, like sisters."

Brandie was all ears, already finishing one of her glasses.

"Before we get started selecting outfits for the LADY OF SOUL and VMA'S, can we talk about Money's party. The most important thang, who not to invite," Luvly demanded, watching Brandie gulp down her other glass.

"Not need to invite?" Brandie inquired in a tipsy voice.

"Girl, you took that straight to the head." Luvly and Caymin slapped hands, acknowledging Brandie's quick drink. "I don't want all of Money's old flames and my enemies at the party. This is a start of a new year and his birthday. We have enough months to weed out all the bad apples."

Brandie jumped up. "I got to go to the bathroom."

"You can't drink girl."

"That's what I was gone ask you Luvly. Salone and Joi are stuck together by the hip. How do you trust her to be around Sap?"

"She ain't crazy. Joi love Sap like her own, and if

all else fail, Chinoe and Money will get in Salone's ass about her. About seven months ago I had to beat her ass at Spondivits."

"Whaddd?"

"She came in there drunk while we were eating. Popping off at the lips, saying shit about my baby being a bastard. I stabbed dat bitch wit' a fork 'cause she hit me in the face with a beer pitcher."

"Whadddddd?" Caymin screamed with excitement. "She is so stupid for playing second all these years."

Brandie walked in the room like she was walking on the catwalk—dead gorgeous. "Not as stupid as I was for being the last on Diamonds list." Luvly downed her second Appletini. "I was just dumb." She said bothered by the whole thought of Diamond. "I really was stupid for him." Admiring Brandie's crème leather pants and halter top, "Girl that is the shit. You gone turn more heads than your super model boyfriend." Luvly quickly started on a third drink, with Diamond on her brain.

"Ok, my turn. Since I'm only going to the Lady of Soul awards this should be simple." Caymin stretched her long legs before going to try on her dress.

"Diamond?" Brandie snapped her fingers, trying to remember, "He Puerto Rican, Cuban or something ain't he? All I know is he fine as hell.

Luvly, very intoxicated, smacked her lips. "He was once Sap's father."

Brandie spit some of her third drink out, "I thought . . ."

"Yeah, she is Money's, but . . . it's a long story that I don't want to tell right now, I'm feeling too good."

"He be at the club a lot. Handing out a lot of cheese. Every girl, including bartenders and waitresses be tryin' to get wit' him. But I don't date men from the club. I only see them as a pay check."

"Thank God for small blessings. You've saved yourself dignity, a broken heart and your pretty face."

"Well, I got to give it to you. Diamond is fine as wine. I can see why you so crazy about him."

"Crazy over who?" Caymin asked, entering the room like a goddess, in a pink sheer, one shoulder dress.

"Diamond." Brandie looked up, giving her full attention to Caymin's dress. "That's cute. It'll definitely work."

Caymin modeled the dress like one of the PRICE IS RIGHT beauties.

"Heartbreaker," Luvly said to Brandie.

"We gon' be the smell on the shit." Brandie snapped her fingers.

"Forget the fire, we gone be the bomb." They both laughed.

Luvly held onto the sofa, cramping up on the floor, with tears running down her face.

"We gone out do Mariah Carey, Mary J and . . . Luvly, girl, what's wrong?" Brandie jumped to her knees.

Caymin kneeled down, touching Luvly's shoulder. "You all right?"

Luvly held onto her stomach, unable to speak. Only to think about the day Diamond truly broke her down.

Sap was two years old, participating in a Georgia Baby Misses contest. Two days before the contest

Luvly took Sap to the mall to pick up her costumes. To get to the store, they had to past Micks.

" 'mell good, Mommie."

"Yes it does, baby."

As Luvly looked through the window to admire the happy families eating together, her heart almost stopped, mid-beat. Her eyes watered without a blink. Her hand was tight in a fist.

With her feet moving, Luvly followed her stare, leading her to a table with a mother, a father, a little boy and a new born baby, both children favoring their father.

"You ain't shit! You knew I was coming up here to pick up Sap's stuff today. You can't even give me that much respect!" Luvly knew what was going on with Diamond and other women, but she never had to deal with it face to face.

"Take yo' ass outside. In here causing a scene." Diamond waved his fork at Luvly, dismissing her like a child.

There was only one young, white couple in earshot. They kept their eyes glued to their own table.

"You can take this mudhole bitch and her nappy headed puppy out to—"

Jordan jumped up out of her seat, "Hold on bitch—"

"Sit cho punk ass down," Diamond directed Jordan. "If ya'll don't shut the fuck up, I'm gone fuck both of ya'll up." Jordan sat back down in her seat, defeated once again.

Once the threats started coming, the white couple grabbed their things and left.

"Muthafucka, that's why I don't wonna be wit' cho trifling ass." She threw her six-karat, white gold, broken promise, ring into Jordan's plate.

Diamond laughed at her like she was a little child putting on a talent show. "Luvly, if you don't . . ."

"Whatchu scared of, Diamond? That another man will do a better job at taking care of what you obviously can't?" She patted her stomach, letting Jordan know that she was pregnant.

Slap! Smack! He knocked her to the floor with all his might. Showing her and anyone else that was looking that she didn't mean shit to him. Sap stood motionless, watching her mother get beat to a pulp.

"Jordan, get Sap and take her to the house!" he screamed.

"Nooo!" Luvly screamed from her bloody mouth. She scrambled hard to get to her knees, but Diamond punched her in the face. "Don't touch my baby!" As Luvly tried again to get to Sap, Diamond grabbed her by the shirt, jean jacket, and hair, all in one try. Dragging her off to the bathroom. *Why did he take my baby? Somebody go get my baby from these monsters! Please help me; he's going to kill me!*

The manager was glad that they had taken it to the bathroom, out of the sight of patrons enjoying their dinner. He didn't want to call the police and disturb his restaurant. He'd only been on the job two weeks and wasn't going to jeopardize losing his position because of some ghetto shit.

Diamond slung Luvly into the bathroom like a rag doll.

"What the fuck is wrong wit' chu?"

Luvly sat back on the wall with tears pouring from her eyes, "Please get my baby back. Go get Sap."

"Why do you make me fuck you up?"

She sat quiet, starring into nowhere.

"Answer me, bitch." He stomped his foot into her chest.

Between breaths, "Why . . . do you . . . treat me . . . like this?"

He released his foot and backed away from her.

Crying, "Call Jordan and tell her to bring Sap back to me."

"Naw, I'm sending Sap to Cuba."

Covering her mouth and stomach with her hands. She thought she was dying. Her baby was going to stay with that treacherous family, making Sap hug and kiss them even when they were mean to her, beating her, starving her when she didn't obey by their rules. Telling her horrible things about her mother.

There was a long silence. He stared at her, secretly admiring her beauty and strength. "When I first met you, I knew you were too young for me. Man, I knew all along that you only wanted me because I was different from what you was use to. But I had to have you. You were a challenge for me." He was smiling now, looking as good as the day they met. "You wouldn't have sex with me no matter how much money I gave you or what I bought you. All my boys thought I was going soft. But I just wanted to make you smile. You was the only girl that ever got to me like that." He looked at Luvly, "But you had other plans all the time. You had to have Money Loan ole punk ass. Mannn, my boys that were sent to watch over you would call me and tell me when ya'll was fucking and you sucking his dick. I loved you so much that I let all that shit go.

Until the day I found ya'll violating our bed." He punched the paper towel holder. "I'll never let you go to him. I'll kill you first."

"I asked you to let me go, Diamond. But you wouldn't."

"I couldn't. I want you for always. Even if that meant you suffer to your death. Now get up and take your clothes off."

"What?"

"I ain't gone ask you no more. Take 'em off. I need time to get Sap to the plane without you making trouble."

Her tears came back forcefully. "Please, please—give me, oooh, baby I swear I'll be good." She grabbed onto his leg, trying to gain strength.

"If you fight me I'll beat cho ass unconscious."

"You can do anything to me, I swear—"

"Whooping yo' ass ain't gone solve nothing no more, so I'm hurting you the sure fire way I know how."

He had finally gotten to her. At this time, Money had promised to stay out of her life and Chocolate was out of town for a month. She was on her own now. Lost. Hurt. Angry.

She removed her clothes and Diamond made her have sex, right there on the nasty, cold, bathroom floor. She could feel her body rejecting her pregnancy. The cramps were horrible, but she dare not reject Diamond or she would lose her life as well.

Bam! Bam! Bam! "This is the manager, I need you to come out, or I'm going to have to call the police."

"I'll take her where you'll never see her again." Diamond threatened Luvly, looking deep into her eyes.

"Yes, sir, I'm fine. I'm pregnant and having complications."

"I'll go get help." The manager went to get help.

Diamond left Luvly on the cold, nasty floor, naked, and raped of more than just her clothes and sex—dignity, control of her life, pride and most of all her child.

What was she going to tell the police? Her mind was steadily racing, trying to figure out how she was going to cover up the mess that Diamond had once again stirred up.

"Talk to me, Luvly. Can you breathe?" Brandie asked, getting a queasy stomach herself.

Luvly exhaled and layed her head back onto the sofa, and spoke with a soft, wet voice, "This alcohol was the wrong thing for me."

"You scared the shit out of me." Caymin held her hand over her chest."

"Talking about Diamond got me upset, I'm sorry I scared ya'll. But I just hate that dirty muthafucka." She wiped her tears away, wishing she could wipe away the memories. "Well, it's my turn." Luvly grabbed her bag and went into the bathroom.

"I'm glad I didn't experience all the bad stuff Luvly did with Diamond, having dated some bad boys myself," said Brandie.

Caymin remembered the day she was at Brandie's house, the look on her face and the guy Sean, was that Caymin had walked in on something that was suppose to be secret.

"Have you talked to Sean lately?" Caymin asked.

Almost choking on her drink, Brandie responded, "Naw."

"I don't know why you still messing around wit' anybody. Chinoe gives you everything and more."

Brandie clenched her teeth and stared at Caymin through mean eyes.

"Chinoe is the only man I need and want. And you right, he'll take care of everything I need," she said in a smart tone. "I just hope Sean, stays the hell away from me." She added in a serious tone.

Luvly walked back in with a two-piece black flower printed skirt and half top set on. "Well, we do need some fine men. I got some single cousins visiting from Italy," I added.

They both stopped mid discussion. "Where you get that from? That is so fire."

"You like? I guess from ya'll tongues hanging out, this is VMA all the way."

"I wonder if I should keep my outfit on and call Dun over here after ya'll leave." Caymin smiled.

"Dun?" Luvly questioned.

"She done had her eye on Dun for some time now. He go to school wit' us. When ya'll start talking?" Brandie inquired, glad to get the subject on someone else.

"About two weeks ago."

"Ahh, you really got your eye on this Dun, Caymin. I know that look, that's how you use to look when you were with Chocolate."

Silence tightened their lips. Luvly being sorry that she'd drank too much, thought she should have kept her mouth shut. Brandie looked stunned. And Caymin looked wild-eyed, because she probably hadn't told Brandie that they used to be together in a real relationship.

Brandie said it real slow. "My Chocolate?" Putting her hand over her heart?"

"It was years before ya'll," Luvly said, trying to compensate for opening up the can of worms in the first place.

"I'm talking to Caymin," Brandie snapped.

"Excuse the fuck outta me," Luvly snapped back.

"We use to be together in high school."

"Ya'll fuck?"

"Nooo, he's, or was a virgin," Caymin said with regret in her voice.

"Oh. Well, that's cool. Ya'll were kids. No hard feelings." Brandie hugged Caymin. But I could see the hurt in Caymin's eyes. She still loved him, and wanted to be with him.

Trying to break the monotony, Luvly said, "Well, what about this Dun, Caymin? You stepping out on Rob?"

"Robert all right, but I never committed to him. So I'm single to mingle."

We laughed and slapped hands.

"Dun look like he can eat some good coochie? Big pretty lips." Brandie said through a huge smile.

"Just make sure he brush his teeth first. I went to the OB-GYN last week. She said that a nasty tongue could give you bacteria."

"Can I ask you something, Luvly? Something I've been dying to know?"

"Yeah, Caymin."

"Who's better, Money or Diamond?"

Luvly gave her a crazy look. "I don't tell." Smiling, "They about the same in bed, Money got 'em by a little bit. But out of bed Diamond is no competition."

Ring . . . Ring. "Hello. Ok, I'm on my way. Brandie,

are you sober enough to drive me down the street to the shop?"

"I'm cool now, I done pissed most of it out."

"Okay. Caymin check on the decorations and half of the crowd. I'll call you."

"Bye, ya'll"

In unison, we said, "Bye."

If what Luvly saw in Caymin's eyes was true, then Brandie better watch out cause the desire Caymin had for Chocolate was serious.

Chapter Fifty-Six

Chocolate

"You nervous, baby?" I asked Brandie, looking all sweet in her brown, burnt orange, and tan stripe Gucci dress that crossed in the front, and hung down over the hips with slits up to her hips on both sides, and burnt orange strap sandals up to her knees.

"Yes. It's just that so many people are here that weren't at the Lady of Soul awards. When I take my position as an entertainment lawyer, I'm going to demand that my clients support all black awards shows and functions."

"That's my baby. Thinking ahead of the game. You look good too boo." We kissed.

"Ahh, nigga, quit that shit in here. If I ain't gettin none, you can't either." Money said with a long lip.

"You shouldn't have been talking about my skirt." Luvly pouted.

"What skirt? Here we go again. You know you stole that shit from Sap closet."

"Fuck you."

Luvly's black flower printed, see-through, two-piece set would have been in the garbage if Brandie had thought about wearing it. But she looked good in it, as long as she wasn't my girl.

Joi and Taeko stayed home to get some quiet time. Thank God for small blessings.

The limo pulled up to the red carpet, "Here we go, baby." Brandie looked like she was praying for something, very uncomfortable.

The paparazzi, media and fans were screaming, "Chocolate, we love you." "Over here, Chocolate." "Smile that million dollar smile right here."

"Damn, I know you fine, but they are going crazy over you," Brandie screamed in my ear, over everyone else.

"But I'm here with you. And I have the million-dollar smile, so they say and pay." Damn, I'm glad Chaise had a shoot to do in Milan. She'd been right up in my face acting crazy.

After doing countless interviews and answering who Brandie was for the hundredth time, we were free to go to our seats. Leaving Money and Luvly behind to do more interviews.

Some one bumped shoulders with me. "Excuse me, brother. Sorry 'bout that. Oh, snap, what's up, Sean?" We slapped hands.

"What's up, Chocolate, right?"

"Yeah, good luck on all six nominations."

Remembering the picture on Brandie's mantel, "You know Sean, right, Brandie?"

"Hey," she said in dry tone, "I got to use the bathroom." She shot off toward someone with earphones to ask where the bathroom was.

He laughed. "Check ya later."

"Later."

Brandie returned shortly after Sean left, like she was waiting for him to leave. "Boo, you a'ight?"

"Yeah."

"I thought that was ya boy. You took a pic—"

"And that was all, a picture at the club. He was and is a nobody." She said sternly, as if she were warning me to drop his name from our vocabulary. "Come on let's go sit down. I'm just amazed at all the people I've seen on TV, and actually seeing them in person is crazy."

"Are you going to be all right when I go up to present the award?"

"Yeah, just come back to me, after being next to Vivica Fox and Lisa Raye."

The night turned out perfect. Even though I didn't get no pussy. I couldn't believe my boyz and I had actually made it—STAR status!

Chapter Fifty-Seven

Brandie

Tonight was wonderful! Being on the arm of the sexiest man at the show, and wearing the baddest Gucci dress that Chinoe had made for me was unreal. It couldn't be recreated. Women who walked the red carpet every week of their life complimented me on my dress.

But that damn Sean had to come in the picture. What was that shit he was trying to pull. He'd already done enough. Raping me in my own home wasn't enough for him. He had to rape me again, in public, in front of my man. I felt like vomiting on him, scratching his eyes out.

Someone I once thought I could be happy with violated my body and worst of all my spirit. But I wanted Chinoe to have a wonderful night, so I ran to the bathroom as fast as I could before I spat in Sean's face.

He thought I was the most precious thing in the world. How could I tell him that I had to get an abortion two weeks ago, because of what Sean did to me?

God, that was the most horrible thing I'd been through, besides what got me in that predicament. Sean was scheming on ways to bust my bubble, but I had to make the first move—sell the house, auction off the truck for the Lupus foundation and tell Chinoe the truth about everything . . . No—way.

It was going to get harder trying to avoid having sex, when I'd been his sex kitten; periods only came once a month, and yeast infections didn't last forever.

Chinoe kept talking about having a family. I didn't want kids right then. He was trying to make me into the little old lady that lived in a shoe, at twenty-two.

My baby looked so handsome in his crème Sean John suit. Fresh hair cut. Enough waves to make an ocean jealous. And a sexy goatee that would make anyone weak, especially when he licked his lips and caressed it with his fingertips. The women and press were going crazy over him, screaming, "Chocolate, Chocolate, you so fine!" "Can I be your lady?" "I love you!" "I wanna have your babies."

I was so nervous with all those cameras and mikes in my face, but Chinoe handled it with a grain of salt. He introduced me as, "Brandie, the DELITE of my life."

I was so proud of him. But the bigger question was if he knew everything about me, would he still be as proud of me???

Chapter Fifty-Eight

Brandie

The sunshine sprayed down on us brightly and selfishly, taking all of our energy for itself.

"Chinoe, this lake is so beautiful."

Rubbing his nose on mine, he murmured, "Not as beautiful as you."

"Boy, what am I going to do with you?"

"Love me, like me, stay with me."

I layed into his chest and closed my eyes. It seemed like we'd been together for an eternity even though it'd only been a few months. We knew what each other's moves were before we made them, finishing each other's sentences. I was not use to being so close to someone like that, but I was trying. It wasn't hard, just frustrating when I wanted to roam free and Chinoe wanted to be in my footsteps.

He walked me down onto the docks where there were three mid-size boats and one large boat.

"I've never been on a boat before."

"I was hoping I could be your first for something."

See that was the type of shit he said that got on my nerves, but I was in love so I over looked it.

"What do you mean?"

"This is my boat." He said with a smile on his face, pointing at the candy painted yellow boat with MYSTERY STAR, painted on the side in silver.

"For real?"

"And the white one is Money's." Sapphire graced the side of the boat in blue and silver glitter.

"That one must be Taeko's?" DREAM CHASER, in black, glided across the red boat.

"Yep, and that one is my mom and dad's."

"How sweet. It has your name on it." SWEET CHOCOLATE.

"Come on, your day of spoiling has begun."

As we got onto the boat Eric Benet's FEMININITY started playing. Three big fluffy pillows that seat two a piece had gift boxes on each of them. On the yellow pillow there were three gifts; a long rectangle box, a square flat box, and a tall octagon box.

With a big smile on my face, I said. "What is all this?"

"Wha'zzzzz up, my people?" I turned around to see Money screaming, with Luvly in his arms.

"Damn Money why you always got to be so loud?" Luvly said, as she reached for a hug from Chinoe then me. "Hey girl. Ooh them shoes are the bomb. Where you get 'em from"

"At that boutique at the mall . . . aah . . . Doll Wear."

She stared at me and then cut her eyes at Money. "Can I see how they look on my feet?"

"Luvly, cut that shit out."

"I just want to try 'em on."

Was this a joke on or something? Luvly's little bitty feet could not fit in my shoes, but I gave them to her anyway.

She slung them toward the lake, Money grabbed her arm to stop her, but Chinoe caught them just in time before they hit the water.

"What da hell? I thought we were cool?" I asked her.

"Oh, we are," snatching away from Money. "It's just where the shoes came from."

"I'll just take them down stairs and put them in the cabin. Ya'll ladies have a seat while we go get the rest of the stuff." Money and Chinoe went down to the cabin leaving Luvly and me to have some girl talk.

Peeping from the door, "Don't open those gifts, Luvly." Money winked at her, but she smacked her lips and turned her head away from him.

"Glad my outfit didn't come from Doll Wear or I'd be naked out here."

She laughed, "Sorry 'bout that. Do you know the owner?"

"Not really. I don't get involved with too many females. I've just seen her a few times."

"Salone ole slimy ass. The one I told you about."

"Oh, yeah, she the one all over the papers and magazines with him?"

"Yep and that bitch gone get what's coming to her too. If not from me, from somebody."

"Yeah, you started telling me about when you was pregnant, but you didn't get into it."

"She tried to make me lose Sapphire. She jumped on me with some of her friends. But what she didn't understand was that me and Money choose each other time and time again. We aren't going to leave each other alone—"

We heard someone step onto the boat. We both turned around and met eyes with Taeko and some unknown woman.

Luvly whispered, "Oh, my God, Taeko is really tripping. Money and Chinoe are gone flip."

"I can't believe him, especially with them all being high profile. I bet the paparazzi are giving their cameras a work out.

Taeko walked up like he didn't have a care in the world, "What's up, Luvly and Brandie."

We both said "hi" in low, hushed tones.

"Where dem boys at?"

"Down in the cabin." I answered.

"Taeko, whatchu you doing?" Luvly asked, staring dead into his eyes.

The female that was with him was displaying comfortable body language. She sat down on the last pillow available. "Hi. How ya'll doing? A sista is hungry. Working out all day," she added, smiling at Taeko, insinuating sex, "brings on a healthy appetite. Ain't you dat girl that go wit' Money Loane?"

"No dis heffa ain't in my business," Luvly said, talking to me.

"Ahhh, Luvly. This is Kenya."

"I don't want no formal introductions. Ya'll need to leave."

"Why? This is a day for all of us."

"What the fuck e'va." Luvly walked down to the cabin.

"So, Brandie," he said as he took a seat next to Kenya. "How you been doing?"

"Pretty good. Enjoying my new life," I answered feeling uncomfortable talking to Taeko. Chinoe had told me about the sixteen-year-old girl.

"Girl me too. Being with a star is the shit!" Kenya didn't notice the frustration on Taeko's face.

"Man, what's up Taeko?" Chinoe asked with an attitude.

"Doing what we planned."

"Naw, this shit wasn't planned," he said, nodding his head toward Kenya.

"Joi and Taeko is what was planned," Luvly added, folding her arms.

"Shidd, I didn't even know if it was gone be you or Salone?"

"Why you inconsiderate muthafucka. I can't believe yo' slimy ass." Luvly threw her glass of wine into Taeko's face, some splashing onto Kenya's cheap dress.

Money came up just before Luvly was about to snap, "What's going on?"

"Luvly just acting her usual self." Taeko said, wiping the wine from his eyes.

"Ummmm, and who are you?" Kenya brushed up against Money.

"Ho, if you don't get yo' muthafuckin' ass off my man—" Money swung Luvly around to the back of him. "Unuh, unuh. Let me fuck his sorry ass up, Money. And that raggedy home-wrecker—" Money covered her mouth.

"Man, you need to leave. All this drama is not what I had in mind." Chinoe said with authority.

Taeko left mad with Kenya on his heels. "Nice meeting ya'll."

"I can't believe he brought that tramp here."

"Luvly you didn't have to throw that in his face," Chinoe said with a slight smile on his face.

"What'eva. I'm tired of his shit."

Chinoe kissed me on the cheek. "You all right?"

"Yes baby."

"Well, let's get this thang started."

Chinoe started the motor and, Toni Tony Tone's "Anniversary" came on, while Money brought the lobster tails, shrimp, oysters, Spanish rice and jumbo fish platter to the middle of the pillows.

Chapter Fifty-Nine

Chocolate

I lay behind Brandie, holding her with relaxation, happiness and promise of a beautiful life, running through my veins.

After we dropped Money and Luvly off at the dock, I wanted some time to myself with her on the water. So I turned the motor off and let us float into a secluded area.

"Are you happy sexy?"

"Yes, yes. I've never imagined being this happy." She held up her wrist flashing the ten-carat diamond bracelet. "Damn, Chinoe, this is so gorgeous."

"So you like it best?"

"Noo. What really got me is the gold key you gave me to your place, heart and our life together." She looked nervous. "I didn't expect all of that. Are you sure you are ready for that or want that."

"Hell, yeah!"

Carl Thomas's "Hey Now" started to play. There were no more words to say, I wanted to make love to her, give my all to her.

I kissed her shoulder as I slid her arms out of her straps. I placed small kisses on the spine of her back until the dress laid on her hips. The intensity in our embrace was stronger than I ever thought was possible.

She stood up and let the dress fall to her feet. No panties! I kissed her polished toes that I had the pleasure of painting. Rising onto my knees, I kissed her entire leg until I got to her thighs. I got a mouth full into my lips and sucked on them both equally. She let out a sweet moan that let me know she loved it.

As I continued to suck her thighs, I gently parted them and ran my fingers slowly between them, parting her wet pussy lips. I slowly pushed one finger in and out of her making sure she was ready to receive me. "Yessss, sissss," she said sweetly.

Spreading her lips with my thumb, I pressed my entire mouth into her, sucking up all her juices. She slightly bent her knees from the overwhelming feeling. Grabbing her cheeks with my hands, pressing her harder onto my mouth.

Her whole body was shaking. "Ooh, shit . . . I can't take this."

I continued to dig my tongue deeper into her, shaking my head slowly at first, then picking up a little speed, making her drop to her knees. "You are so good to me, Chinoe."

"It gets better sexy."

She layed back with me on top of her. My lips still hungry for any part of her body. Her hard nipples were calling me to toss them between my full wet lips. My tongue took control, wanting to taste everything in sight, starting from the bottom of her navel. Holding her revolving hips tight in my hands, in one full motion, I layed a flat wet tongue at the bottom of her navel, up her stomach, to both of her breast smothering them with my mouth, up to her neck, sucking hard as I could without hurting her.

"Mmmm . . . yeah . . . sisssss. That hurts, boy," she said in a sexy voice.

"You shouldn't taste so damn good. Wit' cho sexy ass. Turn over."

As she turned over and rose up on her knees, I unbuckled my pants and proceed to enter heaven.

She was so warm, waterfall wet, but tight as a glove. I didn't want to hurt her, so I took it real slow until I was all the way in, "Damn, yo' pussy good."

"You . . . feel so good." She barely got the words out.

Just as I was getting into it, slapping her ass, making it bounce as she threw it back, a light shined in our face.

"Oh, my God, dude. We are so sorry dude."

We were caught like two deer in front of headlights. A boat with its motor not running floated over toward us, leaving us exposed in front of two white couples. Brandie didn't move, but turned her head away from the lights.

I waved my hand, letting them know it was okay.

As they left we hear them say, "Oh, my God, did you see how big his dick was?"

"Did you see her ass? Damn, baby got back. She can back that ass up any time!" The white couples discussed us as they floated away from us, their voices echoing on the water.

"Hahaha." We both laughed as Brandie fell to her stomach and I fell on top of her.

"I'm truly loving you, Chinoe."

I kissed the back of her head, "I love you, too."

Chapter Sixty

Brandie

"So what are we going to do for Thanksgiving?"

"Love on you all day and all night."

"Chinoe, for real baby."

"I wanna see yo' mama. Umm mm, she sho' is fine."

"You kill me looking at my mom. So you want her now?" I asked, playing. "Since I'm only a dime, you must want a quarter on your arm."

He looked at me with lust in his eyes. "You shouldn't have on this little white tee-shirt and no panties. It can drive a man insane." He walked up on me and rubbed my thighs.

"Chinoe, don't you want to eat, sleep, go anywhere, do anything besides screw all day?"

"Yeah.

"What?"

"Eat your sugar lips, suck on some sweet titties,

and lick you from head to toe. See that's not actually screwing."

He was driving me crazy! Everyday, all day, he wanted to be stuck up under me. I was losing my freakin' mind. It felt like Chinoe had a noose around my neck.

Ring . . . Ring. "I got it." I jumped up from his clutches.

"Hello."

"Hello."

"Hel-lo."

"Is Chinoe there?"

"Yes, he is. Hold on. Chinoe, telephone."

The voice didn't sound familiar. But the way she kept saying hello made me think I shouldn't have been answering his phone.

"I got it."

Holding the phone in my hand, I debated whether I should hang up, or listen. My ears won. Clicking the phone to make it sound like I hung up, but I held the button and let it go slow.

Damn, I had missed the beginning of the conversation!

"It's not your place to be questioning me. You told me what I needed to know."

"Well, it must be serious. You've been dodging my phone calls. What's going on? Is that the new piece of pussy in your life answering the phone?"

I wondered who this woman was, demanding to know what was going on with my man, and asking about who I was?

"Look, go on wit' cho life, Chaise. I thought we had an understanding. We were never a couple anyway."

There was a pause. I started to butt in, but he

had a life before me, so I was going to see if he knew how to handle his business.

Beep.

"Look. My phone is beeping so—"

"Whatever, Chinoe. Dog me out, I should have known—"

He tried to click her off but I was holding the phone.

". . . ass was gone fuck over me! You told her about—"

I quickly and quietly hung up the phone. I wanted to know about this Chaise person. Sounded like there were fresh feelings on her part. Which could cause a lot of trouble.

A few minutes later Chinoe walked down stairs.

"Babe, I got to go to Tahoe to do a shoot. Do you want to come?"

"No. Was that one of your agents on the phone?'

He kept looking through the refrigerator as if I hadn't asked him a question.

"Chinoe."

"Huh?"

"Who was that woman?"

"She used to assist the photographer. I'm going to pack. I need you to drop me off at the airport." He kissed me and ran up the stairs.

"Ummhm." I got something for his lying ass. I don't know why I thought he could be faithful. He knew I wouldn't go to Tahoe with him because of my class schedule.

Fuck this shit! I had his number. Cartel had been hounding my ass too. It was on now.

* * *

Ring . . . Ring . . . Ring.

"Hello."

"May I speak with Cartel?"

"Speaking."

"Hi, Cartel. How are you?"

"Fine, I know this is not Miss Delite?"

"Miss Delite is right. But I prefer Brandie."

He gave me one of those deep sexy laughs, "I been waiting to hear from you. You don't ever stay at home."

"Oh, I've been there, but I stay at my second home, the mall."

"A beautiful woman such as yourself should be spoiled."

I liked the sound of that. He was already talking my language.

"So, Miss Brandie, when can I see you again?"

"Well, I'm on my way to Cumberland Mall, maybe we can do lunch," I responded hoping he would take the hint.

"Sure. I'll be ready in about an hour and a half. See you in the food court."

"Naw, see me in Nine West."

I was riddled with guilt as I went into the mall, but Chinoe was doing it, so why couldn't I?

Walking towards the Nine West shoe store, I felt all the power I used to possess over my life seep back into my body. Cartel wasn't there yet, so I walked on in and started browsing for my invited shopping spree.

About ten minutes later I felt a pair of big strong hands on my waist, "Hey, Miss Delite—I'm sorry, Miss Brandie. See something you like?" I paused for a few seconds before turning around.

"Now I do." Parting my full lips to show all thirty twos.

After he practically bought me the mall he called the limo driver to pick up all of my bags.

"You might as well have bought me the whole mall."

"If that's what you want. Hungry?"

"Starving." I missed the cat and mouse chases. It was so exciting to be chased. It seemed like me and Chinoe skipped that part and went right to the relationship, straight to a marriage.

Cartel and I decided on MICKS.

"So, Brandie, I'm hearing around town and seeing it for that matter, that Chocolate has you wrapped around his finger. Is that why you've been so distant and hard to find?"

I wanted to lie and tell him that it was just a misunderstanding, which was partly true. "I have been seeing him, but there are no fingers wrapped." I held my hands up to show him. "I'm single. You know how the media hypes situations up. You of all people should know that."

"So that big rock on your finger means what, friendship?"

Damn I forgot about that! "Just a present."

"Umm hmmm. So when can I see your lovely face again?"

"Tonight, tomorrow, next week, you pick the day and place and I'll be there."

"What about tomorrow? I'll have everything planned out. And bring an overnight bag."

Damn. I didn't think he would mean so soon. "Deal." I smiled to let him know that all was good.

* * *

When we got to my truck he kissed me before I had time to turn away. "That's what I've been missing? Don't keep it away from me anymore, okay?"

I usually didn't like to be kissed on the lips. Chinoe was the only man that I enjoyed kissing. But Cartel's lips felt just as good and just as comfortable.

I felt so guilty, but at the same time, I was loving it.

Chapter Sixty-One

Chocolate

Damn, I didn't want to deal with Chaise. I knew I just kicked her to the curb, but I didn't make her any promises. So why did I feel so guilty?

After the long ride I just wanted to get in my room, take a hot bath and sleep.

When I reached my room, I headed straight for the Jacuzzi, putting Frankie Beverly and Maze in the CD player. I missed my babe already. I knew I'd been smothering her, but damn, I'd waited for her all my life. I hoped this time away would give her back the freedom that she loved so much.

Sitting in the Jacuzzi, thoughts of our wedding day ran through my head. Money would be standing next to me as my best man with Taeko on my other side. Sap and Trinket would be the flower girls and Trey my ring bearer.

Brandie would be beautiful in a princess dress.

I could see my mother and father now with the biggest smiles on their faces, happy to see me happy.

Knock. Knock. Knock.

"Damn. I wonder who the fuck this can be. I didn't order anything."

I jumped out of the Jacuzzi heading toward the door until I realized I didn't have on anything. "Hold on. Let me get my robe."

Before I could turn from the door, it opened. "Hold on, wait a minute."

"No need to wait. I've seen it all before."

"Damn, how you get the key to my room?"

"Our room."

"No my room."

"When I booked this room, I booked it for us. I am still your photographer."

"I almost forgot." I said in a sarcastic manner. "I need to see about getting that changed."

"I'm the best and you know it."

"I'm going to call down stairs and see if they got another room."

"They're booked." She smiled. "Check if you'd like." She held the phone up to me.

I grabbed my robe and layed across the bed, "I'll take the sofa so you can have the bed."

"Why can't we share it?" She walked up to my head with her pussy in my face.

"Because I'm with someone."

"You're always with someone. And I'm always left being the fuck-partner."

The room seemed like it was spinning. The bitch was dick whipped.

"So what is she like? Is she yellow?"

"No, hell naw. Why bother asking those types of questions?"

"I just want to know what took your concentration off me."

"She's from a long time ago. Somebody I should have been with. And I promised myself that if I had the chance to meet her I would never let her go."

"So you didn't know her, you just seen her somewhere and chased a fantasy?" She hit her forehead with the palm of her hand. "You need some serious help Chocolate. Chasing women is going to be the death of you."

"Chasing me Chaise is going to be the death of you."

Smack. She slapped the shit out of me.

My reaction took over before I could stop it. I knocked her to the floor slapping blood out of her mouth. "Here let me." I extended the same hand I'd just slapped her with, to help her off the floor.

"You've done enough," she said angrily, slapping my hand away.

"I'm sorry, it happened so fast. Let me help you up."

As I grabbed her arms she snatched away from me, "Muthafucka get your hands off of me!" She got off the floor and snatched up her stuff. Pointing her finger at me, "You sick bastard, that bitch ain't gone love you the way you love her." She laughed wickedly, "That bitch probably already fucking somebody else, just like Haven."

I jumped at her like I was going to hit her again and she ran out the door. I kicked at the air, "Son-of-a-bitch!" How dare she say something like that about my baby? Brandie was the real deal.

Chapter Sixty-Two

Brandie

Limo lights pulled into my circular driveway. Why didn't he drive? Maybe he wanted his hands free to roam around. I killed myself sometimes.

I ran to the bathroom to check myself out one last time before Cartel had a chance to feast his eyes on this delightful package.

My hair laid in a side ponytail. My ribbed long halter dress matched my olive green strappy Via Spiegel shoes that he so graciously bought me. I puckered my lips once more before I heard the doorbell ring. *One more time Cartel, I don't run for the first bell.*

Ding, Dong.

"Coming." I winked at myself and prepared to spit game until he's woozy in the head and weak in the heart.

"Damn, you look bad as a devil. And smell like an angel." We embraced.

"How do you know what an angel smells like?"

"I've smelled you inside and out at the club."

I didn't know whether to take that as a compliment or sarcasm.

"Where are we off to?"

"All I asked you to do was look sweet and let me handle the rest. So lay back and relax, it'll be about an hour and a half." I layed back in his arms and eventually fell asleep.

Two hours later, he shook me awake and there were big beautiful trees and a country dirt road. We finally pulled up to an abandoned looking building. "Are you going to kill me?"

He laughed that conniving laugh, "No thickness, I'm about to bring you alive. I've waited so long for the day to be able to have you all to myself."

He kissed my hand as the driver opened the door, "Mr. Cartel, Miss Brandie, this way."

"Thank you."

I felt like a queen. When Cartel opened the door to the building the first thing I saw was a big pink rocking chair with lots of pink and purple teddy bears. It looked like the chairs in the old barbecue places.

I'd talked to Cartel a few times before Chinoe captured me in his palace. I told him about some of the things that I liked and I guess he paid close attention.

Covering my mouth, I walked closer to make sure it was real.

"It's real sweetness, and all for you. Look over there." He pointed to a candle lit table with two big jugs, one filled with cranberry juice and the other with sprite. He walked up behind me and kissed me on my shoulder. "Is everything to your liking?"

"Yes." I turned around and met his lips with a sweet long kiss. It felt different. I guess I was so use to Chinoe that it felt funny kissing someone else. "What's wrong, Brandie?"

"I feel guilty. I mean being here with you when I know I shouldn't."

"You should be where ever your heart desires." He grabbed my hand and led me to the table. The driver turned waiter brought out shrimp, lobster, and crab legs; all my favorites.

"You remembered everything," I said blushing.

"I told you, I've been waiting for you a long time. Now that I'm in your path I want everything to run its course."

After dinner, we ran around and played like children. My mind free, my body felt serene, and Cartel was there for me.

Finally I climbed up into the chair and Cartel followed. The Isley Brothers, LET'S LAY TOGETHER, made the mood complete.

He stared at me.

"What are you staring at?"

"Just admiring how beautiful you are." He leaned over and kissed me. This time it felt right. I pushed my tongue deep down his throat. His hand rested on my thigh. I reached down and pulled it close to feel my heat.

"You feel so good." He unhooked the halter part of my dress without breaking the kiss. He kissed my forehead, then my nose, to my chin. "I want to taste every part of you."

"I'm your feast, you may begin." I said in a foreign voice.

He began with my back, licking down to my tattoo. He sucked my cheeks, licked the back of my leg down to the heel of my foot. Each one of my toes were licked and sucked dry. He made sure I was sitting tightly on the chair. I layed back on one of the pillows as he put both my feet on the arms of the chair. His lips met my hip lips. "Damn, Cartel." Panting heavy. "Umm . . . Um." We had sex all through the night into morning He released all of my frustration. I felt so relaxed, subdued.

The next day, on my way to Chinoe's house, I pulled up next to a bus, and my heart skipped a beat.

The logo on the bus was a picture of Sean and his crew, holding bottles of brandy. "That's the only Brandie he'll ever touch or taste again." Punching the gas, I ran the red light.

I felt terrible for spending the night with Cartel, but Chinoe had to be gotten back. Know telling what he's doing with that woman and whoever else. But the sad thing about it, I think I would have still done it if I had not heard Chinoe's conversation. Once inside the house, I took a deep breath of relief. I was safe and no one knew. I ran up the stairs, grabbed the phone, and ran some bath water, throwing my unpacked night bag into the closet.

Ring . . . Ring . . . Ring. "Hello."

"Caymin, I just had the most magical night of my life."

"With who?"

"Cartel Rizza?"

The excitement left her voice. "Girl, you crazy. Where is Chinoe?"

"In Tahoe."

"You know all of them boys talk. What are you going to do if Chinoe find out?"

"Cartel knows everything."

"But Chinoe is in love, that doesn't mean anything to you?"

"Huh. I swear you act like you in love or Chinoe is your man or something, sometimes."

Ignoring the truthful accusation, "So what did ya'll do?"

The excitement had now left my voice "He took me to this building, had all the things I liked."

"Umm, hmm, so you gonna keep seeing him?"

"Sometimes. I'm not married. He knows about Chinoe so he knows he can't monopolize my time. Well, let me take a bath and get some sleep. Bye." *Click.*

I hung up the phone before Caymin could say bye.

Thank you, Lord, for opening my eyes up to a new beginning, magical moments and sweet endings.

Amen.

Chapter Sixty-Three

TWO DAYS LATER

Chocolate

"I'm home, Babe, where you at?" She must be sleep or at the damn mall. But her car was outside. Maybe she rode with Caymin. I still couldn't believe my luck on that. I was surprised Caymin hadn't told Brandie about us. Maybe she didn't want to cause confusion. Thank you God for small favors. "Damn I'm hungry, a brother got to eat."

Ring . . . Ring. "Hello." Her sweet voice came through the phone.

"Miss Delite, can a brother get some of your sweet stuff."

She giggled. "Yes, you can. When did you get back?"

"About thirty minutes ago. You hungry?"

"No I already ate. There's some lasagna in the

oven. I cooked it about an hour ago. I'm with Caymin at the mall."

"That figures. Pick me up some Polo socks and ribbed tees please."

"I'm going to stop by my house and pick up some more things, and I'll be back later."

"Got'cha, Babe."

"Late'a."

"Bye."

I ran up stairs and threw my things in the closet. Looking at the sandals and dress I bought for Brandie was making me horny, thinking about how good she was going to look in them.

Trying to hang them in her closet, I almost tripped over her Louis Vutton bag. "Dang, this thang full. She don't never put shit where it's supposed to go."

Ring . . . ring . . . ring. "Chinoe," I answered, agitated with her carelessness.

"Why you ain't call and let nobody know you were back. All these planes falling out of the sky. Nigga, yo' family care when don't nobody else do."

"I was gone call 'Mama', but I just walked in and a nigga starving." I said laughing as I pulled stuff out of her bag. Money was going on about something, but this olive halter dress, full of a man's cologne caught my attention.

"Aye, Money, let me hit chu back in a minute."

"Late'a."

"Late'a."

I turned the bag over and dumped it out onto the bed. "New shoes, too, hunh?" As I continued to go through the stuff on the bed, "What the fuck?"

Pictures of her spread-eagled on some type of

platform, and what was this? "Aw hell naw. Fuck this, I'm gone kill 'er."

I couldn't believe my eyes. Brandie was layed on Cartel Rizza. Sitting on his lap with her arms wrapped around his neck. Smiling and shit. She used to look like that when we first got together, but I hadn't seen that smile in a while until then.

"Fuck." I screamed, as I threw the pictures on the floor. "What did I do to deserve this shit?" A tear rolled down my face. I loved that girl. Gave her every thing she desired and more. I didn't want to let her go. What did I do to her for this to happen? Was this pay back for runnin' game, not caring about women who've cared for me—breaking their hearts?

Chapter Sixty-Four

Money

"It's almost Christmas, Sap. What do you want Santa Claus to bring you?"

She put her finger under her chin. "Ahh, Ahh . . . Lemme see. A big girl's bike, a puppy, a store, skates and a baby."

"Girl, you have a million baby dolls."

"No, a baby to play with me."

She caught me off guard. Where did she learn about babies? I had to admit, I'd been thinking about a baby boy lately myself.

"Okay, I'll talk to Mommy about that."

"Okay, Daddy."

I kissed her and left her playing with her dolls. She was getting so big.

Ring . . . Ring . . . Ring. "Hard as Diamond nails, how may I help you?"

"I thought you were working on that."

"What, the name? Yes, Babe, I am, but legal papers haven't come through yet. Diamond has to release the building to me."

"And I told you that we can have you another shop built."

"But all my business and clientele is here on Old National. I like this location."

"Yeah, whatever. Sap asked me for a baby for Christmas."

"That girl has enough dolls to play with. She needs a bike, and a new bedroom suite."

"No, a real baby to play with."

"What? Where did she learn that from?"

"I don't know, but you need to hurry home so we can work on that."

She giggled the way she always did when she agreed with what I wanted, "I'm outta here at eight-thirty. What are we eating?"

"Olive Garden, Chocolate and Brandie are coming."

"Good, call them and ask Brandie if she has found out about what I asked her to do?"

"What did you ask her to do?"

"None of your nosey business."

"Well, no. I'm not calling."

"Please."

"Bye, Luvly."

Damn, I couldn't wait until she got here. I'd been gone for a week and a half. Before that her period was on, so I was ready.

Ding Dong, Ding Dong. "Daddy, Uncle Chocolate here!" Sap yelled jumping up and down.

"What's up, Dawg?"

"What's up?" Chinoe said in a low tone.

"Uncle Chocolate, Uncle Chocolate." Sap reached her arms out to hug him. He pulled her close to him with one arm.

I immediately noticed trouble on his face. "Sap, go to your room and find you some clothes to put on."

"But, but I wanna stay wit—"

"Upstairs now," I said increasing my tone.

Chocolate walked over to the sofa and plopped down.

"But—" Sap tried one last time.

I started undoing my belt. "Get upstairs right now, I'm not going to say . . ." She was up the stairs before I could finish my sentence.

"She is getting too damn grown. I'm glad she with me now." Chocolate's mind was elsewhere. "Where is Brandie?"

"Gone to get her nails done," he answered dryly.

"Why you looking like a mullet?"

At first he was silent, then he let it out, "Man, Brandie cheating."

"On her man with you?" I tried joking with him to bring his spirits up. How would anyone not know they were a couple being all over magazines?

"Man, she cheating," he repeated with tears in his eyes.

"Dawg, come on now, maybe you over reacting. And anyway she ain't the only woman in the world. Nigga, you travel all over the world, Italy, London, Trinidad. Boy, you better open your eyes and close your nose."

"Last night at the club she was all up on Cartel Rizza."

"Cartel, Cartel? He cool wit' everybody."

"Yeah, she didn't see me though. She was doing all the stuff she do for me to him."

"Chocolate, she a dancer. How many dancers just stand around?"

"Naw. It was the expression on her face, the way she was touching him. Like they familiar with each other."

"Cartel frequents that club just as much as any other player." This nigga was actually sitting on my couch in front of me crying like a bitch. He done had hoes fuck up his car, throw bricks through the windows of his house, even had a broad call his mama and claim she was pregnant. But dis nigga crying over one female? Damn her pussy must be platinum.

"Man, you got to suck that shit up and just let 'er put on them track shoes. I can't stand seeing you like dis."

"She got me, Money, she got me bad. The day I got back from Tahoe I found her overnight bag."

"And?"

"She had a new, sexy dress with cologne all over it. There were pictures of her spread eagle. Then there was a picture of her and Cartel. She was all over him, kissing and hugging him; he was touching all over her."

That's why that nigga was so distant lately. "Why didn't you tell me that day? You wanna go get that nigga, Dawg?"

I knew what he was going through. Luvly had this ass layed up sick, throwing up, not eating for weeks. So I knew his pain.

"What do you need me to do?"

"Follow her tomorrow."

"Follow her?"

"Yeah, she has started working on Sunday's, supposedly to hurry up and finish out her contract."

"I'll do it, Chocolate, even though it's against everything I believe in. What time do I need to be there?"

He held his head down between his knees. I ain't never seen my boy like this. He had me wanting to go ring her damn neck myself.

I wonder if Luvly knew about this shit. They been hanging so tight lately, she probably the one schooling her on how to do it and not get caught up.

"Why, Money? I give her everything, no hassle, all my time, love, what else does she need. She got her own money and mine whenever she wants it. I've bought her a new car, sent her on shopping sprees in Milan, Paris, Sicily, what else do she want?"

I know he ain't ready to hear this, but he needed to know, "Word is, Sean the one who bought her that Escalade and that house."

He hit the table. His knuckles started bleeding. I went to the kitchen to get him a towel with ice. "Here, Chocolate."

"What the fuck? I thought she was paying for that house. She makes about three grand a week. Why me? I thought this was the one."

"Tae told me he saw Brandie and Cartel at the mall when you were in Tahoe."

"Why ya'll nigga's always try'na keep shit from me?"

"'cause whether you know it or not you got a bad-ass temper when it come to shit like this. And I just talk to Tae yesterday, he at camp. He said he called you but you were out of town. She walked right past him. Said she was so smooth with her shit."

"Man, I love that girl with everything I have in my body. I don't wanna know anything but her."

My dawg was on the verge of a break down. I had no choice but to help him out.

Chapter Sixty-Five

Luvly

"Luvly, how is your relationship with Money?"
"What do you mean?"

"Are you happy? Is he happy? Do you cheat?"

I paused in mid breath. I hadn't been confronted with that question besides with Money. "Well, I've did my share of dirt, Brandie, but I've learned from my mistakes. Diamond was the biggest mistake that I'm still trying to make up for. But for the most part, I'm happy with Money. I can't answer for him, 'cause I have put him through hell. Why you ask?"

"Chinoe is smothering me. He's at the club all the time. I can't even go to the bathroom by myself. He is driving me nuts."

Smiling at her, I said, "He loves you, girl. That boy has lusted after you before he knew your name. Then he ended up giving you his virginity.

Chinoe has given you his whole self. His mother loves you and so does his extended family. What else could you ask for?"

"Space, individuality, personal freedom."

"Just talk to him about it. Chocolate'll understand."

"I can't breathe."

As I filed and shaped her nail, I asked her, "You don't love him, do you?"

"Yes. I do, very much. But he is drowning me." She sighed. "I'm seeing Cartel Rizza."

"What?" I let go of her hand. "Why, Brandie? Why not leave Chocolate alone and then start seeing Cartel? I can't believe you. Girl, don't you know they know each other."

"I know, but Cartel knows about me and Chinoe."

"Well, Chocolate is crazy about you. And that's my brother. You need to tell him or I will." How could I tell her to confess about her wrongdoing, and I couldn't even confess about my own?

"Luvly, I thought I could talk to you and it be between us."

Brandie was the only female that I talked to lately. Caymin was there sometimes, but she had fallen in love, damn near married. I understood all to well what Brandie was going through.

Taking her hand back in mine to finish her nails, "Okay, Brandie. I won't tell him, but at some point you need to before this shit blows up in your face. This isn't fair to him. Do you want out, to be with Cartel?"

"No, I just enjoy Cartel's assertiveness and his mannerism. Chinoe use to be stronger and more take control, but now he's a puppy."

"You'd rather have a puppy than a snake, in the long run. See women get generous confused with weak, and controlling confused with strength and love. You better open your eyes. How you know Cartel ain't just using you to get back at Chocolate? They had beef some years back over some girl that Cartel was seeing, but she wanted Chocolate. I don't know the specifics, but maybe that's not what's going on."

"I've been thinking about breaking it off with Cartel because it's getting hectic. I do love Chinoe and want to be with him."

I put my arm around her neck. "Let's go eat with our men, I'm starving. Oh, did you check on the hall for the New Year's party."

"Yeah, it's going to be five thousand, two for the deposit."

"Okay."

I felt shaky about Brandie now. She was becoming like a sister to me, but Chocolate was already my brother. Wasn't my loyalty to him? He had always been there by my side, but he never mixed friendships by telling me what Money did. I didn't know what to do about this, but if I told on Brandie, I would have to tell Money that I slept with Diamond a month before Sap's birthday party. And about Chocolate and me, something we said would stay between us forever. And I'm not ready to face those consequences.

Chapter Sixty-Six

Brandie

"Why are you so quiet, Baby?" He was just sitting there looking spaced out.

"Just thinking."

"About?" I asked, rubbing on his leg.

Everyone started quieting down.

"Uncle Chocolate, Auntie Brandie, I made a hundred on my spelling test."

"You are a very smart young lady. I know you can do it over and over again."

"That's good, baby girl."

That's all he could get out? Sap was the icing on the cake to him, so I knew he had more than just that to say. Tears were in his eyes. Then I became worried.

"Brandie, what are you and Chocolate doing for New Year's Eve?" Luvly asked, trying to break the monotony. But the tension was too tough.

I touched his hand and pulled him near me, "Are you okay, Chinoe?"

"Naw, I'm not."

A single tear ran down his cheek. Luvly got Sap and Trinket up and walked with them to the sitting area.

"What the fuck is wrong, Brandie? What have I done that was so bad?"

"What did I do?" I asked trembling from the sound of his voice.

Screaming so loud that everyone turned around, "You know what the fuck you did, and doing. Don't fucking lie to me."

Luvly had walked back over to the table looking nervous.

I started crying because I knew I was guilty as charged. How did he find out? I looked at Luvly for help, but she looked down at the ground. *Did she tell him? I'll beat her gotdamn ass!*

Should I say something about the girl on the phone?

"Look ya'll need to take it outside, ya'll startin' to cause a scene," Luvly pleaded to no avail.

"Did you think Atlanta was too big for all this shit to get back to me. Or you just didn't care?" Standing up over me, his voice got all up in my soul. "Why, Brandie, why?" Anger had stolen his face.

"What do you need that I don't give you?"

"Space, Chinoe. You are smothering me. We do not have to be under each other twenty-four seven. I am use to being independent."

"Space?" He slapped two of the drinks on the table onto the floor. He grabbed my chair, swiftly turning me to face him. He poked his finger deep into my forehead, "Space is not an option. There will always be an us. Do you hear me?"

Money grabbed his arm. "Come on, Chinoe."

Chinoe grabbed me by the throat and squeezed until I couldn't breathe.

"You will never have any space. You are mine. Always will be."

"Chinoe . . . I can't . . . breathe, please, you're . . . hurting me!"

"This is how it felt when I saw you wit' that nigga."

Money couldn't relieve Chinoe's hands from my throat. "Chinoe, man, stop. You gone kill 'er."

The look in Chinoe's eyes was pure anger. I knew I'd hurt him.

"Fuck Cartel again and I'll kill you, Brandie." He finally let me go. I was shivering from head to toe. "Get your shit and let's go."

Never in a million years would I have let a man put his hands on me, but for some reason I felt like I deserved this.

Sitting in Money's great room, no one said a word.

Money took Sap to her room. Luvly was sitting on the couch, looking Chinoe up and down. "What the hell has gotten into you? That was not you in that restaurant."

"She knows what she's doing."

I couldn't say anything to defend myself—I was speechless. Nothing I said was going to fix this mess.

"Chinoe, I'm sorry."

He jumped up. And I jumped up to protect myself, but he moved faster than I could and pushed me down onto the lounge chair, "You are sorry. Sorry as hell!" He towered over me like a big dark thundercloud, ready to throw lightning. "Who else you fucking, Brandie? Hunt, huh?"

He hit the cushion beside my head. "Aaaaaaa!"

"Please, Chinoe, calm down."

"Luvly, she deserves for me to beat her ass."

Luvly came over to him and rubbed his back. "Chinoe, she's sorry. She felt smothered."

Not taking his eyes off me, "I'm all the air she needs." Every word out of his mouth felt like a knife through my heart.

"Baby, I love you. Please tell me you love me. Tell me that it's over with Cartel and Hunt." He stared at me as if he was looking at my soul.

"Chinoe, I do love you, but I need space, baby. I want us to be together, but you need to ease up. I'm not going anywhere."

He lowered his body onto mine, his wet face resting on mine,

"Please, Brandie, you are my everything. I'm sorry." Shaking his head side to side, he mumbled, "Never again."

He kissed me with salty lips and I received his kiss with intentions on leaving his ass, as soon as it was safe.

I had to admit, though, Chinoe did have me wide open. Sexually, he drove me wild, always left me begging for more. Physically, I adored his sexy ass. He looked so damn good! I liked to just sit back and stare at him like a picture on the wall.

And after all of that, I was afraid. Afraid of getting hurt—emotionally. I felt like if I gave him my all-trust, love, honesty, my heart—that gave him room to turn on me and hurt me, leave me wounded. I wanted to do right by Chinoe, I truly did.

I was so glad that Sean was out of the picture, no questions. Cartel, on the other hand, was not going to let me walk away so easy.

Lord, please guide me in the right direction. Don't lead me astray.
I put my life under your guidance.
Help me make strong, sound decisions.
Amen

Three days later, after we'd made love, cuddled and said our apologies. While Chinoe was away, I grabbed all of my important things, stuffed them in a bag and got the hell out of Chinoe's house. His anger, aggression, possessiveness, controlling jealousy, was too much for anyone to bear.

Chapter Sixty-Seven

Chocolate

It had been two months since I'd seen or heard from Brandie. The first day she got a chance to leave, she did. Every time I called to apologize, she hung up. So, I'd been playing a hard ass, to match her game.

I started to kill her that night at Olive Garden. All this time I'd been without her and I finally found her and she go and fuck Cartel Rizza and whoever else. I shouldn't give a shit about her, but I couldn't control it.

"Chocolate, what 'cha over there thinking 'bout?"

"That goddamn Brandie, " Tae said, answering for me.

They both started singing, "I really miss you Brandie. When are you coming back home?" I did want to know when she was coming back home. I missed her. I needed her.

"Fuck ya'll niggas. All I'm thinking about is feeding my stomach. What we gone eat?"

"Waffle House." I should have known it would be there. We were raised on Waffle House late night food.

"Damn! Waffle House. Crunk, shawty!" Taeko shouted.

Before we could get out of the truck people were already surrounding us, "What's up folk?" A dude name Kay, that we use to kick it with sometimes asked.

"What's the word Pimping?" We all dapped and showed respect.

"Ya'll got it." Everyone said to each other.

The girls were ooohing and ouhhhhing about us and someone yelled, "I like that about them niggas. They paid as hell, always on TV and still keep it real in the hood."

A cutie we went to school with name Tess, ran over to me and gave me a hug and a kiss. "I hope you ready to mingle with me now."

Looking at her big breast sitting so pretty and plump, I said, "Let's see about that."

As we walked through the door our eyes locked. I almost ran back out the door like a bitch, but Tess was holding onto my waist like we belonged together, so I played into it.

Not breaking the stare, I hugged Tess closer to me and told her to go find something on the jukebox. Brandie looked away like I meant nothing.

Everyone got in and seated. We had about twenty folks surrounding us.

"Aye, ya'll seen dis pretty nigga right here layed

up in the magazine?" Kay asked jokingly. He put his hand on his hip and poked his leg out and smiled real big. Everyone cracked up. "Nigga you getting paid a lot to do dat?"

"Yeah, nigga. Don't be hating 'cause you can't have the good looks or the benefits of the money and ass that come along with it." I said loud, hoping it carried over to Brandie's ears.

Kay reached his hand out to give me dap. "All I got to say playboy is, do yo' thang. And I 'preciate the fact that ya'll got dem programs for housing. That's good looking out. Ya'll ain't never forgot where ya'll came from."

Receiving his dap and a hug, "I'll never get no bigger than my niggas. That's when you start loosing yourself."

Conversation continued, but my mind was focused on Brandie.

Watching her smile, showing her teeth to this nigga sitting across from her like he was saying something wonderful, her ass was pissing me off.

I wanted to walk up and slap this nigga silly for laughing in her face, but I kept my cool.

The waitress placed their food on the table, the playful way Brandie handed him the salt and pepper got me to a point that I couldn't hold it anymore. Everyone noticed me getting up from the table but they kept the conversation going strong about our high school years, who's still fucking who, who has baby mamas and daddies.

As I stood in front of her table my intoxication took over. She looked so good with her hair parted in the middle, cut around her face, laying long on her shoulders. And her sexy full lips shined with gloss.

The five-carat heart pendent that I gave her, just because, was complimenting her caramel complexion beautifully. "Brandie, can I talk to you for a minute." I asked in an impatient voice, trying to keep my attitude mild.

But from the look on her face I knew she was ready to push my buttons. "Chinoe, as you can see I am on a date and we are about to eat." She said slow and pronounced.

Who the fuck was she talking to like a chump?

She gave her attention back to that fuck nigga, like I was a nobody.

One more time before I cut the fucking fool, "Brandie, can I please talk to you outside?"

She hit the table. "Chinoe, why are you over here trying to start shit? I'm sure your entourage is waiting on you to finish telling 'em your ho stories. I'm trying to fucking eating." She pointed to her food.

"Look homeboy, we trying to eat. She got a phone, dial her number if you wanna spit bullshit in her ear."

I lost it. "Wooo." I put a call to my boys, because I couldn't handle my business with this dusty nigga in the way.

I slung her plate to the floor, hushing the entire Waffle House, "You ain't eating no more!"

By the time her plate hit the floor Kay was standing knee to knee, staring down dude's throat. I had Brandie by her collar.

"Man, don't hurt her," the punk she was with said.

"Shut the fuck up, nigga!" My rage got the best of me.

"Chinoe, let me go." She started tussling and

rustling with me. Then she spit in my face. It seemed like time stood still with us looking into each other's eyes.

From that point we headed out the door with her head and back opening the glass door. She tried to fight back, but I had her tight in my hands and under my control like a rag doll.

"You son-of a bitch. I hate you, I hate you!" Her words slapped me in the face, making my eyes watery.

"I love you though." She stared at me through teary eyes. "Brandie, why did you leave me like that?"

Still tussling with me, "Because we both did wrong. And you started to change. See look at how you acting. Now let me fucking go!"

She slapped me and scratched my face, breaking skin. Before I could control my actions, I snatched the necklace off her neck and slammed her into the hood of a car.

She was screaming and crying, but all my anger was drowning her out, pouring into my hands.

A crowd of people ran out to the parking lot, surrounding us. Money ran to the opposite side of the car, while Taeko stood behind me.

"Chocolate, let her go, man. It ain't worth it, Dawg," Money said, trying to save my sanity. "Come on, Dawg. You know what I done been through with this type of bullshit. Just let her go. We ain't like this, beating on women and shit."

With every word out of Money's mouth Brandie scratched deep cuts in my hands, striking blood with every hit.

"Come on, Chocolate," Taeko said, trying to pry my hands off her neck. She started gasping as I squeezed harder. "Chinoe, she gone die, man. And you know you love this girl, so let her go!"

"Come on, Chinoe!" Money and Taeko both pleaded, using my first name, so I knew they meant business. But I couldn't let go.

"Chinoe, Chinoe, listen to me, Dawg."

Before Money finished, my heart released my hands. Brandie lay in the floor, crying and gagging. Money grabbed her legs and pulled her to the opposite side of the car, close to him.

"He is going to kill me, Money! Please make him stay away from me!" She hugged Money, crying on his shoulder.

Money stared at me with harsh eyes. Taeko stood with both hands on the car and his head hanging down.

"Fuck this shit." I walked down the street to Denny's. Pedestrians got killed all the time on Old National, maybe I could be added to the statistics. My life was over.

Ring . . . Ring.

"You've reached me, now state your case." Beep. I hung up.

Ring . . . Ring.

"You've reached me, now state your case." Beep. I wanted to hear her sweet voice over and over again. I hung up.

I knew she still had to love me. The letter she wrote me told it all.

Chinoe,

I don't know what happened to us, but it has to stop. Chinoe, we hurt each other pretty bad. I did not do this alone, nor did you. No one is to blame. I love you, Chinoe, so much, more than you'll ever know. I've waited a long time for you, but you rushed me and smothered me. I just need sometime to myself. That shit you pulled at the Waffle House was not fair and very selfish of you. Give us time, Chinoe!

Ring . . . Ring. "You've reached me, now state your case." I had to hear her voice one more time.

Chapter Sixty-Eight

Brandie

The club was hype, the music sounded good. Caymin and I were champion stallions walking. All eyes on us. I needed this night to recuperate from all the drama that had been going on in my life.

Cartel was still riding my ass: "Why are you letting Chinoe run your life?" "Why can't you sell your house and let me build us one?" "Are we going to be a couple?" "Why you letting that nigga control you?" "It's not like that, Cartel. I just need my space period."

"I want you nonstop, Brandie! Permanently!"

Ahhhhhhhhhhhhhhhhhhhhhhhhhhh!!!!!!!!

"Shut up!" I wanted to yell.

He didn't understand, nor did I. I longed for Chinoe, but not for his attitude or jealousy.

"Girl, these niggas looking good up in here."

Caymin was looking cute as usual with her hair pulled back in a sleek ponytail matching mine, without our awareness of course.

"Brandie, cheer up. This was a new day, so get some soul back in your spirit."

I let a smile out of hostage, "You right girl, I do need to come back to life."

We stood around for a while taking in the sights. Two men in expensive leather bomber coats approached us.

Black bomber coat smiled at Caymin and showed her he was grilled out. She liked that gangsta shit. "How you doing beautiful?"

She instantly smiled and accepted his invitation for conversation.

The one with the cream leather coat and hat to match approached me. He reminded me too much of Hunt. "Baby girl what's good."

"Standing here trying to figure out why I came." My body language told him I wasn't interested. But his pride wouldn't accept.

"It's like that? Well, I'm here now."

"Hunh? I can barely hear you." I played him.

"I said I'm here now. You can let me take care of your time."

"Oh, mmmhm." I nodded and averted my attention back to the dance floor.

"So, what's yo' name?"

I wished his fake ass would get the hell away from me. "Brandie."

"Like dark liquor?"

I heard him loud and clear, but I wasn't in the mood. He probably wasn't a bad guy. And he was cute at that, but right then I was so beyond his type that it was sickening. "What you say? I can't hear you."

"Ahhh, man, fuck dis shit, you just over here running game. You can't run game on a player. It's all good baby girl, all you had to say was no thank you." He waved me off and patted his boy to let him know that he was going over to the bar.

"Well, girl, I'm going to dance," Caymin said, too excited for me.

"Do your thang ma-ma." As Caymin went to the dance floor, I found myself walking to the bathroom for comfort.

"Excusssssss me, sexy thang." Before I could make it to the bathroom, a short guy with a row of gold in his mouth and stanking breath grabbed my arm. "Can I buy you a dress? I mean a drink, sexy thang?" Goldie asked, looking at my skirt like he could see through it.

"No thank you." I looked around fast as my eyes could travel and I spotted a cutie and grabbed his arm, "My man has my drink right here, thank you, Babe."

Goldie sucked his teeth and walked off. "Hoes always fronting."

"Ehhhhhh," I said as Goldie walked away. "Thank you for lending yourself to me."

"No problem, beautiful." We looked at each other up and down. He was wearing a nice black DADA sweater with some black pants that fit nice on his derriere and some Perry Ellis shoes that I'd been eyeing for Chinoe. My two-piece crème halter and hugging skirt to match made us look like the perfect couple.

Staring at my outfit, he remarked, "How is that

top holding on to you—with those dental floss strings?"

I rolled my eyes. This was just another horn-dog on the prowl.

"Don't get me wrong, it looks good, looks damn good."

"Brandie." Extending my hand, giving him another chance, I relented.

Meeting my hand, he said, "Jason."

"Hunh?" The loud music drowned him out.

"Jason."

"Oh, nice to meet you. Thanks again for saving me from Goldie."

"Anytime, anytime, hey, isn't your name Miss Delite?"

I was about to run to the bathroom, but I didn't want to seem like I was ashamed of what I chose to do for a living.

"Yes, but that's my stage name."

"No offense, but you bad as hell." Holding his hands up like he was under arrest, "That's all I'm going to say on that subject. Where you sitting, can I join you?"

"I . . . I—"

"If you wit' your man I'll understand."

"No, no, it's not that. Let me run to the bathroom."

After I checked myself out in the mirror, we sat and talked for about an hour. I told him about Chinoe and everything that had been happening. I don't know why I told him all my business, but he made me feel so comfortable, he was easy to talk to, a good listener.

As he finished his drink, a slim sister with baby doll curls and glasses walked up behind him. She stood with one hand on her hip, and turned up lips. I stared at her as she stared back at me.

"What's up beautiful, checking out another prospect?" Jason asked me.

I let go of a glamour girl smile that was sure to piss curly que off.

"What the fuck is this?" the ghetto girl shouted.

"Damn!" He slammed his glass on the counter and didn't turn around to greet her.

"Brandie, you wanna dance?"

"Look, I don't want no shit I've been through enough drama to last me a life time." I held my hands out to stop him.

"You right ho, you don't won't no shit." She walked in between us and stood in his face.

I knew she was mad at Jason, taking it out on me, but I still had shit on my chest, so I vented by fucking with her mind. "Yo' man seem to be liking this ho," I responded, popping my lips.

"Bitch, please," putting her hand in my face. "You can buy this ho drinks but you can't buy your daughter no winter coat? Trifling ass." She slapped the glass that he was holding, out of his hand.

"Keonia get out of my face and take yo' ass home. Damn, you make me sick. Always trying to start shit, but not this time." He pushed her to the side just as Jay-Z's, "Sunshine" came on.

"Oooh, I love that song." I was ignoring both of them.

Jason snatched my hand, "Good, come on." We made it to the dance floor without me having to go to blows with her. As we danced, she was sitting in his seat pouring salt into my full, fifteen-dollar drink.

"You have to excuse that girl. She a little crazy."

"Yeah, about you. Why you treating her like that?" Shaking my head, "Cutie pies like you always have that type of drama."

As I turned around, looking down at the floor, pushing my butt into him, I felt someone standing right in front of me. "You look like the ho that you are."

When I raised my head, I met Chinoe's breath, smelling like hard liquor. I quickly turned back around, embarrassed, but I could still feel him there. My heart was beating a mile a minute, scared of the foolishness he was about to cause.

"Take yo' muthafuckin' ass home, wit' that ho shit on." He screamed over the music, in slurred speech.

My eyes started searching the room for Money or Taeko. I knew one of them was with him and would be the only one to make him not cause a scene.

He got closer to my ear, "Did you hear what I said?"

I kept dancing, trying to ignore him until I could spot Money or Taeko. Chinoe was drunk and I knew he was going to act out. I didn't see Caymin anywhere either.

"Brandie," he screamed loud enough for people to take notice, "Or would you prefer me to call you Miss Delite?" He started laughing loud. "You ain't shit!"

"I take it this is Chinoe?" Jason asked."

I was so embarrassed. I wanted to be back in the bathroom digging into the bottom of my purse for change to give to the bathroom attendant, so she'd stop trying to sell me shit that a normal person should have used before they left to come to the club.

"Turn around when I'm talking to you."

Before I could get up any kind of nerve, he was behind Jason with his cup above his head threatening to pour it on him. "Ok, ok, Chinoe."

When I turned to face him he was looking at me up and down like I disgusted him. "Man, go home and put on some decent clothes."

Talking to Jason, "Nigga, if you like hoes, you'll love this one." Pointing at me.

"Chinoe, I'm through with this type of shit, leave me alone!" I screamed, finally getting mad instead of being scared.

"Fuck you," throwing his drink on me. This was the third time he'd embarrassed the shit out of me. "Now you don't have a choice but to take yo' raggedy ass home." Smiling as he walked off.

Jason's baby mama was clapping and yelling, "That's what cha get, ho, for messin' with other peoples' men. Slimy bitch!"

Chapter Sixty-Nine

Brandie

The ride home was even worse. Caymin wanted me to retell the whole awful story.

"Girl, you crazy 'cause I would have stole his ass."

"You would have did exactly what I did, got your shit and left."

She looked out the window like she was remembering something.

"Caymin, are you mad at me for going with Chinoe?"

She quickly answered, "Oh, naw, girl, naw." I knew that really meant yeah. Silence fell upon us.

"I won't be mad if you tell me the truth."

"Umph, umm."

My anger had reached its boiling point, and somebody was going to pay. "Are you sure?" Come on, bitch. I know you still wanna have 'im."

She faced the window. "Yeah, it does bother me that he treats you like I cried for him to treat me. I was truly in love with him not because he fine as hell and has the perfect skin, teeth, and hair, but because he is beautiful and intelligent on the inside." She wiped uncontrollable tears. "I thought I would be with him forever but things didn't work out.

Neither she nor he told me what had happened to them. "So why did ya'll break up if he was so wonderful?"

She turned back to the window for support, "I'd rather not talk about it. He's in love with you now, so why dwell in the past?"

"I do love him, Caymin. I love him deep down in my soul. I want to be with him once he calms down and becomes himself again. Every man I have ever dated has turned pussy on me. If I could have been Tupac's wife I would have had no problems. I would be his perfect women and he my perfect man. Thuggish, roughish, smooth, sexy, intelligent, soft, hard, all of the above and then more than I could handle."

"Yeah, I think he was every woman's fantasy."

"And Chinoe is your . . ."

"My what?"

"Never mind. That was in the past, so why dwell on it?"

"Oh, you wanna play games now?" She pursed her lips. "Look, Brandie, you got Chinoe, so it doesn't matter. You were his first for everything."

I knew that he cared a great deal for her once, so I had just as much to loose from the whole deal. I needed to know if there was space for reconciliation.

"So do you still love him?"

Sighing as if it was a ridiculous question, "I'm with Robert."

"For what?"

She turned and looked at me but nothing came out of her mouth.

"Money, to pass time; loneliness? Caymin, I've done them all so which one does Robert posses over you, 'cause it's certainly not love?"

The truth began to surface and I wanted it signed, sealed, and delivered. "You know Caymin, I've been wondering about our friendship a lot lately. When I told you about that shit with Cartel, you were still more concerned about how Chinoe felt, than how I was feeling."

"That's expected, he was my friend for a long time, before you."

"So admit it, you still love him." I don't know why I was badgering her like this. My suspicion was turning in to hostility because I needed to vent my anger on someone.

"Why, Brandie? Why does it matter? I'm not the one he wants."

"How do you know?"

"What?" Staring at me through squinted eyes, she said, "Just get me home cause you trippin'." She paused for a second then positioned herself in the seat like she was ready for a tongue battle, "Your man, huh? Was he your man when you fucked Cartel or Hunt or what about Sean? Where does he fit in?"

"Bitch you must be silly talking to me like that. You got some nerve talking about who I fucked, Dun don't sound like Robert to me, the one you singing about being with. And now to think about it, you probably the one who told him about them anyway."

"What? Ho, pleazz. You must be dizzy! You don't even know the half."

"Know what? That you trifling!" I slowed down. She was going to tell me why they broke up and if she still wanted to be with him.

"Brandie, you wanna know why we broke up?"

"Yeah, why?" My voice towered over hers.

"Because of you! All because of you! You worrying about me being the man stealer, and you the one that did it to me."

"What are you talking about? Ya'll broke up way before me and him got together."

"But he wanted you long before ya'll got together. I couldn't compete with a fantasy woman. After he saw you in the mall, you was all he thought about. You consumed his thoughts; you motivated his heart. He wouldn't even sleep with me because he was waiting for you. Destiny, Brandie. He slept with you because of who you were, everything he ever wanted, obviously everything I lacked."

"Ahh, Caymin."

"Naw fuck that. Listen, you wanted to know. I couldn't win a competition with a nonparticipating competitor. When I gave Chinoe head it was you that he thought about. He finally admitted that he was in love with a woman that delighted his life and he hadn't even touched or smelled her. How could I win that battle, Brandie?"

I pulled into her driveway, my eyes filled with tears. She jumped out the car before it completely stopped. I didn't know how to say I was sorry.

* * *

As I drove home my cell phone started ringing off the hook. I didn't bother looking at the number because I didn't care who it was.

My first thought was to drive by Chinoe's, but what would be the point? I needed comforting.

As I pulled into my drive way I saw a shadow on my steps. I locked my doors and grabbed my phone. Cracking my window, yelling, "Hey whoever you are go away or I'm calling the police."

I looked around to make sure I didn't over look a car.

"Ooh, shit." Chinoe's face met mine on the other side of the window, "What are you doing out here?" I still had my window cracked.

"Trying to see you. Come on out and let's talk."

"Blow your breath into the crack."

"What?" He asked like I was speaking foreign.

"Blow your breath into the window."

"It's chilly out here, Brandie. Come on."

"You come on. Breathe, please."

"What, you the po-po now?" He blew his sweet smelling breath into the crack of the window.

I got out of the car and we just looked at each other for a few minutes. "Sorry about that." He pointed at the big cranberry stain on my suit, which resembled the sun.

"Ahh, damn, Chinoe. Cranberry juice? I didn't even look at what it was."

He followed me, listening to me cuss about my suit all the way into the house.

I started taking off my clothes as I walked up the steps and he was right on my heels. I left the radio on, 'Gotta Be" by Jagged Edge greeted us as we reached the bathroom. Moving so fast, I reacted before I thought, taking all my clothes off in front of him.

"Will you give me a towel please?"

He shook his head no and stared at me like a dessert he'd been having a sweet tooth for.

"Please, Chinoe," I said, a slight smile on my lips.

"No. Run some water."

I should have been scared, escorting him to the front door, but I was turned on by the tone of his voice and the determination of his stance. I stood still for a minute, admiring his whole person. He sounded like the Chinoe I met that night in a dark windowless room.

Chapter Seventy

Chocolate

As we sat in the water surrounded by darkness, I massaged her feet.

"Why have you been acting so crazy lately?"

I didn't want her to talk. I just wanted to remember the first time I met her and didn't know her name or face or how she felt on the inside.

"Chinoe, please say something to me."

I let silence be my game of choice.

"So you aren't going to talk to me?" Splashing water into my face. "Shit, you the one that choked the shit out of me and threw a drink on me at the club in the middle of the floor while you called me hoes and shit." She snatched her foot out of my hand.

She was making it sound worse than what it really was.

"Fuck this shit, get out!" She jumped up, but I

grabbed her by her hips and pulled her back into the tub.

"Brandie, I'm sorry. Sorry for acting the way I did, but you got to understand I did it out of . . ." Stopping myself, I was sounding like a wife beater trying to make his wife believe he won't hit her again. "Look, I saw you and fell in love with you before I met you. I gave you my virginity and didn't know that you were the woman I was already lusting after. It all fell into place. And I guess I took destiny, ran with it to ecstasy, trying to make it eternity. I couldn't allow myself to fall in love with no one else after I saw you. You were perfect. I know I failed you and me, but I . . . I don't know, Brandie, I just love you, girl."

"So why did you put your hands on me, to hurt me?"

"I overreacted, love took over my heart, and anger took over my hands. I have no excuse to ever lay my hands on you. Hold on, I got something for you." I got out of the tub and put on 'R U Still Down' by Jon B featuring TuPac.

"Chinoe . . ."

"Shhh, listen to every word."

Pulling her closer into my chest from her waist, smelling her sweet hair, touching her soft skin, holding her feminine fingers in my hungry hands; hungry for all her loving, life and future. Being next to her felt like the next best thing to being an angel in Heaven. It made me think about how she use to take care of me, like a woman did for her man, "Brandie, you remember how you tricked me that night I came home from Cancún?"

She laughed, "Yes. We had been arguing, well, not arguing, but debating about how you couldn't resist having sex with me, no matter what."

We both laughed thinking about the outcome.

"And when I came home you were acting like you were sound asleep. That night was so special to me. I came in singing, 'I Really Miss You Brandie', and when I got to the bed you were acting like you was dead to the world. Then I peeked under the cover to see what you had on."

"Yep, and then you had to go take a shower because all I had on was a pink thong and you know you wanted this thang."

I hugged her tighter.

She was right. I wanted her right then and there, but I couldn't punk out. I turned on the radio so only the speakers in the bathroom would come on. After I was in the shower for about five minutes, just enough time to wash my dick, she knocked on the shower door, I flashed a devilish grin, "Yes, may I help you?"

"Is there any room for me in there?"

"I got to check you out first. And anyway, who are you? My girl in the bed sleep."

She flashed a sexy smile and stepped in my full view, "Ahh, Miss Lady, you ain't got no clothes on." I covered my eyes.

She giggled and stepped in the shower. "I told you I need to check you out first, Miss Lady."

"Be my guest." She put one leg on the bench, I smelled the hair on her head, first, the smell always, drive me crazy. Then I kissed her on all her facial parts. Next I kissed, licked and sucked her breast. As I made my way down her side she began to moan. By the time I reached her pubic hair she was about to fall out.

Her pubic hair shaved in the shape of a Hershey's kiss, "Can I have a bite of your candy?"

She nodded her head yes and licked her lips as I dug my face into her sweetness.

After all that she was ready for me to drill her, but I had a point to prove. So I just turned away from her and continued to wash myself.

"You need the rest of this water?"

"Hunh?"

"The water, you want to finish using it?"

She stood looking at me dumbfounded, "You aren't finished."

I laughed at her and left her standing in the shower by herself.

"Chinoe?"

"Yeah."

"Can we have more nights like that?"

This was my invitation to come back home.

She turned around and sat up on her knees, "I love you too baby!" She said sweetly, hugging my neck. I held onto her soft body and inhaled her sweet Ocean Dream.

Chapter Seventy-One

Chocolate

"Christmas is two weeks away. Are you ready Sap?"

"Yes. I wrote Santa a letter, a long time ago."

"Have you been a good girl?"

"Yes, Grandma, I have."

"No, she hasn't, Ma. She didn't eat all her vegetables yesterday."

She poked her lips out. "Uncle Chocolate." She jumped on me and we start wrestling.

"Don't hurt her little bitty self, Chocolate," my mother said, still looking bright and beautiful. She still won't let me move her into a bigger house. She said comfort is better than size.

"Where is Brandie? She loves my collards."

I didn't want to worry her with all of the particulars of our arrangement. "She's at home. Her house." We were back together, but on a trial basis, and she wouldn't live with me until we had counseling and were married.

"When you get a chance call her, tell her to come get some dinner." Putting her hands on her hips, "So what's up with my lights?"

I didn't put up a fight. I headed straight out to hang the lights. My mind was going in five different directions. *Am I making the right choice by staying with Brandie?* My last photo shoot sucked. I have no chemistry with this new photographer. Worrying about Money and if he'd broken it off with Salone, if not, he's in for some serious hell. I know Luvly still messing with Diamond, and that's already hell. I often think about what would have come of me and Caymin if I would have given us a fair chance.

But Brandie was my baby, though. No one compared. She made me whole, complete. It had been going good lately, but she gets timid when we get into an argument. I didn't want her scared of me. I needed to show her that I wasn't a stranger and that I could be the man she first met. I'm just hurt about the whole situation. What man wouldn't be, especially a man like me that has everything to offer.

Whose car was this pulling in my mother's driveway? The tint was too dark to see behind the glass.

Chaise got out of the car looking as good as the last time I saw her. I continued to hang the Christmas lights.

"Hey, Chinoe. How have you been?" she asked, sounding sincere.

"All right and you?"

"Disappointed. Why did you change photographers? Just because we stop being bed partners doesn't mean we had to cut out the business relationship."

"It wouldn't have worked."

"My job is my job. Pleasure is just pleasure. If you don't know that then we never had anything, because you didn't know me."

"You don't even believe that. You were too attached."

"Not too attached, I fell in love and forgot to invite you. And I apologize for that."

I dropped a line of lights, "Would you like me to help you?"

I looked into her eyes, and knew if I gave her an inch she would take a mile. "Naw, I got it."

Getting antsy, putting a hand on her hip she said, "Give us another chance to have a love affair, with the camera. We were good together."

And this was the truth. We were good together. The camera loved the touch of her hands and loved my body and face, "I don't know Chaise. I'll have to think about it."

"Well, I have a shoot lined up for Tuesday. It's for three days and you can be back home Christmas Eve."

"Where?"

"New York."

"Yeah. All right." I needed a break.

My mother came to the door, "Oh, hi, Chaise. It's been too long," She hugged Chaise and cut her eyes at me. My mother agreed that I should have broken off the business relationship with Chaise. She said it would have been conflicting, especially when Brandie came along on trips. "So what brings you around?"

"I have a shoot that's paying major dollars. But I need the perfect face."

"My handsome son?" My mother laughed and shot some soul back into my body. My mother put her hands on my shoulder to show Chaise that she wasn't leaving my side until she did.

"Chaise, what time do I need to be ready?"

"Tuesday at eleven-thirty a.m." The smile on her face was what I'd been missing in Brandie. Chaise's fresh essence sent shock waves through my body. *If Brandie wanted space, space she shall get!*

Tuesday morning seemed long and dreary with all the rain and fog.

"Chinoe, why do you look so down?" Chaise asked.

"Problems. A whole lotta problems."

"Is there anything I can do to help?" The only thing she could do those three days was work and fuck me to sleep.

"No. I just don't understand my girl. Why does she feel like she needs so much space?"

She looked out the airplane window. "The same reason you needed it."

Shit, I needed it because I needed to know where I stood with my life. "Brandie knows what she wants, she's not unsure about her life."

"Are you sure, maybe you forced her into love. Maybe you didn't give her any choices or a chance to venture out."

Maybe so, but hell, Chaise would say anything to get her position back.

We finally got to our hotel room. We had to share one because there was a convention going on and all the rooms were booked. "You sure they're all full?"

"Yes, Chinoe. Check for yourself. Believe me, I'm not trying to lure you away from your problems."

When we got to the room I went straight to the phone, "Could you please be quiet? I don't want her to think anything."

"Ooohhh, déjà vu."

Ring . . . Ring . . . Ring.

"Hello."

"Hey, baby"

"Hey, Chinoe, you made it safely."

"Yes. Finish wrapping presents?"

"Yes. Sap has the whole house mostly."

"You sound happy."

"No. I'm missing you, baby. Just sitting here talking to Caymin and Luvly."

"Where Luvly?"

"In the bathroom."

"So are you really happy? Happy with yourself, us, me?"

"Yes, baby, I am. I love you, Chinoe."

"Love you, too."

"Hurry home to me."

"I will sexy. Keep it hot. Talk to you later."

"Bye."

As I hung up the phone, I felt I had to hurry up and ask her to marry me. If she said yes, I knew she would be in my life, but what if she said no? I can't blame her, especially the way I treated her a month ago.

"Chinoe, do you mind if I take a shower?"

I was confused and strung out on a fantasy. What the fuck was wrong with me? Maybe I needed to test myself, see if I was doing the right thing. "If I can take it with you."

She smiled as if she had won an award, "That's exactly what I wanted."

She dropped her clothes and sexily motioned me to come with her. I let her lead me into a world of pleasure, and guilt.

Chapter Seventy-Two

Chocolate

Christmas morning started at 6:20 a.m. Everyone decided to have it at my house.

My dad, mother, Grandma Loane, Luvly and her parents, Money, Brandie and her parents, Tae and his family and, of course, Sapphire.

Trinket and Sapphire had a toy store in my living room, while Trey rode his scooter outside.

Everyone exchanged gifts. Brandie looked content, but I couldn't tell if it was because she had her family there, and that it was Christmas or me.

"Brandie, are you happy?"

"Yes." Her facial expression was fake and her answer forced.

Brandie was playing happy homemaker. Sashaying like she was queen of the castle. The phone rang and she dashed to the kitchen. Her attention was diverted from me so she didn't pay attention to me leaving the living room. I went upstairs to the guest bedroom and picked up the phone.

"No, no. I told you I couldn't come see you. He knows Cartel. What am I suppose to do."

"Tell that nigga that we are not finished and I'm not going to just let you go."

"Cartel, I'm in love with Chinoe. I don't want to leave him."

"But you wanna keep fucking me? This shit ain't right Brandie. Did you tell him about the other day, while you trying to be so truthful."

She hung up the phone.

"Cartel!"

"Who—"

"Muthafucka you know who this is. I don't blame you for fucking her, she fine as hell, but she is mine."

"I don't give a fuck about ya'll. Brandie is grown and is going to make her own decision. When I met her she was single, so in my eyes she's still single. Fuck what you wanna think."

"Fuck you! She off limits! Nigga, I will kill you!" I hung up the phone. There was no more to say. Brandie was mine and that was the bottom line.

"Chocolate what's up? The women making breakfast," Taeko said with a smile.

"Why you looking like that nigga?" Money asked.

"Cartel just called my muthafuckin' house."

Luvly walked in and flopped down on the bed, "What cha'll doing up here?"

Tae had a furious look on his face. "Man, I can take care of Cartel."

"What's going on?"

"Cartel just called my damn house. This nigga

got some real balls to call my muthafuckin' house and on Christmas morning at that."

"You have to let her go, Chocolate. Let that bitch walk." Tae was going ten steps ahead of me.

"Joi didn't make your whorish ass walk," Luvly said, still mad at Tae.

"Chocolate, look at me. Have you talked to Brandie about this situation, calmly?" Luvly asked in a loving voice.

"Yeah, she told me that she was done with that shit. But when I picked up the phone, he asked her did she tell me about the other day when I was gone to New York."

"Man, I feel like killing that girl myself, but I've been here before Chocolate, and you know no one could tell me right from left. I had to make my own decisions. And you're going to have to do the same."

Brandie walked into the room. "Why ya'll all up here?"

"Discussing whether to bust your ass and leave you stanking. Brandie, why are you still fucking Cartel? Don't you know that nigga don't care about you. He just see this as a challenge towards Chinoe."

She looked over at me, then back to Luvly. "I—I—" She stood in the doorway holding her stomach.

Money walked up on her so that they were exchanging breath, "Stop this shit. That boy loves you. I've never seen him like this. That nigga has had all kind of beautiful women falling at his feet, but he stays true to you. Why is it so hard for you to do the same? I've never seen Chinoe want for shit.

You need to make amends now or walk out of that do'." Money sounded like my father.

Brandie stood in the same spot with tears running down her face, not saying I'm sorry, or that she was wrong.

Looking at her stand there with no remorse, just the guilt of getting caught finally gave me the strength to make a decision for my sanity, "Brandie, get your stuff and leave."

She rushed over to me. "But, I don't want to go, Chinoe."

She kneeled down in front of me, "I love you, Chinoe. I know I've made mistakes, but it's over. Cartel heard you pick up the phone. He made that stuff up to upset you and break us up." Kissing my hand, she said, "Please, don't make me go, baby. I'm in love with you."

My pitiful eyes gazed into her sad eyes. I love this girl till it hurts. Love was not suppose to hurt. But I knew if she walked out the door I'd hurt even worse.

"What do you think I should do, Brandie? Let you keep screwing other men and turn my head? Being embarrassed to shake hands with niggas I've known for years because you might be sleeping with them?"

"I'm on my knees begging you, Babe. No more! No more, just me and you."

My extended family looked on with held breath and hoping hearts. She layed her head on my hand and put my other hand to her heart.

Chapter Seventy-Three

Chocolate

It was two days before New Year's Eve and Money'd been driving me crazy about a ring for Luvly.

He had to have it platinum and it had to be ten karats. What the hell was she going to do with ten karats on her damn finger, get hit over the head, and robbed?

Brandie was layed across the bed asleep. She had been running around with Luvly trying to do something for Money's birthday party on New Years Day.

I layed down beside her, rubbing her silky hair. I wanted to ask her to marry me yesterday, but I knew she wasn't ready. These last several months felt like seven years. I want this woman to have my children, get fat and grow old with me.

I kissed her on the back of her neck. She squirmed

but didn't wake up. I didn't want to wake her, just look at that angelic face.

Ring . . . Ring . . . Ring.

"Hello."

Click.

I knew that was either Chaise or Cartel. Chaise had been threatening to tell Brandie about those three days in New York. I couldn't justify fucking Chaise, but Brandie was cheating on me and I felt like my world was crumbling.

Chaise even wrote a letter to my mother, but I recognized the handwriting and threw it away. She knew my mother's opinion meant everything to me, so telling her that Brandie was cheating and I screwed her in New York would make her hate Brandie.

Ring. Ring. Ring. I held the phone for a few seconds in hope of hearing a voice . . . "Hello."

Click.

"Got damn it." I knew it was Chaise. A nigga wasn't gone keep doing this type of shit. She was waiting for Brandie to answer the phone.

I should have just told Brandie about the photo shoot. I knew what her plan was, but I wanted to get even with Brandie.

Ring. Ring. Ring. I ran into the guest room. *Ring . . . Ring . . . Ring.* "Chaise stop playing on my goddamn phone."

"Put your wifey on then."

"Why? She ain't got nothing to do with this."

"She's in it all right. I was screwing her dick, raw."

"She don't have anything to do with what we did. Damn Chaise, leave it alone. She ain't going nowhere. I love her and want her for the rest of my life."

"Fuck you, Chinoe! Your luck is about to run out. You told me you were leaving her, that we could have another chance. What, you were just running game on me? Fuck that shit! Put her on the goddamn phone!" she screamed like a crazy woman.

"No, so stop calling here. Aren't you in Italy?" I whispered between clenched teeth.

"Yep, see how determined I am. So I will find her and tell her about your promises to me and our fuck fest."

She hung up the phone. "Damn!" Why did I do that shit? What was I thinking?

Ring . . . Ring . . . Ring.

"Stop calling my muthafuckin' house!"

"Why? I love you, boo."

"Oh, Luvly, my bad."

"Who keep calling your house?"

"Chaise."

"Boy, ya'll keep more drama going in that house than I've had in my whole life."

"You believe that if it makes you feel better."

She popped her lips, "Kiss my ass. Did you get the stuff I asked you for?"

"Yeah, I ordered the big ass football cake. And hired the decorators."

"Good, how much was the cake?"

"Why? You not paying for it."

"I just wanna know."

"Five hundred."

"Umm. Glad you're paying for it. So how is everything going with you and Brandie?"

"Good. She's not dancing at the club. Cartel was coming down to the club every night harassing her. So in order for me not to catch a case, she quit."

"Ya'll need a vacation."

"It's on the way."

"Chinoe, can I tell you something and you not tell Money?"

"What did Diamond do now?"

"He came in the shop yesterday and started going off. He smashed two of my glass tables and most of my finger nail polish that was on the front counter."

"Did you call the police?"

"No, I didn't want to make a big scene. He had Pila with him. She was standing on the curb, waiting for him to pull me out of the shop."

"Luvly, you haven't told Diamond about Sap have you?" She got quiet. "Luvly!"

"No! Ok, no! I'm not in love with him any more, but, Chinoe, I don't know how to tell him. He's going to try to kill me."

"You been letting him see her haven't you?" She didn't answer.

"And if he seen her then he's seen you." Punching my hand, "You know damn well I would never let him hurt you. But you have to let us do dat nigga and not get involved."

She started crying, "Yes. I'm falling right back into the same shit I just cleaned up."

"Money is going to find out about yesterday. You know Pila gone make sure of that."

Sniffling, "He won't be back in town until five o'clock New Years Eve. Listen, the reason Diamond did all that is because of an interview in VIBE magazine. He said Money said he loved spending time with his family and especially his girlfriend and their daughter."

"You have the power to stop this."

She whined, "I know, I know."

"Where is Sap?"

"Sleep. She's running a fever and hurting."

"What the doctors at Emory say?"

"The doctor at Emory is contacting a specialist in L.A. They are looking at her blood work."

"Well, ya'll need to let me know what's going on with her."

"Like I wouldn't."

"And, Luvly."

"Yes?"

"I'm always here for you. I'll never let anything or anyone hurt you, not even Money. You just have to let me in."

Chapter Seventy-Four

Brandie

I wonder who keep calling this house and hanging up. I'm going to call the phone company and get those hang-ups traced.

I just wanted the New Year to bring brightness to my life. I didn't know if me and Chinoe were going to make it.

I was torn between love and lust. Cartel gave me the kind of affection that Chinoe could never give. And Chinoe gave me the kind of love and passion that Cartel didn't possess.

Hunt and Sean were out of the picture completely. And after the New Year I would have everything on the right track.

Ring . . . Ring . . . Ring. "Chinoe, catch the phone. I'm in the bathroom."

"All right."

Two minutes later he came in the bathroom, "Hey beautiful, sleep good?"

"Yes. Luvly has been driving me crazy. But hanging out with Sap is cool."

He sat down by the tub and started rubbing my back, "Umm that feels good."

"Brandie," he said in a serious tone.

Oh, Lord, here we go. Whenever we were having a nice quite moment he brought up bullshit. I can tell by how he said my name, "Yes."

"Are you sure you love me?"

I turned and looked into his handsome face, into his hopeful eyes, "Yes, I'm sure I love you, I'm here with you."

"Why do or why did you feel like you had to see Cartel?"

This was my chance to explain my position.

"I don't know, Chinoe. I met him before I met you and then I saw you and I forgot life existed. Once reality hit, all my obligations were still there. Then I thought you were seeing someone else, I'm sorry. I let my assumptions take over my good judgment."

He hugged me tight. It seemed like that question was really for him, but pushing the guilt on me.

Ring . . . Ring . . . Ring. "Let it ring."

"Who keeps calling and hanging up?"

"Don't know. Probably some kids."

Yeah, right. Probably somebody he was fucking. *See, shit just keep going against us.*

"Hungry?"

"Nope."

"So are you ready?"

"Ready for what, Chinoe?"

"To get married, have kids?"

Usually the man was the one who cringed and tensed up when asked that question, because he was unsure or not ready, but today the shoe was on the other foot.

Ring . . . Ring . . . Ring. "Chinoe, go answer the phone. It could be Luvly about Sap. She was sick last night."

Ring. Ring. "Hello."

"Put her on the phone, Chinoe."

"Bitch, stop calling my damn house!"

I yelled from the bathroom, "Chinoe, who is it?"

"Yeah, Chinoe, who am I. Tell her I'm the woman you were fucking in New York."

"I told her."

"Who are you kidding? I know you wouldn't tell her. You don't want to lose her, but you aren't going to play on my emotions. I've been the clean up woman in two of your relationships. Not any-more. If I have to hurt, you and she will too. Shit, she probably still fucking Cartel anyway. But hey that's not my concern." Screaming "Put that ho on the phone!"

"You are in Italy, do your job, and leave me alone."

"Chinoe, who is that, Babe?" Brandie kissed my neck.

"Thank you, Miss Colier I will come down to the agency tomorrow and pick up the assignment." *Click.*

"You have to leave?" she said with a sad face.

"No, something for next week."

I wanted to make love to Chinoe. Show him that he still had claim on me. Make myself believe it too.

Chapter Seventy-Five

Brandie

"Ma, are you bringing that good pasta salad."

"I told you I would, Luvly," Mrs. Starr said, agitated, rubbing her temples.

"Sorry I asked."

"Don't be sorry, just be careful." Realizing that she'd hurt Luvly's feelings, she added, "I just have a little headache is all. Brandie, bring me those two bags on the sofa please."

Grabbing the two bags from the sofa, taking them to Mrs. Starr, I took a second look at Joi. Her hair color had been tamed down, nails cut at to a moderate length and the tight outfit replaced with a cute navy blue and cream velour-jogging suit.

Me, Joi and Luvly were helping Mrs. Starr prepare food for Money's birthday party. Mrs. Starr was making everything from potato salad and fish, to Lobster, ribs, Hawaiian chicken and squash casserole—Chocolate's favorite.

Joi prepared the mac and cheese and baked beans, as I fumbled around with the candied yams, dropping sweet potatoes and brown sugar on the floor.

Luvly seasoned and floured the wings, along with making a green bean casserole—Money's favorite dish. "Is this going to be enough food, Ma?" Luvly inquired.

"If it's not, you always got KFC."

We all laughed.

"I know ya'll need my help in here." Grandma Loane told us as she sashayed through the kitchen. She was getting sicker. She had Systemic Lupus and it was tearing her body apart.

"Noooo, Grandma Loane. We old ladies can handle it." Mrs. Starr said as she gently grabbed her shoulders, trying to direct her back into the den. "Go sit down and be youthful and gorgeous."

Tapping Mrs. Starr on the hand, "Seal you let me be." She sat down at the table and started cutting up celery, "I might be a little ill, but I'm not handicap."

I wondered when Luvly was going to tell us she was pregnant. She thought I didn't know, but I was around her every day, and she'd been putting on weight in her butt and face. She had that pregnancy glow too.

"Brandie, when are you and Chocolate getting married?" Mrs. Starr asked, smiling.

Smiling, cutting my eyes back to the table, "I don't know, sooner than later. We're talking about it."

"The question is, when is Luvly and Money getting married?" Joi asked in a sneaky voice.

"Yes. Now that's what I wanna know." Grandma Loane spoke up.

"Is Mr. Starr coming to the party?" Luvly asked, shying away from the question.

Mrs. Starr blushed, "Yes he is."

"Mrs. Starr may I ask why ya'll are not together, but are together?"

"Brandie, you will understand once you fall so deep in love that you forget that life is proceeding and it leaves you breathless, standing still."

I sat down next to Mrs. Starr and opened my ears, eyes, and heart.

"I have loved Moe for a long time. He was good to me, but he was just whorish like most young men. I had a time with him, but I let him go. Tried to start over with my life, I dated for a while, but he got jealous, then I got jealous and a whole lot of fights came after that. But no matter what, he has always been there for Chinoe.

Baby, people fall in and out of love everyday. Nobody will blame you for falling out of love, but the games played while doing it is where the blame takes place. You have to experience and grow to understand. The secret to everlasting love is both of you can not fall out of love at the same time."

"Well, I just want this New Year to bring prosperity in love, health for all and caring for and from everyone. I've been through to much lately." Joi expressed.

"Joi, how long have you and Taeko been together?" I asked.

"Forever, since we were going to the ninth grade."

"Oooooh wee. That's a long time."

"A hard time."

"Luvly, how long have you and Money been together?" Joi asked, trying to take the heat off herself.

Everyone cleared their throats and sniffed.

"A long time." She wiped the tips of her fingers on a flower printed towel. "I met all of them when I was in the ninth grade. If I knew then what I know now, I would have ran in the opposite direction. I met Diamond and Money the same day, at Mosely gym."

"A woman is the strongest blade in the world."

"Grandma Loane, what you talking about?" Luvly playfully asked her.

"A woman can split a family, a man's heart, and a nation all in one stroke. Women are strong as steel. You young women have a strength and power that you don't even know how to use yet. Your smile can break a man's pockets and make him leave his home. And your hips can start a war between two brothers or a father and son. But the thing you have to remember is the gift is from God. It's to be used for the love of your husband, not to thrown around like loose change in any man's pocket. It's God sent and not to be used on lust."

We were all stunned. Grandma Loane got deep.

The men walked through the door with growling tummies. "Hey Ma, what's to eat?" Taeko asked, rubbing his stomach.

"Dang. Hungry, boy? Can you speak first?"

"Hey, Ma, what you cooking?" Chinoe was looking so damn cute. His crème-cranberry turtleneck Girbaud sweater with large billowy sleeves made him look like the super model he was. He looked at me with a sexy, boyish look, "Hey, beautiful, how are you today?"

I blushed and kept washing the dishes, "What did you buy at the mall?"

"None of your business." The smile on his face soothed me from snapping on him.

Money came in two minutes later, yelling, "Money in da the house!" He looked around at all of us, "Ya'll suppose to be yelling."

"Boy, please. Let Blair Underwood, Denzel, or R. Kelly walk through that door and then we will yell and fall out," Luvly joked with him.

Everyone hugged Money and gave him early birthday licks, "Hey, hey, my birthday isn't until twelve a.m. with twenty additional seconds." Money told everyone as they whooped him around the table.

He hugged Luvly and kissed her like it's the most important thing for him to do."

Sap and Trinket came running in, straight to their grandmother.

Showing no favoritism Mrs. Starr gave each one an arm, "How are my sweet girls." Patting them both on the bottom.

"Why didn't you bring Trey?" Joi asked.

"He was gone with your brother."

"Damn, Luvly, you getting thick ain't chu baby."

So many conversations were going on that Taeko's question went unheard.

"I've been eating a lot lately. You know when I'm depressed or sick I eat.

"I'm sleepy, Mommie." Sap wallowed her head on Luvly's thigh, looking feverish and sick.

"I'll put her to bed," I volunteered. She was such a gorgeous little girl.

Burying her head into my neck, "Auntie Brandie, you smell good." She layed her head on my shoulder.

"She's not too heavy for you?"

"I'm a big girl." I turned to walk away, poking out my butt on purpose.

Chinoe licked his lips. "I'll help you tuck her in. Trinket, you sleepy too?"

With her chin resting in her hand, she said, "No, I'm hungry."

We layed Sap down and I rubbed her hair like Chinoe had done me so many nights and mornings.

"She's so beautiful, Chinoe. She could be yours with her skin color and hair." I turned my lips up and slighted my eyes at him.

"Naw, she's her daddy's child. She looks just like his mother."

Looking into my eyes, she said, "You are beautiful. When do you think you'll be ready to have our first child?"

I wanted to say we could go home and start trying now, but who would I be kidding? We weren't strong enough in our relationship.

"When we are ready." He didn't argue or disagree. He kissed my hand, and I continued rubbing Sap's hair until she fell asleep.

Lord, please bless me with fruitful gifts. Provide me with enough love and strength to give it back. I'm waiting with open arms to receive your gifts.

Amen.

Chapter Seventy-Six

Chocolate

Everyone was looking nice. I was pimping a cream and tan pin stripe Gibaud jean suit. Brandie was matching me with a crème and tan linen Encye pinstripe suit. The top had no back and the wide legs pants fell nicely on her hips.

Money had on a Phat Farm platinum jean outfit and Luvly had on a baby blue platinum Encye dress. She looked a little on the thick side, but it looked good on her. And Sap matched Money's Phat Farm outfit except with a jean shirt.

It was one hour before the new year and everyone had smiles on their faces.

"Hey, sexy, why are you over here alone?"

"Wishing you were with me." I grabbed Brandie, touching her bare silky back, "You look so beautiful tonight."

"So do you Babe."

She gave me a sweet kiss. "I love you, Chinoe Chocolate Starr."

"I love you more."

She walked back to the crowd of people. I scanned the room to see all the familiar and unfamiliar faces.

"So, I see you on the prowl again."

I turned around and met eye to eye with the devil herself. Tightening my grip around my glass, I said in an even voice, "Why are you here? How did you get past the front door?"

"I told you that I would be seeing you soon." Rubbing her hand over her ass, she said, "I got my ways." She reached her hand out to touch my chest. "You should know better than anyone." I walked away from her, closing my eyes, hoping I was just delusional.

She stood at the top of the steps smiling and gloating. She spotted Money and walked over to him. I was trying to place my eyes on Brandie, but she was nowhere in sight.

"What the hell?" Diamond was standing at the door. I knew I needed to go over there and straighten it, but the bodyguards were checking the list; they'd handle it.

"Chinoe, this is a nice party."

"Thank you, Caymin." She had cut her hair into a swinging bob that complimented her sweet face. "Where is your other half?" I asked, referring to her new lover Dun. I quickly turned my attention away from her beauty.

She rolled her eyes and smacked her lips, "He's in the bathroom."

"He don't let you out of his site does he?"

"Maybe it's the other way around."

She twisted off. I had to admit, she was still fine. Looking at her reminded me so much of Brandie. *Brandie. I have to find Brandie.*

My heart was beating ninety miles per hour, my hands were sweaty, nerves jumping.

"Nice party, Chinoe." "This mug is off the chain." Different people were patting me on the back. "Tight gig Dawg." I gave everyone dap and head nods.

I spotted Luvly standing by the cake, talking to some guests, "Excuse me, Luvly I need your help please."

"What's up?" she asked, smacking on pineapples.

"Where is Precious?"

"On the dance floor."

"Look, when I went to New York I slept with Chaise and told her that I was leaving Brandie. And that me and her could get back together."

"Slow down. You slept with Chaise, Chinoe, how could you? After you almost committed murder on Brandie for the same thing."

"I know, but now is not the time for a lecture. She's here and she's looking for Brandie."

"Where is she?"

"I don't know and don't care as long as she's not near Brandie. The good thing is she has never seen her before."

"With all the magazines ya'll have been on?"

"She's been overseas, and besides it always said friend, not Brandie. I've had many pictures taken with other models from the company, so she don't know."

"So you want Precious to be Brandie?"

"You got it."

We both got on a mission to find Precious.

After a few moments of panic, Luvly said, "There she is, Chinoe."

She was all smiles, thinking I wanted to dance with her. "Come on, Chinoe. Show me what you got."

"Precious, come here, please." She stopped dancing and stood close to me.

Any other time I would have pushed her back. "I need a huge favor."

"You've finally come to your senses."

"Yeah, kind of. I need you to be my girlfriend."

She almost knocked me over with hugs and kisses. I spotted Chaise looking at Precious load me down with love. I smiled at her and placed my arms around Precious. "Right now, Precious. I need you to be Brandie."

Chaise walked up with revenge on her mind, "So you are Brandie?"

She looked confused, but caught on quickly. "And you are?"

She licked her lips and dropped her fake smile. "So you haven't mentioned me to her, Chinoe?"

I stood back because I knew the ghetto Precious was going to surface any moment.

"No, so I'm asking you."

"I'm his ex-girlfriend who fucked him a few days ago."

Precious turned and looked at me. She slapped the shit out me.

"So you knew about me and you still fucked him?"

"He wasn't my dog to keep on a leash."

"Bitch, please tell it to somebody whose listening." Precious threw her drink on Chaise's white suit.

"You ghetto ass bitch. I thought Chinoe had better taste in women, but obviously I was wrong."

"You're right, if he chose to be with you." Precious grabbed me by the hand and we walked off.

"Why did you slap me?"

"Because if you were going to cheat, you should have come to me. Chinoe, you know I've been wanting a piece of you ever since junior high. But I like Brandie and know she would have been proud of me."

Brandie walked up on us. "Hey, Babe, let's take pictures. Hey Precious. Babe, they are taking pictures out on the balcony come on."

As we rapped up the pictures, Money came on the mic. "Can I have everyone's attention? Could everyone please come around the platform?" People were still laughing and staggering behind.

"Could ya'll please move your asses before twelve hits. We have thirty minutes before count down." Everyone came to the platform. "First I would like to have my best friends and their ladies come up here. Next, could my extended family join us?"

My mother and father looked so in love. Grandma Loane was too sick to make it. And Luvly's mother and father were in Italy, celebrating their thirty-second anniversary. Tae and Joi stood with Trinket and Trey by their side, hand in hand. Me and Brandie were hugged up like two high school kids. And Luvly was holding Sap in her arms.

"Luvly we've been through hell and back. And no one can predict if we are going back. But I love you and . . . " He paused and took a deep breath, "And our daughter. Give Sap to Chinoe." I took Sap.

Money got down on one knee. Camera flashes nearly blinded us. "Luvly Tanese Mancini, will you be my wife?"

He pulled out the ten-karat rock and almost knocked everyone out.

She was crying but maintaining a big smile. "Yes, Money, I will." They hugged and kissed.

"Okay, since you said yes, Reverend Burns will you please come up here?"

Luvly, still wiping her face, looked confused.

"Will you marry me right now?"

With no hesitation, she said, "I do!"

"I pronounce you husband and wife, Mr. and Mrs. Money Loane." The ceremony was short, but intimate and meaningful.

Everyone began clapping. My mother hugged them both, "I'm so happy for you all. Now maybe all the madness and confusion can leave your lives. And that baby can grow up in a home."

My dad gave Money some dap and a fatherly hug. He kissed Luvly. "Your mother and father are going to be so happy. Money, boy you have finally done it. You have finally become a man, taking steps to have a family. Your grandfather would have been proud, but he's looking down on you, proud as ever."

Brandie and Luvly were both crying. Tae and Money were hugging. Joi was congratulating Luvly.

It was 11:56 p.m. and the whole room was already celebrating like it was 12:00 a.m.

"Excuse me, everyone. May I have your attention, first of all thank you everyone for coming out to help celebrate Money's birthday. Not knowing that it would be my engagement party and wedding. I would like to thank God for all these unforgettable blessings he's blessed me with. I love you Mrs. & Mr. Starr for being my second set of parents. I love you, Chocolate Starr, for being my brother best friend and guidance counselor."

The whole room laughed. "Thank you Tae for being my big brother and protector. Brandie, you're next sister-in-law. Joi, I know we can squash all the madness in the new millennium. And to my beautiful daughter, lots of kisses and hugs, Mommy loves you. And best friend, soul mate, confidant, shoulder, and husband, I love you. And I promise to be the best wife, mother, and friend any husband and daughter could have. I just hope you both can accept our new addition."

The glow in Money's face hit everyone in the heart. "Luvly, you're pregnant?"

"Yes Babe."

He picked her up and the room went wild. ". . . five, four, three, two, one, Happy New Year and Happy Birthday, Money!"

The room went from Yahoo's and claps to screams and stomping feet. Out of nowhere, gunshots rang in the air. I threw Sap on the platform and threw Brandie over her. I covered them both with my body.

My mother and father were on the floor behind the platform. I couldn't hear anything but music, and all I saw was people running! They were jumping through closed windows—glass was shattering everywhere. Gunshots were still blasting.

My side and leg were burning, I asked, "Brandie, are you all right?"

"Yes, what the hell is going on? Sap, are you okay, Babe?"

She shook her head, so I assumed she was just scared, "I don't know Baby, but we are going to find out." My head started feeling woozy. And my side and leg feel wet.

I looked around to see if I could see Money or Tae, but I couldn't.

The gunshots had stopped. People were crying, still running, asking what happened. Some had been hit and grazed.

I was trying to stand up but my body became lifeless. I slowly rolled off Brandie and Sap. "Sapphire, are you okay?" She started crying and layed in Brandie's lap.

"Do you see Money or Tae?"

Brandie was in so much shock that she was speechless, wide-eyed, looking into space. "Brandie, Brandie. Do you hear me?"

"Yes, I hear you,' she whimpered. She began to cry. "Chinoe, you are bleeding!" She layed Sap down on the platform. "Oh, God, Chinoe, you have been shot. Lay still!"

I had no choice. My body was numb. I layed on my side and looked around the room. Sap was laying next to me with her eyes wide open, she wasn't blinking. "Sap, Sappy, talk to Uncle Chocolate. Are you hurt?"

Her eyes remained wide, and her mouth remained silent.

I struggled to turn onto my stomach. When I finally got into the position, I saw Luvly's shoes.

I tried to raise myself up to see further over the platform, but I felt a hand on my boot, "Chocolate, you've been shot. He's been shot!" my mother screamed, shedding tears and holding her hands over her mouth. She ripped her shawl and opened my coat, pressing the shawl into my side.

"Owe, Ma!"

"Sorry, Chocolate, but I need to try and stop the bleeding." I felt faint and my vision was going blurry.

"Hurry up!" she screamed. "Don't let go, baby. Hold on, your father is calling the police."

Through short breaths, "Ma—where is—Luvly, Money? Is Tae okay?"

My mother looked around the room, "I see them, but they're not moving. Where is Brandie?"

"She—call—police."

"Shhh, don't try and talk. Hold this tightly to your side." I could barely see my mother, but she went over to Luvly and Money. "Oh, my God. Oh Lord, why? Luvly, talk to me, honey. Money, wake up baby." My mother cries became loud and deep. "Please, Lord, don't take them."

Tears rolled down my face. My body started shaking and my heart beat faster. *Please, Lord, protect us from this evil.*

Chapter Seventy-Seven

Brandie

"Chinoe, wake up, honey. Talk to Mama." Mrs. Starr rubbed her son's forehead.

"Son, we are here. Right by your side," Moe said as he held his son's hand.

Chinoe's parents were in tears, kneeling by his bedside. He was in critical condition.

When he comes from under the medication, he is going to want to know where Luvly and Money are? What am I going to say? How am I going to tell him? Tears rolled down my cheeks.

"Brandie, honey, don't you want to go home and shower, change clothes and come back?"

I shook my head. "No, Mrs. Starr. I need to be here when he wakes up."

"He needs to see you strong and healthy."

Sucking up tears and hours of hurt, "Mrs. Starr,

how are we going to tell him about Money and Luvly?"

Tae walked in with a tear stained face, "Has he woke up yet?"

"No Tae. He's still under the medication."

"How's Trinket?"

"She's out of ICU. The doctors said she'll be okay."

"That's good. Where are Joi and Trey?"

"Joi's mother came and got Trey. Joi is at Trinket's bedside, I'm going back up in a minute so she can come see Chinoe and go see Sap." We both hugged him. He walked over to Chinoe and talked to him.

Me and Mrs. Starr walked out of the room. It was almost four in the evening, and there were thousands of flowers everywhere.

"I'm going up to see Sap. I want to know if her blood work has come back." Mrs. Starr said, slightly squeezing my shoulder.

"Did you get in touch with Mr. and Mrs. Mancini?

"Yes." Mrs. Starr couldn't hold back her tears and hurt any longer. "Oh, Brandie, how can a mother take this kind of news. And that poor child is never going to be the same. She is too young too understand what has happened."

A doctor in blue scrubs, pulling a white cap off his head asked,

"Are you Mrs. Mancini?"

"I'm Mrs. Starr. I'm acting as Mrs. Mancini. Mr. and Mrs. Mancini are on their way from Italy."

"We've tried everything possible. But Luvly had a gunshot wound to the head, a ruptured stomach and a gunshot wound through her back. We're sorry."

Mrs. Starr fell down, "What about the baby."

"He is fighting, but the bullet went through his stomach. He's holding on. You can see him when you are ready."

"How far along was she?"

"Six months. Anything you all need, just ask."

He hugged Mrs. Starr, shook my hand, and walked back through the double doors.

"Oh, my Lord. What is going to become of Sapphire? That baby has seen her mother gunned down and killed. She's going to be damaged for life."

Two minutes later, another doctor walked up to us, "Mrs. Loane."

"I'm acting in her behalf."

"Money Loane is in critical condition. We've stopped the internal bleeding and removed three of the bullets out of his back. The bullet in his neck seems to be slowly moving toward his heart. So we are taking him into surgery right away."

My heart skipped a beat, "So he's alive?"

The doctor didn't have a positive look on his face, "He is a strong guy, but there are risks with surgery. We will update you once the surgery has been completed."

"Doctor, do you know the update on Sapphire Mancini?"

"She's doing good. She only had two graze wounds, but she has a very high fever and severe swelling of the legs and arm. She is still non-responsive. We are doing several tests to see if any bullet casing are lodged in he blood stream."

"Thank you."

"Mrs. Starr, I'm going to see Money."

"Ok dear, I'm going up to be with Sap. Precious needs to be relieved."

Walking to the elevator, I broke down. All my strength had been broken. Luvly was gone and she was never coming back. She was just about to begin the life she wanted and deserved. Why did her life have to be taken? Why not mine? I was alone, no husband, no kids, and too much sin to keep carrying around.

"Hey Baby, come here." I turned to face Cartel standing with open arms.

I hugged him; fell into his arms, letting his body soak up all the hurt.

"Luvly is gone! She's gone! Money is barely making it. And, oh, Chinoe, he's hurt bad."

"Where is their little girl?"

"She's on the pediatric floor. She's going to be all right. But the long term affect of losing her mother is going to devastate her forever."

"Oh, Babe, I'm so sorry. I'm here now." He held me tight and strong. "Let me take you home. Put you in a hot bubble bath and get you something to eat." He wanted to take care of me even though I was mourning over another man.

Gently pushing away from him, "I can't leave Chinoe."

"You aren't any good to him like this. You have blood all over you. And you are tired and weak."

At this point I was confused and distraught, "I need to see how Money is doing first."

"I'll walk with you."

I was so hurt and sick inside. Was it something I did wrong, why did this have to happen?

Chapter Seventy-Eight

Brandie

When I got to Money's room, some woman with short pretty hair was laying on his chest. "I still love you, Money. I always will. And I know that you still love me. I know that you want to marry Luvly, but I will still make myself available for you."

She didn't know that I was listening, but I wanted to jump on her for Luvly.

"Excuse me."

She wiped her eyes and turned to me, "Oh, hi. Who are you?"

"Just a friend that was at the party."

"Are you hurt? Do you need a doctor?" She got off the bed and walked towards me.

Holding up my hands, I said, "No, I'm fine. This isn't my blood."

"Do you know what happened?" She asked concerned, folding her arms.

"No. I was celebrating and after the count down gunshots started firing."

Her face looked familiar. Like I'd seen her in the mall or someone described her to me.

"On the street I'm hearing Luvly's boyfriend did it."

"Money is right here, so how could he do it?"

In a nasty tone, she sneered, "No, her boyfriend is not Money. Diamond."

"But I was there when Money asked Luvly to marry him. And they got married"

Tears begin to fall instantly. "He . . . asked her . . ."

She looked back at the bed where Money lay helpless and unaware that the love of his life, his wife, was gone.

"Yeah, and she was pregnant." I stuck the words hard into her heart.

"Pregnant? Damn!" With big, hopeful eyes, "You said was? She lost the baby?"

"No, the baby is in ICU. He's going to be fine."

She rubbed her chest, exposing L shape scars on her chest. That's where I knew her from. Salone!

"So how is Luvly?" Salone reached up to hold her neck, like she was praying for the worst.

I almost broke down, but I held my composure, "She died." The bitch almost smiled.

She stared at me for a second, "So who did you say you were?"

"I didn't." I walked over to Money and held his hand. "You have to make it for Sap and your baby boy. Chinoe . . ." My tears got caught in my throat.

"He's going to be okay . . . so you have to, too. Maybe your spirit and his can meet and tell each other to wake up."

My heart was broken and my spirit torn. Money lay wounded, inside and out, and for what, jealousy, and rage?

"Well, I'm Salone. You look familiar. Do you shop in Southlake Mall?" she asked in an authoritative voice.

I chose to ignore her demand for information.

"Has anyone informed his grandmother?"

"No, she's too ill to be told right now."

"You sure do know a lot to just be a friend partying."

My patience was wearing thin. "Look, Salone. I'm not interested in carrying on a decent conversation with you."

Knock. Knock. Knock. "Is this Money Loane's room?"

"Yes," we both answered and then looked at each other like neither one of us had the right to answer.

A petite, but very shapely woman, who had the same complexion and face as Sap, stood in the door. "How's he doing?"

"He's going into surgery in twenty minutes," Salone spoke up.

The lady looked to be in her late twenties. "Who did this to my baby?"

Salone turned up her nose. "Your baby?" Salone walked in front of the lady, interfering with her touching Money.

"Excuse me, but who are you?"

"Look, li'l bitch, back the fuck up off me or I'll

slice yo' ass up in here!" Cutting her eyes at Salone, she added, "Get the hell out of my way!"

"Mommie, Mommie."

"I'm right here, baby."

A little girl looking like Sap's twin ran in the room. "Is that my brother, Mommy?" she asked, grabbing her mother around the leg, pointing at the still body in the bed.

"Yes, it is, M&M."

Money's mother was beautiful. Chinoe mentioned her once. But she didn't look like a typical crackhead. "Hi, Mrs.—"

"Lopez."

"Mrs. Lopez. I'm Brandie, Chinoe's girlfriend."

She smiled. "He always did have good taste with everything. Where is Luvly?"

My smile quickly faded and the tears swelled up again. "She passed earlier today."

"Oh, my God. Are her parents here?"

"No. They are flying in from Italy."

"They have a daughter . . . Sas ahmmm . . . Sapphire?" Placing her hand on my arm, "She is all right, isn't she?"

Salone spoke under her breath, "Damn shame. Junkie ass, don't even know the child's name.

"Yes, ma'am." I talked over Salone.

"Chile, I ain't old enough to be called ma'am. Call me Maynea."

"Maynea." I gave her a slight smile and looked over at Salone, who was standing with her arms folded and a mean stare on her face. "She had another baby. He was taken before she passed. He's on life support."

"A baby boy, born on Money's birthday. Have

they named him yet?" She looked dreamy-eyed and hopeful.

"No, not yet. I'll leave you to visit with your son."

"Brandie, what room are Sapphire and Chinoe in?"

"Seven-o-six, and Chinoe is in Six-seven-seven."

"Thank you so much." We hugged and I walked out of the room.

I felt Salone on my heels. "Brandie." She said my name like it was a bad taste in her mouth. "So you're the prostitute Chinoe's tucked his tail between his legs for?"

"And you are the slut that Luvly stabbed and left her mark on?"

She walked up close to me. Her breath blew my bangs. "Bitch, you ain't shit, just like Luvly wasn't shit. Ya'll hoes think because you pretty and your pussy holes tight that you can write your own script for life; taking other peoples' man, taking the whole damn cake, fuck you and your broken theory. Chinoe gone find out how sleazy and slimy you are."

I was about to bust her ass and show her how this pretty bitch could work it. "Brandie, I've been looking for you."

Caymin hugged me. She looked at Salone with evil eyes, "its okay, Brandie." Tears were steaming down my face. "Come on, Chinoe is up."

"Chinoe's up!" My spirits were lifted. *Thanks for looking out, Luvly.* I almost broke my legs trying to get to the elevator.

"Brandie, is Cartel downstairs?"

I felt ashamed, but he wasn't there upon my request. "Yes, but he came on his own."

She fell back onto the elevator rail, "I can't believe all of this. I'm going to miss Luvly."

"Me, too." Me and Luvly probably had gotten closer in the last few months than her and Caymin in all the years they were friends.

Once I reached room 677, seeing Chinoe sitting up in bed was the best present he'd ever given me. "Hey, Babe. How you feel?"

"Good as can be expected," he answered in a groggy voice. "Get over here and give me some healing kisses." He raised up slowly. "How are you?"

"I'm not hurt on the outside." I gave him a kiss, trying not to put any pressure on his body. He still looked good, all wrapped up.

"Where is Money? Is Tae and Luvly okay? Ma told me Sap was all right. I want to go see her."

"Tae wasn't hurt, but Trinket was shot in the leg." Chinoe took in a deep breath. "But she's all right baby. And Money is going into surgery in about two minutes."

"And Luvly, how is the baby?" Mrs. Starr looked me in the eyes. She looked sad and confused. I was trying to read her mind. But I didn't know how to tell him about Luvly.

"Please, lay back, Chocolate." *Knock. Knock.* "Come in," Mrs. Starr said.

Maynea walked in, holding M&M's hand. Mrs. Starr's expression was that of joy and thanks for interrupting us telling Chinoe the truth.

"Maynea, how are you?" They hugged, "Who is this little princess?"

Maynea picked M&M up and put her on her hip. "M&M, say hello to everyone."

"Hi." She buried her head into her mother's neck.

Whispering to Mrs. Starr, "How is Chocolate, Seal?"

"He's going to be all right. He's strong just like Money." Mrs. Starr winked at Maynea.

"Maynea?"

"Yes, Chi-Chi. It's me, boo."

She went over to his bed with Malaney on her hip. "This is M&M."

"I would swear this was Sap. Or maybe it's all the medication. Have you seen her yet?"

"Only through the window, the doctors were in there."

"Well, let me get back up stairs with her. I need to speak with the doctors," Mrs. Starr said as she kissed Chinoe.

"I'm going too. I want to meet my grandbaby."

As they walked out of the room, Chinoe's father stuck his head in the door, "Hey there, Brandie." He gave me a hug and grabbed his son's hand. "Glad to see you up, boy. You had us all scared."

"Old man . . . you know I'm a soldier." Chinoe's voice was hoarse.

"I just wanted to make sure you were up and all right. I'ma go up here and see Money before he go into surgery."

"All right, Pop." Chinoe sat all the way up in the bed trying to clear his throat.

"You thirsty, baby?"

"A little. Now what did you say about Luvly and the baby."

My eyes became watery and I couldn't look him in the eyes. So I called the nurse to the room to buy some more time. "Look at all your flowers and gifts."

"Who sent all this stuff?"

"Fans and family."

The door squeaked, "Hey, Chinoe. How you doing?" Caymin walked to the other side of the bed.

"I'm cool." He looked me in the eyes. "Where is Luvly, Brandie?"

I held back my tears and tried to push it out of my mouth, "She, she umm . . . she . . . passed a few hours ago."

Slow hard tears dropped out of his eyes, "Naw. Stop playing."

I was shaking my head from side to side. "No, she's gone, baby."

"Oh, Brandie, why? That was my dawg. My baby. It's always been me, her, Money and Tae." Saliva ran out of his mouth uncontrollably, "I'm going to kill that muthafucka." He started moving hysterically. Tossing and turning, he screamed "Whyyyyyyyy?" so loud that the nurses finally ran into the room. His monitor started beeping.

More nurses pushed past me and Caymin. "Excuse me, ma'am. We need to get to him." "Somebody get them outta here."

Chinoe's eyes rolled back into his head. "He's going into shock. Page the doctor," one of the nurses said.

I covered my mouth in shock. "What's happening?" I screamed. "Is he ok?"

"No, he's having a seizure." I let out a loud scream. "Get them outta here, now!" one of the nurses shouted.

* * *

Two hours later, everyone was calm. Chinoe was stable and Luvly's parents were due in the next hour.

Cartel had left and told me to give call him. But Caymin was still by my side. "Girl you can go home and get some rest." I lazily told her.

"You sure?"

"Positive." She hugged me and left.

Mrs. Starr was still up stairs with Sap. Mr. Starr was in the chair opposite mine. "Brandie, why don't you go home and get a hot bath and some clean clothes? Bring everybody something back to eat." He pulled out his wallet.

"Oh, no. No money. I got it. Any requests?"

"Popeye's will be good."

"Anything in particular?"

"White meat for Seal, and sweet tea for both of us. Since we got here by ambulance, see if Maynea will let you use her car. "

"Okay.

Chinoe was resting, so I kissed him on the forehead.

A short chocolate sister with thick, shoulder-length hair walked past me as I walked out. Probably from the agency or some family I hadn't met. I headed to Money's room to see if Maynea would let me use her car.

"Excuse me, Maynea. Did you drive here?"

"Yes."

"Is there anyway you will let me, a stranger, use your car to go home and take a shower."

"Sure. I'll take you. M&M needs to lay down, and I'm starving."

Taeko met us at the door. "How was his surgery?"

"He's out of the woods."

"Good." Taeko let go of a deep breath.

"And your baby?"

"She's doing fine. Maynea, I'm glad you here." They embraced, Taeko rubbing up and down Maynea's back.

"We are about to go get something to eat. Would you and Joi like me to bring something back?"

"Yeah, something for Joi, she hasn't eaten since yesterday."

Me and Maynea headed to my house.

Chapter Seventy-Nine

Brandie

Pulling into the driveway, Maynea's mouth dropped open. "This is your home?"

"Yes."

"Girl, what the hell did you do—rob a bank?"

"No, pockets." We both laughed. "I was a dancer and the house was a gift."

"From a sugar daddy?"

"A friend."

"Umm, hmm, girl. I'm not stupid. Friends buy you cards and flowers, not a damn castle."

We walked through the door and she got over excited. "This is some beautiful furniture. That is gorgeous." She pointed to the curio full of teddy bears. I'm gone keep my eye on her and my things. They both might come up missing. "Very expensive taste I see. How long have you and Chinoe been together?"

"Physically seven months. Mentally, a lifetime."

"What do you mean mentally?"

"I use to think about Chinoe ever since I saw his picture on his mother's desk in school."

"Oh, you were in homebound school? Little smart ass, hunh?"

"Yeah. And when he graduated, he saw me in the mall and has been in love every since. He didn't get a chance to talk to me though. Not until the night of Sap's birthday party."

"That little girl looks like she could be mine." Maynea had tears in her eyes. "I don't think that little boy is going to make it though. His lung collapsed." She wiped her tears. "Did you know Luvly?"

Tears filled my eyes, "Yes, we had gotten real close over these past few months." The hurt punched me in the soul.

"Yeah. When I used to come in and out of town, she would be my comforter, no matter how much wrong I did. Have you seen her father?"

"No."

"Umm Um, he is fine, Italian, with that mocha skin and big curly hair. We dated once."

"When?"

"When Luvly's mother was pregnant with her. Her or the boys don't know about that though." Maynea winked and put her finger up to her lips.

"Oh."

"I used to be wild, Brandie. On drugs, selling my ass. Everything was an open door for me. Despite my mother and father being great parents, I was just a bad child. But I'm straight now. My life is in order. I just want my family back." She hugged her body as if it were her family.

"Money and Malaney have different fathers, but I am their mother, damn it! Money's father has always been around him, even though he doesn't know him as his father. He's so proud of Money. So am I.

"I have a young daughter now, I can't have my nose open and still raise her. And those babies have lost their mother. But I'm young enough to help raise them. I won't leave their side again."

She was very open and honest. I guess that could be taken as good and bad. "How old are you, Maynea? You look good—around my age."

"I've been blessed. The drugs didn't destroy my looks. I'm thirty-eight."

Damn, she had Money young.

"Yeahhhhh, I was extremely young when I had Money. Pregnant at thirteen, fourteen when I gave birth."

My coochie was hurting for her. "You want something to drink?"

"Yep."

"I don't know what's in here. I've been at Chinoe's for about two months straight."

"Water is fine. Can I lay her down?"

"There's a bedroom around the corner to the left."

The mail was piled up, bills that I'd been neglecting. The one piece that caught my eye was a huge bright pink envelope with silver writing. FRAGILE was posted on the front.

"So you and Chi-Chi are serious?"

"Yes. We've had our share of problems, but we're working them out." I gave her a beauty queen smile.

"You are a pretty girl. Rare to see a true beauty."

I smiled at her and continued to open the package marked FRAGILE.

Oh, hell Naw! It was pictures of Chinoe naked. I turned them over to see if they had a name on them, where they were taken, or any evidence that this was not my man.

The dates on them were when he was in New York. A letter dropped out of the envelope.

I didn't want to be rude to Maynea and show my natural ass, so I slid the package into a drawer. I pinched myself and took in a deep breath. I opened the drawer one more time hoping all of sure they were real. And yep, there they were.

I was puzzled. There was no return address. And my last name, nor my address were on the envelope. So who ever delivered it came to my house. Who?

"So Chinoe is a super model now?"

I slid the drawer close. "Yep, he's a big time model now." Obviously, he posed nude for somebody.

"I always knew these boys would make something out of themselves. Just, I wasn't there to see it with my own eyes. That bothers me so much. Shidd, them boys got mo' money than my Daddy ever won or seen. "

I was listening to her, but my mind was focused on the envelope of pictures. It was eating me alive. *What the hell has Chinoe done?*

Chapter Eighty

Chocolate

I was trying to calculate everything that happened, but nothing added up.

Luvly was gone and Money was fighting for his life. It was all my fault! I saw Diamond standing at that door. I knew he was up to no good, but I was too interested in saving my own ass. I could have saved all of us, but being selfish cost me more than I ever expected to lose.

I opened my eyes to another nightmare. "What are you doing here?" My dad was sitting behind the curtain taking a nap. I hoped he didn't wake up and hear me get rude.

With tears streaming down her face, "I heard about what happened, on the news. I'm sorry about Luvly. Are you okay?" She reached for my hand, but I snatched it away.

"Yeah, you've said your piece so go."

"I'm sorry for being such a bitch. But I was and still am in love with you. I couldn't help myself. And to be honest if I had to do it all over again, I probably would."

The look in her eyes was the same look Nikki had the night of graduation.

"Thanks for the apology, but it's not accepted." She was the reason I neglected seeing about Diamond.

"But, Chinoe, what did you expect me to do? Take what you told me in New York and then forget it once we got back to Atlanta. Love doesn't just die when you want it to. If that is the case, I would be in Italy still. I know you never loved me but the pretending was nice. I never thought I would be standing in front of a man spilling my guts to him." She kneeled down beside my bed. Her teary eyes glued to my face. She looked helpless and innocent. No makeup, hair pulled back. "Tell me that you really love Brandie and I will leave. Tell me those three nights in New York meant nothing. I can't say that I won't keep trying."

"I do love her. I want her to be my wife, be the mother of my kids, want to grow old with her. I regret New York." She put her head down on my hand, "I was hurting and wanted to drown, and you happen to be the available alcohol. I used you, and that was wrong."

Crying, she pulled herself to her feet, "Bye, Chinoe. I'm not going to stop until you are mine."

I watched her leave out the door, wishing it was my life she was walking out of.

"Son, don't fall into your old man's past. Let

these women know the truth in the beginning. Leading them on only makes matters worse."

"I know, Pops, but I slipped. I'm man enough to admit I've made a bad situation worse."

"I'm not the one you need to admit it to. Son, I'm about to tell you something that I think you're old enough to know. A long time ago I met your mother after I had been involved with another girl. I knew that I didn't want to have a long-term relationship with this girl, but she was fine and setting it out. She was young and naive. But so was I. I screwed her without love or protection. That's why I never pressured you to have sex. I wanted you to hold your manhood until you found a worthy woman to share it with.

After I slept with this girl in April, one week later, I met the woman of my dreams. Seal was out of sight. The baddest thing I'd ever seen."

I had to admit, my mom was bad. She was good-looking as a young woman. And now she looks even better.

"We started dating and we fell in love. I was in love the first day I saw her. Five months later your mother was pregnant. We were young but very much in love. When this other women found out, she started claiming me daddy to her child. When I calculated the days and months, it was possible. She had her baby January 1st and your mother had you June 5th. I kept this a secret for four years. But when I moved your mother to Atlanta, there was no more hiding it. The other woman was hoeing, strung out on drugs and I felt like it was because of me. She had my son, but her parents had money so I stayed in the background of his life, always there, but not letting my identity be known."

"So . . . I have a brother?" I asked confused, angry.

"Yes, you do; a best friend and a biological brother. Your mother and I were never able to get over that secret. We stayed together despite what I'd done, for you. And I still loved Seal, but she couldn't trust me, and a lot of the time I couldn't trust myself."

"Where is my brother now? What's his name?" I asked intensly.

"Money Loane."

"What, Money? Money? My mother knew and never told me? Why? Goddamn ya'll!" My fist hit the bed. My father sat back and let me vent. He knew that the news caught me off guard. "All this time, that's why we've been in each others life for . . ." Tears got caught in my throat, like a sour pickle.

"Never wanted you separated."

My dad hugged me with no arm between us. Heart to heart.

"Sitting in this hospital seeing both my boys and my grandbaby suffering, I'm losing my mind. Running from room to room, not knowing if ya'll was going to make it. I made up my mind that today was the day that both of ya'll would know the truth . . ."

Maybe that's why I always felt so close to Money. I closed my eyes and tried to think myself back at the party having fun, celebrating the new millennium and Money's birthday. But when I opened my eyes, I was still in the damn hospital bed with tubes running all through my body. My dad was still sitting in front of me looking sad, disappointed in himself.

I needed Brandie by my side. I wanted to be laying next to her, rubbing her silky hair, telling her how much she meant to me and how wonderful I was going to make our life.

Chapter Eighty-One

The Resting of Luvly Mancini

A loving daughter, caring mother, trusting friend, and an adoring lover lay in a yellow marble, and platinum casket that sat high above the pews. Closed and concealed from the world, her body never being viewed by her loved ones. Several pictures of her from first born to a sixty-inch picture from the night of her departure surrounded the casket. Yellow, purple, and white flowers accent the heavenly site.

Money slumped lifelessly in the front pew with a wet face, holding on to his daughter for dear life. She was the only sanity he had left. Why Luvly, his first love, his one and only true love, why not him? Why did her mother and father have a closed casket? They wouldn't even let him see his baby one last time.

Stop playing, Luvly. Walk yo' silly ass around the cor-

ner or jump out of the casket and yell "surprise." Come on now . . . stop runnin' game! Oh, baby . . . what am . . . what am I going to do without you? There is no substitute. You are my wife . . . my wife . . . ahhhh, mannnnn.

Money jumped out of his seat, almost dropping Sap and ran to Luvly's casket, "Baby, I'm sorry . . . please, come back," He beat on the casket, making it rock. "I'm gone kill that muthafucka. I swear on everything, he is dead!

"Ahhhhh, Luvlyyyyy, come backkkkkkk!"

Chocolate and Taeko tried to pull him back, while everyone in the church stood and gaped at the star studded event. Only when Moe kneeled down beside him and gently patted him on the back, whispered something in his ear, did Money release the casket and return to his seat.

"Just come back to me love. No matter how mad you made me, got on my nerves and shitted on my heart, I never wished anything bad to happen to you. Luvly, I can't eat . . . I can't sleep, it's so hard to swallow. There is a big lump in my throat and it won't go down. It's so hard to breathe, baby, please come back to me, I can't breathe!"

How can he live without her? All he can think about is how to revenge her death and how to make her come back. Is any of that possible? And now his crack-head mother is trying to slither her way back into his life, introducing his precious little sister and finally his father. Should he be grateful or hateful????

Chocolate mourned next to Money with his head resting in his hands, crying, crushed, confused, dead on the inside. More so for the fact that he seen Diamond and could of prevented it. Or realized it was just the fact that Luvly was gone? What about Sap? What about Money? Mannn . . . Money, his best friend—brother—homeboy—brother—dawg—brother. *What did I do, Luvly? Oh, shit, what did I do? I seen that nigga at the door, but ignored it for my own selfish reasons.*

That nigga will pay, slowly and painfully, he will pay. Man, we done been through so much together, you was my sister, my conscious, my best friend, and my confidant. Thank you for always being there for me . . . my insides felt like they've been ripped out and trashed.

That day in my basement . . . you were almost my first. Your sexy ass laying on my bed, naked and hot. The air-conditioner was broke and we were trying to stay cool by using ice cubes on each other. We both thought since we were like sister and brother that our attraction would stay calm.

But I've always wanted to be with you, and when you told me that you felt the same, it was on. The way your lips felt, how soft your body was, the way you caressed my skin. Ummm, I wanted you so bad. When the head of my dick entered you, I thought I was in heaven. I lost myself.

If Money had not meant so much to me, I would have made love to you til the sun came up. And when Money came to the door, we both looked at each and instantly turned our feelings off. You've taken that secret to your grave and I'll take it to mine. And don't you worry about Sap. I'll be her second daddy. You know that. Now when she get in her pre-teen years show up or something and tell me how to handle her, especially if she's anything like you were.

Luvly, I'm still calling on you for your help—please send Brandie back to me. I love you, Luvly Lady.

* * *

Taeko sat next to Chocolate with a blank stare on his face, while Joi and the kids sat on his opposite side crying uncontrollably. That little lady was like the sister he never had. She always got on his nerves, fussed at him continuously, and constantly ate out of his plate because they had the same taste in exotic food. All the boys fell in love with her at the same time, but it was Money who won her heart. Good, Taeko thought, because he could never have been any good to her. Or could he? If he had been Luvly's lover, Diamond's throat would have been sliced a long time ago. Taeko would be wearing Diamond's heart as a charm around his neck. *Ahhh, Luvly, baby girl. I'm so sorry. It should have been me, me who took those bullets. All the terrible shit I've done, it should have been me! I'm gone miss yo' ass, girl.*

And you know it was always you that Money loved, he gon' miss you. I don't know what's gonna make it all right for him. And Sap, I'm gone do everything in my power to take care of her and give her everything you would have. Dammmmn! Why didn't they kill him when Luvly was layed up in the hospital barely alive from that nigga's hands? But when they find him, ooooh, when they find him, won't be nothing nice.

Joi wiped her tears constantly, trying to stay strong for her kids. Her and Luvly were just starting to talk and become closer. Both young mothers dealing with trifling men, other women, battered bodies, and broken hearts. They should have been more like sisters than enemies. Their daughters were best friends and so they should have been closer. Joi could remember when she first heard

Luvly cuss Taeko out for being a whore and doing her wrong. *Thank you so much for taking up for me. I should have done more about you and Salone's situation. I'll take care of Sapphire, raise her along with Trinket like she's my own.*

Brandie sat on the opposite side of the family, in the guest section, praying to God to help her to stop crying, to be able to eat and sleep. She had been sick with grief. *Girl, you were my road dawg, best friend, the sister I never had. What are we going to do with out you? Lord, have mercy on us all. I will treat Sap as if I birthed her myself. And your beautiful son, I will do the same. But if I fuck up, please, don't come and visit me. It will scare me to death. Hahahahaha. I'm gone miss you girl.*

And you know Money is going to be lost without you. Your parents are taking this rather well, but I can't say the same about Moe and Seal. They miss you dearly. Caymin sends her love; she was in a bad accident and had to stay in the hospital. You know her no driving self, ran into the back of a parked truck. I don't know what to tell you about Chinoe. I just can't do it anymore, if you would have seen those pic—forget all that. Rest in peace and continue to shine your love down on us.

Brandie was mourning her loss for Luvly and Chinoe. How could she keep her promise to Luvly about the kids, and stay away from Chinoe, too??? ???????

Four disguised women sat scattered about the pews. One in particular, wore a smug on her face, a slight smile on her lips. The bright red slutty dress would have caught any man's attention in the club, but here, at Luvly's funeral, it was meant to show disrespect.

Salone popped chewing gum loud and carelessly, dangling one leg over the other, while she admired her new, red, pointy toe Jimmy Cho's. Hot like fire—the devil herself. Her only thought was that Luvly was finally out of the picture for good.

The only thing that's bad about this situation is that it took too long. Diamond should have been knocked your slimy ass off. I've waited so long for this. I tried my best to kill yo' ass at the gas station that time, but yo' stanking ass had to survive and so did that little bitch. As soon as me and Money are married that little heffa is gone. Either with your parents or with Diamond, I'll make sure of that. I got a trick up my sleeve that is fool proof; it will guarantee my happiness. Me, Money and the baby I'm carrying, hahahahahahaha!!!

Jordan sat in the back of the church with big sunglasses, a blonde wig, red lipstick, and a black lace dress. She went unnoticed as she thanked God that Luvly was gone, out of her and Diamond's life. She had to come and make sure it was really true. When they make it to the gravesite, she had a jar of spit that she'd been saving for all the years she thought Luvly made her life hell.

Pila stood at the crowded door with tears in her eyes, trouble in her heart. This was the day that she prayed would come. She even went to a witch doctor and lit candles, stole hair from brushes left at Diamond's house, clothing and articles from the nail shop. She wished for Luvly's destruction.

I was so tired of hearing about how much Diamond loved you and how he would kill you if he couldn't have you. That hurt me night after night, him laying with me, but knowing he was truly loving you. Calling your name while I sucked his dick, while I let him enter my ass and violate my body in so many degrading ways . . . sleeping with Jordan to appease his sick pleasures. My wishing death upon you has left me living like a dead woman.

Every time he thinks about what he's done to you, he beats my ass to a pulp. My once-prized smile is now missing three teeth and a permanent dent in the corner of my mouth. I don't mean shit to Diamond, never have.

Me, Jordan, nor the other babies' mamas, or the kids, mean shit to him. All he talks about is stealing his daughter and running away to Cuba with her. I want to run up to Money and tell him so bad so that he will protect himself and her. Your words haunt me everyday, about how Diamond would do me. I'm sorry. I'm so sorry . . .

Chapter Eighty-Two

Money

"Finally, I'm home. It doesn't feel like home though." Felt empty. No nail polish left open on the table. No fake nails with art on them strewn across the floor and couch. No Luvly with Sap between her legs, doing her hair, screaming at me about being out and not calling her.

"It will, as soon as you get back to functioning and moving around."

"So how long are you staying this time, Maynea?" I asked, irritated just by the sound of her voice.

She looked at me with a sad look in her eyes. "Always and forever."

"Hahaha, you still telling that same ol' lame-ass story."

She slammed the door and put my bags at the bottom of the steps. Mad that she couldn't straighten me about the words or action I was using towards her. She understood that she was like garbage to me.

"Are you going back home or a hotel?"

She snickered to herself. "Well, Chinoe's girlfriend invited me and M&M to stay with her."

"Brandie? Naw, don't invade her life like that. She ain't use to being around nobody like you. She don't know to lock all her shit up."

Maynea slammed her glass down. "Okay, Money, you win dammit! I'm the world's worst mother. I chose the streets over you. There I said it. I was a ho, a prostitute, strung out on drugs. I'm sorry! Now your best bet is to talk all yo' shit now because I still have guts and dignity. I've graveled much too long to go back. I've cleaned up my life and I'm trying. I can't make up for the last twenty years, but I can start trying for the next." She flopped down on the couch.

"I don't want your time or your sob stories. You left me! I don't feel sorry for you. You made all the choices that determined your welfare. I feel sorry for M&M. She got you for a mother."

"Money, what are you going to do about Sapphire?"

"What do you mean, do about her? I've been there since she came out of her mother's womb. I cut her strand to life. I've help raise that little girl even when I didn't know if she was mine. She had a father even when she didn't know what a father was."

Maynea put her hands over her head. "You act like I wanted to . . . Money, please understand why I had to let Mama and Poppa raise you."

Leaning against the kitchen counter, I gave her a chance to explain. "I got nothing but time."

"When I was thirteen turning fourteen, I met a handsome, charming boy. He was a little older than me so I was fooled into thinking everything he said was gold. We slept together and two weeks later he told me that he was seeing someone else. She lived in Columbus or somewhere down there.

"A month later I found out I was pregnant. I was a young girl with dreams and a whole lot of talent. My mom told me that an abortion was out of the question. This baby was heaven sent and meant to be. We barely had enough money to feed me.

"But my father took another job to support this child. Your father came back two months before you were born and told me that the girl he was dating was pregnant. And that his cousin called him and told him I was pregnant too. He told my father that he would take full responsibility for what he was responsible for. He sent me a hundred dollars a week and the weeks he couldn't send that, he sent what he could. He always remembered your birthday and sent you Christmas money and presents."

"Sooooooo, he wasn't here in my face. The only two men that made me who I am, was Grandpa and Moe. Chinoe and I shared a father. Moe was always there at my little league games, my proms, broken bones, when I went to jail, he was there."

"When you were four your father said he couldn't take not seeing you, being in your life. So he moved his family to Atlanta. I couldn't take seeing him married to another woman with another child. So I destroyed his life, told his wife and my life ended that very day." She let out a long sigh. "And you're right, Money. Moe did do the right thing by you. It was me who ran away from my responsibilities."

"So you are thanking Moe for being what you couldn't. Tell 'em personally."

"Listen to me, damn you!" she screamed. "Money, you have always had a father." She paused, like she was scared to keep talking. "Moe . . . Moe is your father, and Chinoe is your brother.

"What!" I waved her off. "Man, go on back to wherever it is you came from wit' them lies. "

She jumped up from the sofa. "I put that on my father's grave."

"You didn't even show up for the funeral. Get outta my house."

She grabbed both my arms. "Look at me."

I started to punch her lights out, but something told me to listen to her plea. She now had tears pouring from her eyes. "I know I wasn't a good mother to you, but trust me on this, Moe is your father and Chinoe is your brother."

It was true. And I didn't know whether to be happy or mad. I had a dad who I always thought of as a dad, but really was my dad. I'm glad that Sap would not have this shit to worry about.

"Why didn't he tell me?"

"He thought you would be better raised by Mama and Dad. His wife, Seal, had left him and their life was shaky after I told her."

Man, was my life getting better or worse? I couldn't decipher between the two.

Ring . . . Ring . . . Ring . . .

"Hello."

"Money, are you okay?"

"Yes, Ma." Seal must have known Maynea was going to tell me about Moe—Pops—Daddy.

"I was just calling to see if you needed anything. The community Luvly lived in wants to know if you plan on selling the house or moving someone in? There are a lot of big bids for it."

Damn, she ain't been gone, but a month and a half. I didn't want to sell it or have anyone move in, "I don't know. Ma, you sure you don't want a bigger house?"

"I keep telling ya'll boys to leave me in my comfort zone."

"How's my baby boy?"

"He's still breathing through tubes. They don't know if he can breathe on his own."

"I'll be back up there later."

"Money, you just got out of the hospital. Take your time and relax. We have everything under control. Hold on some one wants to talk to you."

"What's up, Cash Money?"

"What's up, Dawg?"

My brother was my dawg. My dawg was my brother. I liked the idea.

"You being strong? Handling Maynea?"

"Yeah, I'm cool." I held back my tears, "Are you coming over later. I need to talk to you about some important decisions."

"You got it, bro." His response made tears form. I lost my lady, best friend, love of my life, but gained a father and brother.

Chapter Eighty-Three

Money

"Is Sap still not talking?"

"No, not yet. I'm taking her to therapy starting Monday. The doctors say it's shock and not to worry. She'll talk when she's ready."

"She's got you and Luvly in her; she's strong."

"Call me later and I'll try and talk to her when she wakes."

"Okay, Mrs. Mancini. Thanks for everything." *Click.*

My son didn't make it, but I knew Luvly had him, holding him close to her heart.

I didn't think that me and Chocolate could get any closer, but we did as rediscovered each other as brothers.

"So you haven't talked to Brandie at all."

"Naw she don't want to see me. I don't blame her. I almost wrecked shop when I found out about Cartel. Plus Chaise fucked everything up by sending them pictures."

"I can't believe Chaise had a camera, snapping pictures of ya'll fucking. She was the baddest bitch."

"Not my problem anymore. My only girl is Sap. I'm here for her and Ma."

"Yeah, my baby girl has been through so much. But she's going to make it."

"Is Maynea enjoying your old house?"

"As long as she don't come over here. I don't care what she enjoys. All I want is to know Malaney. She's innocent. Her and Sap deserve to know each other."

"You heard from Salone yet?"

"She had the baby in late May or early June."

"Is she going to let you see the baby?"

"Yeah, she's been by here three times. She done got huge. I didn't think her little body could stretch like that. But I won't let her in the house, so she been trippin'. I told her this is me and Luvly's house."

"Well, how you gone see the baby?"

"I don't know. I have two or three months to figure that out."

"Have you seen Tae's new ride?"

"Yeah, he need that Excursion for all those kids he about to have."

"I can't believe that nigga bout to have twins."

"I talked to that doctor from L.A. They're going to test Sap's blood again. They got a positive reading for Syphilis. They said that sometimes fever could cause a false reading. I don't know, but I'll be hearing from them later on in the week."

"I need to call the agency and see when my next

shoot is. They left a message on my machine yesterday."

"Why you going back to work so soon."

"I need to get away, go on an island somewhere."

"Just pray Chaise ain't no where stalking you, hiding behind a bush or something."

"Man, I'll throw her ass in the water."

We laughed and talked about the good days, the bad days, and the future.

Chapter Eighty-Four

Beginning of the Ending

Chocolate

Diamond escaped the law and us. That pussy-nigga relocated while all of us were experiencing the worst time of our lives. It's been said that he went back to Cuba with his family, but he was still on our hit list. We would not rest until his body did—six-feet under.

Salone had Money's son on my birthday. His name was Spencer Money Loane. He's the next baller in the family, weighing eleven pounds, twelve ounces when he was born. That's my li'l dawg.

My dad was a good grandfather. He loved both his grandchildren and both of his sons. He and my mom keep bugging me about when I was going to have mine. And I kept telling them, "When Brandie comes back home."

* * *

"You sure you ready to go into this club. It's been a long time since you seen some pussy, you might bust one on the spot," Money joked.

"Nigga, please. Come on."

Me, Tae, and Money walked into Platinum Kat, being announced by the DJ, as we took our seats by the stage.

The music was pumping, the drinks were already coming, and me and my boys were together. The atmosphere was long over due.

Dances were swarming our table like bees to honey.

"Girl, football players in da house!!!"

Chapter Eighty-Five

Brandie

Fifty girls ran to the back, talking about putting on their baddest outfit.

Musta been Cartel and his crew. I didn't mess with him anymore, but he still came to see me every weekend.

I'd been trying to recover from New Years 2000. I stayed home and toasted to the peach drop on TV this year with a few friends. I admit that Chinoe never left my mind, but neither did those pictures of him fucking Chaise. Or the letter she sent me.

Brandie,

I know you don't know me, but I know your man, physically and mentally. He was once my man. We had a relationship until May 24th. You came in his life and wrecked mine. So, in return, I'm wrecking yours. When we were in New York for that three-day shoot, there was no shoot. I did tell him there was one, but when he got there he could have left, but he chose to stay and fuck me raw without a condom, licked my ass and my pussy, while you were getting yours licked by Cartel Trems.

Me and Chinoe were on our way into bliss until you came into his life. So now, Bitch, die on the inside. Leave him. He deserves to feel what you did when you saw his dick in me, his mouth on me.

Good RIDDANCE, BITCH
Chaise

That bitch had real nerve. Even though I thanked her for not letting me play the fool, I better not ever see her face as long as I live.

"Girl, you better hurry up and get out here and catch you one."

As I walked out the door, I could see the house was packed. I did my usual routine, walked to the DJ booth to request my music. *I was in a slow, mellow mood tonight.* I wanted something sexy and sweet. The first thing I asked for was some Prince. "Hey, Mr. DJ. Can you play, IF I WAS YOUR GIRLFRIEND, by Prince."

"If you be my girlfriend."

"We can arrange that." I winked and smiled at him.

He dropped his headset. "For real, Brandie?"

"Yes, Cappers, for real."

"What else do you want to hear?"

Looking through the albums, JUST ME AND YOU, by Toni Tony Tone. And ONE MORE CHANCE remix.

After confirming my first date with Cappers, I went to the bar to get my regular drink. The bartender already had it waiting, "Thanks."

I turned to look at the crowd to see who I could see. I almost fell off my seat, and choked on my drink. There he was. Sitting by the stage, my favorite spot to dance. He was looking sexy as hell, too. *Stop it, Brandie! Don't look at him.* But I couldn't help it. My revenge was getting the best of me. I knew he probably thought that I didn't work here anymore, but I had something for his ass.

"Please, gentlemen, welcome to the stage, Miss Caramel Delite."

The crowd went wild as usual. Cappers played JUST ME AND YOU. I danced straight down to the middle, in front of Chinoe's face. He had a dazed look on his face.

Money and Tae were waving money in the air. Money winked at me, motioning for me to come closer, holding the money over Chinoe's head.

I stopped in front of Chinoe. At first he sat motionless. I made my body sing the song to him. He licked his lips, looking me up and down from head to toe. "Like it?"

He nodded his head yes.

Prince came on next and I moved more seductively, making my hips and pussy call his name. "You want it?" He nodded yes again, his lips shiny and wet from licking them.

I untied one side of my bikini and shook my hip, almost touching his lips. I turned to the back and moved my ass slow and sensual, making it jiggle just a little.

He leaned forward putting a hundred dollar bill in the crack of my butt. I turned around to the front and untied the other side. My bottoms dropped to the floor and he picked them up, taking a deep whiff of the seat. He placed them tight in his fist.

"One More Chance" thumped through the club, and I fell in love all over again.

"You want me."

He nodded yes and dropped the panties to the floor, smiling and licking his lips. He stood up, so that we were face to face, my breath exchanging for his.

Money and Tae started hollering, "Get that thang, Chocolate. Take 'er back home wit' chu, nigga."

We didn't break the stare down. Our breath was intertwined. I was searching his soul and he was searching mine.

I wanted to see if he suffered from my absence. I needed to feel his pain, and know if he was sorry for what he had done.

"I love you, Brandie."

I continue to look deep inside him for the answer.

"I want you in my life, Brandie, I'm miserable without you. Please come home, baby."

Looking at him stand at my mercy, made me want to take him back. He was sorry for what he'd done, wasn't he? My love for him could over take what he'd done, couldn't it?

The music was thumping so hard, and everything was moving so fast that my concentration was off. How could I take him back, welcome him back into my heart? He slept with Chaise and I'd given myself to Cartel.

As our lips were about to touch, I pushed him back. "We can't do this."

"Why not? I love you, Brandie. You are the only one for me."

"Too much hurt has pinched my heart. I don't want this again."

I stood fragile in front of him, fumbling with my hands, trying to decide if I should stay or walk away.

Money, Taeko, and the entire club were staring at us like we were on a movie screen.

If I stayed, problems would always follow us. I could still see those damn pictures of him and Chaise in the front of my mind. I could see him eating her pussy, licking her ass and raw-dicking her.

How could I forgive him? And most of all, how could I forgive myself? I was just as wrong as Chinoe. I slept with Cartel because I felt smothered. Who's to say that Chinoe wouldn't smoother me even more if we got back together?

"I can't do this to me or you. We both have done too much to save it." I walked away not looking back.

I didn't want to see him anymore. *Did I really mean that? Or was it that I wanted him so bad that I couldn't handle it?*

I knew he wouldn't follow. He still had pride. His boys weren't going to let him fall prey to me again.

I walked straight to the dressing room and grabbed all my stuff. I was walking away from Chinoe, the club, and the lifestyle. I was finished!

As I was about to walk out the back door, "Brandie, please talk to me. I know that we both did some low-down shit, but baby, time has healed all that. We've been through so much to just let go."

"Look, Chinoe, we don't need to repeat the past. We need to learn from it."

I tried to walk around him, but he grabbed my arm and made me think of the night at Red Lobster, when he choked me.

"Chinoe, please take your hand off my arm."

"I just want to make you understand that I love you." She stared at me like I was foreign to her. Why did I have to meet her in the first place? Why couldn't she have just stayed a fantasy and a one-night stand?

"What do you want from me, Chinoe? Love? Companionship? To be your trifling whore?"

"All of you."

Wanting to say yes, I swallowed the lump in my throat. "We tried that once already." I shifted my bag to the other shoulder. Heat was rushing through my body.

"Look, just give me your number. Mine is still the same. Please, Brandie, let's just start over; set a date to talk about everything." I promised myself that I wouldn't wimp out if I seen her again. But seeing her has made my heart tell my mind that everything could be possible again.

Chapter Eighty-Six

Chocolate

It's been one month, three weeks and two days since she stood cold and heartless in front of my face and told me she didn't want me. Maybe, she had moved on with her life.

I saw a picture of her and some busta, who was said to have the hottest club in Atlanta, in Ebony. She looked like his princess that belonged on my throne.

"Chinoe, why are you sitting out here?"

Why was this bitch bothering me while I smoked my problems away? "I'm just smoking one. I'll be back inside in a minute."

"It's cool out here, and all you have on is a tank top and boxers."

"Damn! Are you my mother now!" I pushed her hand away from my chest. "I don't need a piece of pussy trying to be my care taker."

Shit, I needed Brandie . . .

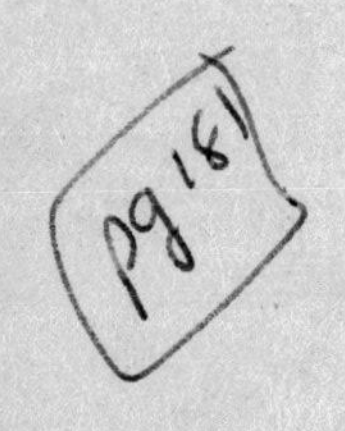